PRAISE FOR STINA LINDENBLATT

"A feel good, sensual, intoxicating and sexy love story; if you love contemporary romance you do not want to miss *Decidedly Off Limits*." —Slick, Guilty Pleasures

"Sweet, sexy and invigorating, *Decidedly off Limits* is a friends to lovers story that is truly a breath of fresh air!"—Read & Share Book Reviews

"Oh my goodness this book was so much fun!!!"—For the Love of Books (*Decidedly With Baby*)

"There are steamy moments but you are just left with feel good melty moments more."—Books Are Love (*Decidedly With Baby*)

"Be warned dear reader, this book will have you giggling and blushing as you devour it."—The Subclub Books (*Decidedly With Love*)

"...a truly unique and utterly swoon-worthy romance." —Mary Dubé at Frolic/USA Today's HEA (*Decidedly by Chance*)

"This is a great read, fresh, funny, sweet and romantic, with amazing characters and lots of surprises." – Blog on the Run (*Decidedly by Chance*)

"Stina Lindenblatt writes an emotional, heartfelt story about single parenthood, friendship, and love. Add to that great chemistry and tons of feels and this is a great book for anyone who enjoys this trope." – Ari at Red Hatter Book Blog (*Decidedly by Chance*)

"I can't wait for more Daniels brothers."—Mary at USA Today HEA (*Cowboy Most Wanted*)

"Are you in the mood for a fun, hot, sweet, romantic read that will have you blushing, laughing and glued to the pages then look no further than *Cowboy Most Wanted*."—The Subclub Books

"HOLY HOTNESS!! Not only this book was a fun read, but it was so sexy as well!"—Blog on the Run (*Cowboy Most Wanted*)

"I'm loving this series!"—Red Hot Blue Reads (*Once Upon a Cowboy*)

"Filled with emotion, intensity, a lot of sexual tension and the perfect amount of heat."—*About That Story* (*This One Moment*)

"Romantic angst powers this fast-paced novel, and readers will return to the series to learn more about the enigmatic side characters whose own stories are waiting to be told." —Publishers Weekly (*My Song for You*)

"A just-right balance of comedy, tragedy, heat, and ice."— Publishers Weekly (*Heat It Up*)

ALSO BY STINA LINDENBLATT

CONTEMPORARY ROMANCES

Carson Brothers Series

One More Chance

One More Secret

One More Betrayal

One More Truth

SPICY ROMANTIC COMEDY NOVELS

By The Bay Series

Decidedly Off Limits

Decidedly with Baby

Decidedly with Love

Decidedly with Mistletoe

Decidedly by Chance

Decidedly with Luck

Decidedly with Wishes

Copper Creek Series

Cowboy Most Wanted

Once Upon a Cowboy

Fix Me Up Cowboy

Visit stinalindenblattauthor.com for more books

DECIDEDLY WITH LUCK

STINA LINDENBLATT

Cover design: Stina Lindenblatt
Editing: Bev Rosenbaum and Flat Earth Editing.

Special Edition Paperback ISBN: 978-1-990177-59-0

eBook ISBN: 978-1-7772625-1-8

To my family, whom I love with all my heart...

DECIDEDLY WITH LUCK

PART I

1

KIERA

December

For as long as I could remember, I'd always loved fairy tales. Even before becoming an elementary schoolteacher.

More specifically, I'd always loved Disney's versions of the classic fairy tales.

Have you ever read Hans Christian Andersen's original story of *The Little Mermaid*? There are no singing lobsters, no happy endings. The little mermaid doesn't sail away into the sunset with her handsome prince.

Nope, not at all.

Spoiler alert!

She sacrifices herself so the prince can live, and the sea witch transforms the little mermaid into sea foam.

Unlike the original fairy tales, Disney leaves you with hope for a happily ever after, hope for a new beginning.

This was all fine and wonderful, but as I stood at the entrance to the hotel ballroom—my glittering silver stilettos feeling as though they were glued to the floor—I questioned if that would be the case for me.

Of course, it will.

Embracing that flicker of hope, I resumed reciting in my head my goal for the evening: *Project Kissing Under the Mistletoe.* A kiss under the mistletoe from a handsome stranger. A happy-for-now ending to the night—and a baby step toward moving on after my husband's death a year ago.

I scanned the sea of ball gowns and tuxes and elaborate masks, searching for a particular blonde in a dress of black tulle. *That's right.* In addition to the Jingle Balls ball being a fundraiser for testicular cancer, it was a masquerade ball.

My sister waved at me from across the ballroom, next to the grand Christmas tree decorated with a flurry of gold and red ornaments.

Brittany and her husband were the reason I was here tonight instead of back home in San Francisco, knitting mittens for foster kids in Boston. They were the reason I was wearing the mask covering the upper portion of my face and the stunning burgundy gown.

Don't worry. This wasn't the anniversary of my husband's death. That had passed a week ago with me spending the day reading the love notes he used to leave all over our house.

Love notes I'd saved in a big floral box every time I found one.

On the day of the one-year anniversary, I'd sipped a glass of Enchanted Springs Chardonnay, the same wine we'd served at our wedding, and read the notes aloud.

Roses are red, violets are blue, I want to have hot sex with you.

A poet, he was not.

And then there was the note I had saved for last:

If I die before you, I want to be the star in the sky that grants all your wishes.

I inhaled a long, fortifying breath, channeling my inner Disney princess, and wove my way through the throng of merry partiers.

The conversation I'd had with Stephen after I'd found that note sashayed into my head. The conversation where he told me that if he did die before me—way, way, *way* down the line—he wanted me to fall in love again.

After this, he proceeded to list all the men he thought were viable options, in case they were available at the time.

"But definitely not Stinky Pete," he'd said.

"I don't think you have to worry about me ending up with the villain from *Toy Story Two*."

Stephen barked a laugh—the laugh he always made when he thought I was being cute and adorable. "I was talking about my teammate. Pete Mundy. His hockey skates smell like he melted Limburger cheese in them."

I grinned at him and kissed him sweetly on the cheek. "Okay, no, Pete Mundy. Anyone else?"

"Logan Mathews."

"Is he a yah or a nah?"

"A definite yah."

"I'm sure his wife would have something to say about that." Logan had been Stephen's best friend and teammate in college, and his best man at our wedding. Now, he played in the NHL—with the Chicago Blackhawks, last I'd heard.

"All right, I'll add him to the list," I'd said with a grin, even though my heart had been splitting into a billion fragments at the thought of Stephen possibly dying before me.

My sister's red lips curved into a wide smile under her black-feathered half mask as I approached.

"Kiera." She beamed at me like I was a baby who'd taken her first wobbly steps. "Let me introduce you to the charity's biggest supporter and my dear friend." The way she said it, you would've thought she was talking about royalty. "Lucinda, this is my little sister, Kiera. Kiera, this is Lucinda Mathews." The woman's surname came out in a hushed whisper.

I bit back the urge to curtsy to the much older woman standing next to Brittany. Lucinda's gold-and-cream gown, diamond earrings and necklace, and spritz of floral perfume gave her a queenly air.

"Hello, my dear." Her voice was dry and brittle, like antique parchment paper, yet filled with warmth and a spark of something.

Amusement, perhaps?

Remember the part about me resisting the urge to curtsy?

It would seem my body failed to get that message. Luckily, I'd had spent years perfecting the skill as a kid, back when I believed in fairy godmothers and dreamed of one day marrying my own prince.

Lucinda chuckled, and I felt my face heat as I straightened.

"And this is my grandson, Grayson." She gestured with a wave of her hand to the tall, dark-haired man next to her. His half mask was simple and black. If the way his tuxedo embraced his body was any indication, the man made keeping in shape a top priority.

I held out my hand for him to shake—because heck if I was curtsying for him. But instead of shaking it, Grayson lifted my hand to his mouth and pressed a soft kiss to it.

At the feel of his mouth against my skin, my body shouldn't have reacted like hot lava swirled within its depths. My breath shouldn't have hitched with sudden longing. And my lips shouldn't have tingled, craving to taste his mouth on mine.

None of those things should have happened—with a stranger, no less. A stranger who might not even be single.

Desire wasn't alone under the hotel chandeliers, their lightbulbs twinkling like stars. Hanging out with it was regret. Regret in knowing that Stephen was looking down from heaven and shaking his head at me, disappointed that the stranger I wanted to kiss under the mistletoe wasn't on the list of approved men he'd jokingly created.

"Brittany mentioned you're an elementary school-teacher," Lucinda said.

I nodded and smiled warmly at the thought of my students. "That's right. I teach second grade."

"Oh, such a delightful age. My great-granddaughter is in that grade. Such a precocious little thing, just like her father was at that age."

My gaze flicked to Grayson, but he gave no indication the child belonged to him. So maybe she was his niece.

He chuckled, drawing my attention to his mouth. *Don't look at his mouth. Look away from his...* "I'm sure her father will be thrilled you said that. I know for a fact that he took great pride in keeping you on your toes."

She flashed him her perfectly straight, angel-white teeth. "I daresay you're right."

"And what about you?" I asked Grayson. "What do you do for a living?"

"This and that" was his non-answer.

Truth? I sort of appreciated that he was evading the question like a spy at a royal tea party. I preferred the mystery surrounding him. It made him even sexier—not that he needed help in that department as far as I could tell.

"Brittany also mentioned you live in San Francisco," Lucinda said to me.

For a masked ball, where our identities were a secret,

my sister was certainly spilling the jelly beans when it came to all there was to know about me.

Please tell me you never mentioned my deceased husband.

"That's right," I said.

"She mentioned you used to live in Boston—"

I sensed she was going to say more, but Grayson coughed as though clearing his throat, and her words came to an abrupt halt.

She threw him a subtle smirk. He gave a barely perceptible shake of his head.

"Do you live in San Francisco?" I asked him. My tone was edged with a curiosity I shouldn't have felt. I really didn't want to know anything about him. If I found out too much, the magic of the moment would be reduced to glitter.

"No, Chicago." His deep, sexy voice left my insides quivering like leaves caught in a stiff breeze.

"That's quite the drive just to attend the ball."

"You might say I happened to be in the neighborhood, and my grandmother asked if I would attend as her date."

Aww, that's so sweet.

"My poor Alfred died ten years ago from testicular cancer," Lucinda explained, "which is why this charity event is important to me. And why awareness and early detection is vital."

"I'm so sorry for your loss," I said to them both, praying Brittany didn't decide this was a good time to inform them about *my* dead husband.

Luckily, she remained silent on the topic.

"Thank you, my dear," Lucinda said. "I was fortunate to have a supportive family and friends to help me get through it. And you know the best part?"

I shook my head, clueless at what it could be.

"Just because you lose someone you loved doesn't mean

you'll never love again." She winked at me, confirming she did know the truth. What else had my dear sweet sister shared? My social security number? "I found a new prince, and I'm just as much in love with him as I was with my sweet Alfred."

"I'm glad to hear that." My words had more to do with her falling in love with someone new than the chance of that happening to me again.

I shifted on my feet and twisted toward the orchestra, now playing a new piece.

I could almost imagine Cinderella and Prince Charming waltzing to the music with the other couples dancing.

"Would you like to dance?" The question was a low murmur against my ear, and my insides quivered once again, in a way that would make a bowl of Jell-O envious.

2

LOGAN

The blue-eyed, blonde beauty had turned to the dance floor, where couples were moving in time to the music. Some clearly knew how to waltz—unlike me.

I was a hockey player, not a dancer. But that hadn't stopped me from asking Kiera if she wanted to dance. I'd sensed she wanted to escape my grandmother's questioning as much as I did.

This wasn't the first time I'd met Kiera. Her husband, Stephen Ashdown, had been both my teammate in college and best friend.

The last time I'd seen her was at his funeral a year ago.

And Christ, she still looked as beautiful as she had back then. Beautiful, but not as sad.

How did I know she was the same Kiera I'd met in college?

I'd seen her checking into the hotel with a man a few hours ago. Although at the time, I hadn't realized he was her brother-in-law.

The unnamed emotion I'd experienced when I saw her

with the man I thought was her new boyfriend hadn't been alone. Shock, excitement, desire had all been its teammates, along with unease. The unease felt when you're slammed into the boards during a game, and you pray you haven't just exacerbated a previous injury.

I shook the thought aside. Happiness—that was what I should've felt at seeing her. And I had. Because Kiera being here, not far from the ski slopes where Stephen had lost his life, meant she was moving on. Which was exactly what he would've wanted.

Kiera looked at me and smiled. It was the smile I'd missed seeing all these years. A smile that had been absent the day of Stephen's funeral. In its place had been the reserved, relieved-to-see-me smile, but nothing beyond that.

This smile? It was all dimples and had been responsible for a few of my morning hard-ons in college.

She tilted her head to the side. "I would love to dance. Thank you."

I held out my hand and led her to the dance floor, silently thanking my daughter's love of *Cinderella* and *Beauty and the Beast* for teaching me what I was supposed to do in situations like this. It wasn't as if playing with the Chicago Blackhawks had prepared me for this moment.

Away from my grandmother's prying eyes, I parked my hand on Kiera's waist. The zap of electricity from earlier, when I kissed the back of her hand, hummed through me again.

Kiera's gaze locked on mine. Her lips parted slightly, and the tip of her tongue traveled slowly along her lower lip. The move sent a shot of red-hot desire to my cock.

I don't think she even realized she'd done it. The move seemed subconscious.

With one hand still on her waist, the other holding her

hand, I started swaying to the music. Her soft floral scent that I remembered so well prompted a kaleidoscope of memories. Memories of sitting next to her in geology class. Of studying with her. Of introducing her to my best friend at a party. I'd never had a chance with her after that.

The soft waves of her dark-blonde hair brushed teasingly against the fabric of her low-cut dress. Without meaning to, I let my gaze wander down to her mouthwatering cleavage. But what did you expect? I was a hot-blooded man, after all.

The gold scripted letters of her necklace glinted in the light, and the adrenaline rush of an overtime goal pulsed through my veins.

She still has it?

I'd given her the "Believe" necklace as a graduation gift after I'd seen it in a store while the Blackhawks were in Nashville for a game. I ended up missing part of practice when I failed to return to the arena on time, and the head coach rightfully reamed me out. My punishment? Sitting out that night's game as a healthy scratch.

But the look on Kiera's face when I gave her the necklace had made it all worth it.

I couldn't believe she still had it.

"Are you enjoying the ball so far?" she asked, yanking me from my thoughts.

"I can't say it's my scene," I said, adopting a slight yet undistinguishable accent so that she didn't recognize my voice. "But it's for a good cause."

"I'm sorry about your grandfather." She smiled softly at me.

"Thank you." I swallowed down the urge to tell her I was sorry about her husband. To do that would've given away too much. "Did you come all the way to Lake Tahoe just for the ball? Or are you also here to hit the slopes?" I didn't believe it was the latter. Stephen had told me Kiera wasn't much of a skier.

"Just the ball. I'm returning to San Francisco on Sunday. Winter break doesn't start for another five days. What about you?"

"I have a flight out tomorrow morning." The Blackhawks had a game scheduled in Anaheim for Sunday afternoon. As it was, I was lucky the team had granted me permission to miss two practices to be here.

The smile returned to Kiera's lips. And the sudden need to kiss her powered through me.

I wasn't the only one who seemed to share the sentiment. Her gaze dropped to my mouth, and I leaned down without any thought to what I was doing. All I could think about was what she would taste like.

"Sorry to interrupt," a man said next to us. I jerked away from Kiera. His name tag claimed he was a member of the hotel staff. "There's a call for you, Mr—"

"Okay," I said, cutting him off before he had a chance to finish the sentence.

Kiera's sister had already mentioned my last name when she introduced Kiera to my grandmother. Still, I didn't want Kiera to link it to me if she hadn't already. As it was, I was lucky my grandmother preferred to use my middle name, Grayson, than the one everyone else called me. I couldn't explain why, but I didn't want Kiera to learn it was me.

At least not yet.

You're probably thinking that Mathews isn't exactly an uncommon last name. You'd be right about that. But I still didn't want to give her a reason to add two and two together and start asking questions.

Whoever was calling me must've been doing so with

good reason. Only a few people knew I was here, and I'd left my phone in my room to charge.

"I'll be right back," I told Kiera, then followed the man toward the main ballroom doors.

At the front desk, he handed me the phone.

"Hello, Logan Mathews speaking."

"Hey, sorry to bug you," Stacy, my ex-wife, said. "But Livi has a stomachache, and she wanted you to sing to her. I told her you were busy—"

"No, that's okay. Give me a minute, and I'll FaceTime her from my room."

I could hear the smile in Stacy's voice when she said, "Thanks, Logan. I keep telling Tony to take singing lessons since it's not always feasible for you to sing to her when she's sick."

I chuckled. Most men would probably be jealous if their ex-wife's new husband wanted to sing to their child. And maybe I should've been.

But Tony had been there for Livi when I couldn't because of my hockey career—a career that had eventually led to Stacy and me divorcing over a year ago.

Not wanting to risk some asshole swooping in on Kiera like a ravenous vulture because I left her alone for too long, I jogged to the elevator.

"Hey, baby girl," I said a short time later on my phone. I was sitting on the wing-backed chair in my hotel room. Olivia was lying on her bed at home, surrounded by a billion stuffed animals.

"Hi, Daddy." At the sound of her sweet, seven-year-old voice, my heart drooped like a wilted plant thirsty for water. *Shit.* I missed her, even though I'd seen her just yesterday. "Have you danced with any princesses yet?"

I laughed. "It's not that kind of ball."

Her face screwed up into a comical look of disappointment. "Great Granny said there would be lots of princesses there. And at least one on-duty fairy godmother, just in case."

Stacy's laugh came through the speaker even though I couldn't see her. She must've been holding the iPad.

I smacked my palm against my forehead. "Oh, that's who that was with the purple dress, wings, and magic wand. I didn't recognize her."

The disappointment smoothed from Livi's face, and she smiled, revealing a hole where one of her baby teeth used to be.

"Mommy told me you've got a tummy ache," I said.

Livi pouted and nodded.

"Do you want me to sing it better?"

She nodded again.

So, I sang "Frosty the Snowman," her favorite Christmas carol.

Followed by "Rudolph the Red-Nosed Reindeer"—because I really missed my baby girl.

3

——————

KIERA

How did I feel Project Kissing Under the Mistletoe was going?

I thought it was going well. But what did I know?

Flirting and reading the signs had never been my superpower.

Not even close.

But as far as I could tell, Grayson seemed interested. I was positive that before we'd been interrupted, he was leaning in to kiss me.

Or maybe that was wishful thinking.

But if he had kissed me on the dance floor, would it have counted when it came to my goal for the night? It wasn't as if there was mistletoe hanging where we'd been standing.

I surveyed the crowded ballroom but couldn't find a single sprig of the plant anywhere.

That was okay. As an elementary schoolteacher, you learned to be flexible.

A kiss was still a kiss. The lack of mistletoe didn't change that.

Through the etched glass of the double French doors, I caught a glimpse of the mountains. Moonlight reflected softly off the white snow.

For some unknown reason, the mountains beckoned to me the way a rich, creamy brownie beckoned to a chocoholic. I'd never been a skier. That had been all Stephen. He'd loved the thrill of racing down the slope, taking the sharp turns with high precision.

Me? I was more a fan of the bunny slope—and sitting by the roaring fireplace in the ski lodge, savoring a mug of hot chocolate.

Not expecting the doors to be unlocked, I tested one. Delight swelled in me when it clicked open. I briefly scanned the ballroom to check if Grayson had returned yet. When I didn't see him, I slipped outside.

The freezing mountain air instantly wrapped around me like an ice blanket. But the white Christmas tree lights on the shrubs skirting the large balcony called to me, their festive holiday magic hard to resist. Other than the potted plants and a few old-fashioned lampposts, which added a romantic glow to the area, the balcony was empty.

The Christmas lights weren't the only things that looked magical. Thousands of stars twinkled above me. I swirled on the spot, taking them all in.

"God, it's beautiful." Puffs of white clouds rose with each word.

"It is," a female voice said from behind, startling a gasp out of me.

I whirled around to find a woman I hadn't noticed before step from the shadows. Her long-sleeved, pale-blue gown shimmered in the light from the nearby lamppost.

Her thick white-blonde hair was pulled up in a poufy style popular in the 1960s.

Unlike everyone inside the ballroom, she wasn't wearing a mask.

"Oh, I'm sorry, dear. I didn't mean to frighten you." Her voice held the faded edge of an English accent. "I had to sneak away for a second to have a quick smoke. I'm trying to quit, but I haven't quite got there yet."

I smiled reassuringly at her. "That's okay. I was just admiring the stars. I don't see them very often in the city."

"Aren't you cold?"

I figured the goose bumps on my arms and shivering were enough of an answer. Besides, I couldn't imagine she was doing much better. "It's okay. I won't be outside long enough to turn into an icicle."

She glanced skyward again. "It really is magical out here."

"It is."

"Well, I'm going back inside to mingle. You're welcome to borrow my shawl while you're out here. It really is nice and toasty."

"Oh, I couldn't do that."

"I insist." She slipped the royal-blue cashmere shawl from her shoulders and spread it across my bare skin. The soft fabric was surprisingly warm, and my arms and body sighed with relief.

My gown was breathtaking, but the sweetheart neckline and the spaghetti straps weren't exactly practical for winter in Lake Tahoe.

"Thank you," I told her. "I'm Kiera."

"Nice to meet you, Kiera. I'm Helena. Well, toodle-oo." She wiggled her satin-gloved fingers at me, and with a swish of her skirt, hurried inside through the door I'd used.

Happy to stay outside a little longer, I walked over to the

stone balcony railing to get a better view of the mountains and the stars. The tangy scent of pine trees greeted me. It was like standing in a Christmas tree lot, only better. I could almost hear the ringing of sleigh bells and a hearty "*Ho, ho, ho.*"

I inhaled a deep breath, suddenly feeling a little lighter. Lighter than I'd thought I would feel returning to the area.

A small voice inside my head urged me to go back inside, so Grayson could easily find me—assuming he was still interested. But another voice told me that being out here, on the balcony, couldn't be more right. It was peaceful. Romantic.

A break from my regular life.

Who knew masquerade balls could be so freeing?

The breeze brushed against my cheek in a brief kiss. "I miss you," I whispered to it as if the wind would carry my words to the stars.

At the thought of kissing a stranger—the first baby step in moving on with my life—my heart clenched to the size of a prickly pinecone. "What am I thinking?" I asked the breeze. "The last thing I should be doing is kissing another—"

I didn't have a chance to finish the thought out loud. A sudden gust of wind tugged the shawl from my shoulders.

I gasped and pivoted to catch the shawl before it could hit the ground.

Standing behind me was the man who had the power to still the air in my lungs. The blue fabric was grasped in his hand, a sexy one-sided smile on his face. "I take it this is yours," Grayson said.

Now, you might be wondering if I believe in ghosts or the paranormal.

Or signs from beyond the grave.

Not really.

But that didn't stop the air rushing from me at his inexplicable timing.

Or maybe it was just relief that he had saved the shawl from a disastrous fate.

"No, it belongs to a guest at the ball. She loaned it to me so I could stay outside for a bit and enjoy all of this." I gestured with a grand sweep of my arm at the wintery scenery.

"Here, let me put it back on you. I wouldn't want you to get cold." His white, wispy breath merged with my own.

He leaned in closer, his body almost touching mine, and draped the shawl around my shoulders. The pads of his fingers traced across my skin, igniting a trail of tingling goose bumps. My pulse thrummed loud and rapid in my ears, blocking out all other sounds, and I inhaled a soft breath.

"I really want to kiss you," Grayson said, his voice low and husky.

The wind picked up behind me, nudging me forward.

Or maybe I'd imagined that.

"I want that, too," I whispered.

At this point, I didn't care about the lack of mistletoe. Kissing under the stars was just as magical—maybe even more so.

Sure, tomorrow, this would all be a distant memory. Grayson lived in Chicago, and I lived in San Francisco. But that didn't matter. At least then, I'd have something special to remember about the masquerade ball.

Something to tell my grandchildren one day.

He lowered his mouth to mine—his touch like the wings of a butterfly brushing against a petal. My body shivered slightly, but it had nothing to do with the cold temperature. As far as I was concerned, we were standing on a Hawaiian beach at sunset.

The next moment our lips touched again, the lingering uncertainty vanished like a puff of smoke. This time our mouths moved together in unison. And with each brush, flames licked my body with a burning desire.

My lips parted, begging him to deepen the kiss, to relieve the need smoldering in me, to stoke it, to reduce me to ashes.

His tongue stroked mine, and I released a soft moan.

The sound was met with his answering one. He threaded his fingers through my hair, cradling my head. His other hand slipped to the curve of my lower back, and he pulled my body against him. Even with the fabric of my dress and his tux between us, I could feel his length harden.

My heart rate picked up, excited by the wicked possibilities.

I pulled away slightly, my breath coming out in rapid white pants. "God, this is going to sound crazy. I don't normally do one-night stands, but—"

I got no further than that. Grayson's mouth was on mine again, answering the question I hadn't yet asked.

4

LOGAN

What was my first thought when Kiera insinuated she wanted to have sex with me?

That Christmas had come early. I couldn't begin to count the number of times I'd fantasized back in college how it would feel to be buried deep inside her.

But as my mouth moved against hers, I was reminded of one crucial question: How would she feel if she found out I was the one kissing her?

I'd kept my identity a secret from the moment she entered the ballroom. I had kissed her and still hadn't told her the truth.

Okay, I know what you're thinking. She had no idea that I knew who she was, so she couldn't possibly get mad at me.

Or maybe that's not what you're thinking. Maybe you're thinking I'm an idiot for holding my tongue on the whole identification thing.

You're probably right about that.

Kiera pulled away as if she'd bounced off an electrified force field that had sprung up between us. Christ, I hoped she hadn't suddenly developed the ability to read minds. "There's something you should know first," she said.

"What's that?" I asked, voice huskier than before.

"It's been a long time since I was last with a man that way." She swallowed. "I used to be married. I don't want to talk about it, but my husband died last year."

I nodded in understanding even though I had no idea where this was going. "So, you decided your first time would be with a stranger?"

"More than that. I hope you don't take this the wrong way, but I want us to keep the masks on."

O-kay.

I wasn't sure what I thought of that. It could've been taken so many different ways. So I asked the one question echoing in my head like a gong struck by a puck. "So, you can pretend I'm him while I'm fucking you?"

I hadn't meant for the words to be so crass. But now that they were out there, there was no taking it back.

Besides, who was I to talk? What kind of man slept with his best friend's wife?

A crappy one.

Sure, Stephen was dead, but did it really make a difference?

Of course, it makes a difference, either the voice of reason or the devil on my shoulder—it could have gone either way —said. *It would only be immoral if her husband was still alive.*

But what about the part where I was keeping the truth about my identity a secret from her?

Both the voice of reason and the devil pointed out that it was Kiera's choice to keep the masks on because it would be easier for her.

And who was I to argue with that?

Kiera adamantly shook her head. Her eyes were as wide as an owl's that had sat on a downed power line. "No...no, not at all. It's just this isn't something I normally do. It's completely out of character for me. Being adventurous. And well, having sex with a stranger while we're both masked seems sexy and forbidden." She clasped her lip between her teeth for a heartbeat before releasing it. "I know this sounds strange, I mean, I don't even know you. But my sister knows your grandmother, so in a way, we're not complete strangers."

I had to smother a laugh at that logic.

But she'd also handed me a solution to my dilemma. If we kept the masks on, she'd never have to find out I was less of a stranger than she imagined. "Okay, the masks stay on."

Kiera shivered and pulled the shawl tighter around her arms. "I should probably find the woman who loaned me this, so I can return it to her first."

"Good idea. But it might also be a good idea if we didn't disappear quite yet. Otherwise, my grandmother will send the army to drag me back to the charity event." Which wouldn't be a problem if we were having sex in Kiera's room.

Plus going to Kiera's room would solve several issues, one being the picture of Livi, Stacy, and myself on my bedside table. I always brought it with me on the road. Tony took the photo of the three of us last summer.

Kiera and I strode to the doors leading inside. I twisted the handle of the one I'd come through. It didn't budge. We tried the other four doors. They, too, remained locked.

Fuck.

I peered through the glass. Everyone was turned away from us, listening to the woman on the stage. No one seemed to notice we were out here.

"I think she's telling everyone about the silent auction

prizes," Kiera whispered, even though no one inside could hear us.

I surveyed the balcony for another way inside. Spotting a potential route, I lightly grabbed Kiera's arm. "This way."

I guided her to the stairs leading to the ground level and helped her down the steps until we reached the path.

Or at least where the path *should've* been.

"Oh!" she said, staring at the snow-covered ground.

Whoever had been responsible for clearing the path had been sadly negligent in their duty.

"I guess you aren't wearing winter boots under your dress?" I asked with a smirk.

Kiera pulled up the hem of her skirt, revealing shapely calves, kissable ankles, and stilettos that looked like they'd been covered with silver glitter.

And just like that, the image of Kiera wearing the mask —and only the mask—pushed aside the argument of whether it was morally acceptable to have sex with her.

I wasn't sure I could last five more minutes, let alone another hour or two, before giving her a night we would both remember for a long time.

In the near distance, cabin lights glowed warmly in the dark. In addition to the regular rooms, the hotel also boasted secluded cabins. I'd never been inside one, but I'd overheard a guest gush about the elegant rustic interior, the fireplace, and the faux bearskin rug.

Like a honeymoon suite—only better.

In the opposite direction and around the corner was the main hotel entrance.

"Looks like I'll be carrying you. Climb on," I said, turning away from her.

"I can't do that!"

I chuckled at her scandalized tone and peered over my shoulder at her. "Why not?"

"Because I'm not a little girl. I'm a grown woman."

"So I've noticed. What's that got to do with anything?"

Her breath came out as a huffed sigh. "It means I'm heavier than a little girl."

"Yeah, so?"

She didn't reply. She just gaped at me. I'd bet my seven-figure annual salary she was wearing an *Isn't-it-obvious?* expression under her mask.

"I guarantee I can carry you without straining a muscle." She wouldn't have doubted that for a second if she'd ever witnessed my pre-season training.

An icy wind swept down from the mountains, reminding us that it wasn't getting any warmer outside.

"All right," Kiera said on another sigh. She hiked her skirt up and climbed awkwardly onto my back.

Once I had her securely in position, her arms wrapped loosely around my neck, I plodded through the ankle-deep snow. My feet were getting cold from snow sneaking into my dress shoes—there was no way Kiera would have survived walking in those shoes.

Her warm breath brushed against my ear, and my skin hummed, my cock stirred, and the pounding of my heart thundered through the valley, shaking the snow from the trees. Never in a million years in college had I imagined a moment like this. With Kiera. And I was positive I'd never have a moment like this again.

I didn't mean that because Kiera lived in San Francisco and I lived in Chicago. I'd made the mistake once before of marrying a woman when I was already married to my career. I had no intention of doing that again.

Not that I would ever call Stacy or Livi a mistake.

But my career and my daughter were more important to me than anything else. As long as I was playing hockey, I had no room in my life for another relationship. Lesson learned.

We arrived at the hotel entrance a few minutes later, and I lowered Kiera to the sidewalk. The doorman and the valet managed to keep what they were thinking off their faces, but you couldn't mistake the lewd thoughts glinting in their eyes.

Fortunately, Kiera was too busy straightening her skirt to notice.

I leveled a get-your-mind-out-of-the-gutter glare at them.

Both men got the message, despite my mask, shifting uncomfortably on their feet. My size had the benefit of intimidating more than just my on-ice rivals.

The doorman gave us a welcoming nod. "Good evening, sir. Madam."

"Hi," Kiera said brightly, as though she had stepped out of a golden carriage made from a pumpkin, instead of riding on my back while wearing a ball gown.

She moved forward. The automatic glass door slid open, and we entered the building.

Warm air instantly hugged us like Aunt Sonia's bear hugs.

"Oh, God," Kiera said on an erotic moan, rubbing her bare arms under the shawl. "I forgot how amazing heat feels."

"Why don't we get a drink? That'll warm us up." Although after that moan, a dunk in the icy river might be in order for me.

"I'll catch up with you in a minute. I need to return the shawl to its owner before she wonders what happened to it." Without waiting for my reply, Kiera strolled toward the ballroom.

I started to follow her but changed my mind, veering toward the front desk.

5

KIERA

It took me all but a few minutes to locate Helena. She was talking to two good-looking men. Like the other men in the ballroom, they were wearing tuxes, but as with Helena, they had forgone the masks.

"Kiera, let me introduce you to Eli Lawson and Kai Korhonen from the San Francisco Rock hockey team." She grinned at the two men. "Gentlemen, this is my dear friend, Kiera, who I've only known for a few minutes, but I can already tell is a wonderful person."

Her smile faded, and her expression turned puzzled. "Have you been outside this entire time?"

I nodded. "Turns out the doors are only unlocked from the inside." Except, she hadn't had trouble re-entering the ballroom through them.

Her mouth formed a perfect O. "How did you ever get back inside?"

"The stairs leading from the balcony to the ground level."

"You were alone out there?"

"No, I had a friend with me." I swiveled to see where Grayson had disappeared to. He was nowhere to be found.

I returned my attention to Helena and the two hockey players.

"Do you like hockey?" she asked me.

"I haven't watched it in a while. Not since..." I left the rest of the sentence dangling, having already met my sad-story quota for the day when I informed Grayson of my widow status.

The three of them looked at me expectantly while I fumbled for an alternative answer.

When one failed to materialize, I went with, "What positions do you play?"

"Goalie," Kai said.

"Forward," was Eli's reply.

"I heard the team's doing really well this season." Even though the sport was no longer part of my life, I wasn't deaf to the comments from some of my students. They were huge hockey fans.

The two men nodded. "We are." Eli smiled smugly. "The Blackhawks didn't know what hit them when they lost to us yesterday."

"Now, now," Helena said, her English accent coming in a little stronger. "I thought Logan Mathews was on fire. If it hadn't been for your goal during the power play in the last two minutes of the game, things might've turned out differently."

A warmth filled me at the mention of Logan, a name I hadn't heard in a while.

Eli's and Kai's gazes darted to something over my shoulder. A hand rested on my lower back, and the sensation of two dozen fluttering fairy wings settled in my belly. I didn't have to turn around to know the hand belonged to Grayson.

I grinned at him, but his gaze wasn't on me. It was locked on the two hockey players. Maybe he was a hockey fan and recognized them. He did live in Chicago, after all. For all I knew, he'd watched the Blackhawks' game against the Rock last night.

But if he did recognize the two men, he didn't say anything. He just nodded at them.

Eli and Kai were eyeing him as if they were trying to place him. I guess he had one of those faces that seemed familiar when it wasn't, especially when you couldn't see it in its entirety because of the mask.

"Would you care to dance?" Grayson asked me, not giving the two men and Helena a second glance.

Before I could reply, he was guiding me away from the trio.

"Have fun, you two," Helena called after us.

For a second, I considered asking him if he liked hockey, but decided I didn't care if he did or not. We only had this one night together, and damned if I'd spend it talking about the sport.

The less I knew about him, the better.

The night wasn't about getting to know him because I wanted a happily ever after with him. It was about enjoying unforgettable sex. Unforgettable sex that I could relive while I was pleasing myself during my next Sahara of a sex dry-spell.

"That's a gorgeous necklace," Helena said a while later, after Grayson and I had returned from the dance floor. The two hockey players had since left her side. Her gaze was directed at the gold charm resting above my cleavage: the elegant script spelling the word "Believe."

She smiled softly at me, the pale blue of her eyes sparkling like an icicle in the sunlight. "Magic exists if you believe. Do you believe?"

Does that quote sound familiar to you, too?

I was certain I'd heard or seen it somewhere. "I'm not sure the guy who gave it to me was thinking about magic when he bought it."

"A fellow? Is he special?"

A man dressed in a gray suit stepped up to Grayson. Grayson moved away from my side to talk to him.

"He was a friend back in college. He gave it to me as a graduation present."

She seemed to contemplate that for a second. "Whatever happened to him?"

"I have no idea." If it had been someone other than Logan Mathews, the hockey player she'd been referring to earlier, I would've told her he played in the NHL, was married, and had a child. But who he was didn't matter. He'd been part of a life that no longer existed.

Grayson stiffened briefly, having since returned to my side after the brief exchange with the man.

Helena cocked her head to the side, the sparkle still in her eyes. "You never said if you believe in magic?"

I laughed. "If I say no, does that mean another fairy falls from the sky, or whatever it is that happened to them in Peter Pan?"

She giggled. "Something tells me that's not how it works." Her purse buzzed. She removed her phone and checked the screen. "Looks like my assistant needs me to call her. It was nice meeting you two. Good luck with everything." She bopped her head in a brisk good-bye and hurried toward the doorway.

"What do you say we make our escape now?" Grayson asked. His grandmother was talking to a group of people on the other side of the ballroom. My sister was dancing with her husband.

"Deal."

In the lobby, I turned to the elevators. Grayson reached for my hand and pulled me in the opposite direction.

"Aren't we going upstairs?" I assumed we were heading to his room. We hadn't actually discussed whose room we would end up in.

"No. I've got something else planned."

O-kay.

We stepped outside as a white SUV pulled to the curb. Grayson reached for the front passenger door and opened it. "Your chariot, Madam."

"Will it turn into a pumpkin at midnight?" I asked on a giggle.

"I'm pretty sure that only applies to golden carriages. SUVs are exempt from the rule."

I climbed into the vehicle. Grayson shut the door, retrieved his keys from the valet, and walked to the driver's side.

Part of me was expecting a long drive to wherever our final destination awaited us. So I was surprised when the trip lasted less than two minutes, and he parked in front of what looked like an adorable log cabin behind the hotel. A soft glow came from between the closed curtains, and smoke curled up from the chimney.

It wasn't the only cabin here. From what I could tell, there were about a dozen of them, randomly located away from the road.

Grayson opened the passenger door and helped me down.

"What is this place?" I asked as we strolled up the short path.

"The cabins are like hotel suites but more secluded.

Plus, they have something the rooms in the hotel don't have." He unlocked the door with a key card and pushed it open.

And I instantly understood what he'd meant.

A roaring fire greeted us from the fireplace on the opposite side of the large room. In front of it was a white fur rug that fortunately looked more fake than real.

Add the king-sized bed, the iron headboard with the intricate swirls, and the crimson bedding, and the place looked like it belonged to royalty, but with a rustic elegance to it.

"It's gorgeous," I whispered.

Grayson wrapped his arms around me from behind. "I thought you might like it," he murmured in my ear.

At the husky sound of his voice, my pulse beat a fast rhythm in my ears, my skin tingled, and that sensation of fairy wings in my gut went berserk.

I smiled. "Very much." I'd never seen anything like it.

I twisted in his arms and gently kissed him. "Thank you." My heart swelled at the generosity of this man. I had opened up and told him about my husband, and he decided to make my first time with another man—with him—more special than a regular one-night stand.

"You're welcome." He guided me backward into the cabin and clicked the door shut behind him.

Then my mouth was on his, thrilled the wait was finally over.

His lips parted, and our tongues moved together in a slow tango. Every nerve in my body came alive, fuses lit, ready for the countdown for the firework display to commence.

I moaned into Grayson's mouth, needing more than just this contact, but at the same time, never wanting his kisses to end.

Grayson must have felt the same way. He kissed me like a man appreciating an exquisite glass of whiskey, each sip savored and lingered over. Each sip an unearthed treasure.

My hands smoothed over the front of his shirt, appreciating the taut muscles under the fabric. They moved up again, under the tux jacket, and I pushed it off his shoulders, hinting at what I needed.

Him.

Naked.

Now.

It took him but a second to shrug off his jacket and let it fall.

And another second to be free of his shirt, a shower of buttons raining on the hardwood floor.

He cupped my breasts, covered by the bodice of my dress. His thumbs brushed across my nipples. They tightened, and wetness rushed to my core.

"I've imagined all night what these beauties look like," he said, dragging his thumbs again across the highly sensitive buds.

Another moan escaped my mouth, captured with his lips pressed to mine. He then kissed my neck. I moved my head to the side, giving him greater access, humming my pleasure. I was incapable of saying anything beyond that.

His hands inched behind my back, and with the skill of a man who knew how to unzip a dress while blindfolded, he slowly slid the zipper open. His fingertips deliberately skimmed along my skin as his hand traveled south. Each spot he touched sizzled with want, sizzled with desire. If he didn't pick up his pace soon, I would simply combust.

And wouldn't that be a shame?

The only sounds in the room were the crackling fire, our heavy breaths, and my heart pounding hard against my sternum, the big bass drum in a parade.

He peeled the thin straps down my arms, releasing my breasts from the confines of the fabric.

Baring my nakedness for him to see.

"Fuck," he groaned under his breath and palmed the heavy weight of my breasts in both hands.

While he did that, I went back to appreciating the fine cut of his muscles. Neither of us had bothered to turn the light on, so I memorized with my fingertips the ridges and valleys that made up his abs.

But the exploration could only go so far, with impatience cheering in the shadows for us to shed the rest of our clothing. I shimmied out of my dress, leaving on my purple lace panties and silver stilettos.

In the dim light, I could make out Grayson's blue eyes darkening behind his mask. Before you could say, "Bibbidi bobbidi boo," he shucked off the rest of his clothes. The only thing still on him was his black boxer briefs, which housed a very impressive erection as far as I could tell.

I ran the tip of my tongue along my lower lip in anticipation and slipped off my stilettos.

Unsure what to do next, because it had been forever since I last seduced a man, I walked over to the fur rug. Then I looked at the bed.

Both held all sorts of delicious and wicked possibilities.

Wow, look at you. Add a mask, and you really are a different person.

I mentally giggled at the thought.

But it was the truth. In the light of the fire, with the mask on, and with a man I'd never see again, it was all bringing out someone I hadn't known I could be.

I felt less vulnerable.

I felt free.

Grayson bent down and removed his wallet from his pocket. From it, he extracted several foil square packages.

"Wow, you come fully prepared," I said, relieved he'd put that much thought into it. I'd come to the mountains hoping to kiss someone under the mistletoe. I hadn't actually planned to have sex with them.

A lopsided smile slid onto his face. "What can I say? The gift shop came stocked."

His comment surprised me.

"Are you telling me you didn't come to Lake Tahoe with those condoms?"

His shoulders raised in a slight shrug, a boyish grin on his face. "You aren't the only one who doesn't make one-night stands a regular habit."

"So, you're more like the relationship type?"

"Not at all. At least not these days. My career comes first."

I opened my mouth to ask him what his career was, because his comment conflicted with what he'd said earlier about doing "this and that" when I asked him about his job. But then I remembered—I didn't want to learn anything else about him.

I smiled instead. "Fair enough."

Grayson strode the short distance to the bed like a panther stalking his prey.

And judging from the way he was eyeing me, I was most definitely on the menu.

"On the bed." The low rumble of his voice smoothed over me like hot fudge daring me to eat just one bite.

Let me tell you now...when a man talks to you that way, there's only one thing you can do.

Yep, you guessed it.

Normally, I would've felt self-conscious being so exposed, both figuratively and literally. It wasn't as if I were skinny. After Stephen died, after the initial mourning phase had passed, I'd become intimate with two men by the name of Ben and Jerry.

Once I'd moved past that phase, I began working out again and became consumed by other distractions, but some of those new curves were reluctant to leave.

Thankfully, the firelight was far more forgiving of them than I was.

Grayson climbed onto the bed and started kissing me again. I slowly rolled over to my back, absorbing his weight and his heat.

He shifted down my body, and his tongue lavished one of my nipples. Not to be outdone, his fingers pinched and tormented the other. Wetness raced to my core, and I squirmed on the bed, desperate for so much more.

My fingers brushed against the short strands of his hair, careful to leave his mask undisturbed.

Aren't you just a little bit curious what he looks like? a voice in the recess of my mind asked.

What's the point? I mentally replied. *So I can imagine him when I make myself come? Probably not a good idea.*

Grayson's mouth moved from the breast he'd been toying with, and he planted slow, languid kisses across my stomach to the waistband of my panties. Each feathery kiss felt as though he were worshiping me, taking time to memorize every inch of my body, like I'd done with his abs.

A soft, gratified moan escaped me.

He hooked his fingers under the elastic and pulled the lace over my hips and along my legs.

I knew it wasn't appropriate, but I couldn't help comparing his actions to those of my husband. Stephen had been the kind of man who removed his clothes and expected me to do the same, and we would climb under the covers and make love. He had never undressed me. He had never taken the time to appreciate my body that way.

Don't get me wrong, he had been great in bed. But this —with Grayson—was so different.

Like ice cream. You can eat a flavor that makes your taste buds sing. You can't imagine anything finer.

But then you try a different one. A creamier flavor. A flavor worthy of the heavens.

Grayson was that flavor—the available-for-a-limited-time flavor.

A sad realization trickled through me at the last part.

But I didn't have time to dwell on the realities of the moment. My panties sailed merrily over the side of the bed. Grayson pulled my legs apart, exposing my sex to him. Any hint of shyness I might've otherwise felt bailed to join my underwear.

He positioned himself between my legs, his breath a tickle against my clit. My body zinged, and I unconsciously fisted the sheet with both hands.

"You don't know how long I've imagined this moment," he murmured.

Huh?

I pushed myself up on my elbows. "What did you say?" I must have misheard him—or misunderstood what he meant.

His gaze darted to my face. "I've thought about doing this since we first kissed," he clarified.

"Oh, okay." That made sense.

It wasn't as if I hadn't imagined a few times after that kiss what it would feel like to have him inside me.

I lay back on the pillows, propped up enough to watch him.

For about three seconds.

That was as long as I lasted once his tongue teased my clit, sending my eyes rolling skyward. "Oh, God, Grayson," I groaned, already racing to the abyss, a place I'd been heading for since our first kiss.

Just as I thought I couldn't last much longer, he pushed a finger inside me, then another, curving them into my soft heat. He plunged them in and out a few more times, his tongue still worshiping my clit.

Those lit fuses? They quickly burned to the end, and with the next flick of his tongue, fireworks ignited deep in my belly, shooting me skyward.

Shooting me to the stars.

I cried out his name, the sound explosive on my lips.

As awareness slowly seeped into my satisfied thoughts, I heard the ripping of a foil package.

I pried my eyes open in time to see him roll a condom onto his impressive length.

Noticing that I'd partially recovered from the mind-blowing orgasm, he grinned devilishly at me, positioned himself against my entrance, and slowly pushed his way in.

I groaned as my body stretched to accommodate him.

He paused. "You okay?"

A liquid smile spread on my lips. "Definitely. Please don't stop on my account." I wrapped my legs around his hips, encouraging him to keep going.

He plunged inside me, and I released another satisfied groan. Then our hips moved in time with each other, taking...and giving so much more in return. And with each thrust of his hips, I climbed higher and higher.

"*Christ*, Kiera," Grayson husked against my ear.

The sound of his voice was all it took.

A tsunami of contractions swept through me, and my inner muscles clenched hard around his length. I'd thought the last orgasm was intense. That had been nothing compared to feeling him inside me, feeling him branding me even though I wasn't his to brand.

I cried out his name again. This time it was met with him grunting his own release, the sound both animalistic and all male.

41

6

KIERA

Cinderella only had until midnight with her prince before her carriage returned to its pumpkin form and her dress switched back to rags.

Fortunately for me, I didn't have the same time constraints.

But as the embers in the fireplace began to slowly die away, I was reminded I couldn't stay here, in bed with Grayson, any longer.

At that somber thought, my rib cage shrunk one size, making it harder to breathe. All the more reason for me to leave now and not once the sun had risen.

The man in question slept in what seemed like a peaceful slumber. His mask was slightly askew, but not enough for me to see his features in the dimly lit room.

Was I surprised that he was asleep? Not at all. After the fourth round of sex, I'd be shocked if he didn't sleep for eight hours straight.

We'd also cuddled in front of the fireplace and talked. Talked about nothing in particular—nothing that would give away too much about our real lives outside the cabin walls.

As tempting as it was to stay here until morning, it would be better to follow Cinderella's lead and hightail it out of here.

But unlike in the fairy tale, there would be no prince combing the kingdom to find the runaway girl. This prince would be returning to Chicago, and I'd be returning to San Francisco.

I adjusted my mask. Then, careful not to wake Grayson, I scooted off the bed.

I wasn't familiar with the rules of one-night stands, but I did know one tended not to overstay one's welcome. The awkward morning-after was always best avoided.

"Good-bye," I whispered, wishing the night could've lasted longer. Yet thankful for the gift I'd been given, even if what we'd shared had been for only one night.

I retrieved my clothes from the floor and soundlessly put them on.

One thing Cinderella never had to worry about was doing the walk of shame. She also didn't have to return to her hotel room through falling snow while wearing stilettos.

She had no idea what she'd missed out on.

I certainly would never regret it.

Nothing about this night would ever be a regret.

7

———

LOGAN

Three weeks later, I pulled the small package out of my condo building's mailbox and checked the return label. It was from the hotel in Lake Tahoe, where I'd stayed.

Curious as to why they were sending me anything that would fit in a small box, I ripped open the brown paper while walking to the elevator.

The door opened as I approached. I entered and pressed the twentieth floor.

Inside the package was a piece of paper. I unfolded it and read the brief note:

> Dear Mr. Mathews,
> The enclosed necklace was found in the cabin you stayed in while you were a guest at our hotel.

I removed the lid from the box. A gold necklace with the familiar script "Believe" gleamed in the elevator light.

My gut tumbled two stories, the cable cut clean through. Kiera's necklace—the one I'd given her as a graduation gift.

It must have come unfastened during one of our super hot sex-a-thon sessions.

According to the date stamped on the wrapper, the package had been sent a few days after Kiera and I stayed in the cabin. But I'd been on the road a lot since then, and it was probably delayed in the mail due to the holiday season.

For a second, I considered what to do with the necklace, but in the end, I decided to do nothing.

It had been from me and not Stephen. It would've been a different story if he'd given it to her.

The elevator door pinged open, and my legs made quick time to my apartment.

Had I thought about Kiera since that night? You'd better believe it. But what she and I had shared was nothing more than a single night of incredibly hot sex.

A one-night stand.

A forbidden romance with my best friend's wife.

I entered my condo, walked to the dresser in my bedroom, where the photo of Livi, Stacy, and myself sat, and pulled open the first drawer.

Smiling at the picture, I dropped the box with the necklace inside, on top of my underwear. Then I returned to my living room and retrieved the iPad from the coffee table to FaceTime with my daughter before I was due at the arena for tonight's game.

"Hey, how's the weather in San Francisco?" I asked her after she'd told me about her day at school, and all about Mrs. A—the best second-grade teacher in the whole wide world....

PART II

8

KIERA

March

"Put your math workbooks away. We're starting an art project based on the stories you've been reading during quiet reading time." Twenty-nine eager second graders peered up at me from their tables. A moment later, this was followed by the shuffling of chairs across the tile floor and chatting voices.

A sudden need to yawn powered through me. I gave in to the urge, barely managing to cover my mouth in time.

How many times had I yawned in the past fifteen minutes?

At least seven.

I'd love to say I only had thirty minutes left of work; then I could go home and nap. But unless the classroom clock was lying, I still had an hour to go until lunch break.

And after that, I had to survive the afternoon before I was done for the day.

The reason for my exhaustion was a mystery. It wasn't like I'd stayed up late last night. I'd gone to bed around 10 p.m. after finishing a pair of children's mittens I'd been knitting for my aunt in Boston.

And then there was that incredibly erotic dream I'd woken up from. The same erotic dream I had experienced regularly ever since the night with Grayson at the ball. My body still dreamily sighed whenever it reminisced about it —which was often, lately.

I collected the stack of white papers from my desk and handed them out. "I want you to take a favorite scene from the book you're reading and draw a picture, showing what's happening in it. You can use colored pencils or crayons or both. Any questions?"

How about a blueberry smoothie? a voice in my head blurted.

Weird. Since when did I crave blueberry smoothies? Sure, they were probably yummy, but my favorites usually revolved around strawberries or raspberries.

Once I'd answered my students' questions, I walked around, checking on how everyone was doing. A murmur of quiet voices followed me through the room.

I approached the table where Livi and Tyler were sitting. The other three students with them were hard at work on their projects, talking among themselves.

"It's an amazing book," Livi animatedly told Tyler. Her blonde pigtails were slightly askew and had been that way ever since she'd returned from morning recess. "The best book in the whole wide world. The series is the best in the whole wide world."

Her face glowed with excitement and awe as she explained the plot to him. A plot I recognized because I'd already read the middle-grade urban-fantasy series.

Ava Quade—my friend and a fellow elementary school teacher—wrote the series under her pen name, AJ

Versteeg, but most of the kids and teachers at the school knew she was the author.

"Max exaggerated the truth about what the Fates told him," Livi said, "and it caused a huge, disastrous mess."

"You mean he lied." I smiled at the way she described it.

"Yes, but he did it to protect those he loved."

As Livi explained the story, her colored pencils glided across the paper, and a griffin took shape. Its head, claws, and wings belonged to an eagle, its body that of a lion—except Livi's eagle looked more like a colorful parrot.

Tyler's page was still blank.

His gaze shifted from her picture and landed longingly on her book, *Max Thunder and the Ocean of Secrets*. His book was the same one he'd been reading for the past three months. It wasn't even his. It belonged to the school.

"How's your book, Tyler?" I asked him.

He shrugged. "Okay."

I crouched to their level. "You can change books if you want. You don't have to keep reading it if you'd rather read something else. You should be reading a story you can't put down, one that excites you. You should be reading a story you can't stop thinking about, one where you're practically counting the minutes until you can disappear into its world again."

Livi nodded, her face alit with a wide grin. "Like the book I'm reading."

His gaze returned to his book, his eyes lacking the glow that Livi's held, and I could almost read his mind.

Tyler was a foster kid.

Don't worry, his foster parents were nice. They were nothing like the horror stories you hear about. I could tell they weren't in it for the money, but they also didn't have a lot of money to spare on things such as new books.

My heart broke for him. His biological parents had died a year ago in a boating accident. Books had been my savior when I was a kid, especially when I felt alone or sad or scared.

"Would you like me to check if the school library has a copy of the first book in the Max Thunder series for you to borrow?" I asked.

With wide, hopeful eyes, he nodded.

I smiled and mentally crossed my fingers and toes. Then I silently wished on all the four-leaf clovers in the playground that I wasn't about to let him down. "Okay, I'll check at lunch."

How did my trip to the library go?

Not so great.

As expected, all the copies were signed out, and the book had a super long waitlist. School would be out for the summer before Tyler could borrow it.

And it wouldn't be much better with the public library.

My heart aching that I didn't have better news for Tyler, I headed to the staff room. As I made my way there, I deliberated my options for getting Tyler a copy of the first book.

And after that, the rest of the series.

By the time I entered the staff room, the only solution I'd come up with was that I would buy them for him and anonymously donate them to him. It would be worth the money if the series got him excited about reading.

Chloe, my best friend, and Ava were sitting at our end of the long table. Their lunch bags were open, the contents spread in front of them.

I yawned once more. God, why was I so tired?

Did I have some terrible disease that sucked energy

from a person like a vampire draining blood from its victim?

Oh, God, please tell me that isn't it.

"Are you okay?" Chloe asked. Both she and Ava were studying me, eyebrows raised.

I took my usual seat next to Chloe. Her copper-colored hair shone softly in the sunlight pouring through the window near us.

"I'm fine. Other than being a little tired. I haven't been able to stop yawning all morning."

"Late night? Maybe a hot date?" Chloe's hopeful expression caused me to snort a laugh.

I know, I know. I'd promised myself at the Jingle Balls ball that it was time to stick my broken pieces together— either with tape or white glue, whatever was available— and move on.

Easier said than done.

It didn't help when the memory of that night enjoyed tormenting me with those erotic dreams. What if I couldn't find another man who sizzled in bed like Grayson?

I mean, sure, sex wasn't everything. But damn, it was still important.

And thanks to Grayson, the bar was now higher.

Darn him.

My hand moved subconsciously to my chest, where the pendant Logan had given me once rested—until I lost it at the ball. I'd called the hotel the next day after realizing it was missing, but no one had turned it in.

And no one got back to me to tell me it had been found.

The taste of bitter regret sat in my throat, and I lowered my hand. "Sorry to disappoint. No hot date."

"Let me guess," Chloe said, "you were up late, knitting mittens for foster kids in Boston."

Like I said, she knew me well—even if she was wrong this time.

She lowered her sandwich with a heartfelt sigh. "I think it's wonderful that you're making them, Kiera. Your aunt's charity is making a big difference to the foster kids who receive them. And those encouraging messages you slip inside each mitten are sweet. But you've been using them as an excuse for why you're always too busy to meet someone new. You deserve to find someone just as wonderful as Stephen. You deserve to have a second chance at love."

"Are you telling me I should stop making them?" My stomach twisted into a tangled knot at the suggestion.

"Not at all. The charity's important to you, and I love that you knit them. But it's time to start putting yourself first. You've been doing a crappy job at it, and I've been a crappy friend for not saying anything sooner."

I grinned. "You're not a crappy friend. You're the friend who's madly in love with her super hot boyfriend and wants everyone to be as happy as you." I gestured at Ava with a wave of my hand. "Same deal with you. You've both found amazing men and want everyone to be as happy as you are. And I don't blame you. I did exactly the same thing to you, Chloe, because I was madly in love with Stephen... in case you're forgetting."

She cringed, no doubt remembering how annoying I had been, and I laughed.

"Anyway, that's not why I'm tired. I went to bed at a decent time. But my waistband's been getting a little tight lately. Maybe I'm gaining weight, and that's zapping my energy."

Ava's eyes widened, and her gaze dropped to my breasts.

Okay, that was unexpected.

She leaned forward, and in a hushed tone, asked, "Are you pregnant?"

A laugh burst from Chloe. That blush on her face? I guess she hadn't expected to laugh any more than I had expected Ava to check out my breasts.

"Sorry, I didn't mean to laugh," Chloe said. "But don't you need to have sex to get pregnant?"

"Not always," Ava replied. "One of my friends had a baby last year, thanks to an anonymous sperm donor."

They both turned to stare at me.

I rolled my eyes. "I didn't get artificially inseminated, if that's what you're thinking."

"You *are* pregnant?" Chloe asked, almost squealing.

I could feel the other teachers' eyes peer our way. I didn't think they heard what she'd said, but the unexpected sound was bound to have gained their attention.

I shook my head—which started out adamantly at first but trickled away to something less sure.

Could I be pregnant?

I mentally counted the days...well, more like weeks... um, months since I last remembered having my period.

Oh. God.

"You had sex and didn't tell me?" You'd have thought from Chloe's reaction, I'd just found out I'd won a billion dollars in last week's lottery.

I shrugged, my mind still spinning like a top at the possibility I could be pregnant. "Apparently. You were busy with everything that had gone down between your cousin and Landon." She'd met her hot boyfriend in the fall when he was undercover at the school as a substitute kindergarten teacher. He'd been hired to protect her due to her past association with the Russian mafia. "I didn't think the fact that I'd had sex the one time was all that newsworthy."

All right, that wasn't entirely true. Grayson and I had engaged in earth-shattering sex several times that night.

Was it any wonder that I'd had been plagued by erotic dreams ever since?

But I was hardly admitting this to Chloe and Ava, especially not when I could sense a few of the other teachers still straining to hear our conversation.

Have you ever had to deal with that super friendly person who loves to be in everyone's business? She's positive she's the one who can solve your problems—along with world hunger?

No, I didn't mean Chloe.

Meet Kristine Richmond.

The tall, pretty brunette slid onto the seat next to mine. "I'm planning a get-together for Sunday afternoon at my house, and I'm hoping you can all attend. It will be so much fun." She winked at us.

Oh, did I forget to mention Kristine had a side business that I was positive would cause some parents to freak if they found out about it?

Kristine's party planning company was wildly popular with bachelorette parties.

You guessed it. Her business involved ensuring your sex life was the best it could be—assuming you had a significant other to share it with.

I could feel my face heat up a thousand degrees. Not because of what she sold. If timing were a dartboard, she'd hit the bull's eye. It was as if she had heard my conversation with Chloe and Ava.

But just how much had she heard?

Did she know I could *possibly* be pregnant?

"Is this one of your sex-toy parties?" I asked.

"I prefer to call it a 'Be Good To Yourself' party, but yes, there will be sex toys and sexy lingerie and other sexy indulgences. So can I count you all in?"

Grinning, Chloe and Ava were quick to say they would

be there. I stuffed my sandwich into my mouth. It wasn't like I had anyone to have sex with or seduce.

I didn't need to seduce my fingers into pleasing me. They were easy and willing—especially after one of my Grayson-induced dreams.

"Perfect. I'll see you three there." With that, she sashayed back to her seat.

"She seriously doesn't expect me to go, does she?" I asked.

"Not only does she expect you to go," Chloe said, "we do, too. It'll be fun. And you know what else will be fun?"

I shook my head. "No, what?"

She exchanged a knowing glance with Ava before turning to me. "You'll find out after school."

And with that, my friends stood up and left the room to get ready for our afternoon classes—leaving me to wonder how I was going to get out of attending the party.

I might not have wanted to go, but I also didn't want to disappoint my friends by not showing up.

Although in light of my possible impending mother-hood status, disappointing my friends was the least of my problems.

9

LOGAN

"Got any plans for tonight?" Eli Lawson asked Travis Hamilton and me in the locker room following afternoon practice.

Chatter from the other San Francisco Rock players filled the space, occasionally punctuated by laughter from one group or another.

That's right. A month ago, I was playing with the Chicago Blackhawks. Two weeks later, I was traded to San Francisco.

And I couldn't have been happier.

Did I expect to be traded, or had I heard rumors circulating in the media about the possibility as the trade deadline approached?

Not at all—nor would I have paid attention to it. My focus was on the game and not on media speculation.

But either way, there was no city I would've rather been traded to than here.

Where my daughter lived.

"You mean other than playing with my daughter and making love to my beautiful wife?" Travis smirked at us. I suspected the smirk had more to do with the latter part than the comment about his daughter.

Unlike Eli and myself, Travis didn't have to hook up with women to get laid. But while I couldn't speak for Eli, hooking up with women wasn't something I did.

Who was the last woman I'd had sex with?

That would be Kiera Ashdown. And no, I hadn't tried to contact her since moving here. It had nothing to do with me being too busy. It was because what happened at the masquerade ball stayed at the masquerade ball.

I didn't see a point in contacting her.

At least not right now.

Maybe I would later on, to see how she was doing. But merely from the point of view of her former husband's best friend—and not the guy who at one time had been secretly in love with her.

"I'm spending the evening with my daughter and ex-wife," I told the guys.

"You want to explain how that works?" Eli asked.

"What do you mean?"

"Conroy and his ex-wife can't stand to be in the same part of the city, never mind in the same house, without hurling accusations at each other."

"That's probably because he cheated on her numerous times while we were on the road," Travis volunteered. "The guy is as faithful to a woman as the moon is likely to be made of draft beer."

"You have a point there."

"Things are different with Stacy and me," I said. "We're close friends. We fell out of love, but that doesn't mean we can't be friends anymore. Livi's our first priority."

"And you don't have issues with her new husband?"

"Should I? He had nothing to do with my marriage breaking up. That was all on me. I'm just glad I get to spend more time with my daughter than I would've if I hadn't been traded here."

"And maybe she has a friend she can hook me up with."

I laughed. "Don't hold your breath. I've been warned to keep away from her friends. Stacy doesn't want to be responsible for picking up pieces of their broken hearts." Her words, not mine. And from the way she'd glared at me when she said it, she'd been damn serious.

Eli yanked his T-shirt on over his head. "How about if *I* hook up with them? Is that allowed?"

"I'm pretty sure her warning was for all hockey players."

"What does she have against hockey players?" Travis asked, grabbing his jeans from his locker.

I shrugged, knowing damn well what her issue was with us. But I couldn't say I blamed her for feeling that way after how our marriage fell apart.

I'd been so focused on my hockey career, training harder, studying plays harder, pushing to be better. And then there were the late game nights, the road trips, the afternoon pregame naps, plus, the community involvement expected from each player.

All of this had added up to less time available for my wife and my daughter.

"Damn, you must have really done a number on her," Eli said, "for her to be against our kind."

Travis and I burst out laughing.

"You make hockey players sound like some kind of species of animal." That got me a towel thrown in my face.

I yanked it down and glared at Eli. It was the same towel he'd had tied around his hips a short time ago.

This only made the guys laugh harder.

"I take it you've got plans for tonight that don't involve kids, wives, or ex-wives," I said to him. The team didn't have a game tonight, and we had three days at home before we were back on the road.

"Some of us are going out, getting drinks, and watching whatever game is on TV. You want to join us after your daughter goes to bed? Or are you, your ex-wife, and her husband doing some sort of meditating, we-are-besties crap together?"

I could only shake my head, a half grin forming. "Yep, that's exactly what we're doing tonight. We're also hoping to summon a few ghosts and paint each other's toenails."

I STROLLED OUT OF THE DRESSING ROOM.

"Daddy!"

At the sound of my daughter's voice, relief and pride squeezed my heart like an accordion. A month ago, I would never have imagined Livi showing up after practice to see me. The closest I'd come to that was via FaceTime.

I was still thanking my lucky stars (and my lucky briefs) that Chicago had traded me to the Rock.

Livi raced toward me, grinning my favorite grin. Stacy was smiling in that confident way that always turned heads —like the security guards who were currently checking her out.

Stacy was gorgeous. In college, she'd done some modeling, mostly to help pay her tuition. Even now, she had agencies trying to get her to sign with them.

But that was all in the past. Being a mother, a supportive wife, and managing a small online business were her only goals these days.

I caught Livi in my arms and hoisted her up. "Hey, princess. How was school?"

She wrapped her arms around my neck. "Mommy's

gonna have a baby," she blurted, beaming. "I'm gonna be a big sister!"

"Congratulations," I told Livi, meaning it.

Stacy flashed me a sheepish grin, her hand resting protectively against her still-flat stomach. I gave her a one-armed hug. "And congratulations to you and Tony."

Her expression slipped into a grateful smile, and she returned my hug. "I hadn't quite planned to tell you this way. Livi's been bouncing off the walls since I told her about it after school."

"How far along are you?"

"Twelve weeks. Tony and I were at the doctor's this afternoon, and everything's looking great so far." The words came out like a torpedo.

I smiled at my daughter. "So, what should we do to celebrate the big news?"

"Ice cream!"

"Are you okay with that?" I asked Stacy.

"That sounds like a perfect idea. Let me text Tony to tell him the plan. He's making dinner to celebrate hearing his baby's heartbeat."

Did I do a good job keeping the cringe off my face?

Already Tony was proving to be a better father than I ever was from the get-go. My hockey schedule had prevented me from making it to most of Stacy's prenatal appointments when she was pregnant with Livi.

And even when I hadn't been on the road, I'd done a lousy job of ensuring I made it to them.

I felt an eyebrow lift. "I take it you were originally planning to tell me the news at dinner?"

Stacy had always idolized Martha Stewart and a host of other lifestyle bloggers, who I couldn't name if I tried. I swear, part of Martha's fortune was thanks to Stacy's love of anything associated with the woman's name. So you could imagine what our wedding was like, especially if you've ever read one of her wedding magazines. (And yes, I'm man enough to admit that I have.)

I was positive the dinner would include pastel balloons, handcrafted paper ornaments, and tiny cakes with baby-themed decorations.

"I thought it would be the perfect time to tell you. Tony and I wanted you to hear it from us first."

I lowered Livi to the floor so she could open the door. "Instead of from our daughter?"

The sheepish look was back on Stacy's face, and I laughed.

We stepped outside the arena and headed toward the rear parking lot.

"You really couldn't expect her to keep silent about something like that," I said. "She's been dying to be a big sister."

Stacy had wanted another baby while we were married, but I'd felt that it wasn't the right time to have another child. My hockey career had come first.

I'd had enough trouble being there for Livi the way I should've been. How I would have balanced two young children had been beyond me—and I still felt that way.

Livi skipped ahead of us, leaping over cracks in the sidewalk.

"I guess not." Stacy was quiet for a moment before saying, "So, how are things with you? Have you met anyone yet since you moved here?"

"Met? As in dating?" Or screwing around with any woman who was interested in having sex with me?

Stacy knew what it was like with some of my team-mates. Even though she'd known I was faithful while we were married, I suspected she believed I had joined that lifestyle as soon as the divorce papers were signed.

I hadn't even been like that in college. Back then, I'd been more focused on my coursework and hockey than I had been on getting laid.

She bumped shoulders with me in her teasing way. "Of course as in dating. I want to make sure she's good enough for you."

A small laugh escaped me. "Are you seriously planning to vet any woman I date?"

"Naturally. That's part of my job as your ex-wife. It was in our wedding vows, in case you've forgotten." She grinned at me.

"Fortunately for you," I said, "you won't have to worry about that."

"Why not?"

"I screwed things up when we were married and put my hockey career first. I'm not repeating that mistake. Lesson learned."

"So what? You're never planning to settle down again? Our marriage didn't work, so you're throwing out the baby and the rubber duckie with the bathwater?" Based on the level of exasperation in her tone, I was surprised she didn't stomp her foot against the sidewalk like I'd seen Livi do.

I bit back a laugh. "No, just not while I'm playing hockey. And I'm hoping I still have several years left in me before I have to worry about it ending."

The Blackhawks hadn't traded me because I was no longer a good hockey player. They'd done it for strategic reasons.

I could tell Stacy wanted to say more on the subject but had decided to keep silent. For now, anyway.

We approached my car, and I unlocked it with my key fob. Stacy's mom-van was a few spots down.

"Oh, before I forget," she said. "I was scheduled to volunteer in Livi's classroom tomorrow, but now I have a time conflict. The mother who organizes the classroom volunteers told me your clearance has been approved. Can you fill in for me?"

She told me the time.

"Sure, why not? I'm looking forward to finally meeting Livi's teacher."

10

KIERA

"You ready?" Ava asked.

She and Chloe were standing in the doorway of my classroom.

I slipped the nonfiction book I was holding into its spot on the bookshelf. "Ready for what?"

"We're going shopping. And then we'll go to your house and wait while you take the test."

"I take it you don't mean a spelling test?"

Neither answered because it was obvious what test they were referring to.

That plunging sensation in my stomach?

I didn't need a test to know what it was going to tell me.

But it would definitely explain the odd blueberry-smoothie craving, which hadn't lessened any since lunch.

"Where am I getting the test from?"

Translation: Are we going to the mall so I can finally deal with this craving?

I grabbed my purse from my desk drawer and a small stack of files to take home.

"I was hoping we could go to the mall," Chloe said. "I

need to buy a baby gift for one of Landon's sisters while we're there. I told him I'd get it for him. He's clueless about these things."

And blueberry smoothie it is.

The three of us drove our cars to the shopping center. The entire drive over, I prayed my body was pranking me.

That I wasn't really pregnant.

That my recently expanding waistline, my larger-than-normal boobs, the blueberry-smoothie craving, the tiredness, and how I was several months late were due to something else.

Something temporary and benign.

Not once during the drive to the mall did I wonder how I would explain the pregnancy to my colleagues and my family and my friends.

Nor did I think about how I was a pregnant widow whose husband died well over a year ago.

But the moment I stepped from my car, the reality of my situation came crashing in on me.

What the heck was I planning to do?

Okay, first things first.

I needed to take the test—or several tests—and see what the verdict was. There was no point in getting all worked up if they were negative.

Something inside me—possibly my ovaries—started laughing their heads off.

Right, ovaries don't have heads, but you know what I mean.

"Are you going to tell us who the father is?" Chloe asked, voicing what was no doubt also on Ava's mind.

We walked toward the entrance.

"All I know is his first name. We didn't share last names. I didn't think it was necessary. What happened between us was a one-time thing."

Grayson's last name *might* have been Mathews. But just because that was his grandmother's last name, it didn't mean he shared it. She had remarried, so it probably belonged to her new husband.

"All I know is, he lives in Chicago."

"Chicago?" Chloe echoed. "That complicates things."

Don't I know it.

"There's a chance I'm not pregnant."

Those pesky ovaries? They started laughing hysterically again.

"If you're pregnant, are you going to tell him?" Ava asked.

"I don't know. First I need time to process that I'm pregnant. *If* I'm pregnant. Having this conversation in person would be tough enough, but I'll have to tell him on the phone. I need a few months to wrap my brain around this before I even think of trying to track him down."

"If you don't know his last name," Chloe asked, "how are you planning to find him? Finding a needle in a haystack would be easier."

"True." I explained about his grandmother.

"Maybe Liam can find out information about the guy," Ava said. "His team has quite the connections."

That didn't surprise me. I didn't know a lot about what her husband and his company did beyond what Ava could tell us, but I did know he had connections with the FBI.

"I'd rather not go that route until I've spoken with Grayson. Let me see what he wants to do about the baby, and then if I feel like it's necessary, Liam can look into his background afterward."

Just because the condom had forgotten its function in life didn't mean I wanted to snoop around in Grayson's private life.

I already knew he wore boxer briefs. What more did I need to know?

"So what did the guy look like?" Chloe asked, eyes bright with curiosity.

"I'm not really sure. We wore masks the entire time."

"Even during sex?" She sounded slightly impressed by that.

And intrigued.

I momentarily grinned at my vivid recollections of that night. "Yep, even during sex. That was my choice. I didn't want to know what he looked like."

In retrospect, that had been an epically bad idea. Although at the time, my rationale for the secrecy about our appearance had sounded great in theory. I hadn't wanted to risk fantasizing about him while I was pleasing myself. I didn't want to have a face to think about during the act.

So instead, I had erotic dreams about a masked stranger.

"What *can* you tell us about his appearance? Or was he wearing a potato sack over his head?"

I laughed as we entered the mall through the automatic doors. "No, he wasn't wearing a potato sack. He had short light-brown hair and blue eyes. And he was tall and athletic."

There had been something familiar about him, but I couldn't place what it was. It was probably nothing more than my imagination.

After I picked up the box set for Tyler from the bookstore, we headed to a store that sold high-end baby products for the gift Chloe needed to buy.

"Oh, this is adorable!" I picked up a onesie from the display of onesies, sleepwear, and bibs, and showed it to them. It read, *Daddy says I'm not allowed to date. Like ever.*

Ava held up another one. "No, this is perfect."

The front of it read, *Mommy doesn't want your advice.*

"I can't tell you how many times I got unsolicited bad advice when Cassie was a baby. And now I'm getting unwanted advice on how to parent a toddler."

Chloe took them from us and added another one that read, *Future Hockey Player.*

"The baby comes from a long line of hockey players," she explained. "Her grandfather, her uncle Landon, and her mommy all used to play hockey."

A neatly folded oatmeal-colored onesie caught my attention. It simply said "Love Bug" on the front.

I didn't return it to the stack.

Chloe and Ava studied me, eyebrows raised.

I lifted my shoulders. "I figure if the test comes out positive, this will be my first step in acknowledging the truth."

"And if it comes out negative?" Ava asked.

I grinned at her. "Well, Cassie isn't going to be an only child, is she?"

Chloe's grin was bigger than mine. "Or maybe they're already trying for Cassie's sibling." We eyed Ava expectantly.

Her face flushed. "I'm not pregnant, if that's what you're asking?"

"So, you're admitting that you're trying."

"There's a possibility that we may or may not be trying to get pregnant again."

Chloe and I laughed. "We'll take that as a yes, you're trying," Chloe said.

"I'm hoping that if I'm pregnant, you quickly get pregnant too, so I'm not doing this alone." I cringed at how that came out—because the truth was, I really was doing this alone.

I would be a single mother.

Not at all how Stephen and I had envisioned things when I'd stopped using birth control three months before the accident.

We had been excited about the possibility of being parents, of filling our child's world with love and happiness.

I guess the joke was on me.

During the three months we'd tried to conceive, nothing. And then one night with a masked stranger and I was possibly knocked up.

Go me.

An unexpected tear trailed down my cheek. I wiped it away.

Chloe pulled me into a hug. "Hey, it's going to be okay. And you won't be alone, no matter what. I know this isn't how you had planned things, but it really will be okay."

I hugged her back. "I don't even know why I'm such a mess."

"Pregnancy hormones will do that to you." Ava's expression clearly stated, "*so you'd better get used to it.*"

Yep, the evidence was definitely stacking in favor of the test swinging in the positive direction.

God, how am I going to explain this to everyone?

Maybe I could claim it was an immaculate conception. Was that even a thing?

We continued shopping. Chloe grabbed several more baby items, oohing and aahing over everything as we went. By the time we left the store, her baby gift had acquired quite the collection of adorable items, including a cute floppy giraffe.

"Do you mind if we hit the Smoothie Hut?" I asked. "I've been craving a blueberry smoothie all day."

I could see Ava mentally add another check to her rapidly growing list of signs I was pregnant.

At this rate, I didn't need to buy a pregnancy test. Ava's list said it all.

The food court was busy when we arrived. We lined up at the Smoothie Hut and ordered our drinks, then headed to the drug store.

"Kiera, how are you doing?" Mrs. Wasserman, my parents' seventy-five-year-old neighbor, stood in the middle of the parenting aisle, holding a box of tampons I was positive wasn't for her.

I had known her forever. She was sweet and friendly and a bit of a gossip.

Correction, she was a huge gossip. If you wanted everyone in the neighborhood to find out something, you just had to tell her, and everyone would hear about it by the end of the day.

The internet had nothing on her.

Which meant the last thing I needed was for her to spot me buying a pregnancy test. Not unless I wanted my parents to know about it before I had a chance to pee on the stick.

I threw Chloe and Ava what had to be a panicked glance and turned to the elderly woman. "Hi, Mrs. Wasserman. I'm good. What about you?"

"I'm doing great. My grandson took me to see the latest *Fast and Furious* movie. That Dwayne Johnson is a nice piece of eye candy." She winked at me. "Don't you agree?" The question was directed at all three of us.

At Ava's startled reaction, Mrs. Wasserman chuckled. "I'm seventy-five years old, young lady. I'm not in my grave yet. I can appreciate the fine male species just as much as someone your age."

I introduced her to my friends.

"And what are you three up to?" she asked.

Yep, she was definitely looking for some juicy details to

share with the Grapevine Express (I kid you not. That was the name of her group of friends who helped spread the gossip. They even had T-shirts and mugs with the name and logo on them).

"We're just shopping. Chloe needed to buy a baby gift for her boyfriend's sister."

Rule #1 when dealing with a gossiper?

Distract her with irrelevant details that have nothing to do with you. If you're creative enough, she'll never realize what you're up to. Your secret will be safe.

"And what did you buy there?" Her gaze fell knowingly to the bag in my hand—the one with the store logo that matched the bags in Chloe's hands.

Oops.

Right, I was never a good liar.

"Umm. It's for a baby shower...gift. For a colleague. At school."

Somehow I kept from covering my face with my hand.

"Oh, that's so sweet. And what are you doing down this aisle? You ladies aren't by any chance buying condoms, are you?"

I inwardly flinched at how loud she said that. I'd be surprised if the entire store hadn't heard her.

Fortunately, she lowered her voice for her next question. "Have you tried those glow-in-the-dark ones? They sound like quite the hoot. Too bad they weren't invented until after my eggs turned to dust."

Chloe, Ava, and I shared a look. Only one of us showed any hint of mortification at the question. The other two were highly amused.

Please don't repeat this conversation with my family, I silently begged Mrs. Wasserman.

Oh, who was I kidding? Of course she'd repeat it to my parents.

Better they think you're buying glow-in-the-dark condoms than purchasing a pregnancy test.

"That's exactly what I'm buying." Chloe grabbed a box from the shelf.

"What about you, Kiera?" Mrs. Wasserman asked, her expression on the hopeful side of things.

"Chloe has a boyfriend. I don't."

My parents' neighbor's gnarled hand reached for a box and passed it to me. "I bet you'd have a boyfriend if you used these."

Heat rushed to my face. Was it too much to ask for, to buy a pregnancy test without any witnesses who knew my parents?

Speaking of condoms, Grayson and I had used them every time we'd had sex. Brand new condoms. At least I assumed the ones in the hotel gift shop hadn't exceeded their expiry date.

So I couldn't possibly be pregnant.

Yes, yes, I know. Even though the box might state a 99% efficacy rate, real life wasn't quite as perfect. Something like fourteen out of a hundred women who used condoms wound up pregnant.

But why did I have to be one of those fourteen women? Until that night, I hadn't had sex in over a year.

Why couldn't Murphy's Law have given me a little leeway? Made me an exception to his stupid rule?

Just when I thought I couldn't be any more mortified than I was, someone decided to prove me wrong. Nick Wasserman, the man angels wept over because he was that handsome, walked toward us. His gaze dropped to the box of condoms in my hand, then shifted to my face.

If I thought my face was hot before, that had been nothing compared to now.

"Nick, you remember Kiera, don't you?" his grandmother said. "Ed and Beth Nickleson's daughter."

"I do. The last time I saw her was during their Christmas party, wearing a sweater with Rudolph on it. And Rudolph's nose glowed." He seemed to be working double time to keep from laughing out loud.

Ah, yes. The infamous ugly Christmas sweater Mom had given me for the party.

"Yes, that would be me." Chloe and Ava had seen photos of the outfit, complete with reindeer antlers attached to a headband.

The ensemble hadn't exactly been my dream outfit for the night, but it had made Mom happy, so I'd worn it.

"Kiera was just mentioning to me that she's still single," Mrs. Wasserman said. "Nick's single, too."

That sound? It was the angels tooting their trumpets in triumph.

Only I didn't share their sentiment.

Not to say he wasn't a nice guy. He was. Even Stephen had liked him—but he also hadn't made Stephen's list of men that I could marry if Stephen died before me.

And even if he had, it was too late for that if I failed the test I was about to take.

Or would be taking once I could sneak a pregnancy test past Mrs. Wasserman's prying nose.

Ava and Chloe peered on with interest. Chloe flashed me a *He's-hot, double-thumbs-up* message with her eyes.

"Maybe we can get together for coffee some time," Nick said.

"Absolutely," Chloe replied. "She would love that."

I flashed her a *What-the-hell-are-you-doing?* expression.

Hers responded, *Getting you a date with a hot man.*

Are you forgetting I might be pregnant? was my answering reply.

Her eyebrows raised as if to say, *It's just one coffee. You are allowed that when you're pregnant.*

I ignored her.

———

An hour later, Ava, Chloe, and I sat in my living room, waiting for the three minutes to tick down on my phone. In front of me on the coffee table was an array of peed-on pregnancy tests.

Yes, I did eventually buy them, after Nick got my phone number. And no, I didn't buy the glow-in-the-dark condoms. Chloe did, though, as a joke for her boyfriend.

"Sooo," Chloe began, "if the test is positive, what are you going to tell everyone when they ask about the father? Even though it's none of their business, people *will* ask."

"Maybe I should just tell everyone it's Stephen's baby." The corners of my mouth twitched, giving away the fact that I was kidding. "That would certainly make things easier if Grayson wants nothing to do with the baby. Heck, maybe I shouldn't even try contacting him." At least that would be one less person to disappoint because I'd let a super hot kiss morph into super hot sex.

Ava snorted a laugh. "That won't work, Kiera. Stephen's been dead for over a year now. So unless you're an elephant, no one's going to buy that your baby is his."

She had a point there.

"So I guess it won't fly if I tell people that Stephen and I had been attempting to get pregnant for a while, and because things hadn't gone as planned, we'd been seeing a specialist? And I used his frozen sperm to get pregnant?"

Chloe chuckled. "Well, that would be one way to explain how your gestation period ended up resembling that of an elephant."

"I'm not sure if that's how it works," Ava said. "I think they only do that if the husband has a disease that will eventually impact his fertility, and the couple isn't ready to have a baby yet. But I could be wrong."

That was too bad, because it would be easier telling people the frozen-sperm explanation than letting them know the truth. And then the baby would never have to know that they were the result of Mommy having a one-night stand with a stranger.

Plus, I wouldn't have to worry about disappointing my parents (or anyone else I cared about). I had disappointed my grandmother when I was nine years old.

She died.

Lesson learned?

It was always best to do whatever it took to avoid disappointing those you loved.

Sure she didn't die of disappointment, but I'd still let her down.

The timer on my phone went off.

Oh, fudgesicles. The moment of denial was over.

I hit stop...and stared at the tests. They were all flipped over so I couldn't peek at them before the time was up.

A long, God-I-can't-do-this breath slipped out between my pursed lips. I continued staring at the tests.

Yep, because that would ensure they were negative.

"Do you want me to look?" There was enough compassion in Chloe's tone to fuel a jet plane from San Francisco to Uranus.

I nodded, gaze still locked on the tests.

Everything was about to change, but I couldn't take that first step in confirming what we already suspected was true.

Chloe picked up the first test, inspected it, and handed it to Ava.

Ava smiled. It was the kind of smile you gave when you

were happy with the news, but you weren't sure how the other person would feel about it. "You're going to be a mom."

She handed me the stick.

"It could be wrong." That was why I'd bought the other four tests.

I flipped them over, one by one, each test confirming the results of the first one.

I was pregnant.

And just like that, my world changed once again.

11

LOGAN

When was the last time I'd entered a classroom? I'd have to say when I was a kid.

Stacy had been the one to attend Livi's parent-teacher conferences.

I'd always been too busy.

Which was why when I stepped into Livi's classroom the following afternoon, it was like entering a spaceship. Everything felt foreign.

But that was why I was here.

To change that. To be more involved with my daughter's life. To not let my career steal more of my precious time away from her than was unavoidable.

The woman who I assumed to be her teacher was talking to a student, her back to me.

Livi was at the same table. She looked up as the door shut behind me, waved at me, and said something to the woman.

Her teacher straightened and turned around.

And at the sight of her familiar features, framed by equally familiar blonde hair, it was as if a wave had swept

79

up the shore with vengeance, then pulled away, dragging the sand from under my feet.

Holy shit.

Happy laughter from a nearby table echoed inside me, blending with the shock that now sat firmly in my gut.

The last person I'd expected to see was the woman I'd made love to several times the night of the Jingle Balls ball.

Livi had always referred to her favorite teacher as Mrs. A, but Stacy had never mentioned that A was short for Ashdown.

Had Stacy ever met Kiera?

Yes, a few times when Stacy and I were first married.

If Stacy had figured out Stephen's wife and Livi's teacher were the same person, she'd never mentioned it.

Kiera stared at me as if seeing Santa's ghost, and the possibility crossed my mind that she had already pieced together everything from that night.

But since I hadn't hinted at the ball that I knew her true identity, she wouldn't know I had purposefully kept mine a secret. She wouldn't know I had altered my voice that night so she wouldn't recognize me.

Even though the world had unceremoniously dropped from beneath my feet, my body remembered how it felt to kiss her, to hold her, to make love to her.

That's in the past, I reminded it. *It won't happen again.*

I walked toward her. A murmur of young voices sprung up as several kids recognized my face.

I approached the table and smiled at my daughter.

"Hi, Daddy."

"Hey, Livi."

The eyes of the boy sitting next to her were as round as pucks, and I could have easily fit a puck into his wide-open mouth. "Wow. You're Logan Mathews. You used to play with the Chicago Blackhawks, and now you play for the Rock."

"That's right. And you're?"

"Tyler."

"He's one of my best friends," Livi proudly told me, and I instantly recognized the name. There was a chance she had mentioned it several hundred times in the past five months.

"Nice to meet you, Tyler." I fist-bumped him.

I turned to Kiera, who was still staring at me. "I had no idea you were Livi's father." Her voice was soft and a little off-balanced compared to the last time I'd seen her. "I had no idea you were living in San Francisco."

"The Blackhawks traded me to the Rock a couple of weeks ago. I've been meaning to contact you to see how you're doing, but I haven't had a chance yet."

That sounded better than the truth—that I had been avoiding her.

Her lack of awareness about the trade surprised me. The Kiera I remembered would've known about it. She and Stephen had become Rock fans when they moved to San Francisco. Maybe that had ended with Stephen's death.

I could feel Livi's gaze dart between us. She'd been a toddler the last time she'd seen Kiera, so she wouldn't have remembered her. And I couldn't remember the last time I'd sent Stephen pictures of Livi.

For a second, Kiera looked as though she had numerous questions swirling in her head, but then the confused frown smoothed away. In its place, a grin, complete with the dimples I loved, brightened her face.

The same grin and dimples that always stole my breath away ever since college.

After all these years, I still wasn't immune to it.

"Well, it's great to see you again," she said.

"It's great to see you, too." I waited for another sign that she had pieced together that I was Grayson, but instead, she asked Tyler if he wanted to be the first to read to me.

He practically fell off his chair in excitement at the question.

Kiera directed her breathtaking smile at him. "Tyler, you can take Mr. Mathews into the hallway to read." To me, she said, "It's quieter there. Have him read to you for about ten minutes, then send him back in, and I'll send out another student to read to you."

Tyler scrambled off his chair and grabbed a book from the table. I followed him into the hallway, and he showed me the two chairs we were to sit on.

"What are you reading?" I asked. He handed me the skinny paperback, and I read the blurb. "Are you enjoying it?"

He shrugged. "It's okay."

I wasn't familiar with the book—not that I considered myself an expert when it came to kids' books. My only experience with them was when Livi read them to me or gushed about a novel she loved.

And this one fell under neither category.

Tyler opened it and began reading to me.

Reading clearly didn't come easy for him. He was slow and struggled with some of the words. He also didn't share the same enthusiasm for reading that Livi did.

But based on what I'd heard so far from him, I couldn't say I was too surprised. The story wasn't all that gripping. It was the kind of book you read when it was 2 a.m., and you were desperate to fall asleep and counting sheep had failed.

Hell, I was barely staying awake reading along with him.

"That's the last of them," I told Kiera two hours later. It was almost the end of the day, and the kids were tidying up to go home.

"Thank you so much, Logan, for your help. I'm sorry I didn't clue in sooner that you're Livi's father. It's been years since Stephen..." Her words paused for a heartbreaking second. "Since he last showed me a photo of your daughter."

"To be honest, that's probably because I did a crappy job sending any to him. I'm not surprised you didn't recognize her. She's talked a lot about you, but Stacy never mentioned you were her teacher."

Kiera laughed softly. "I'm not sure even she remembered me. I certainly didn't recognize her. It's been a long time since your wedding, and I think that's the last time I saw you two together."

That was mostly my fault. I'd always been too busy with hockey, so we'd rarely done things together. It became habit. And habit led to divorce.

Not wanting to talk about any of that, I decided to switch topics.

Topics that also didn't include the masquerade ball.

Did I think Kiera recognized me from that night?

If she did, she didn't show it.

But that wasn't all too surprising. Neither of us resembled the same individuals as that night. My hair had grown longer. Kiera's long hair had been cut to just below her shoulders. She had looked beautiful that night. Now she looked fucking gorgeous.

She had the sweet look about her that always got my dick hard.

Okay, let me rephrase that.

The sweet look that always left me mentally cursing how my best friend got the girl, and I just got to be her pal.

"How are you doing?" I asked.

"Good. Busy."

Busy? As in busy dating other men?

Some men might resort to persuading their daughter to ask the hot teacher if she was single. I wasn't one of those douchebags.

So I went with a simple, "Busy?" and hoped that was enough to get her to answer the question I hadn't asked out loud.

"With my job...and other things."

"What kinds of other things?"

You're probably wondering why I didn't come straight out and ask her if she was seeing anyone.

Well, here's the thing. The only time a guy ever asked that question would be if he was asking the woman out on a date, and he didn't want to risk rejection.

It was his saving grace.

If the woman wasn't interested, she could take the easy way out and say yes, she was seeing someone—even if she wasn't.

It was the coward's way of coping with an otherwise awkward situation...on both ends.

If I asked Kiera if she was seeing anyone, she might automatically assume I was asking her out when I wasn't.

I was just curious—on Stephen's behalf.

And please don't give me that crap about him watching Kiera from heaven, so he knew if she was dating or not.

You don't know what he was doing up there. They might have rules against watching your loved ones on Earth. Hell, he might've been too busy to keep an eye on her to ensure that she was all right.

And that was where I came in.

I could make sure she was okay. Make sure she was

doing what she had promised the night of the ball—finally moving on.

"I've been knitting mittens that my aunt in Boston donates to kids entering the foster care system," she said. "That way, they have warm mittens for the cold weather." The smile on her face was as warm as the mittens no doubt were.

"That's really great. I didn't know you could knit."

She laughed. "YouTube is a wonderful place if you want to pick up a new skill. I was struggling at first when Stephen died. Curling up in a ball sounded like a better idea than facing another day without him. Aunt Trudy told me about the mittens she and a group of her friends were making.

"I lost the man who I'd loved, but those kids in foster care had lost so much more. For some of them, they lost hope after losing their parents. For others, they never had hope to begin with because of their living situations until family services stepped in." Kiera picked up a kid's book from her desk. "Knitting those mittens helped pull me out of my depression."

"Have you been doing anything else to help you move on? Have you been seeing someone?"

Okay, I'll admit it. That could be taken in so many different ways. And yes, a large part of me hoped she would interpret it as I had intended.

"I did meet with a grief counselor for a bit. It was my mom's idea. That helped, too."

Not quite the answer I'd been fishing for.

But it was good to know that she hadn't been dealing with her husband's death on her own.

"What about other men? Have you been dating again?" I aimed for a casual, shooting-the-breeze tone, not one that suggested I wanted to go out with her.

Her gaze dropped to the book in her hand, then she looked up again and smiled. Something was off about it, but I couldn't put my finger on what it was exactly. "I've been too busy to date. Or prospect for dates." She lowered her voice on the last part in a way that almost caused me to laugh out loud.

I interpreted that to mean she hadn't been having sex with other men—other than me. Nor was she ready to admit to having sex with Grayson.

Before I had a chance to comment, she blurted, "I've decided to create a fundraiser. I love making the mittens, but they aren't in high demand in San Francisco, as you can imagine. I want to do something for the foster kids in the city. For kids like Tyler." She waved in the general direction where he'd been sitting.

"What are you thinking of doing?"

"When I was his age, my dad's job transferred him to Boston. It was during the summer, and I didn't know anyone there. I was shy, so making new friends was harder for me. My aunt gave me *Harry Potter and the Sorcerer's Stone*. I hadn't been an avid reader prior to that. But by the end of the first chapter, that all changed.

"After that, there was no stopping me. I read the series several times. Then started to read books by other kid-lit authors. I loved disappearing into the worlds they created. And they taught me that I could be anything I wanted to be. I just needed to have the determination and courage to achieve it." She grinned my favorite smile once again, causing something deep inside me to stir. "And the best part? I had something to talk about when I started at the new school in the fall. I quickly made friends with kids who also loved those books."

I nodded like I understood what she was talking about —which I partly did. Hockey had been like that for me.

"Livi told Tyler all about the series that she's been reading. The one by AJ Versteeg."

I knew the books she was referring to. Livi had been reading them to me, and I could see why she loved them. They had everything I would've loved as a kid—if I'd read more than I had.

Let's just say I could relate to Tyler a lot more than he realized.

My parents had pretty much bribed me to read more as a kid. In retrospect, I'm glad they had. It meant I'd been able to attend college and impress NHL scouts while I played for the Boston Eagles.

And it meant I had an education to fall back on after my hockey career came to an end.

Way.

Way.

Way down the line.

"She loves those books," I said. "I gave her the new one for Christmas."

"That's because you could. But for kids in foster care, most of them don't have someone who can buy them books. And that's where I come in. I want to raise money to provide books for kids in foster care. But not just a single book. I want to give box sets to kids who want to read all the books in a popular series. So they aren't left waiting until it's their turn on the massively long library waitlist for the next book in the series."

You know how when there's a sudden break in the thick clouds, and rays of sunlight illuminate the ground, turning drab into breathtaking? That was how Kiera looked as she explained her idea. The only difference was that she was already beautiful. Her enthusiasm for the project increased it a hundredfold.

"I think that's a great idea. What can I do to help?" The

words hustled their way out before I knew what I was saying.

But I meant it. Every word of it.

For a second, Kiera looked stunned, as if she hadn't been expecting me to say that. "That's sweet of you to offer. I'll let you know once I have a better idea of what I want to do. Are you still going to be volunteering in the classroom, or will Stacy be back next week?"

"Stacy will be back. But I would like to volunteer as my schedule permits. I'll talk to Joyce tonight, and maybe the next time I'm here, we can discuss your plans after school."

I wanted to bring up the topic of her dating life again, but really, what would I say?

Tell her to get out there—that Stephen would have wanted her to?

It was true; he would have. As long as the man was good enough for Kiera.

But did I really look like a dating cheerleader?

Someone who shook their pompoms from the sidelines when it came to someone's dating life?

No, I didn't think so either.

12

KIERA

"**S**weetheart," Mom said, drying her hands on the kitchen towel.

It was late Sunday morning, and as per tradition, I was at my parents' for our weekly brunch.

"Hey, Mom." I stood in the entranceway, gripping a bunch of tulips so hard, I was surprised the stems hadn't snapped in half.

I didn't usually bring Mom flowers for brunch, but I figured they'd help soften the blow of my big news.

They certainly couldn't hurt.

I hugged her, which wasn't new. Even though it had only been a week since I'd last seen her, I was positive she could tell I was expecting.

Seriously, how had I even missed that I was pregnant?

The signs were all there—like a billboard in Times Square.

If my oversized T-shirt surprised Mom, she didn't let it show. I'd worn it over my black yoga pants, which were about the only pants I owned that weren't now tight in the waist.

I handed Mom the flowers. "These are for you."

"Thank you! They're gorgeous. But since when do you bring me flowers for Sunday brunch?"

"I just figured they would add a special touch to your great food."

"That's so sweet of you, Kiera." She walked to the sink, ankles peeking from under the hem of her tie-dyed purple skirt, and placed the flowers in a vase. "I saw Mrs. Wasserman yesterday."

Oh, fudgesicles. Please tell me she never mentioned the condoms.

"Oh, really? How's she doing?"

"Probably the same as she was on Wednesday when you saw her." She smiled proudly at me like she had when I got accepted into Boston College.

Okay, maybe she didn't know about the glow-in-the-dark condoms.

"You mean happy?"

"Over-the-moon happy. She told me that you have a date with her grandson, Nick." It would seem that Mrs. Wasserman wasn't the only one over-the-moon happy at that news.

"I wouldn't get too excited about that. It's just coffee." Plus, once the man discovered I was pregnant, he would be running for the hills faster than Julie Andrews in *The Sound of Music.*

"Just because it starts out as coffee doesn't mean it can't become something more."

Dad thankfully picked that moment to enter the kitchen, saving me from the awkward conversation. One awkward conversation a day was more than enough, and I was reserving the quota for what I was about to tell them.

Dad hugged me, and I took a deep breath.

"I'm pregnant," I blurted.

The room went silent, other than the reprimanding *tick-tock tick-tock* from the clock on the wall.

Since I'd done a great job of shocking them, I figured I might as well leap in all the way, headfirst. "And it's Stephen's baby."

Oh, damn.

I hadn't meant to say that.

So why had I said it?

I mean, other than me being an idiot.

I'd been thinking on the way over about how much Stephen had wanted a baby. And about how he would've been an amazing father.

To be honest, I'd been thinking about that a lot lately.

And then one look at my mom and the idea of admitting that I'd been knocked up by a masked stranger suddenly seemed less appealing.

I could see my mother mentally counting the months since Stephen had died, and I prayed to the god of lying that he would help me with this doozy.

Right, I know what you're thinking. Just tell her the truth.

I was going to eventually track down Grayson and let him know about his impending fatherhood status. So why let her believe that Stephen was the baby's father?

Because what if he didn't want to acknowledge his child?

What if he wanted nothing to do with us?

I was confident that his bucket list didn't include knocking up a stranger.

For all I knew, he didn't want kids.

"Stephen and I were trying to have a baby before he died," I attempted to explain, grateful neither parent worked for the police department or the FBI or the CIA. Basically, anyone who could tell when someone was lying to them. "Things didn't go as planned, so we went to see a fertility specialist...and they froze some of Stephen's sperm...er, just in case."

Please don't know anything about in vitro. Please don't know anything about in vitro.

Prior to her retirement, Mom had been an advertising executive, so there was a good chance she was clueless about the process of artificial insemination.

Much like me.

"So, you got pregnant with Stephen's Popsicle sperm?" Dad asked, looking more amused than anything. But that was my father for you. He was always one for rolling with the punches with a dash of humor tossed in.

"I'm thrilled for you." Mom's voice wobbled, but not enough to keep her from beaming. "I didn't realize you were planning to do this."

That made two of us.

"I didn't want to say anything in case it didn't work out." I inwardly cringed at the lie.

Some people were natural liars.

I wasn't one of them.

Yes, eventually, I would tell my parents the truth—assuming Grayson wanted to be part of Love Bug's life—but for now, it just seemed easier to let them believe what I'd blurted out.

Love Bug?

That was the baby's name until he or she was born.

Even though I hadn't planned to be a single mom, I wanted the baby to feel loved from the get-go. So Love Bug it was—for now, anyway.

SEVERAL HOURS LATER, CHLOE SWUNG BY MY PLACE TO PICK me up for what Ava, Chloe, and I had dubbed "The Sex Party."

"Do you want to explain to me again why I'm joining you and Ava? You two have significant others. You have someone who'll appreciate anything you buy at the party. I'm going to feel ridiculous there."

Especially now that my pregnancy had been confirmed and my first prenatal appointment was for the following week.

"Maybe Nick will appreciate it. Has he called you yet?"

I laughed. "He hasn't, and I can guarantee he won't now. I told my parents this morning I'm pregnant. I suspect by now Mrs. Wasserman and her grandson know."

"How did your parents take the news?"

"They couldn't be more delighted...that I'm having Stephen's baby."

"You told them Stephen's the father?" Chloe's gaze darted briefly to me before returning to the road.

"I hadn't planned on it. It just kind of came out."

"Does that mean you're no longer planning to tell the real father that he's going to be a daddy?"

"No, I'm still going to tell him. At some point. Before I have the baby."

"And then you'll tell them the truth?"

"It depends on Grayson. If he wants to be part of Love Bug's life, I'll tell them the truth."

"And if he doesn't?"

I lifted my shoulders even though she couldn't see the movement. "I guess my parents will keep believing that Stephen is Love Bug's biological father. It'll be better that way. Then my baby will always believe that he or she is the result of two parents who loved each other. That's gotta be better than the truth if Grayson isn't interested in being a parent to our child."

"Aren't you worried they'll tell Stephen's parents?"

"Not at all. They haven't spoken to them since his funeral."

I still talked to his mom from time to time, but since Stephen's parents lived in North Carolina, there was no reason for them to find out I was pregnant.

"That's good, I guess. It'll definitely make things more awkward if they think you're having their grandchild when you aren't."

Don't I know it.

"So now that we've established I'll be dateless until Love Bug is in college, you want to remind me again why I'm going to The Sex Party?"

"Because it will be fun. Besides, what else were you planning to do today? Other than knit mittens."

All right, she had a point there.

My phone pinged as we approached Kristine's house. Thinking it was Ava, I checked the message.

Logan: Hey, Kiera. Stacy gave me your number. Are you busy tonight? Thought you could come over for dinner, and we can discuss the fundraiser.

Me: I have plans for the next few hours, but I should be able to escape by then.

Logan: Sounds intriguing.

He texted me his and Stacy's address. Typically, I wouldn't go over to a student's house for dinner. But this was different. Logan and I had been friends in college.

I'd always liked Logan. He was cute and funny and smart. He knew how to make me laugh. Before I met

Stephen, I'd wanted to date Logan, but I was shy and awkward. Telling a guy that I was crushing on him wasn't my style.

So, I flirted with him. Well, had attempted to flirt with him. Some girls are brilliant flirters; it's in their DNA. Me? Not so much. But either way, Logan never asked me out or gave any indication he liked me the same way I liked him.

And then I met Stephen.

Stephen was a take-charge kind of guy.

The kind of guy who wasn't afraid to go after what he wanted—case in point.

The moment Logan introduced us at a party, Stephen became an outrageous flirt.

I could've taken some serious lessons from him.

He made me laugh so much, it was impossible to turn him down when he asked me out.

One date became two, then three, and then ten.

And before I knew it, I was his girlfriend, the woman who cheered the loudest at his games. The woman who fell in love with him.

And Logan remained my friend.

Logan's and my friendship did fade over the years—no fault of ours.

He was drafted by Chicago. After that, Stephen and I married and moved to San Francisco. And over time, Logan and I saw less and less of each other, even though we still had Stephen in common.

Ava's car was parked on the street outside of Kristine's house when we arrived. Chloe found an empty spot not far from there.

"So what's the plan?" she asked. "Are you telling people that you're pregnant?"

I shook my head. "Not yet. For starters, I should probably tell Principal Woodnut first."

"Right. That might be a good idea. Okay, I won't say anything."

After brunch with my parents, I'd gone home and changed into a light-pink sundress that hid my stomach. I'd also slipped on a lightweight cardigan to mask that my boobs were bigger than they used to be, which was painfully evident from the way the bodice strained to contain them.

"Do I look pregnant?" I asked Chloe as we walked along the sidewalk to the house.

She stopped and openly appraised my body. "Nope, I think you should be safe for now. But I'm not sure how much longer you'll be able to hide your situation."

Despite my reluctance to be there, I burst out laughing. "You sound like someone from the eighteenth century." I pretended to fan myself and spoke in a falsetto voice. "Oh, heaven forbid people discover my virtue has been tarnished by my unwed pregnant status."

Chloe snickered and looped her arm with mine. "Would you care to take a turn around the room while we discuss how that roguish man got you in such a scandalous state?"

That only made me laugh harder.

And for a moment, I temporarily forgot my predicament of being knocked up, thanks to a masked stranger.

Temporarily forgot the embarrassment that thrummed deep in my veins.

Temporarily forgot how I had betrayed Stephen's memory by claiming the baby was his.

At the front door, I rang the bell. Laughter came from inside, and the door opened a moment later, revealing Kristine. Her navy knit dress clung to her slim body, making it clear she didn't have a baby bump to hide, unlike me. With wavy chestnut hair tumbling over her shoulders, smoky makeup, and never-ending legs, the woman was sex-on-a-stick, and then some.

Which, I suppose, was ideal if you were planning to sell sex toys to a bunch of giggling women—including one who was sex-starved.

She smiled her usual bubbly smile, slightly easing my trepidation at being here. "Everyone's in the living room."

We entered the house, removed our shoes, and joined the eight women, including Ava, sitting on chairs in a circle.

Like a support group.

Only this support group was here to confess that they loved sex and to buy naughty toys and lingerie.

Chloe and I sat on the two empty seats on either side of Ava.

"I'm thrilled you could all make it," Kristine said before the three of us could say anything to each other. "I thought we could start off by introducing yourselves and telling us if there's a certain somebody in your life you're hoping to spice up your sex life with." Her gaze briefly touched on me. It wasn't long enough to single me out, but it was enough for me to wonder if she'd figured out I was pregnant.

Or had decided I was just packing on some extra weight lately.

"And remember, what we say here today stays here. This is a safe environment." She nodded at Chloe.

Ava and I exchanged amused glances at Kristine's comment.

"I'm Chloe. I have a boyfriend who I've been with for about three months."

I bit back the urge to say, "*Hi, Chloe,*" support-group style.

"Do you mind if I ask if you and he have had sex yet, or are you waiting?" Kristine's smile hinted she knew the answer. We all did. Chloe glowed in that way of someone who was getting sex on a regular basis.

This wasn't to be confused with the glow that she, Ava, and my mom claimed I now sported—the glow of being knocked up.

All eight of us peered at Chloe in eager anticipation, even though Ava and I were well aware of the answer.

Chloe's glow switched to a full-out blush. "Yes, we're sexually active. And it's really good."

Everyone nodded, satisfied with her reply—and maybe in my case, a little envious—then we turned to Ava.

"Hi, I'm Ava. I'm married to an amazing man. Our sex life is already great, although it can be challenging because we have an energetic toddler."

A few of the others nodded in understanding.

Someone muttered under her breath, "Amen to that."

That was one thing I didn't have to worry about. Love Bug could be as energetic as they wanted to be as a toddler. It wasn't like it could impede my already nonexistent sex life.

Now it was my moment of truth. Well, half-truth. "I'm Kiera, and I'm single." Most of the women in the group knew I was a widow, but that didn't mean I wished to witness pitying looks from the others.

"Is there anyone you're interested in seducing?" Kristine asked.

Good thing I wasn't drinking anything. I would have accidentally spewed the beverage over everyone.

How exactly was I supposed to answer this?

If I told them I was seeing someone, there would be lots of questions about my fictitious boyfriend once I announced to my colleagues I was pregnant.

And sure, I could pretend he was the father, but that

would be messier than pretending Love Bug was the product of Stephen's frozen sperm.

"No." My answer came out as a squeak.

The women I didn't know stared at me with wide-eyed horror, as if they couldn't imagine not having at least one person to lust over.

For a second, Logan's image popped into my head.

I shoved it away.

What was I thinking? The man was happily married.

Besides, even if he wasn't married, it wouldn't make a difference. He wasn't interested in me that way. And he certainly wouldn't be interested once he found out I was pregnant.

The rest of the group introduced themselves and shared about their special someone. I wasn't the only one who was single, but Crystal had her eyes set on someone whom she hoped would one day be more than just a friend.

"I can guarantee by the time we're finished today," Kristine said, "he won't be able to resist you."

She introduced us to a line of bubble baths, candles, and massage oils that were, in her words, bound to get our man's blood pumping.

You know what else I learned about that line of products?

Well, it was more like what I learned when it came to pregnancy and certain smells.

"Are you okay?" Ava asked me a few minutes after I'd excused myself and raced outside.

I was standing on the front porch, breathing in the fresh rain-scented air. The sudden nausea from the overwhelming smell of the products had since subsided.

A light spring shower was wetting the ground, the droplets creating a rainbow in the sky ahead of us.

"I'm better now. The smell got to me." I flashed her an

amused grin. "I guess I won't be buying any of those products for the boyfriend who doesn't exist."

"For me, it was olives—the open ones in the grocery store. Every time I passed them, I thought I was going to hurl. I used to give them as wide a berth as I could, just to avoid them.

"I also couldn't drink orange juice while pregnant. Even thinking about it made me nauseous." She scrunched her nose, and I chuckled.

"So far, I haven't had that problem with orange juice. Do you think it's safe yet to go back in?"

"I think so. We're modeling the lingerie next."

"Modeling?" My voice sounded like a squeaky toy. "As in, trying on sexy lingerie and parading around Kristine's living room?"

Ava nodded.

"I can't do that. Everyone will know I'm pregnant."

"They'll figure it out sooner or later. It's not something you'll be able to hide much longer."

That might be true, but it didn't mean I was ready to start lying to everyone.

I was still getting used to the newly found skill; I wasn't ready to go big-time yet.

"Don't think of it as lying," the devil hanging out on my shoulder said. "Think of it as acting. Or like writing fiction. It's not like Ava's stories are true."

Two points to the devil.

I waited for the angel to respond, but she was too busy knitting a muffler to pay attention to the conversation.

I was positive if she wasn't too busy, she would've argued that writing about mythological creatures wasn't the same as telling people that Love Bug was the result of Stephen's Popsicle sperm.

Besides, I'd never taken an acting class in my life, which pretty much explained why I wasn't a good liar.

"I need more time," I told Ava.

The devil snickered something about me being a coward, and the angel popped her head up and asked if she'd missed something.

"I know," Ava said. "But don't worry about the modeling part. I'm sure Kristine has something that will hide the fact that you're pregnant."

I nodded because I didn't want to ruin Ava's and Chloe's fun. And that was precisely what would happen if I spent the rest of the party outside, trying not to feel sorry for myself.

We headed inside and selected our outfits to try on.

What was mine?

A black lace baby doll nightie that was fitted in the chest but flowed loosely around my thighs. The front was open, but it still hid the fact that I was pregnant.

I felt sexy, and based on the girlish wolf whistles I got when I stepped out of the bathroom, I wasn't alone in thinking that.

"Thank you." I gave them a little curtsy.

Even though no man would ever see me in it, I decided to order it. At least I could wear it while pregnant.

Ava and Chloe also bought the outfits they had tried on.

"Next up," Kristine said, gaining our attention. "Now for the moment you've all been waiting for—the sex toys."

Right.

Exactly what I'd been waiting for—if I were someone else.

She picked up a purple vibrator that seemed like the kind of thing that would glow in the dark, much like the condoms Mrs. Wasserman got excited about.

Embarrassed giggles broke out among the teachers, and Kristine explained the virtues of this particular model.

Ava nudged my arm with her elbow. "You should get it," she whispered.

"Why?" I didn't need one when my fingers already did a pretty decent job.

My clit certainly hadn't logged any complaints in the orgasm department.

"Because second trimester is when you'll be super horny." Her eyebrows lifted as if to remind me that I'd just entered that period of my pregnancy.

"Did you use one when you were pregnant?" I whispered back.

"I didn't need to. I had Liam. Most of the time. When he wasn't away on a mission. Which fortunately wasn't all that often or for long while I was pregnant."

He'd made sure of that. His pregnant wife had been his #1 priority.

I glanced at the vibrator, again, that Kristine was still holding. My body chanted that I really, really, *really* wanted to buy it. My lady bits would love me forever if I did.

I chewed on my lip for a second, contemplating if I wanted to buy it in front of everyone—including my colleagues.

Ava must have sensed my dilemma. "I'll get that for you," she said under her breath. "Consider it my early baby gift to you."

She might have said that, but her tone implied something else. Something that suggested I might want to buy an extra-large pack of batteries to go with it.

Maybe condom companies should start supplying coupons for them in the box, along with the message, "Sorry that you fell into the one percent failure rate. Here's a free box of batteries for the vibrator you'll now need if you're single. Enjoy!"

Wonderful.

13

LOGAN

"Do any of you know anything about fundraisers?" I asked Travis and Eli in the team locker room, my body and hair still damp from the shower.

We'd just finished a particularly grueling practice, thanks to yesterday's embarrassing loss to the Calgary Flames.

Yes, the Flames were killing it this season and were number one in the Pacific division, but that didn't mean we should have lost 5-1.

Playoffs were rapidly approaching, and we were in a wild card position.

We couldn't afford to lose a game.

As our head coach needlessly pointed out.

"Emma did one a few years ago when we first started dating," Travis said over the whining of a blow-dryer one of our teammates was using.

"What kind of fundraiser was it?" Yes, I might've been fishing for details. I wasn't exactly the fundraising type.

I was more the type who donated money or participated in whatever activity the team I played for had organized.

Like visiting sick kids in the hospital.

But the Kiera I'd known in college had been the kind of girl who would pick up a coin from the ground and donate it to the nearest donation collection box.

Her reasoning?

That maybe it would bring someone else luck.

She'd also volunteered at the children's hospital, doing kindergarten tours, so the place wouldn't be quite as scary if the kids ever ended up there as a patient.

She'd even convinced me one year to volunteer as an elf at the local emergency women's shelter, to help hand out Christmas presents to kids staying there.

That was when I'd first begun falling for her...and not only because she'd looked damn cute in her outfit.

She had helped so many people over the years, which was why I was adamant about helping her with her fundraiser in whatever way I could.

"Some of the guys on the team and I did a PG-rated *Magic Mike* routine as part of the charity event," Travis said. "It included a silent auction."

A laugh erupted from me as I dropped my towel from around my waist and grabbed my boxer briefs. "That was *you?*"

I'd heard about the infamous *Magic Mike* act, but I never paid attention to who was involved.

"Yep, that was me. It raised a lot of money for the community center for underprivileged kids where Emma volunteers." He regarded me for a moment. "Why are you asking? You thinking of doing some sort of fundraiser?"

"Not me specifically, but a friend of mine is. She wants to raise money to buy books for foster kids. It's something she feels passionately about."

"She should definitely talk to Emma and her best friend, Hannah. They both grew up in foster care, and I'm sure they'd love to talk to your friend about it."

"I'll tell Kiera. She's coming over for dinner. I'm sure she'd be happy to talk to them."

"You've got a date?" Eli asked.

"It's not a date. She's coming to brainstorm ideas for the fundraiser." I removed my jeans from the locker and pulled them up my legs.

"You've only been in San Francisco for a month, and you've already got female friends?" Amusement and surprise wrestled for top spot in Eli's tone, as if the idea of female friends was a foreign concept to him.

"Is she like a friend with benefits?"

I shook my head, worried my voice would betray how Kiera and I had hooked up at the ball.

The same charity ball Eli had been at but had failed to recognize me, thanks to my mask. It also helped that I'd been introduced as Grayson, and he hadn't clued in that I was the same guy who played for the team he'd beaten the day before.

Thank Christ for that.

Because heaven help me if he figured out I was Grayson, and then he met Kiera—especially if she recognized him as one of the hockey players she'd met that night.

He didn't look as though he believed me about Kiera and I not having a friends-with-benefits arrangement.

"She's the wife of a close friend of mine," I explained.

"So, you're not sleeping with her?"

Rule #1 when you don't want to confirm that you have indeed slept with the woman in question?

Do.

Not.

Hesitate when answering.

Because when you do, it's a dead giveaway you've done exactly that. And no matter how many times you deny it, you're just digging a deeper hole.

"I don't sleep with married women."

Technically, it was accurate when it came to Kiera (and all women). But she was a widow now, so it was okay for her to have sex with whomever she wanted. Marriage vows were "till death do you part." You weren't expected to remain faithful long after your partner died.

"Okay, you're not sleeping with her," Eli said. "How about fucking her?"

"I'm not fucking her, either."

Again, not a lie.

Based on technicalities.

First, his question was in present tense. What happened between Kiera and me occurred three-and-a-half months ago.

Second, I didn't fuck her that night. I made love to her.

Yeah, yeah, in his eyes, I'd be a pussy if I told him I'd made love to a one-night stand. It didn't matter that I'd known her for years.

"She's really just going to your place to talk about a fundraiser?"

I almost laughed at the disappointment in Eli's voice. "Yep."

Thinking the Q&A was over, I grabbed my long-sleeved T-shirt and pulled it on.

"How long have you known her?" he asked.

"Since college."

"So, a long time."

"Pretty much."

"And it's just you and her having dinner together?"

Travis snorted a laugh. "You're as bad as my wife when

she and her friends get together. When did you trade your balls for ovaries?"

He was referring to Eli.

I had to agree with him there.

Eli shrugged. "Just curious."

"Her husband died over a year ago," I said. "So if you're wondering why he's okay with her and I having dinner together, that's why."

"Is she single?"

"Why are you asking?"

"If she's single, then you don't have an excuse not to fuck her. It's not like her husband will chuck lightning bolts at you for making moves on her."

"You're right—he wasn't Zeus. But that doesn't mean I'm going to make a move on his wife." Even though, technically, I already had. "Plus, she's my daughter's teacher."

"And there're laws that you can't sleep with your kid's teacher?"

"Can't say I've looked into it."

It didn't matter if it was allowed or not, I wasn't going there again with her.

She needed to move on with her life. And I needed to do the same. While I might've had friends who had figured out how to make their relationships work—including some who were hockey players—I didn't trust myself not to screw things up again like I had with Stacy.

So as far as I was concerned, Kiera was off-limits.

THE CONDO SECURITY APP ALERTED ME TO KIERA'S ARRIVAL.

I buzzed her into the building and finished dishing out the Thai food from the takeout containers onto the serving plates.

Kiera's knock on the door came several minutes later. I went down the hallway and let her in.

Shit, she looked good. But that came as no surprise. Even in jeans and a faded maroon T-shirt that looked…

"Is that my old T-shirt?" I vaguely remembered giving it to her in college after she'd come over to my apartment to study but got caught in the rain. She had been soaked, so I loaned her one of my T-shirts.

She glanced at it. When her gaze returned to mine, her eyes were lit up, as if from the same memory. "Oops. Now that you mention it…it is yours."

"You kept it because you thought it was Stephen's?" I didn't believe for a second that she had kept it because it was mine.

A blush reddened her cheeks, making her look even more adorable, but instead of answering my question, she sniffed the air. Smoke still lingered from my failed attempt at dinner, the burned remains of which rested in the garbage. RIP.

Her eyes widened with concern. "Is everything okay?"

"I had a little accident with dinner. But not to worry, I have it covered."

Kiera laughed that sexy sound of hers that made my body tingle like I was standing out in an electrical storm. I had always loved her laugh. "I see your cooking skills haven't changed much since college."

I grinned at the memory of making her dinner for a study date. That hadn't gone down too well either, even though I'd only attempted to make melted cheese on toast. "I promise you my culinary skills have improved since then —they just went on strike tonight."

And maybe the choice of recipe, which had been slightly beyond my skill level, hadn't helped. Being distracted while talking to Livi on FaceTime might have also added to the recipe's downfall.

I led her to the living room. Her gaze surveyed the area that in no way resembled my apartment in college, which I'd shared with Stephen.

But that was only because Stacy had decorated my condo.

I'd returned from being on the road shortly after I was traded to San Francisco, to find the boxes unpacked and my condo looking nothing like the one I'd left in Chicago.

By that, I meant, my post-divorce apartment had been sparse in the decorating department. It wasn't as if I'd cared about how it looked when I spent a good portion of my time away from home.

After Stacy was finished with it, the walls, the sofa, the armchair, and the coffee table were various shades of dark gray. Everything else, including the cushions, was either cream or burnt orange.

The large matte, black-and-white photos on the wall were of Livi, Stacy, and me that had been taken during the past seven years. Candid photos that I didn't realize existed until recently.

"Your place looks amazing," Kiera said.

"Thanks. Stacy gets full credit for it. Do you want the guided tour?"

My condo wasn't large, but it was a decent size, considering I was the only person living here for now.

After showing Kiera the spacious living room and kitchen, I led her to the bedrooms.

"Wow, this is gorgeous." Kiera walked around Livi's room, inspecting the green bedding with daisies, the white furniture, the green rug on the hardwood floor.

"One of my teammates will be painting a mural on the wall this summer."

Turns out, Travis Hamilton wasn't only a talented hockey player, he was somewhat of an artist, too.

"I bet Livi's excited about that."

"She is."

"How come Stacy and Livi moved to San Francisco while you were still with Chicago?" She glanced around the room as if expecting them to magically disappear. "And where are they?"

"Tony—Stacy's husband—was offered a job he couldn't turn down."

"You and Stacy are divorced? When did this happen?"

"Almost two years ago. I thought you knew that."

She shook her head. "Did Stephen know?"

"I told him about it after we filed for divorce. I was away a lot because of my hockey schedule, and when I was home, my mind was still in the game and not on my wife and daughter. Stacy was miserable. We finally realized that even though we still loved each other, we weren't *in* love."

"So, you got a divorce?"

"Yep. I figured I wasn't being fair to Stacy. She wanted everything I couldn't give her, and she deserved more than that. She and Livi deserved more than that."

"How did Livi take it?"

"Given I wasn't around as much as I should've been, I don't think it made much of a difference to her. The divorce was my wake-up call that I needed to do a better job with Livi."

Was I surprised Stephen hadn't told Kiera about the divorce? A little. It wasn't like it had been a national secret. But he also hadn't been the type of guy who went around sharing about other people's personal problems.

Even with his wife.

"Are you seeing anyone?" she asked.

Remember how I said that if a man asks a woman if she

was seeing anyone, it meant he was interested in going out with her?

Kiera might have said those words, but she didn't give the impression that she'd asked the question because she was interested in going out with me. Like when I'd asked her the same the other day, her question seemed more to do with curiosity than an interest in dating me.

"My hockey career and Livi are my priorities right now. Once that career is over, I can consider being in a full-time relationship."

Kiera nodded, her expression thoughtful.

And I splatted away the sudden urge to tell her I was the man she had sex with the night of the ball.

There was really no point going there.

Both of us had moved on.

14

KIERA

My reaction when Logan told me he was divorced?

Shock didn't even begin to describe it.

It wasn't so much that Logan was divorced—which was surprising in itself. I was shocked that Stephen had never mentioned it.

I had wondered, though, when Logan showed up at school today, why Livi had been my student since fall, yet Logan had just been traded to the Rock last month.

Part of me had sadly thought that perhaps he and his wife were divorced. The larger part assumed they had decided they wanted to live in San Francisco, and Stacy and Livi had moved here first. Logan would have joined them once his team was finished for the season.

"But maybe next time things will be better," I said, referring to how Logan would only consider a relationship with a woman once his hockey career was over. "You learned your lesson, and now you know how to avoid making the same mistakes." I ran my hand over the fluffy green cushion on Livi's bed. The comforter was also green and covered in daisies. A lamp resembling a mushroom with a white-spotted red cap stood on the night table, a happy garden gnome leaning against the tall stalk.

"I don't think it's as easy as that. Playing in the NHL is tough on families, especially if the player gets traded. The family is uprooted and has to adjust to the new city—or country if they end up in Canada."

"But didn't Livi and Stacy have to do that anyway? They were already living here when you were traded to the Rock."

"That's because Stacy's husband was offered a great opportunity he couldn't turn down."

"Even though you're Livi's father and were living in Chicago at the time?"

"I couldn't expect him to turn down the promotion because I lived in Chicago. I'm not the only one who should get to have a job that he loves."

That was one thing I had admired about Logan when we were friends in college; it wasn't always about what he wanted. He'd worked hard to excel at everything he did. He loved the challenge, the thrill of success. But he was also not the type of man who would trample over others to get there.

"In the end, it worked out for everyone," Logan said. "But I got lucky when Chicago traded me to San Francisco. They could have just as easily traded me to a Canadian team or Tampa Bay or anywhere else far from Livi. And there's no guarantee the Rock won't trade me next year to another team."

Which meant he wouldn't be in Livi's life as much as he was now.

My heart ached for him, just thinking about that.

"What if you become a scout?" I pointed out. "From

what Stephen told me, that job requires a lot of traveling, too. As does being a coach."

"That's true. But by the time I'm ready to hang up my skates, I'll want a career that doesn't involve traveling all the time. Someone has to make sure Livi isn't dating until she's at least thirty."

I laughed.

Next on the tour?

"Wow, this is your bedroom? I can't believe Stacy decorated this place. She did an incredible job."

Not exactly what you'd expect an ex-wife to do.

"If it weren't for her, I'd no doubt be living out of boxes for the next two years."

Nothing about Logan's bedroom or condo suggested a woman lived in it.

It looked...handsome (because beautiful and gorgeous didn't exactly apply here). It made a statement. A statement that said he wasn't interested in having a woman in his life to disrupt his manly domain.

I didn't know if that was the message Stacy had consciously been aiming for, but she'd certainly succeeded in conveying it.

We continued our tour. Every room, including the bathroom and the kitchen, was as impressive as the living room.

"I can't remember the last time I ate Thai food," I said, walking over to join him at the dining table, practically drooling. The rich, spicy scent hadn't faded any since I'd arrived. It only made me hungrier.

Stephen hadn't been a fan of Thai food.

"You want red or white wine?" Logan asked.

"I'm fine with water, thanks. I have to drive home."

Not exactly a lie.

Why not tell him I was pregnant?

It wasn't like it would be a secret much longer.

While that might've been true, I also wasn't ready to lie to Logan about who the father was—and I wasn't ready to contact Grayson yet. I wanted to do that before I announced my pregnant status to Logan. Admitting that I got knocked up by a one-night stand who I couldn't even identify in a lineup wasn't high on my priority list.

"I was talking to one of my teammates about doing fundraisers," Logan said. "His wife organized one a few years ago to raise money for the center where she volunteers. It helps underprivileged kids."

"What kind of fundraiser did they do?" I took a bite of the cashew chicken and almost purred in contentment, although part of that might've had something to do with Logan being so willing to help me.

Like when I had convinced him to dress as an elf in college and help hand out gifts to the kids at the women's emergency shelter. He had been so sweet and adorable with the children.

He'd helped them forget for a short time about the sad hand they'd been dealt.

"Some of the guys on the team did a PG-rated *Magic Mike* number."

That was something I would've loved to see. For a heartbeat, I imagined Logan ripping off his T-shirt, baring his magnificent abs, and tossing the piece of clothing at the gawking women.

My hormones sighed at that image, too.

And without warning, a desperate need stirred between my legs.

Oh. Damn.

Not what I needed right now...or ever.

Ava's warning paraded through my head, with balloons, banners, and dancing dildos.

Maybe I'd find a good use for that baby gift after all.

As soon as I got home.

Assuming I lasted that long.

"I was thinking of maybe doing a silent auction."

Except, I had no idea what kinds of things I could auction off.

It would have to be something exciting.

Something that would get people talking.

"Travis suggested you could talk to his wife about what she did. She also had a silent auction. He figured she would be happy to talk to you about it. She grew up in foster care."

"That would be great. Thanks."

"Do you have any idea what kinds of things you want to auction?"

Even to my ears, my sigh sounded super dejected. "Nope. I want to do something exciting. To have prizes that are unique and will generate lots of interest. But that means asking people to donate prizes, and I'm not good at that kind of thing. I can convince second graders to practice their math equations, but I suck at convincing people to donate prizes for an auction."

Plus, I didn't know enough people and businesses I could approach.

"I could ask my teammates if they'd be interested in donating something—like signed Rock jerseys."

I smiled. "I bet that would be popular." It was definitely a start.

"Let me talk to them tomorrow and see what I can do."

My smile widened, my pulse quickened, and my insides vibrated like a bee drunk on pollen. And for once, it had nothing to do with Logan.

Much.

"That would be great, thanks."

15

LOGAN

Three days later, I was sitting in the dressing room with my teammates and coaching staff, waiting for Coach Fusco to finish the team meeting. We had a game that evening against the Pittsburgh Penguins, and we had to win it if we hoped to remain in the wild card position.

Our playoff aspirations were dangling by a weathered thread.

"Does anyone have any questions?" Fusco asked, standing in the center of the team's logo on the carpet in front of us. A reminder of what we were made of.

Metaphorically speaking.

In the game of Rock, Paper, Scissors, I was positive Rock crushed Penguin.

As long as Penguin didn't peck Rock to pieces, we were gold.

We shook our heads, adrenaline pumping to get on the ice...after we went home and napped, which was the standard pregame ritual.

"All right, Logan has something he wants to discuss with you." He nodded for me to go ahead.

I thanked him with a returning nod and stood. Thirty men watched me, curious about what I had to say.

Even Travis and Eli had no idea of my reason for wanting to address the team.

"First, I've already talked to Don McDonald." The general manager. "He's given me the okay to discuss this with any of you interested in helping out." I'd spoken to him on Monday, but he'd wanted to confer with the legal department before giving me his okay. "A friend of mine is organizing a fundraiser to provide book box sets to foster kids." I explained Kiera's rationale for wanting to give the kids the box sets.

"Are you asking us to do another striptease?" Mark Milone performed a dance move I could only guess had come from the fundraiser Travis's wife had organized. His antics elicited a round of laughter and wolf whistles.

"Move like that on the ice tonight," Eli called out, "and we're bound to beat Pittsburgh."

Coach Fusco looked mildly panicked at the suggestion.

"No, I figured that's already been done. This fundraiser will be a silent auction that will occur after the playoffs and will have nothing to do with the team. But I wanted to see if any of you were interested in donating anything."

"Could we auction off Eli?" Milone asked with a laugh. "The highest bidder gets to go on a date with him."

Was he joking?

Absolutely.

But his suggestion also had merit.

Coach Fusco's mildly panicked expression shifted to horror.

A smirk slid onto Eli's face. "You're only saying that because you know the women will be clambering for a date with this." He gestured at his body. "Whereas no one would be interested in your ugly mug."

"You got that right," Milone said, grinning and ignoring the part where he was happily married.

From what Stacy had told me, her friends thought both men were hot. I had to take her word for that. But if that was the general consensus among women, that meant there must be some who'd be willing to bid on Eli for a date.

"By date, don't you mean fuck?" Kai Korhonen asked. "You don't date, Lawson."

I could've sworn Coach Fusco was going to pass out, his blood now pooling in his feet.

I took pity on him. "I can guarantee the team and the league would be against that version of a date, even if the fundraiser has nothing to do with the team. But as long as the date includes the stipulation of no sex, it should be fine."

"What if the lucky woman and I want to fuck on the date?" Eli shrugged, open to the possibility.

"Then I suggest you ask her out on a second date for that. Remember, this is a fundraiser to benefit kids in foster care. It's got to be kept clean, or else my friend could find herself being dragged through the media in the worst possible way."

Eli's smirk turned downright mischievous—or evil, depending on your take. "Even if I could raise more money by prostituting myself out?"

The men around him chuckled.

"And that's my cue to get out of here," Coach Fusco grumbled. He stood and left.

I shook my head at Eli, doing my best not to grin. "No prostituting yourself."

"Well, now you're taking all the fun out of this. But either way, count me in."

"You honestly want to auction off a date with you?" Yep, that was definitely incredulity in my tone.

But underneath it, I was mentally high-fiving myself at the brilliance of talking to these guys.

"Sure, why not? I take a woman out on a date, strictly platonically, of course"—he hastily added the last part—"and it benefits a bunch of kids when it comes to reading. I'd say that's a definite win for all concerned."

"Is there anyone else who's interested in donating to the silent auction?"

"What about two hours of one-on-one coaching?" Travis asked. "My wife would definitely not be okay with me auctioning myself off for a date—and she's the only person I'd want to date. But I'm all for offering my services when it comes to coaching."

Four other players said they, too, would be game for that.

I wrote down their names. Two players figured that if Eli could auction himself off for a date, they could do the same.

Several other suggestions were put forth: a gourmet dinner for the lucky winner (with up to four guests) cooked by Sean Burrows, a fair number of players were willing to donate signed jerseys, and our strength and conditioning coach offered to donate an hour and a half of personal training.

When I'd initially told Kiera I'd ask my teammates if they would be willing to help out, I thought maybe I could convince a few of them to donate signed jerseys. I'd never expected anything like this.

Everyone left shortly after, and I checked the time. Livi was due to finish school in four hours. Enough time for me to squeeze in my nap first.

I texted Stacy.

Me: Okay if I pick Livi up from school?

I wanted to tell Kiera the great news in person.

Stacy: I know she'll love that.

———

TYPICALLY, IF I PICKED LIVI UP FROM SCHOOL, I WOULD WAIT with the other parents near the front doors. This time I entered the building and headed to the office.

"Hi, Jeanine," I said to the receptionist. "Could you let Kiera Ashdown know that I'm here and would like to talk to her once class is over?"

I smiled brightly at her. Experience had taught me with women of all ages that this smile usually got me what I wanted. It was like magic.

Stacy had once described it as my panty-dropping smile. As long as it worked in my favor, I didn't care whether that was true or not.

Jeanine smiled at me from behind her computer. "Let me check if she can see you. Give me a moment."

"Thanks. Can you also let her know that I'm picking up Livi while I'm here?"

She nodded, and a minute later she gave me the answer I was hoping for. "Just wait for the bell to ring, and then you can head to her classroom."

The bell rang several minutes later, and I made my way through the sea of giggling and chatting students streaming toward the two main exits.

Livi was talking to Kiera when I entered the classroom. As soon as she saw me, she squealed, "Daddy," and raced over to me. Her skinny arms wrapped around my waist, and she peered up at me. "I didn't know you were coming to get me."

I ruffled her hair. "I need to talk to Mrs. A, so I told your mommy I'd drive you home."

I turned to Kiera. She looked as beautiful as she usually did, but there were also light shadows under her eyes. "Are you okay?"

"A little tired, but other than that, I'm fine." She smiled softly at me. "So, you needed to talk to me?"

"I spoke to my teammates about the auction."

"You did? How did it go?"

I told her the list of things that were being donated. And for a second, her breath appeared stalled, her eyes as big as a new roll of hockey tape.

The air in her lungs rushed out in a squeal. "I can't believe you got all those players to agree to donate those prizes. Thank you, Logan." She shifted slightly as though to hug me, but then seemed to change her mind. "Thank you so much for arranging that."

Several memories of when she had hugged me over the years paid me a brief visit, like a whisper on the wind. They tugged at my heart, reminding me of how much I missed that Kiera. The Kiera who had been happy to hug me—even though it had only been as a friend.

"You're welcome," I said, quickly pushing the sentiment aside. Pushing aside the memory of her soft floral scent.

"Did three players really offer to auction off a date with them?" Her expression said she didn't know if she should laugh or be shocked. It could have gone either way.

"Yep, that surprised me, too." For my daughter's and Kiera's sakes, I skipped the rest of the conversation that had accompanied Eli's offer.

"The Rock are flying out east tomorrow and I'll be gone for a week, but I thought you and I could get together once I return to discuss the fundraiser some more."

"That sounds like a good idea. I talked to Emma Hamilton last night, and she and I are meeting for lunch on Saturday to discuss what she did with her fundraiser."

"I'm glad you had a chance to call her."

An odd, satisfied feeling stirred in me at Kiera's news. Usually, an NHL player only introduced his new girlfriend to the close-knit group of hockey wives and girlfriends once she hit serious girlfriend status.

Casual relationships didn't usually make the cut. It was tidier that way.

Kiera wasn't my girlfriend, yet it couldn't have felt more right, introducing her to my teammates' wives and girlfriends.

Yes, I know, it wasn't quite the same thing.

She was meeting with Emma to discuss the fundraiser.

A fundraiser that Emma's husband was donating a prize for. But knowing that didn't change the satisfied feeling— the feeling that everything felt right in the world.

For now, anyway.

The urge from the other day to tell Kiera the truth about the ball bit at my ass. Until that night, I'd never lied to her before...if you didn't count how I had felt about her in college.

Which I didn't—because before she met Stephen, my inability to tell her the truth was due to me being chicken.

I hadn't wanted to wreck our friendship if she hadn't felt the same way about me.

And then after she met Stephen, it was too late.

So, not telling her about my feelings for her in college didn't count as a lie.

But while I hadn't outright lied about knowing Kiera the night of the ball—since it had been her idea to keep our identities a secret from each other—I should probably tell her I was actually Grayson.

I opened my mouth to fumble my way through that awkward conversation.

"Daddy," Livi said approaching us, reminding me that we were still in the classroom, and Kiera and I weren't alone.

"What, sweetheart?"

"I don't feel well..." That was as far as she got before puke covered my shoes.

16

KIERA

Aphrodite's Boutique.

I'd heard about the store back when Stephen was alive, but I'd never stepped inside. Ava had recommended it because a friend of hers was the owner.

What she had failed to mention was that her friend was the wife of a San Francisco Rock player.

The store was like nothing I'd seen before. A large fountain with a stone statue of the Goddess of Love stood in the center. The rest of the store displayed an array of lingerie—everything from innocently sexy to sultry siren—candles, toiletries, love-themed decorations. Soft, romantic music played in the background.

I couldn't believe this was the first time I'd been here. Now that Chloe was in a serious relationship with a man who worshiped her, I could see her having a lot of fun in this store.

Me? I would've loved to come here when Stephen was alive. Now, it was a reminder of just how alone I was.

Well, not completely alone.

My hand cradled my baby bump, hidden under the

loose dress I'd bought the other day after my doctor's appointment.

The appointment where she confirmed that I was, without a doubt, pregnant.

I'd even heard Love Bug's heartbeat for the first time.

And in case you're wondering, yes, I did tear up at the sound.

It wasn't a sad tear. It was a tear of awe at the miracle growing in my belly.

A miracle who I'd get to see in three weeks when I went for my ultrasound.

If Stephen were alive, he would have done everything in his power to be there for all my prenatal appointments.

I couldn't feel sad that he was missing out on any of those things, because Love Bug wasn't his. Grayson was the one missing out on the appointments—and he didn't even realize it.

On the other hand, he might not have cared either way.

A small bronze plaque on the fountain wall proclaimed that all coins tossed into the foundation were donated to The James Bell Youth Center. I removed my wallet from my purse and tossed in a handful of coins.

I scanned the store for Emma and spotted her with a customer. Or at least I assumed it was her. She'd told me that she had long, curly, red hair, and the woman definitely fit that description.

It was the person she was talking to who caused the air in my lungs to freeze.

Dr. Lakin.

She was the one person in the store who knew the secret that I wasn't ready to share with the world yet, beyond Chloe, Ava, and my parents.

My gaze darted around the store, searching for a suitable spot to hide. But unless I was willing to climb into the fountain and pose alongside the goddess, the number of options was minimal.

The fitting room was on the opposite side of the store from where the pair was standing. I slowly reversed, keeping my eyes on them, like one would do when moving away from a hungry tiger.

You know how some people seem to have eyes in the backs of their heads?

Or at least it seemed that way when you were a kid, and your parents knew you were up to no good, even though their back was to you.

Well, I was definitely *not* one of those people.

My calves hit something solid behind me. Before I registered what was happening, I stumbled backward, arms flailing, and landed on my butt in the fountain.

Water splashed on impact, ensuring every inch of my dress was soaked.

I wasn't hurt—as long as we weren't referring to my ego. I had used my hands to cushion my landing.

"Kiera," Dr. Lakin said as I crawled to the side—my dignity as bedraggled as I was—and all hopes that no one had witnessed what happened came crashing down like a house of pretzels. "Are you all right?"

Emma was with her, a look of horror on her face. The kind of horror that came right after a grimace.

They helped me to my feet. Emma retrieved my purse. Water dripped from it and my dress, creating a puddle on the floor.

And there was no missing the way the wet fabric clung like a neon sign to my baby bump.

"I'm fine," I reassured Dr. Lakin. "Sorry about the mess," I told Emma.

Emma's face paled. "Don't worry about that. Are you sure you're okay?"

"I'm more embarrassed than anything." In more ways than she could possibly imagine.

"Well," Dr. Lakin said, "I'd feel better if you dropped by my office in about two hours so I can double-check that everything is all right with you and your baby."

I winced because there was no hiding the truth now, but I agreed to meet her at her office. Better to be safe than sorry when it came to Love Bug.

"Why don't you come into my office?" Emma suggested. "Believe it or not, I actually have some dry clothes you can change into." She grinned at my surprised expression. "Let's just say I've had at least one run-in with the fountain that left me drenched."

She led me to a room at the rear of the store that contained a desk and several unopened cardboard boxes. She removed a dress from the closet and examined it for a moment, then her gaze gave me a once-over.

She smiled again. "Give me a second. I'll be right back."

She left with the dress—a dress that I doubted would fit me. We weren't exactly the same size, especially given my pregnant status.

When she returned, she was carrying what looked like a sundress covered with small hearts in a rainbow of colors. She handed it to me. "This dress will fit you better. And I grabbed you some panties and a bra. All on the house."

"You don't—" I started to say.

"Consider it an early baby gift—not that your baby will appreciate it." She laughed softly. "Get changed, then we'll go to the café around the corner for lunch. Hannah will be meeting us there."

"I can't believe we've both been friends with Ava all this time, and we've never met until now," Emma said after the three of us had ordered our food from the counter. We were seated at a table near the window. Riley, Hannah's adorable newborn son, was asleep in his car seat on the chair next to her.

For the past few minutes, we'd been discovering just how close our inner circles were without us realizing it until now.

You know what they say about the six degrees of separation?

Turned out, Chloe's boyfriend worked in the building Hannah's husband owned.

"Wes told me Landon's back at work," Hannah said.

"More or less. Chloe said he's on restricted duty until his physician gives him the final stamp of approval. But he's been working hard on his physical therapy, and his shoulder's getting better."

He'd been shot while working undercover as Chloe's fake boyfriend. The FBI and the security firm Landon worked for had been trying to locate her cousin, the head of a Russian mafia crime family.

Chloe's family tree made most people's look super boring...but I'd take my boring family any day over what she went through.

But in the end, injury non withstanding, everything worked out great—Chloe wound up with an amazing boyfriend.

"So, tell me more about the fundraiser you want to do." Emma took a bite of her fruit salad.

I told them about Tyler and his struggles with reading. I told them about my idea for providing box sets to kids like him who wanted to read the books, but their foster parents couldn't afford them. And I told them about the prizes that Logan had secured from his teammates.

"I would love to add some prize bundles to it," Emma said. "And I bet there are businesses in my building who would love to help out, too. They were super supportive when it came to donating prizes for the silent auction I did with the *Magic Mike* number. As long as the businesses are credited for the donation, it's a win-win for everyone."

"And I know some nurses at the children's hospital where I work who run small businesses on the side," Hannah added. "They might want to contribute prizes, too, if it helps get the word out about what they do."

"That would be wonderful. Not everyone will be a hockey fan and bid on the prizes Logan drummed up."

Emma laughed. "Have you seen Eli Lawson and the other two players? I don't think there's a single woman alive who wouldn't want a date with them. Although I wouldn't suggest pinning their hopes on the guys wanting a second date. As far as I know, none are looking to settle down."

"So, like Logan," I pointed out.

She nodded. "Yeah. So, how do you know him?"

"He was my husband's best friend and teammate in college, and he and I were in the same geology class. So you could say we've been friends for a while." Even if we hadn't seen much of each other over the years.

"What does your husband do?" Emma's gaze dropped to my hands as I was about to take a bite of my grilled-chicken sandwich.

The wedding and engagement rings she was obviously looking for?

They were at home, nestled in the box with the notes Stephen had given me during our marriage.

"My husband died in a ski accident over a year ago." At

their sympathetic expressions, I quickly added, "It's okay. I'm not saying it's been easy, but I am starting to move on."

Kind of.

Although it would be a lot easier to move on if I wasn't about to tell everyone I was pregnant with his fictitious Popsicle sperm.

I didn't want to lie to Emma and Hannah. What had started out as a simple, blurted-out lie had morphed into a big, tangled mess.

And now I had two more people I'd have to come clean to after I spoke with Grayson.

If Emma's husband wasn't Logan's teammate, I might have told her the truth. Neither she nor Hannah seemed like the kind of people who would judge me for getting pregnant with a stranger's sperm.

"The baby belongs to my husband," I told them. "We were trying to get pregnant before he died...and well, I used his frozen sperm."

Hannah's eyebrows rose up for a brief moment, and her mouth slipped into a genuine smile. "Welcome to the club."

"The club?"

"My toddler son was the result of an anonymous sperm donor. It was before my husband and I...um...started dating."

Emma chuckled under her breath and resumed eating her salad.

Hannah flashed her a quick smile, then returned her attention to me. "I wanted to have a child, but I hadn't found anyone to settle down with. So instead of doing things the old-fashioned way, I went the scientific route. And I couldn't be happier."

"And she and Wes also have a beautiful five-year-old daughter," Emma said.

"Everly is Wes's niece," Hannah explained. "Her parents died over two years ago."

It sounded like Everly and I had a lot in common when it came to losing someone we loved.

The three of us talked for a while about the fundraiser, about how we met our husbands, and about Emma's and Hannah's experiences in the system.

The one thing I did avoid mentioning was my feelings for Logan in college.

No one needed to know about that.

The more we talked, the more I enjoyed spending time with them. The two women were sweet and funny and giving. They were my heroes for everything they had gone through growing up—instead of turning them bitter, it had made them stronger.

Listening to them made me happy I had decided to do the fundraiser to help kids like they had been at one point.

But despite that, the thought of starting new friendships with a lie sat like sour milk in my stomach.

Hannah had actually gotten pregnant via in vitro.

I had not.

She had intentionally gotten pregnant, even though she was single, because she wanted a child.

I'd gotten pregnant because I was turned-on by a masked stranger. A hot, masked stranger, mind you. But he had been a temporary escape from the loss of my husband, and I would never regret that.

The one thing Hannah and I did have in common?

Neither of us knew the identity of our babies' biological fathers.

Although from the sound of it, that didn't matter when it came to Hannah's son. Her husband loved him regardless.

My heart released a happy, dreamy sigh at how things

turned out for her in the end, momentarily nudging aside my guilt.

"Can you do me a favor?" I asked as our lunch drew to a close. "Can you not mention to anyone that I'm pregnant? I want to tell Logan before I mention it to anyone else. Stephen was his best friend, so I'd prefer if he heard about the baby from me."

And when exactly are you planning to tell him? a voice in my head asked, tone slightly mocking. *When the baby is in college?*

I inwardly rolled my eyes. *No. I'll tell him soon.*

Once I'd figured out the best way to do it.

And once I got around to contacting Grayson.

Soon. Very soon.

17

LOGAN

"**W**hat do you think of this crib, Daddy?" Livi pointed to the one in question, white with royal blue and white bedding.

The puking incident that happened in her classroom four days ago had fortunately only been a twenty-four-hour thing.

Livi was back to her old self.

"It's nice, sweetheart," I told her halfheartedly. To Stacy, I said, "You want to explain to me again why I'm helping you and Livi find baby furniture? You're married to Tony, and he's the baby's father. Shouldn't he be doing this?"

"Oh, I'm just looking. You're here because I need your help planning his surprise birthday party next week."

Livi inspected the matching chest, pulling open the top drawer and checking inside.

"Since when did I become a party planner?" I asked.

That had always been Stacy's role while we were married. I'd just done what any sane husband would do—nod in agreement with everything she said.

"You're a man."

"Glad you haven't forgotten that. I was beginning to think it had slipped your mind, given you're asking me to help plan his surprise party."

I glanced over to where Livi had gone, and spotted Kiera. She was talking to a woman with hair the color of a new penny. Like Livi, they were inspecting cribs.

I wasn't the only one who spotted Kiera. "Isn't that Livi's teacher?" Stacy nodded at the two women.

"Yes. I take it you don't remember her from when she was married to Stephen Ashdown, my best friend and teammate in college?"

Stacy squinted at Kiera and the other woman as if that would jar her memory. "I thought she looked familiar. I just figured it was my imagination."

As if sensing we were talking about her, Kiera looked up from the crib she and her friend were inspecting.

She smiled at us. It was the same beautiful smile that I'd come to associate with her, although something was slightly off about it.

As if it had been spray-painted on. Even her dimples seemed half-committed to the action.

"Hi, Mrs. A. I'm going to be a big sister," Livi proudly told Kiera as Stacy and I approached them.

"Congratulations." Kiera grinned at my daughter. This time the smile was genuine. "I bet you're excited."

Livi nodded, the movement so fast her head was almost a blur.

Kiera directed her smile at Stacy. "Congratulations." She then smiled at me, but this time it held an edge of uncertainty.

Her purse pinged. She removed her phone and checked the screen.

"Looks like we better get going," she told her friend. "My mom needs my help with something. It was nice seeing you." She said the last part to Livi, Stacy, and me. "I'll see you tomorrow in school, Livi."

She hooked her hand on her friend's elbow—her other hand full of bags—and practically dragged her away.

"I didn't realize she was seeing someone," Stacy said.

"Who's seeing someone?" I halfheartedly asked, still looking in the direction Kiera and her friend had gone.

"Livi's teacher."

That got my attention—not to mention an unexpected jolt of jealousy to my gut. "Why do you think she's seeing someone?"

"Because I'm positive she's pregnant. Well, I'm about ninety percent positive that she's pregnant."

"Why do you think she's pregnant?" Great, now I sounded like a three-year-old who had discovered the power of asking "why" when it came to driving his parents nuts.

"She's been wearing baggier clothes lately, and the baby bump kind of gave it away. But the bags she was holding confirmed it."

"How would bags confirm that she's pregnant?"

"They're from the maternity clothing store in the mall."

"Maybe she was carrying them for her friend." Made sense to me. More so than Kiera being pregnant. She'd already told me she wasn't seeing anyone.

"Kiera was the one who looks pregnant, not her friend. I'd say that she's probably early in her second trimester."

Confession time. When Stacy was pregnant with Livi, I hadn't been the most attentive husband when it came to knowing all those things about pregnancy I probably should've been aware of.

So, I had no idea what Stacy was talking about.

"What the heck does that mean?"

She snorted a laugh. "You really weren't paying attention to the things I said when I was pregnant with Livi, were you?"

I didn't answer because I figured that was a rhetorical question.

Stacy decided to put me out of my clueless misery. "That means her baby was probably conceived early to mid-December. Give or take a week. This is assuming she's not pregnant with twins."

Holy Fuck. Kiera told me the night of the ball that I was the first man she'd had sex with since Stephen's death.

So unless she had a one-night stand with another man after me, that meant the baby was mine.

My body turned cold, as if a red slushy had been injected into my veins. "Why didn't she tell me?" I muttered under my breath.

"Who didn't tell you what?" Stacy asked, frowning.

"Nothing."

How was she supposed to tell you? the voice of reason asked. *She has no idea you're Grayson, the man she fucked that night.*

But even then, she could have still told me that she was pregnant. We were friends.

Or at least we used to be friends in college. It wasn't like we had seen each other since Stephen's funeral.

I shoved my fingers through my hair, an inch from racing after Kiera and asking her if it was true—if I was going to be a father again.

"Are you okay?" Stacy was studying me like I was a bug under a microscope.

Pull it together, man. There's no point in freaking out just yet.

"I'm fine. So, back to our discussion about Tony's surprise party." I didn't exactly want to talk about how there was a good chance Tony wasn't the only one having a baby.

For starters, Kiera was the one I needed to have this discussion with.

Only I wasn't sure how I was supposed to do that.

It wasn't like I could ask her, *"Hey, how's everything going? Oh, by the way, are you pregnant with my child?"*

And I suspected the topic wasn't exactly covered in *What to Expect When You're Expecting.*

Which I might have known if I had bothered to read the book when Stacy was pregnant with Livi.

18

———

KIERA

Several hours after Chloe dropped me off at my house, my doorbell rang.

I put aside the mittens I was knitting and pushed myself off the couch. I wasn't expecting anyone—and I definitely wasn't expecting to see the man who was standing on my front stoop, the setting sun glowing softly behind him.

"Hi?" was my brilliant response.

"I need to talk to you," Logan said.

"Okay." Curious about why he was here, I opened the door wider and let him in.

He stepped inside, and his gaze dropped to my belly.

Oh. That was what he wanted to talk about. I guess the cat was out of the proverbial bag.

Or more accurately, out of the "Lily's Maternity Boutique" bag.

"*Ta-da.* Yes, I'm pregnant."

"Why didn't you tell me before that you're pregnant?"

"I wasn't sure how you'd react." And deep down, I'd

141

thought that maybe he had already figured it out but didn't feel the need to say anything.

He shoved his fingers through his hair, gaze still glued on my belly as if it were housing a baby fire-breathing dragon.

In all the scenarios that played in my head, in not one of them had he reacted this way. "Why don't we go into the living room? You probably have questions."

Like who the father is.

Dammit, what was I going to tell him?

I wasn't ready yet to tell everyone the truth. Not until I'd fully come to terms with my new reality.

And not until I'd told Grayson.

Because if he wanted nothing to do with the baby, then I'd rather people believe the alternative story. The story involving Stephen's sperm.

But this was Logan. I had never lied to him before.

Logan followed me, and I sat on the sofa. He chose to stay standing and started pacing.

Wow. I hadn't expected him to respond this way to the news.

Stephen had died over a year ago. It wasn't like I'd betrayed his memory by being with another man.

Stephen hadn't wanted me to stay alone for the rest of my life. He'd wanted me to find love again. Sure, this wasn't exactly how he had envisioned things (that made two of us), but he would've been fine with it as long as I was happy.

And I was.

"It's Stephen's baby," I blurted when it was clear Logan planned to keep pacing.

Well, I guess that answered my question about what to say to him.

Maybe this blurting thing of late was a symptom of pregnancy brain.

Sounded like a logical explanation to me.

Logan stopped abruptly but still didn't sit.

Oh, God. He'll know I'm lying. He was once my friend, and he was Stephen's best friend. He would see through the lie as easily as if it had been made from glass.

"What do you mean, it's Stephen's baby?"

That expression on his face?

Shock—as if Zeus had struck him with a lightning bolt (without singeing his hair).

But it wasn't only shock; there was an odd air of relief about him.

I open my mouth to respond but didn't get that far.

"The last I heard," Logan powered on, "Stephen died over fifteen months ago. How can you possibly be pregnant with his child? What—did he come down from heaven and knock you up like in that Patrick Swayze movie?"

"Technically, Patrick Swayze didn't knock up Demi Moore." That would have been a little tough because he was acting through Whoopi Goldberg's body.

And he was a ghost.

Logan leveled his steely blue eyes at me. The intensity in them caused a shiver to skim through me.

In a good way.

In a delicious, my-body-was-getting-riled-up way.

Now's not the time, I reminded my hormones. *One problem at a time, please.*

"So you're telling me that Stephen visited as a ghost and got you pregnant?" The tone of his voice implied he believed the opposite.

"Fortunately, modern technology doesn't require ghost hauntings to get someone pregnant." I toyed with a piece of lint on the couch. I couldn't look Logan directly in the eyes. I couldn't risk him seeing the lie gleaming back at him. "I got pregnant through artificial insemination. Stephen and I had tried to have a baby the old-fashioned way. It didn't work, so we chose to go in vitro. A few months ago, I decided that I didn't want to wait any longer to find a man who was right for me, fall in love, get married, and then begin a family. My biological clock was ticking."

Well, that was partly true. It was ticking—but I had several more years before I had to worry about it.

Logan frowned and sat next to me on the sofa. "I didn't realize you two were going through that."

"And I didn't realize men talked about their fertility woes."

"We don't, typically."

Which was good news for me. It would have been a lot harder to pull off my lie if they had talked about these things like women did.

"So, there you have it," I said. "The reason you didn't know about his Popsicle sperm."

I mentally fist-pumped the sky even though the guilt from the other day, when I told Hannah and Emma about the baby, returned in droves.

Like everyone else, Logan was oblivious to the truth.

"Well, I guess congratulations are in order." Logan smiled at me, and my woman bits let out a dreamy sigh.

Damn his sexy smile.

Between that and my incredibly horny hormones—which hadn't let up despite my request for a reprieve—I was in serious trouble.

I squirmed on the couch, aiming to dull my vamped-up sex drive.

It didn't work.

And it definitely didn't help when Logan leaned in to hug me. His scent—a combination of whatever antiperspirant or aftershave he used and his own smell—shifted my horniness into overdrive.

A breathy moan escaped me, and I closed my eyes.

There was something familiar about his scent, but I couldn't identify what it was.

Logan released me, and my body silently whined at the loss.

His eyes were dark, his breath came in faster than before.

If I didn't know better, I'd say he was as turned-on as I was.

But this was Logan. He didn't feel that way about me—especially now that he thought I was knocked up with his best friend's baby.

Clearly, my hormones were causing me to imagine things.

Great. As if being horny and single wasn't enough.

"How are you feeling?" he asked.

"Good. A little tired, but nothing I can't handle."

"How was your meeting with Emma the other day?"

I told him everything, including the incident with the fountain and why I'd been trying to avoid my physician.

"Stephen was your best friend," I said, "so it only seemed right that you were first to find out about his baby."

He smiled at me and nodded as if that made sense. "Let me know if you need any help around the place. When are you due?"

"Around September fifth."

"So before hockey season officially begins."

"That's right. When's Stacy due?"

"October sixth."

"And you were crib shopping with her and Livi today?"

Stephen would have found the irony hilarious. It wasn't every day you went shopping with your ex-wife to buy a cradle for the baby conceived from another man's sperm (unless the man was a sperm donor).

"Not really. She and Livi were just checking them out. Stacy's throwing Tony a surprise birthday party, and she wanted my help with it. She needed someone to help her carry anything heavy—"

"Because she's pregnant," I finish for him.

"That's right."

"Well, I think that's really sweet of you."

He grinned at me. "Glad you think so. So make sure you don't forget that when you need help."

"I won't."

"Do you have an appointment yet for an ultrasound?"

I told him the date. A twinge of disappointment twisted in my stomach at the knowledge that I would have to do that without Stephen.

Sure, plenty of women had prenatal ultrasounds without their partner and survived. But it was just one of those things that he and I had wanted to share together once I became pregnant.

But the reality was, Stephen wasn't alive, nor was he the father.

"Who's going with you?" Logan asked.

"I'm going on my own." I could've asked my mom, but I was afraid she would discover I was lying about the baby's father if I did that.

As it was, she had already told me that she'd be more than happy to be there for me in the delivery room.

But I wasn't sure I wanted that either. As much as I loved my mother, I had a feeling she would drive me bonkers while I was giving birth to her grandchild.

"I might be able to go with you," Logan said. "To the ultrasound. It just depends if the Rock are in the playoffs, and as long as we aren't away for a game."

Okay, not what I was expecting.

"I'm honestly fine with going on my own. It's an ultrasound. I'm not going under to get my wisdom teeth removed."

"Stephen would have moved the world to be there. To see his baby for the first time."

"True. But that doesn't mean you have to take his place because he's dead." As sweet as the thought might be. "You were his best man at our wedding, but that doesn't mean you have to do the things he would have just because he's no longer here to do them."

"I seem to remember I was also your friend in college. That counts for something, too."

You know that look a puppy gets when he wants something?

I'm not saying that Logan was flashing me puppy eyes, the kind that melted your heart, but it was pretty damn close.

No mere mortal could resist.

"All right, if you really want to be there," I said, smiling, relieved I wouldn't be on my own at the clinic after all. "I'd be happy to have you join me. But just so you're forewarned, I can guarantee I'll tear up when I see the baby. Are you sure you want to be there for that?"

Truth? I cried at every Pixar movie I'd seen. *Toy Story 4* pretty much did me in when the little girl got lost.

And don't get me started about the movie *Up*.

So if I couldn't handle those movies, it was a given I'd be more than tearing up at seeing Love Bug for the first time.

"I'll bring the Kleenex." Logan winked at me, and I laughed.

"I guess you're a pro at going to prenatal ultrasounds. Or at least you're a pro compared to me."

He winced and shook his head. "Not exactly."

"You must be. You went to Stacy's when she was pregnant with Livi, right?"

"Like I told you before, I was a crappy husband and father. Stacy had scheduled it so I wouldn't be away on a road trip, but I forgot about it and stood her up."

Ouch.

So basically, what he was telling me was not to expect him to actually show up for the ultrasound. There was a good chance he'd forget, and I'd be there on my own after all.

"You can guarantee her husband won't make that mistake," Logan said.

"You like him, don't you? Even though he's the one married to the woman you were once in love with, you still like him."

"Let's just say when it came to husbands, she upgraded to a better model with husband number two."

Smiling broadly, I gave him a gentle shove on the shoulder. "You might've been a crappy husband, but I seem to remember you were an awesome friend."

And he was proving that he was still the same awesome friend.

It was me who was the crappy friend.

The friend who was lying. Lying because she was afraid of what people would think—of what Logan would think—if she admitted the truth.

19

KIERA

April

Two weeks after Logan learned I was pregnant—and the Rock made it into the Stanley Cup play-offs—I parked in my parents' driveway for our weekly Sunday brunch.

The rain from last night had tapered off, and the late morning sun was doing its best to poke through the clouds. Nick Wasserman was kneeling on the ground next to one of his grandmother's flowerbeds, digging in the dirt. Daffodils, crocuses, and tulips bloomed in a rainbow of colors, adding cheer to the small space.

"Looking for buried treasure, are yea?" I asked with a fake accent that would make a pirate cringe.

He turned to me and grinned. "I wouldn't be surprised if ten-year-old me had buried treasure somewhere in the backyard." He stood up and wiped his hands on his jeans, smearing dirt on his thighs. "Congratulations, by the way."

His gaze dropped to my obviously pregnant belly, no longer hidden under baggy clothing.

My floral maternity sundress brushed against my calves. Unlike the baggy clothing I'd worn before, this dress proclaimed I was pregnant and proud of it.

All right, the circumstances surrounding my pregnancy weren't ideal, but that didn't mean I couldn't embrace that I was growing a little miracle inside me. Maybe the baby wasn't quite the miracle everyone believed him or her to be, but that was okay.

I still loved my baby no matter who the father was.

"I'm sorry I didn't realize you were pregnant when I asked you out for coffee," he said.

"That's okay. I wasn't a hundred percent certain at the time, either."

Had it stung that he hadn't called me after he heard that I was expecting?

Not at all. It was better that way.

Dating someone while I was pregnant with another man's baby wasn't high on my priority list. On the other hand, I wouldn't have minded having sex with a real flesh-and-blood man instead of with my vibrating buddy.

Don't get me wrong, I adored my purple orgasm-maker. It made my horny hormones a little less frustrated. But every time I used it, my naughty thoughts conjured up Logan as the one giving me the orgasms.

And that was only when I wasn't imagining Grayson as the creator of all things magnificent in the department of euphoria.

At the thought of both men, heat rushed between my legs, and I had the sudden urge to dry hump something. Anything.

Where's Logan when you need him? my body asked on a sigh.

No, no, no, I can't think of him that way. He's just my friend, I reminded myself.

My hormones disagreed with me. Have you heard of friends-with-benefits? It's all the rage.

Fortunately for me—not so much for my horny hormones—Mrs. Wasserman stepped outside.

"Oh, don't you look lovely?" She smiled warmly at me. "Doesn't she look lovely, Nick?"

"She does."

I got the sense that she was going to say something Nick wouldn't be interested in, so I begged a hasty escape. "I should get inside. My parents are expecting me for brunch. It was nice seeing you again, Nick, Mrs. Wasserman."

I strode across the grass and entered my parents' house. Voices came from the kitchen. I couldn't make out who they belonged to, but it was clear my mom wasn't the only female here.

Curious to see who she was talking to, I quickly removed my sandals and walked into the room.

Only to be brought up short.

Oh. Crap.

Standing next to the sink, in gray slacks and a yellow top, was the woman I hadn't seen in over a year.

As she turned to me, her dyed-blonde bob swung against her shoulders, and her bright smile caused my stomach to drop like a twin-engine plane whose engines had stalled.

Judith Ashdown.

My mother-in-law.

Double crap.

"Kiera, sweetheart," she exclaimed, rushing toward me. Tears glistened in her eyes, and she enveloped me in a huge embrace.

Well, as close to an embrace as she would get given my growing stomach.

"You can't imagine how excited I was when your mother told me the great news."

Triple crap with whipped cream on top.

I tried to say something, but all I could do was open and close my mouth.

I should have realized Mom would've contacted Judith even though I told her I would do it. Of course, I'd only said that so Mom didn't bother. I'd had no intention of telling my mother-in-law I was pregnant.

"I called Judith and told her you have your ultrasound this week." Mom beamed at me.

No, no, no. Please tell me they aren't planning to go to the ultrasound clinic with me.

I might have thought that, but I just nodded, still unable to speak.

"We had a wonderful idea," Judith said. "Your mom and I decided to throw you a gender reveal party."

I blinked. Twice.

This wasn't happening.

Please tell me I'm hallucinating.

That was it. I was suffering from a pregnancy-associated hallucination.

Great. I went from horny to hallucinating, all in a matter of seconds.

"I hope that's okay with you," Mom said.

Both women wore the look of children hoping for chocolate ice cream for dinner.

"Aren't those dangerous?" God knew enough raging wildfires had started, thanks to gender reveals gone wrong.

Judith smiled knowingly. "Don't worry, we won't be doing anything that involves pyrotechnics or anything else flammable. It will be safe and fun. Mostly just a way to celebrate the little miracle growing inside you. It's something I've been dreaming of ever since you and Stephen announced your engagement."

When she put it that way, I couldn't say no.

Not when she looked so happy.

Breaking hearts just wasn't my style.

And I couldn't remember the last time Mom had been grinning like a girl who had just been nominated for prom queen.

"Sounds like fun." That sounded optimistic, right?

When Stephen and I had gotten engaged, I had also envisioned us one day having a party to celebrate being pregnant. Granted, at the time, this vision also included the father of my baby being at the party, but hey, we couldn't always get what we wanted.

Life was brilliant at throwing curveballs that way.

I glanced at my stomach.

Case in point.

"We thought we could have it on Sunday. We know that doesn't leave a lot of time. But we've been brainstorming for the past two weeks, and you don't have to do anything."

"Other than show up because you're the guest of honor," Judith added.

The door to the backyard opened, and Stephen's dad and my father stepped into the kitchen.

Joe's face brightened. "And there she is. The mother of our grandchild."

Before I had a chance to say anything (assuming I could find my tongue), he strolled over and gave me a hug to rival his wife's. "You don't know how ecstatic we were when your mom called to tell us the happy news."

Those tears in Judith's eyes?

They were now sliding down her face.

Oh, God, this can't be happening.

"When we lost Stephen," his father said, "we were devastated. He was our only child, and we thought we'd never be blessed with the pitter-patter of little feet from our grandchildren. But you made that possible."

Judith dabbed at her tears with the tissue Mom had given her. "We didn't realize you and Stephen were trying to get pregnant before he died."

"We were," I squeaked because that much was true.

Tell them the truth.

And then Judith was back to hugging me. "Now, don't worry about the party. Your mother and I have everything under control. You and our grandchild just have to show up." She patted my baby bump. "We wanted to make this a surprise party, but that wasn't exactly feasible. But we still want you to be surprised when the gender is revealed. So we'll come with you to the ultrasound and ask the technician to only tell us. That way, you'll be surprised like everyone else."

Tell them the truth.

I opened my mouth to do just that, but those weren't the words that came barreling out. "A close friend of mine is coming with me."

That caused them all to pause their excitement for about ten seconds.

Disappointment flickered momentarily on their faces before Judith piped up again. "That's okay. We'll give you the card for the technician to write the sex on, and then you can give it to us. But don't peek." She waggled her finger at me.

"Okay," I said meekly.

I can't tell them the truth, I told the voice of reason before it could berate me for being a coward. Again.

I couldn't break their hearts, not after everything they

had gone through. They were so happy about getting to be grandparents; who was I to destroy their dream?

Closing my eyes, I turned my back on the frustrated yelp at how big a mess the lie had become.

Seventeen weeks ago, I'd finally taken a baby step toward moving on with my life after Stephen's death. That was what that hot, steamy night of incredible sex with Grayson had been about.

But instead of moving forward, all I'd accomplished was two giant leaps back.

I was no closer to moving forward than ants were to moving the Golden Gate Bridge to Timbuktu.

20

LOGAN

From my living room couch, I heard my apartment door click open.

"You home?" Stacy called out.

Yeah, it was a little odd to have your ex-wife walk into your apartment as though she was still married to you. It was probably even weirder when she still had a key to your condo.

But I guess when you and your ex-wife had been destined to be close friends and nothing more, it shouldn't have been all that surprising.

We'd married for the wrong reasons—because it was the right time and because our friends were getting married. We had never been super in love (as Stacy put it when we decided to divorce). Certainly not in the way she and Tony were.

"I'm in the living room." I set the book I'd been reading on the coffee table.

"You decent?" Her voice moved down the hallway toward where I was sitting.

I chuckled. "It's not like you haven't already seen it. But yes, I'm decent."

Right, there was one time last month when Stacy entered my apartment and found me sitting on my couch in my boxer briefs. Hell, it was my condo, and I could do whatever I pleased—within reason.

If I wanted to sit on my couch butt-naked, that was my choice.

Anyway, she got in a tizzy over it. And I had a good laugh because, like I'd said, it wasn't as if she'd never seen me naked.

It also helped that I knew Livi wasn't with her. It had been past her bedtime.

Much like now. The sky outside the living room windows was dark.

Stacy entered the room—and the first thing she zoomed in on was the book I'd been reading.

She picked it up, eyes wide. "*What to Expect When You're Expecting?* Is there something you haven't told me?"

"I'm not pregnant, if that's what you're asking."

"You never read this when I was pregnant with Livi. So what? Now that I'm pregnant with Tony's baby, you've finally decided to check it out?" She flipped it over as if expecting to discover it was something entirely different from what the front cover claimed.

I took the book from her and returned it to the coffee table. "That's not why I'm reading it."

"So, why are you reading it?"

"Because you were right about Kiera Ashdown. She's pregnant."

"Wow. I wonder who the father is." Stacy walked into the kitchen, grabbed a glass from the cabinet, and helped herself to the milk in the fridge. "You want something to drink?"

Even when she wasn't in her own home, Stacy couldn't stop playing gracious host.

"Sure, I'll have what you're having."

She removed another glass, filled it, and handed it to me.

"It's Stephen's baby," I said.

She stared at me, stunned, mouth open, eyes ready to pop out of her head. "Stephen? As in her dead husband, Stephen?"

How had I felt when Kiera told me that?

Shocked. When I saw her at the ball, she'd seemed like she was finally ready to move on.

She certainly hadn't come off as a woman who had just gotten pregnant with her dead husband's frozen sperm. Maybe I was wrong, but that didn't seem like moving on to me.

It was more like clinging to his memory.

In a big way.

I had no idea what she was even thinking. Hell, I had no idea what Stephen would have thought of that. No, I knew exactly what he would have thought.

The idea of leaving his child without a father would have upset him. He'd been close to his parents. He'd worshiped his father. He used to tell me stories of all the things he and his dad had done together when he was a kid.

My father was a good man. Maybe he'd pushed me hard at hockey when I was growing up because he'd had ambitions for me to one day be drafted in the NHL, but he was still a good man. Only, he was nothing like Stephen's father.

Stephen would have been a great dad, too.

He would never have wanted his child to grow up

without a father—which was precisely what was going to happen.

Stacy continued staring at me as if I'd told her I was moving to the moon.

In my underwear.

"Kiera's pregnant with her dead husband's baby?" She said the words slowly, shock dripping from them like chocolate syrup. "How is that even possible?"

"She used his frozen sperm."

"I guess that's one way to do it. But why would she do that? I mean, I get that she loved him and wants to keep a part of him with her, but a baby? And to do it alone?"

"She's not going to be alone." I pointed to the *What to Expect* book on the table.

If I'd thought Stacy looked shocked before, that was nothing compared to now.

"What do you mean she's not going to be alone? You're not planning to take Stephen's place as the baby's father, are you?"

"Of course not. I'm going to be the friend she needs."

"I'm sure she already has friends, Logan."

Right. She did. "I'm not just doing this for Kiera. I'm doing it for Stephen, too. It's what he would've wanted me to do."

Stacy walked to the couch and sat down. Hard. Milk sloshed over the side of her glass onto her hand, but she didn't seem to notice.

"Stephen wouldn't have expected you to become the baby's surrogate father."

I sat next to her. "Who said anything about being the baby's father? You know I'm not good father material." I waved in the general direction of Livi's secondary bedroom.

"You're a good father, Logan. Don't let anyone tell you otherwise. No, you weren't around for our daughter as much as you should have been, but we were young when we had her. We weren't ready to be parents."

Christ, she made it sound like we were teens when Livi was conceived. Granted, we hadn't exactly been married when Stacy discovered she was pregnant, but we had been engaged.

"We weren't that young," I reminded her. "Anyway, Kiera's got the ultrasound appointment this week, and I'm going with her."

"Aren't you supposed to be focusing on the playoffs? This isn't the kind of distraction you need."

"I hardly think taking a pregnant woman to her ultrasound appointment counts as a distraction." At least I didn't think it did. But what did I know? I didn't exactly have a world of experience in that department.

Stacy took a sip of her milk. "Are you sure this isn't something more than you helping out a friend?"

"What more could there be?"

No one had been aware of my feelings for Kiera in college.

And that included Stacy.

Nor did she know that I'd had sex with Kiera at the ball.

So I had no idea what she was getting at.

Kiera and I were friends. Plain and simple.

She needed a man like Stephen. A man who would never let her down. I'd already proved I wasn't that man. Nor was I looking to be him.

Her eyes studied me for a second. But I guess whatever she'd expected to find was missing, because she lifted her shoulders and changed topics.

"You're coming to Tony's surprise birthday party on Sunday, aren't you? It's in the afternoon."

"Yeah, sure. I'll be there. I don't suppose a woman in a

bikini will be jumping out of the birthday cake?" I chuckled, knowing full well that Martha Stewart would never consider having someone jump out of a cake, clothed or otherwise.

Stacy flashed me a *What-do-you-think?* look that made me laugh harder.

"I need your help distracting him so I can set up the party. Can you invite him out somewhere, then bring him home in time for the party?"

"Me? Doesn't he have friends who can help you out?"

"Yes, but you're *my* friend, and I'm asking *you* to help me out."

"Where exactly am I supposed to take him? A strip club?"

She rolled her eyes.

I flashed her a one-sided grin. "I take it that's a no on the strip club?"

I wasn't one for that kind of entertainment, and I assumed Tony wasn't either. It wasn't a topic we had ever discussed.

Now, don't get me wrong. There's nothing sexier than watching a woman dance while removing her clothes. But I preferred when it was done in the bedroom with an audience of one: me.

The last thing I wanted was to watch a woman strip in front of a bunch of drunk, slobbering fools. Call me selfish if you must, but it just wasn't that appealing.

Besides, when one-on-one with a woman you crave to taste, you both enjoy the benefits post removal of clothes.

Those drooling idiots can't say the same.

"So, any idea where I'm supposed to take him?" I asked. It wasn't like he and I did things together, just the two of us. When he and I were together, it was always with Livi and Stacy.

"You could take him to the gardening center. He'd like that."

"Really? The gardening center? Since when do I need to hang out at a gardening center?" I spread my arms wide, gesturing to the fact that I lived in a condo. "It's not like I need lawn fertilizer and bedding plants."

"You could get some herb plants for your balcony. Actually, you'd be amazed at what you could do to turn it into a little oasis out there."

Stacy's eyes took on the gleam that I recognized only too well. It was her Martha-Stewart gleam. What did that mean? She was visualizing exactly how Martha would renovate my poor balcony.

And it would mean a helluva lot more than a few potted herbs.

It would definitely be safer to take Tony to the gardening center than it would be to take Stacy.

"All right, I'll take him to the gardening center. What time do you need him home by?"

"Three. I'll need two hours to set everything up."

"Two hours? What the hell do you need two hours for?" Right—did I really need to ask?

"Danielle's coming over to help me. Otherwise, I'd need more like three hours just to be safe."

Something told me I'd gotten the better end of the deal. I had helped Stacy set up for parties when we were married. Let's just say I didn't envy Danielle one bit.

21

KIERA

"What am I going to do?"

Ava, Chloe, and I were sitting in the staff room, eating our lunch. My ultrasound appointment was that afternoon, and this was the first I'd been able to tell them about my in-laws' surprise visit.

"Wow. Your mother-in-law is really throwing a gender reveal party?" Chloe inspected the invitation I'd given her on Judith's behalf.

I had to admit it was adorable. The cartoon boy elephant was holding a hockey stick, and the girl elephant wore a pink tutu.

Clichéd? Maybe a little.

But I did take ballet when I was four years old. Three years later, my aspiration of being a ballerina fizzled, and I stopped the classes.

Underneath the elephants, the card read:

Little He or Little She

Join us to see what baby Ashdown will be…
Sunday, April 19th at 3:30 pm.

"Looks like it," I said. "Please tell me both of you can make it. I need all the support I can get to survive the party."

Chloe and Ava grimaced.

Never a good sign.

"We're supposed to help Liam and Landon with one of their missions." Ava was referring to her husband and Chloe's boyfriend. "Normally, we have nothing to do with their jobs, but they need our help this time to pull it off."

Even though I tried to keep my face a disappointment-free zone, I must have failed. Ava hastily added, "But I can text Liam and see if something else can be worked out so we can be at your party."

Before I could say anything, she was typing on her phone.

Chloe flashed me a reassuring smile that missed the mark. "Are you telling your mom and mother-in-law the gender beforehand, or do they have to wait for the reveal like everyone else?"

"The reverse. I'm supposed to give the ultrasound technician the envelope with the card inside to write the gender on. Judith will take care of everything else. I'll learn it the same time as the guests."

Ava returned her phone to the table. "I thought you weren't planning to find out what you're having until the baby is born?"

"I wasn't, but I could hardly tell Stephen's mother that after she and her husband flew all this way to throw the reveal party."

"But it's not even her grandchild." Fortunately, Ava

lowered her voice so no one else could hear that minor technicality.

"I know that, and you know that, but she doesn't."

"When exactly are you planning to tell her?"

I winced. "I have no idea. Maybe I don't have to tell them. Is it really wrong, letting them think Love Bug is their grandchild?"

At Ava's and Chloe's raised eyebrows, I rushed on. "You should have seen how excited she was. Stephen was Judith and Joe's only son. When he died, they were devastated, partly because that meant there would be no grandchildren for them."

"So, you were going to tell them that you're pregnant?" Chloe asked.

I shook my head. "I figured since the baby wasn't Stephen's, there was no point in them ever finding out."

"How did they find out?"

"My mom. She was so excited to share the news even though I told her I would tell Stephen's mom. I thought that would be enough to keep Judith from finding out about the baby."

"You could have told his mom the truth when you saw them the other day," Ava pointed out.

I could have in theory, but it was too late for that now.

"You're blonde, and so was Stephen. But you said the baby daddy had brown hair."

"That's right."

It took a second for Ava's point to sink in, and my stomach suddenly felt as though a frantic fish was flopping inside it. "I don't remember genetics very well. Is brown hair a dominant or recessive trait?"

Chloe and Ava exchanged looks and shrugged.

Chloe whipped out her phone and tapped away on the screen. "According to the website I'm looking at, if both parents are blond, the child will be blond. So as long as you and Stephen were natural blonds, Love Bug would have been blond if Stephen had been his father.

"But since you're blonde, and the baby daddy has brown hair, it's more likely Love Bug will have brown hair. But there's also a chance he or she will be blond. It depends on Grayson's parents. If one of them is blond, Love Bug could wind up being blond. There's a fifty percent chance of that happening."

I perked up at hearing this. "So there's a chance Judith and Joe will never have to know the truth about Love Bug if I decide not to tell them in the end. They can keep believing they're going to be grandparents."

Even though I should've been relieved, a large part of me was swimming in the pool of guilt, clinging to an inflatable swan.

Waiting for a bird to peck at it.

"It's a slim chance," Chloe conceded, "but it's still a chance."

"Are you sure you don't want to tell them the truth?" Ava asked.

"I will tell them the truth if Grayson wants to be Love Bug's father. But you should see how happy Stephen's parents have been since arriving in San Francisco. I can't tell them the truth and destroy that—even though I might have to in the end."

Ava's phone pinged, and she read the screen.

I didn't have to ask what it said.

Her face revealed it all.

"Sorry, Kiera. But Liam said it's impossible to change the plans at this point."

I smiled brightly at them until my cheeks began to smart. "Oh, that's okay. I'm sure the gender reveal party won't be all that bad."

Have you ever watched the Pixar movie *Finding Nemo*?

There's a scene where Dory the fish says, "Just keep swimming. Just keep swimming" in a singsong voice.

That same voice was now saying, "Just keep smiling. Just keep smiling." The predicament I was in when it came to everything that was happening wasn't Ava's or Chloe's fault.

It was all on me.

But if the gender reveal party took away even the tiniest amount of Judith's pain after losing her son, it would be worth it.

All I had to do was listen to Dory—and keep smiling.

22

KIERA

"How are you doing?" Logan asked after I climbed into his car. He'd offered to pick me up for the ultrasound appointment since I was on his way to the clinic anyway.

"Not bad. What about you? Ready for tomorrow night's game?" The Rock had survived the first two playoff games against the Oilers, winning them both. Thursday's and Saturday's games were in San Francisco.

"Definitely. We're feeling good after the two wins on Oilers' home turf. But it won't be easy. They're desperate after losing those games. They won't be handing us the wins, that's for sure."

"I'm excited to watch you play." It was the truth. I might've taken a one-year hiatus from watching hockey, but part of my moving on involved watching it again. I'd loved the sport when Stephen was alive. Why should that change?

Besides, maybe Love Bug would one day be a future hockey star—even if the baby turned out to be a girl.

Or maybe they would excel at another sport or at math or at writing.

The realization that I had no idea what genetic strengths Grayson brought to the table snapped, crackled, and popped beneath the surface. I could thank the conversation at lunch with Chloe and Ava for that.

"If you want," Logan said, "I might be able to swing tickets for one of our games." He flashed me a cocky grin before returning his gaze to the road.

A cocky grin that had my horny hormones sitting up and taking notice.

Not going to happen, I reminded them.

"Really?" I tried not to squeal my excitement. "Would you be able to get three tickets? I know my best friend, Chloe, and her boyfriend would love to see a game, too. Landon used to play in the same recreational hockey league as Stephen."

"I'll see what I can do."

At the ultrasound clinic, I was given a form to fill out while I waited for my turn. Once I was finished with it, Logan asked me all kinds of questions about my day and about Livi.

"Are you sure you're okay?" he inquired after we'd been sitting there for five minutes.

"Yeah, why?"

"You've been squirming in your seat for the past few minutes."

Well, wasn't that appropriate? My stomach felt the same way.

And my hands were clammy enough to extinguish a forest fire.

"I'm just a little nervous, I guess."

All right, more like elephant-sized nervous.

"What are you nervous about?"

The compassion in Logan's eyes and voice just about melted my heart, and I was taken back to college when we had studied together for our geology exams. He'd always had the same look whenever I got nervous about an upcoming test.

His superpower? The ability to ease my nerves.

What was I nervous about?

Lots of things—but mostly if Love Bug was okay.

And if the technician would discover that Love Bug's father wasn't the same man I claimed it to be?

Luckily, the last one was a stretch, unless Love Bug was holding a sign that read, *My daddy's name is Grayson, not Stephen.*

"I'm hoping they don't find anything wrong with the baby." I cradled my hands around the rapidly growing bump and smiled at it, letting Love Bug know that everything would be all right.

We would be all right.

Logan tentatively reached toward my belly. "Would it be okay...?" His voice trailed off, but I understood what he was asking.

I smiled at him and nodded.

He rested his palm over my T-shirt, fanning his warm, strong fingers across my belly. "Have you felt the baby kick yet? Or is it too early?"

I was aware that he'd asked me a question, but the way my pulse pounded like a percussion drum in my ears at his touch momentarily distracted me.

My gaze flicked upward, only to be sidetracked by his mouth, and a surprising—and totally inappropriate—thought bounced around in my brain. *What would it be like to kiss him?*

Would he be as good a kisser as Grayson?

No, no, no. Don't think about the mysterious man from the ball—the one who got you pregnant.

I let my gaze continue its journey up to Logan's eyes.

"I'm not sure," I said, replying to his question. "I've felt something, but it's barely there, so I can't be sure."

"What does it feel like? The quickening?"

I grinned at him. "For someone who claims he wasn't involved in his wife's pregnancy like he should have been, you certainly know more than I expected."

He returned the grin. "There's a chance I've been reading *What to Expect When You're Expecting*."

Wow. I definitely hadn't been anticipating him to say that. "Because I'm pregnant? Or just something you felt like doing on a whim?"

He laughed softly. "It definitely wasn't on a whim. I felt like I should be better prepared than I was when Stacy was pregnant with Livi."

"Because she's pregnant now?" I guess better late than never.

"Because *you're* pregnant. Stacy might know what the heck she's doing this time around, but I definitely don't. I might not be the father of your baby, but that doesn't mean I shouldn't be prepared."

"As sweet as this all is, Logan, you really don't have to be prepared. Stephen would never have expected you to take his place like you seem to think you have to. I know we were friends in college, but that still doesn't mean you need to take his place while I'm pregnant." I quickly added, "That's not to say I don't appreciate it. It's just that it isn't necessary."

"I know. But I want to. Because he would have done the same if our places were reversed. Plus, it's the least I can do. Stephen was there for me in college when I got in trouble with the team's head coach. Through no fault of my own, mind you." He chuckled.

"What happened?"

"One of my teammates was sneaking around with the coach's daughter. The coach thought it was me, except he never let on what the problem was. It was Stephen who eventually figured it out and set the coach straight."

"What happened with the teammate and the daughter?"

"They eloped, and she threatened to disown her father if he took it out on his player—her husband." Logan chuckled again as if he had witnessed what went down and was remembering it. "But if it hadn't been for Stephen, I could have been kicked off the team, and that might have ended my NHL career before it even began."

I patted his hand resting on his thigh. "Well, regardless of your motives for helping me, it's very sweet of you. You never know, this could be the start of a new business for after you retire from the NHL." There was a strong possibility my mouth slid up to one side.

His face mirrored back my smile. "What kind of business are we talking about exactly?"

"The substitute father—hired out to single mothers-to-be who want to have the temporary support of a man while she's pregnant. You know, someone who tells her that she doesn't look fat in her maternity clothes, and her swollen ankles definitely don't look chubby."

He snorted a laugh. "Suggestion duly noted."

"Kiera Ashdown?" a woman in scrubs and holding a clipboard said, standing next to the reception desk.

Logan and I stood up and walked to her.

"Hi, I'm Kiera," I told her. "This is my friend, Logan."

The woman's eyes went wide like a full moon, and she stared at him.

Either she wasn't used to seeing hot guys, or she recognized him from the Rock.

My money was on the latter.

"Hi?" I asked, seeing if that would snap her out of whatever had her shell-shocked.

She blinked, looked at me, and a friendly smile reappeared on her face. "I'm Debbie. Follow me, please."

She gave Logan one more curious glance and led us to a dim room. Logan helped me onto the exam table and sat in the chair next to it.

"Before we get started," Debbie said, "did you have any questions?"

"I'm supposed to give you this from my mother-in-law." I handed her the unsealed envelope. "She wants you to fill in the gender if you can. It's for a gender reveal party."

"I take it you don't want to know what it is prior to that?"

"That's right."

"Okay, I'll do what I can as long as the baby isn't shy."

Debbie had me adjust my maternity top and pants, exposing my belly.

A slight heat rose in my cheeks. Logan had seen me in a bikini when I was dating Stephen. But that was a lifetime ago. I didn't resemble that girl anymore—in so many ways.

I didn't dare look in his direction, not wanting to see on his face what he was thinking.

You're being silly. He doesn't see you as anything other than a friend—and the wife of his dead best friend.

Which was fine with me. My number one priority was my baby. Just like Livi was *his* number one priority.

We had that in common.

"I'm going to put some gel on your stomach. It shouldn't be too cold."

She squirted the lukewarm gel on my belly and slid the

ultrasound wand over it, spreading it. Every several seconds, she paused to tap away at the computer keyboard.

The entire time, I watched her expression, waiting to see if she would give anything away. Her face stayed emotion-free. But that meant nothing. She was no doubt trained to keep what she was thinking from her face.

I rubbed my damp palms against the cotton fabric of my pants.

A big strong hand rested on top of mine, warm with reassurance.

I turned my head to find Logan smiling at me.

That smile and the feel of his hand worked like magic. The tension in my body leaked out like water through cupped fingers.

"So, what exactly is a gender reveal party?" Logan asked. I couldn't tell if he really had no idea or if he was just trying to distract me while Debbie did her job.

"I'm not exactly a pro on the topic, having never been to one myself. It's a party, like a baby shower, where the parents-to-be announce the gender of the unborn baby. Sometimes the parents themselves don't know what the baby will be. It's a big surprise. But they don't just announce it. They do something that reveals it in a fun way. Like silly string."

At Logan's confused frown, I explained, "The parents-to-be are each given a can of silly string. If the baby is a boy, the string will be blue—pink for a girl. The cans are covered, so the parents and guests can't see the color. Then the parents-to-be spray each other with the silly string, revealing the baby's gender."

"Is that how you're doing it?"

I lifted my shoulders. "My mother-in-law and my mom are planning the party, and I have no idea what they have in mind. It's all been very hush-hush."

The corners of Logan's mouth twitched. "When is it?"

"Sunday afternoon. I don't suppose you'd like to come, would you?" At least then I wouldn't feel so alone since Chloe and Ava couldn't be there.

"What time is it?"

"Three thirty p.m."

His smile this time was more on the sad side. "Stacy's throwing her husband a surprise party, and I said I would go. But I'll try to get away if I can and go to your party."

The hope I was feeling a second ago fell to the ground like a mosquito that had been splatted midair.

Knowing that Livi would be at her stepfather's party and Logan would want to spend as much time with her as possible, I poured on a bright smile. "Don't worry if you can't make it. It'll probably be boring. I'm sure if Stephen were alive, he would have found an excuse not to be there." I feigned a chuckle.

But the truth was, it wouldn't have mattered even if it were a female-only event—he would have moved mountains to be there.

He would have wanted to know the gender of his baby.

But Logan wasn't Stephen.

And neither man was my baby's father.

"All right," Debbie said, fortunately saving me from any more awkwardness. "I'm finished. Would you like to see your baby now?"

That was all I needed to hear. My lips curved into a genuine smile, and my heart swelled in my chest. It was a good thing Logan was still holding on to my hand; otherwise, I would have floated away. "Yes, please."

She turned the computer around so Logan and I could see the screen. "Here's your baby."

At the sight of my little miracle, my breath caught, and

tears blurred my vision. "I can't believe that's Love Bug," I whispered.

"Love Bug?" Logan asked. "You're naming the baby that?"

I laughed, ignoring the tears shimmering down my cheeks. "Until I know the gender and have finalized their name, yes, that's the baby's name in the meantime."

Still staring at the screen, I wiped my hand against the tears. I wasn't sure exactly why I was crying. Because Stephen wasn't here to share this with me? Because the real father wasn't here?

Or because seeing Love Bug's image on the screen made it that much more real?

I didn't know what Logan thought of my crying. I was too busy watching the computer.

"Would you like a picture?" Debbie asked.

I nodded, too speechless to say anything. That little miracle on the screen was *my* little miracle. Sure, Love Bug kind of derailed my plans to move forward with my life. But it wasn't like I had anyone in it who I was interested in moving forward with.

Love Bug was just a different way of moving forward than I had originally planned. On the bright side, I wouldn't have to worry about anyone trying to set me up on dates.

Not for now, anyway.

I was free to focus on what was important: my baby.

"Here you go." Debbie handed me the ultrasound picture and the white envelope. "I filled in your mother-in-law's card. So you're all set for your gender reveal party. Good luck with it."

After Logan and I finished at the clinic, he drove me home.

"Thank you for being there for me," I said once he'd

stopped outside my house. I leaned over to kiss him on the cheek.

It was only supposed to be a friendly peck.

A thank-you.

But he turned his head to me at the last moment, and my mouth landed on his.

For a second, I froze. The only thing I could think about was how soft his lips were. My brain tried to tell my mouth that this wasn't a good idea—Logan didn't feel that way about me.

I needed to back away.

Only, somewhere between my brain and my body, the message got lost in translation.

My mouth wasn't the only thing that didn't seem to agree with my brain. Logan wasn't in any particular rush to separate either.

Neither of us moved.

And then his hand did. It cradled my head, and his mouth opened to mine.

My lips followed suit.

Logan's tongue entered my mouth, and all thoughts of how it wasn't a good idea vanished in a pouf of blue-and-pink smoke.

Once upon a time, I had imagined how it would feel to kiss Logan. Never in my wildest imagination had I expected it to be like this.

With each brush of our tongues, every cell of my body vibrated with lust and joy. I couldn't remember the last time a man had kissed me like this.

During the Jingle Balls ball, a tiny voice in my mind cheerfully pointed out.

Except this is Logan, not Grayson, I reminded it.

But other than that, the voice did have a point.

But it wasn't as if Grayson was the only man who could

be an incredible kisser. It wasn't like he had a monopoly on the talent.

Logan was a talented hockey player.

Clearly, that wasn't the only thing he was talented at.

Even though I didn't really want the kiss to end, I pulled away, my breath coming in fast, and rested my forehead against his.

Words of apology sat on the tip of my tongue, but I couldn't push them past my lips.

I didn't want to apologize.

I wanted to keep kissing him.

The horniness between my legs cheered on that thought—hinting loudly that it wouldn't mind a little action of its own.

Action that didn't involve my purple dildo buddy.

Logan's lips curved into a slight smile. "I'm not sure if I should be apologizing for that or telling you how long I've wanted to do that since I first met you." His voice came out low and gravelly and only succeeded in making me hornier.

Wow. I didn't think that was even possible.

I straightened, and my gaze flicked to his. "I thought it was only me who felt that way."

"Which way?"

"Both."

The world outside the car was a low hum of activity—the occasional vehicle driving past, a small dog barking, the sound of kids playing tag. Inside the car, silence filled the space like cotton candy—sweet and surprising and delicious. My heart was fluttering in my chest, a hummingbird hyped up on sugar, the sound oddly quiet.

My body ached for me to lean in again and steal another kiss.

My brain told it me wasn't a good idea. I wasn't a

teenage boy ruled by his hormones. I was a pregnant woman who was much stronger.

Wiser.

In control.

For the most part.

"Why didn't you tell me you felt that way when we first became friends?" I asked.

"I could ask you the same."

I lifted a shoulder. What could I say? I was a coward when it came to telling guys that I crushed on them.

But instead of saying that, I went for the easy cop-out. "I should go. My mom and Stephen's mom are expecting me to show up for dinner so I can give them the envelope."

It was the truth, at least.

Logan and I had just admitted to having wanted to kiss each other when we first met. The last thing I needed was for him to jokingly ask me how I felt about him now.

Why?

Because I was the world's worst liar—even if I did seem to be getting in a lot of practice lately.

And because things were complicated.

For Logan.

For me.

23

KIERA

"Stacy told me you want to start gardening," Tony said as we walked into the gardening center. It was early Sunday afternoon, and I had to keep him preoccupied for the next...

I glanced at my phone.

Right, I had to keep him busy for the next hour and thirty-five minutes.

Which also included the time required to drive him home—unless Stacy alerted me via text that she needed more time to set up.

Hopefully that wouldn't happen, because if I was supposed to make an appearance at his party, it wouldn't leave me much time to get to Kiera's gender reveal afterward.

Was I curious if she was having a boy or girl?

Not really. I'd been more focused on the kiss we had shared.

Probably the only time I hadn't dwelled on the kiss was during the games versus the Oilers on Thursday and

Saturday—we won Thursday's game, in case you were wondering—and during practice.

The rest of the time had been free rein when it came to remembering the feel of her mouth against mine, her sweet taste.

The kiss was just as I remembered from the night of the ball.

Was it any wonder I'd been craving to kiss her again for the past four months?

"That's right," I said. "I'm growing an herb garden...on my balcony."

"An herb garden?" Yep, definitely disbelief in his tone, although I had no idea why.

"That's all I have room for."

"Right. Sorry, I forgot you don't live in a house. Guess you won't be needing a leaf blower then."

I laughed. "I don't get too many leaves on the twentieth floor. But if you want to check them out, go ahead." He had that look a man gets when he wants to investigate a new toy —whether it be a sports car, power tool, a leaf blower, or a ride-on lawnmower.

He practically drooled as we walked down the leaf-blower aisle. Unfortunately for him, Stacy wasn't the kind of woman who would give her husband a leaf blower for his birthday.

But at least the aisle kept him busy, so that made my life a little easier when it came to killing time.

The store didn't have a large selection of leaf blowers— or maybe there weren't that many models available in the world, period. I honestly didn't see the appeal to them, but they certainly got Tony excited.

I would've understood it better if he got hard-ons over a chainsaw. Something with power. Something that at least cut wood in half.

After Tony spent ten minutes checking over the leaf-blower product specs, we strolled to the plant section.

"What kind of herbs do you want?" he asked.

"No idea. I just know I need an herb garden." Because Stacy told me I did.

"Are there certain herbs you like to cook with?"

I randomly listed a few I used. The ones that came to mind.

"Okay, well, that's a start."

He rounded up several plants and lowered them into the shopping cart.

When he wasn't looking in my direction, I quickly glanced at my phone. I still had to keep him busy for seventy-eight more minutes.

"Are you and Stacy going to throw a gender reveal party?" I asked as I pretended to deliberate the various style of plant pots on the shelves.

Tony gave me a puzzled look. "Funny, you don't come off as the kind of guy who knows what that is."

He was right about that. Usually, I wouldn't, but I was more enlightened about the topic now, thanks to the conversation during Kiera's ultrasound.

"I take it you know what it is?" I said.

"I've never been to one, but a few of Stacy's friends have thrown them."

"Are you guys planning to have one?"

"Nope. Stacy and I decided to wait until the baby is born to find out the gender."

Okay, so much for my plan to kill time with that topic.

We were silent for several more minutes while I continued to deliberate which pots to buy.

"So, how do you know what gender reveal parties are?" Tony's gaze wandered down the row of pots, and I caught the slight shake of his head.

Exasperation because I was taking too long to pick out some goddamn pots?

Perhaps.

"A friend of mine is having one this afternoon."

A friend of mine who I kissed after I drove her to her prenatal ultrasound. The friend who I hadn't planned to kiss, but when she went to kiss me on the cheek, my body said the hell with that, and I captured her mouth with my own.

But Tony didn't need to know about that.

"I wasn't sure if I should bring a plant with me." All right, that was pretty random—but desperate times call for desperate made-up excuses for why we couldn't leave the store yet.

Plus, I was getting fucking bored, pretending to figure out what pots to buy.

"That doesn't sound like a bad idea," Tony said.

I grabbed whatever pots were closest to me and lowered them into the shopping cart.

"Do you have any shelves to put them on? Or are you lining them up along the wall? That would work, too."

"Maybe I should get some shelves." Especially if that killed time.

My phone pinged in my jeans pocket. I pulled it out and checked the screen.

Stacy: Had some technical delays. Please don't return until 3:30pm.

Shit. That was when Kiera's party began.

Me: Okay.

"Is everything all right?" Tony asked.

I stretched my mouth into a broad grin. "Yeah, every-thing's great. Just one of my teammates."

"You sure about that?"

"That it was one of my teammates? Yep. Positive."

"So, it wasn't Stacy telling you she needs more time to finish decorating for my surprise party?"

He laughed at what was no doubt my "Busted!" expression.

"How di—"

"If you ever want to keep a secret, never tell it to Livi."

I chuckled. So true. I couldn't believe Stacy didn't know that cardinal rule. "So, all this time, you knew we weren't here because I suddenly couldn't live without an herb garden?"

"Yep." He surveyed the contents of the shopping cart. "Should we put these back, or do you actually want them?"

"It probably wouldn't hurt me to grow some herbs."

"You'll want some soil, too." He nodded toward where it was stocked. "So how much longer do you need to stall me for?"

"Until three thirty."

"Perfect. Let's get you that soil; then I can check out the hedge trimmers I don't need but want to look at anyhow. What time's your friend's party?"

I told him. Luckily, the address where it was being held wasn't too far from where Tony and Stacy lived. I would've been screwed if it was across town.

But either way, I was still going to be unfashionably late —assuming I could get away from Tony's party.

"Does Stacy know about it?"

"Are you kidding? She almost had a heart attack when she found me reading *What to Expect When You're Expecting*. I'm sure if I told her I'm going to the gender reveal party for my dead best friend's Popsicle-sperm baby, that would push Stacy over the edge."

Tony stared at me for a moment, digesting what I just told him, and burst out laughing. "Wow, you hockey players lead an interesting life."

He didn't even know the half of it.

"Daddy!" Livi ran across the backyard and flung her arms around my waist. She was wearing a light-green party dress with white butterflies. "I missed you."

I gathered her up in my arms and hugged her. "I missed you too, baby girl."

Now that it was the playoffs, I had even less time to spend with her than before. We still FaceTimed daily, but I hadn't seen her in person for three days.

"I love your dress," I told her. "You look very pretty." It went with the tea-party theme Stacy had organized for the event.

Livi grinned. "Thank you, Daddy. Let me introduce you to everyone."

I couldn't help but laugh. She sounded like her Martha-Stewartesque mother. "Sounds like a plan."

I lowered her to the ground. She grabbed my hand and tugged me this way and that way, through the crowd, introducing me to Tony's and Stacy's friends.

And damn, there were a lot of them.

Some were eager to talk about the playoffs—something I hadn't really wanted to do while I was here. I politely answered their questions, then found an excuse for why I couldn't stick around.

Luckily, I didn't need much of one with Livi playing host.

It wasn't as if she wanted to spend time standing around chatting with the adults.

"You have to see the birthday cake," she stage-whispered to me at one point. "Tony isn't allowed to see it yet, but Mommy won't mind if you do."

That was probably not true. Stacy, no doubt, wanted everyone to be surprised when they saw it.

"Where is it?"

"In the kitchen." Her voice held a "no-duh" note that made me chuckle.

We entered the house without anyone else asking me what I thought of the team's chances of winning the playoffs.

As much as I wanted the Rock to win, I didn't want to jinx the team with any predictions.

Yes, hockey players were a superstitious bunch.

For good reason.

Livi pointed to the cake on the kitchen table, not that I could have missed it. The elaborate cake resembled a backyard, complete with a little man (Tony?) gardening. There was even a miniature wheelbarrow and leaf blower.

It wasn't the kind of cake you found at the local grocery store. It was the type you specialty ordered from someone other than the supermarket.

"Wow, that's really nice," I told Livi, who was beaming proudly at it. "Did you make it?"

She giggled. "No, silly. One of Mommy's friends did. Do you like the garden gnome?" She pointed to a tiny gnome with a tall red cap perched on his bearded head.

"He looks yummy."

Her face paled and twisted into a horrified expression. "You can't eat him, Daddy. He's mine. I asked for a garden gnome on the cake."

I'd figured that. Some girls loved fairies. Livi was all

about garden gnomes. Which was why Travis would be painting a mural on her bedroom wall with lots of gnomes on it once the playoffs were over.

A quick glance at the microwave clock warned me it was four thirty. If I didn't leave soon, I'd be beyond fashionably late for Kiera's party.

I couldn't explain the compulsion to be there. She had already told me it would be boring and that it was just as well I had other plans.

But something about the way she'd said it—well, more like the emotion in her eyes—told me she needed me to be there for a reason that was beyond me.

Livi and I returned outside to the party. Tony approached us and told Livi one of her friends—who was also at the party—was looking for her. She hugged me again and skipped off to join a small group of young children playing miniature golf.

"You ready to bail this party and go to your friend's gender reveal?" Tony's gaze scanned the yard like a man looking for a quick escape route.

I was torn by what I wanted to do.

I'd only been here an hour. If Livi wasn't here? Yes, it would be a no-brainer. I would have left thirty minutes ago.

But the party was my chance to spend time with my daughter, who I wouldn't get to see much during the playoffs.

"You can always come back after you're finished with the other party." Apparently, Tony had recently acquired the ability to read my mind. "Then you and Livi can have a quiet evening together—assuming this party is over by then."

I was about to tell him okay, right after I checked with Livi first, but Stacy prevented me from doing that.

"Logan," she said, approaching us. "Can you help me with something?"

"Will it take long? There's—"

Tony was standing behind her, shaking his head and waving his arms and mouthing, *Don't say it.*

He looked so comical, it was a miracle I didn't burst out laughing.

That didn't mean, though, I was capable of keeping the corners of my mouth from twitching.

Stacy spun around, possibly searching to see what had me so amused.

But all she found was Tony, wearing an innocent *Can-I-help-you?* grin.

Shaking her head, more to herself than for our benefit, she turned back to me with the expectant look I was more than familiar with from our marriage.

"What do you need help with?" I asked.

"One of the balloons on the arch deflated, and I need your help changing it."

"I can do that," Tony said.

She swiveled to him. "No, you can't. You're the birthday boy."

That got a snicker out of me, and an eye roll from Tony.

"The last I looked. I'm hardly a boy."

This time I couldn't keep from bursting out laughing. "All right," I managed to say, realizing with a hard kick to the gut that there was no way I'd be escaping the party to get to Kiera's. "Where's the replacement balloon?"

The smile that flashed on Tony's face, too quick to be caught by his wife?

It was his *I've-got-your-back* sly grin. "Stacy, Livi needs you."

She glanced over her shoulder to our daughter, who was still busy playing with the other kids. "She does?"

"Yes, she just waved that she needs you."

If anything, that was the last thing Livi looked like she needed.

"You should probably see what she wants, first," he told Stacy.

"Oh, okay."

No sooner had she gone, than he got down to business.

"The best escape route is to the side of the house." His voice was low, like a highly entertained 007, and he jerked his head in that direction. "You don't have enough time to make it to the house before she realizes I lied about Livi needing her. Now, go. And good luck." He smacked me on the arm, half shoving me into action.

And like when a player gains control of the puck during the other team's power play, I broke away from the party and hightailed it to the side gate.

24

KIERA

I can do this. I can do this. I can do this.

I parked my car in an empty spot along the street and eased out a long breath. My parents' home was several houses behind me, an archway of light blue and pink balloons decorating the entrance.

If this was what the front looked like, I was afraid to see the backyard.

Remember, you're doing this because it's making Judith happy.

I'd been reminding myself of this ever since I dropped off the envelope with Love Bug's gender inside on Wednesday.

It wasn't the reveal that was the issue. It was the guilt bouncing inside me like a rabid bunny.

But the guilt of breaking her heart would be a hundred-fold worse than me lying to her, so I just had to suck it up. For now.

Had Mom or Judith told me their plans for the party? Or at least hinted what was in store for me?

Not at all. They'd clammed up tighter than an oyster at

190

a clambake as soon as they heard me enter the house. By the time I'd walked into the kitchen, Mom had covered everything on the table with a tablecloth.

I had tried not to dwell on what the two women had planned, which I'd been slightly more successful at than not thinking about Logan's kiss.

I had tried not to dwell on the kiss while in bed.

I had tried not to dwell on it while coping with bouts of horniness (which happened more frequently than I cared to admit).

I had tried not to dwell on it while standing in front of my class, teaching addition.

Or spelling.

Or reading.

I had tried not to dwell on it while watching the Rock versus Oilers games on Thursday and Saturday night. This might've been easier to do if Logan hadn't been nabbed to do an interview during the second intermission last night.

The more I'd tried not to think about the kiss, the more the soft feel of his lips against mine played out in my mind.

That wasn't the only thing I'd thought about during the past few days. His confession had played in repeat mode. I hadn't been the only one who'd had those feelings while we were in college.

Or at least it had been that way until Stephen came into my life and bulldozed me off my feet.

I know that doesn't sound romantic, but the truth is what it is. Stephen hadn't taken his time to woo me. He'd seen what he wanted and gone after it.

In the best possible way.

Maybe if Logan had been like that, things would've been different between us. Instead of me dating Stephen, I could have ended up with Logan...and ended up in the same place his ex-wife had found herself.

A car drove past my vehicle, loud rock music jarring me from my thoughts.

"Okay, time to get inside before the guests arrive," I muttered to myself. Cradling my hand against my stomach, I smiled at my protruding belly. Despite all the craziness that was currently my life, this, with Love Bug, felt oddly right.

I removed the key from the ignition, grabbed my purse, and climbed out of the car. The warm afternoon air clung to my bare arms and legs. I'd worn my favorite floral maternity sundress, which emphasized the swell of my belly.

Not to mention, it highlighted my newly voluptuous breasts.

Typically, I would open my parents' front door without knocking first, but for some reason that didn't feel right this time. This time I felt more like a guest in their house than a daughter.

Mom answered the door a moment later, and her face lit up. "I love that dress. It looks beautiful on you, sweetheart."

Two things I've learned so far while pregnant?

First, hormones turn you into a hot mess. One minute you're ready to hump everything in sight. The next, you're weepy.

No secret there.

And the second?

I don't know about the horny part (and I didn't care to find out either way), but a pregnant woman's hormones do quite a job on her mother.

On cue, Mom's eyes glistened.

"Thanks," I said, hoping that was enough to curtail the tears. I stepped into the house, only to be brought up short by Judith.

Turns out mothers-in-law weren't immune to hormones either.

She engulfed me in a hug, squeezing me a little tighter than usual. "Your mom's right." *Sniff.* "You look gorgeous." She released me. "Every bit as pretty as you did on your wedding day." *Sniff. Sniff.*

All right, not what I needed to hear. Now it was my turn to sniff back the tears.

At this rate, by the time everyone showed up, we would be a sobbing disaster.

But for different reasons.

"Do you need any help?" I asked, walking farther into the house, desperate to escape the potential sob fest.

"No, we're all set."

If I thought the front of the house had been a little much with the balloon arch, that was nothing compared to the backyard.

A white-washed wooden sign greeted guests when they stepped onto the deck. A large blue-gray elephant was holding a hockey stick. Another elephant wore a tutu around her middle. Beneath the two elephants, the sign read, "Welcome to Kiera's gender reveal party."

The rest of the deck and yard mirrored the tutu and hockey theme. Bunches of light pink and blue balloons were tied to the wooden railing, and paper lanterns hung from strings crisscrossing the lawn from tree branches.

It was both pretty and depressing.

Sure, Stephen had been a talented hockey player, but this wasn't his child. Grayson was athletic, but for all I knew, he was into martial arts and couldn't have hit a puck into a goal even if he wanted to.

If Love Bug was a boy, did that mean everyone—especially Stephen's parents—would expect him to also be a star hockey player?

Would they expect him to have ambitions of playing in the NHL?

Would they be disappointed if he didn't possess an ounce of the talent Stephen had?

I picked up a puck sitting on the railing and turned my gaze skyward.

God, was Stephen watching from heaven, with a bowl of popcorn, laughing at my predicament.

"Easy for you to laugh," I muttered at the sky. "You weren't the idiot who tried to move on with your life after losing someone you loved."

Naturally, I was referring to the night of incredible sex in Lake Tahoe. The baby and the gender reveal party? Not so much.

The guests started arriving soon after, and I spent the next while milling around, talking to them.

I was chatting with a couple of my mom's friends when a pair of hands covered my eyes.

Definitely female hands.

"Guess who." Chloe masked her voice so it didn't sound like her.

But I knew better.

I squealed and turned to throw my arms around her.

And then did the same to Ava, who was standing next to her.

"I thought you couldn't make it."

Ava exchanged glances with Chloe. "Things went down a little faster than expected."

Both women appeared a bit disheveled. Chloe had a smudge of dirt on her face. Other than that, they looked good.

But it wouldn't have mattered if they were covered in mud and wearing ripped dresses. I was just happy they were here.

They weren't alone. Emma and Hannah were with them. Along with Travis and Wes. Wes was holding Riley in his arms.

"Surprise," Ava said, nodding at the four people I hadn't expected to see. But I also knew they were Ava's friends through her husband and his sister. "Emma told me how you, she, and Hannah have recently become friends, so I asked your mom if it would be okay if they came to your party, too."

I hugged her again. "Thank you. Having you all here is the best surprise."

And I meant it.

She surveyed the decorations. "This is so adorable." She then dropped the volume of her voice so only Chloe and I could hear her. The others were momentarily distracted with something Emma was telling them. "I don't suppose the mystery father played hockey, did he?"

"It didn't exactly come up," I whispered and peered through the window, checking the time on the microwave. Everyone my mother and Judith had invited was here, but there was no sign of Logan.

Not that I had expected him to make it. Livi came first, as it should be.

"Hi, everyone," Judith called out, causing me to turn to where she was standing on the deck. "For those of you who don't know me, I'm Judith Ashdown, Kiera's mother-in-law, and her precious child's grandmother." She beamed at me, and I silently groaned.

"I don't know about you, but I'm excited to find out if Kiera's carrying my granddaughter or grandson."

Chloe leaned closer to me. "I thought she was the one who set up the reveal."

"She did. Maybe she got someone else to look inside the envelope."

A warm hand settled on my lower back. I spun around to see who it belonged to. Logan was standing there, smiling.

And my heart made like a kangaroo and bounced into my throat.

"Sorry I'm late," he said. "Did I miss anything?"

Before I registered what I was doing, I flung my arms around him. "You made it!"

He returned my hug.

I could feel curious gazes on us but didn't care.

"You didn't think I would miss it, did you?" He flashed me a cocky smile. "I just got held up at Tony's surprise birthday party."

I removed myself from his arms and grinned. "You're just in time."

He surveyed the area. "Nice decorations. If I didn't know better, I'd say Stacy was responsible for this." He nodded at a bundle of balloons near us.

I laughed. "Maybe I'll have to introduce her to my mom and Stephen's mother."

I introduced him to Ava, Chloe, Hannah, and Wes.

"Hey, I didn't realize you were going to—" he began to say to Travis.

Judith cut him off. "Before we find out what the little miracle will be. Beth and I have organized some games that we're going to play first. So if everyone can join us on the grass, we'll get started."

She was standing next to a chalkboard set up on an easel. The board was decorated to look like a hockey scoreboard, with the Boston College hockey team logo on it. The timer was frozen at 12:45, and instead of HOME and VISITOR, it read BOY and GIRL.

"As some of you might know," Judith said, "my son was

a talented hockey player, just like my grandson or grand-daughter will be."

How I kept from cringing was beyond me. I could feel Ava and Chloe cast me sympathetic glances.

I let my gaze drop to Logan's lips, prompting the memory of the kiss in his car to replay in my head. I was half aware of running the tip of my tongue along my lower lip, capturing the feel and taste of him all over again.

I really wanted to kiss him.

Here.

Now.

But that wouldn't exactly be a good thing to do. Not with everyone here to bear witness.

My eyes flicked to his. The intensity in them had deepened.

"I want to kiss you again," he murmured.

"I want that, too."

"This probably isn't the best time or place for that."

"You're probably right."

"Beth and I came up with a fun game to predict the gender," Judith announced. She gathered up a hockey stick and walked to the practice goal. Each corner contained a net pocket that you were supposed to shoot the puck into. Or at least attempt to. Mom and Judith had attached two signs on the top bar. One proclaimed BOY, the other, GIRL.

"Normally," Judith continued, "Stephen would have used pucks when he practiced, but they aren't as easy to use on grass. So we're using balls instead. The goal—excuse the pun—is to score on your gender prediction." She pointed to the two pockets on the right side of the goal for GIRL. Then did the same for the other two pockets, which repre-sented BOY. "You'll be allowed three attempts to get the ball into a pocket."

She held the hockey stick toward me. "Kiera, as the mother-to-be, you go first."

You know how two people who are alike are supposed to be attracted to each other?

That's a pile of pigeon poop.

Stephen might have been born with a golden hockey puck in his mouth, but that didn't mean it had been the same for me.

Just the contrary.

But luckily for me, Stephen believed that talent was due to not just genetics. It was honed through practice. Lots and lots of practice. Even though he didn't get drafted into the NHL, he still practiced often—both on and off the ice—so he'd be sharp for his highly competitive recreational team.

I accepted the stick from her, nudged the first ball into position, and shot at the goal.

And missed the pocket I'd been aiming for.

Replaying in my head all the pointers Stephen had given me over the years, I aligned myself with the second ball and hit it with the blade of the hockey stick.

This time it went exactly as planned. In the upper corner, no less.

Cheers broke out among the partiers.

Grinning, I curtsied.

"I didn't know you could play hockey," Logan said as he took the stick from me for his turn.

I laughed. "I can't. That's about the extent of my skills."

What I'd failed to mention was that the extent of my skills went slightly beyond that. But there weren't many opportunities to demonstrate your talent of shooting at the goal while your husband thoroughly kissed your neck.

Logan's first shot went in no problem.

"So, you think I'm having a boy?"

He shrugged. "Heck if I know. What about you? Is your mother's intuition telling you that Love Bug is a boy?"

I grinned cheekily at him. "You want to know why I predicted it's going to be a boy?"

Commissary groans rose from the group as Emma missed the goal pockets on her third shot. Travis told her he still loved her regardless of her crappy puck handling ability. Laughing, she smacked him in the chest.

Logan leveled a goofy grin at me. "You cheated and looked in the envelope?"

I shoved him playfully on the arm. "Nope. I flipped a coin."

He barked a laugh. "I guess that's one way to do it."

Ava, Chloe, and Hannah went next. None got the ball in the pockets they were aiming for. All three had predicted a girl.

Like Logan, Travis got the puck in one go. Girl.

It took Wes all three attempts to score on the same.

"And it looks like the winner is 'boy,' " Mom said once everyone had finished their turn.

We played several more gender-reveal games, after which Mom announced, "Let me get the napkins from inside the house. We can have cake first; then we'll do the gender reveal."

"I can get them." I needed to go pee anyway. I didn't know if Grayson had been a hockey player or a soccer player or a kickboxer, but Love Bug was having a great time kicking my bladder.

"Oh, that's okay, sweetheart. You're pregnant."

"So I've noticed, but that doesn't mean I can't lift napkins." I hustled off before she could argue otherwise.

And because my bladder was sending SOS signals.

After I finished relieving the poor organ of its burden and washed my hands, I opened the bathroom door.

Logan was leaning against the opposite wall, and my breath caught at the heat in his eyes.

LOGAN

Remember when you were a kid, and your mom told you not to eat cookies before dinner because it would ruin your appetite?

But you did anyway.

It wasn't because they were forbidden, and that only made them more enticing. It was because you were hungry, and let's face it, cookies taste a helluva lot better than cut-up pieces of raw broccoli.

At the Jingle Balls ball, Kiera had been like that cookie. She certainly smelled and tasted as mouthwatering as one.

Now?

Not so much.

Don't get me wrong...she was definitely tempting. But not in the tempting-because-she-was-forbidden kind of way.

Now it was due to something else, but I couldn't figure out what that was.

I stepped forward.

The heat in her eyes went straight to my cock.

Christ, I so fucking wanted her again.

Kiera reversed into the bathroom counter. I shut the door behind me and clicked it locked.

I moved closer to her until we were sharing a breath. For a heartbeat, neither of us said anything, our gazes saying it all.

Kiera's hands shifted to my chest. The warmth from them sank into my skin. I stilled, the air in my lungs not daring to move as I waited for her to come to her senses and push me away.

But she didn't.

Her hands fisted the cotton of my T-shirt. "Please, kiss me."

Her voice was a low purr, barely heard over the beating pulse in my ears.

That was all I needed to hear. My lips crashed onto hers, and everything else was quickly forgotten.

After I'd dropped her off at her house the other day, I had entertained the idea of kissing her again. I'd imagined taking things slowly, savoring the moment.

However, instead of taking my time like I wanted to, a sense of urgency pounded through me. Someone could show up at any moment to use the bathroom.

But even though I knew I should step away and leave, I couldn't.

What I wasn't expecting was for Kiera to slightly pull away. "God, I want you so badly," she panted, her voice rough with need. "Fuck, I'm so horny."

I stilled for a second, positive I'd imagined her saying that—especially since Kiera had never said fuck before in that context. Of course, what did I know? My only experience with her that way had been the night of the ball.

"Sorry," she whispered and smiled. "That was a little crass. But it's been a while since I last had sex, and being pregnant is making me awfully horny."

I chuckled. "I remember Stacy being frustrated when I was on the road while she was pregnant with Livi. I wasn't around as much as she wanted so I could satisfy her needs."

"I swear I need to find a temporary boyfriend, so I have someone to fuck while I'm pregnant. Or at least until I'm not horny all the time."

I leaned in, breath tickling her ear. "I'd be more than happy to take the edge off while we're in here."

She gasped softly.

"Would you like that?" I tenderly kissed her neck. It probably wasn't the smartest thing to do, but in this moment, my willpower was at an all-time low when it came to Kiera.

A small moan escaped her, and she nodded. "Very much."

"We probably don't have much time before someone will need to use the bathroom. And your mother's got to be wondering where you've disappeared to with those napkins." She was the one who had told me that Kiera had gone inside to fetch them.

Which was too bad. I wanted to take my time, exploring every part of Kiera like I had the night of the ball.

We would have to save it for next time—if there was a next time.

She nodded and reached for the top button of my jeans. Her hand lightly brushed the hard-on pressing against the fabric.

Her touch did nothing to help my situation. A situation that would have to wait until I got home and had a cold shower.

I linked my fingers with hers, stopping her hand from inflicting any more torture. "No, you need this more than I do."

She grinned impishly at me. "I think your cock disagrees with you."

"It doesn't get much say in the matter." If my dick could talk, it would've booed me.

I cupped her breasts in my hands, feeling their full weight. They were a lot heavier than in December. I ran my thumbs across their peaks.

Kiera nipped her lower lip between her teeth. I suspected that was to hold back a whimper or a moan.

I craved to yank down the top of her dress and worship her breasts. But there wasn't time for that.

I gave the peaks one last teasing caress and shifted my hands to her expanding waist. The baby inside her belly might not have been mine, but that didn't stop the unexpected rush of protectiveness that swelled in me.

For a heartbeat, I imagined the baby was mine from the night of the ball. I mean, it was a good thing that it wasn't, because I didn't have room in my life for another child, not while I was still playing professional hockey. But knowing that didn't stop the protectiveness from taking a firm hold on me.

I lowered to my knee and raised the hem of Kiera's dress, exposing her lace panties and stomach. Before I realized what I was doing, I planted a tender kiss near her belly button.

Kiera sucked in a soft breath.

Hooking my thumbs in the waistband of her panties, I slipped the cotton fabric over her hips. Once I'd rid her of them, I stood and carefully lifted her onto the counter.

Fuck. I needed more time to enjoy this, to enjoy her, but the cavalry would be banging on the door at any moment, checking if she was all right.

She squirmed under my gaze, and a smug smile slipped onto my face.

I trailed my fingertips along her inner thigh to the apex and brushed her sex with my thumb. A moan tumbled from her lips. "*Christ*, you're so wet," I husked against her ear.

That only made her moan again, except this time a little louder.

I slanted my mouth on hers and continued kissing her while my thumb shifted to her clit. I could feel it throb under the light pressure.

I pressed one and then a second finger inside her.

Kiera wasn't kidding when she said she was horny. That was all it took before her soft heat convulsed tightly around my fingers. With my mouth still on hers, I swallowed her sexy groan, which I still remembered vividly from December.

Someone knocked on the door. "Kiera, are you in there?"

"Yes." Kiera's voice sounded like she'd just smoked a pack of cigarettes. Her eyes were wide with panic but also a little dazed. "I just had to go to the bathroom. The baby's been busy kicking my bladder. You know how it is. I'll be out in a minute." Her cheeks flushed—although that might have been partly due to the orgasm—and her head flopped on my shoulder.

"All right," her mother said. "Don't worry about the napkins. I'll grab them on the way out."

"Okay." The reply was slightly muffled, but I didn't think it was enough for her mother to wonder what was going on in here.

We stayed still for a moment while listening for her retreating footsteps. Once we were sure she was gone, I helped Kiera down and into her clothes.

I wanted to give her another kiss, but we didn't have time for that.

"Are you feeling better now?" I asked, instead.

A dopy grin grew on her face. "Most definitely. I don't suppose we could do that again at some point? But next time, we're both left satisfied." The grin shifted to an embarrassed smile. "At least now, I'm not quite as horny and don't want to hump everything in sight."

Relief washed through me at her request. "I think that can be arranged." At the very least, it would help take the edge off between home games.

"You should sneak out first to make sure the coast is clear. I'll be out in a minute." I was certain Stephen's mother wouldn't be thrilled if she believed I was fucking her daughter-in-law while Kiera was pregnant with her grandchild.

Kiera quickly washed her hands and escaped the bathroom. It took me a little longer since I had to get my hard-on under control first.

Everyone was eating cake by the time I joined them outside.

"Would you like a piece from the boy or girl side of the cake?" Kiera's mom asked me as I approached the table. I needed to walk past it to join Kiera and our friends.

"Either side is good with me. But just a sliver, please." Cake wasn't part of my playoff diet.

She sliced a small piece from the hockey side of the cake and handed me the plate. "We'll be doing the gender reveal next."

I thanked her and walked down the deck steps. Kiera was standing with a woman I didn't know near the bottom when I reached the last one. "Wow, you really are glowing," she said to Kiera. "I swear you're glowing even more than you were before you went inside." She scanned the back-yard as if searching for the cause of the glow. "Whatever it was that caused it, I wouldn't mind getting some for myself."

Kiera shrugged, her expression somewhat sheepish. "What can I say? I'm really happy. And I'm going to find out the gender of my baby soon." She rubbed her stomach like it was a crystal ball.

She then smiled at me and hurried over to where Chloe, Ava, Emma, and Hannah were talking. And naturally, I couldn't help but watch her sexy ass as it swayed away from me.

"What's really going on between you and Kiera?" Travis asked, joining me. From the way he and Wes were eyeing me, it was clear they'd overheard the woman's comment to Kiera.

"No idea what you're talking about," I said. "We're just friends."

Wes chuckled. "Right, you're just friends. That's why the two of you disappeared for ten minutes, and Kiera returned looking more satisfied than before she left."

"She was in the bathroom. You both know what pregnant women are like. They always need to pee, thanks to the baby."

The corner of Travis's mouth curled to the side. "Right. And that's why we know the difference between the satisfied look a pregnant woman gets after she pees versus after she gets laid. And the latter is definitely how Kiera looked when she returned from the house."

"Hate to say it, but you're both hallucinating." The last thing I wanted was to admit the truth to either of them—for Kiera's sake. And for my own.

"All right," Stephen's mom announced several minutes later. "Time for the moment we've been waiting for. Kiera, over here, please. And Joe, bring in the balloon, please."

Stephen's father walked over, carrying a large black balloon.

Judith handed Kiera a thumbtack. "You just need to pop the balloon, and we'll see if you're having a girl or a boy. And now, for the moment of truth." She nodded for Kiera to go ahead.

Joe lifted the balloon. Kiera reached up and stabbed it with the pin.

Nothing happened.

She tried again.

Still nothing.

And the same thing happened on her third attempt.

Judith's and Beth's faces shifted into disappointed frowns at the balloon's reluctance to reveal their grandchild's gender.

The same couldn't be said about Kiera.

She was laughing hard.

Seeing her like that brought back memories from when we were friends in college—when seeing her laugh made things a lot brighter. Our collegiate hockey team could have lost a game the night before, but it didn't feel quite as weighted once I heard her laugh.

Would I feel that way if we lost the next game against the Oilers (hypothetically speaking, of course)?

Probably not.

But you get the point.

Kiera tried popping the balloon a fourth time.

When that proved useless, Stephen's mom tried to pop it.

Wes laughed. "Maybe the baby doesn't want to reveal its gender."

Hannah elbowed him in the gut. "It just takes a special skill."

"She's got a point." Judith's gaze zoned in on me. "Since Stephen isn't able to do it, how about the next best thing. Logan, you were his best friend and teammate; not to mention, you play in the NHL. If you can't pop the balloon, no one can."

I was pretty sure playing in the NHL didn't grant me any special skills for the destruction of balloons. Still, the hopeful expression in Kiera's eyes was all it took.

I accepted the pin from Judith.

"He would have wanted you to do this on his behalf." Her voice was low enough that only Kiera and I heard what she said.

"Is everyone ready?" Unlike before, Judith began counting down. "Three...two...one."

I reached up and pushed the pin into the balloon.

Clearly, the seventh time was the charm.

A loud pop accompanied a shower of blue confetti.

Everyone cheered. I heard Kiera's grandfather say, "I knew that boy had it in him. As if it would be anything but a son." His chuckle was paper-thin but hearty.

Without thinking, I pulled Kiera into a hug. "Congratulations. I don't suppose you want to predict who's going to win Tuesday night's game?"

I released her. Kiera opened her mouth. Before she could respond, I pressed my finger against it. "On second thought, I might not want to know. I'll stick with my prediction that we're going to beat the Oilers' asses."

She laughed. "That would have been my prediction anyway."

Judith wedged herself between Kiera and me and squished her with a hug. "I'm so excited for you." She wiped at a tear. "I can't believe it. Stephen's having a son."

Did anyone else notice that?

Kiera flinch?

I had to admit Judith was starting to piss me off a little with her constantly mentioning Stephen. It was time she let Kiera move on. Stephen was dead. He wasn't coming back.

He wasn't going to be holding his baby or watching over his wife and child.

And her constantly clinging to his memory was only hurting Kiera.

THE PARTY WOUND DOWN AFTER THE GENDER REVEAL. I wanted to talk to Kiera more, but that was impossible with everyone waiting to say good-bye to her.

And I needed to head out so I could spend the evening with Livi.

Smiling, Kiera hugged me. "I'm glad you were able to come. I'll see you soon," she whispered the last part, her meaning clear.

"I'll text you once I return from Edmonton."

We stepped apart. "I'll be watching your game Tuesday night. Emma invited me over to watch it and do some more planning on the charity event."

The door clicked shut behind the last couple to say good-bye to Kiera. She and I were temporarily alone.

She kissed me on the cheek, lingering longer than a quick peck good-bye. "Good luck in Edmonton."

Wanting more than what she was giving me, I knotted my fingers in her hair. I was taking a big risk, but fuck, I needed more than a quick kiss to get me through the next few days.

I should have simply said thank you.

That would've been the smartest thing to do.

But smart was a distant cousin when it came to being around Kiera.

I caught Kiera's mouth against mine and gently nipped her lower lip.

"Oh. My."

26

KIERA

One second, Logan and I were kissing, the next, we were springing apart at the sound of Mom's voice.

Heat pricked my cheeks—a giveaway to the guilt and embarrassment rising inside me.

"Hi, Mom," I said casually, as if she hadn't just caught us kissing.

But while I might have been aiming for casual, that wasn't how it sounded, even to my ears.

Mom lifted her eyebrows in a *Do-you-care-to-explain?* expression.

Not particularly.

"I was just wishing him luck for Tuesday's game. Go Rock, Go." I pumped my fist in the air to the beat of the chant.

Okay, that wasn't helping things.

So I went with Plan B. I rested my hand on the bulge of Logan's biceps—damn, the man had nice muscles—and nudged him toward the door. "It was great seeing you,

Logan. Good luck with the game. I know the kids at school will be cheering for you."

He smirked at me, unseen by my mom, and turned to her. "It was nice seeing you again, Beth."

"You too, Logan. Good luck with the game."

I practically shoved him outside, but not before appreciating his muscles one final time, and shut the door. Slowly, I swiveled to face Mom and flashed her what I hoped passed as an innocent, nothing-to-see-here smile.

"Is there something I should know about you two?" Her voice hovered above a whisper.

"We're just friends," I whispered back.

"That didn't look like just friends."

I wasn't positive what she was insinuating—nor did I care to ask—so I raised my shoulders in an It's-not-what-you-think shrug.

"The three of us should go shopping while I'm still in town." Judith strode purposefully into the foyer, hopefully, oblivious to our conversation. "We can start getting you some supplies for my grandson."

That look in her eyes?

I recognized it. It meant she wasn't taking no for an answer.

"That's a great idea, Judith. What about tomorrow night?" Mom's question was directed at me.

Both women grinned at me, their hopeful expressions impossible to ignore.

A list of excuses paraded in my head, some doing impressive backward somersaults. Unfortunately, that was the only impressive thing about them. "Tomorrow works for me."

I needed to get out of there before I agreed to anything else I probably shouldn't, so I told them it was time for me to go home to have a nap.

"Yes, you take care of my sweet grandson." Judith hugged me for what must have been the hundredth time since arriving in San Francisco.

My stomach twisted into tight knots, each one more tangled every time I let people believe Love Bug was Stephen's son.

"I thought we could go out for dinner, the four of us"—Judith patted my belly—"and discuss baby names. Stephen's grandfather's name was Neil. I thought that would be a good one."

"That would be a perfect name," Mom said. "Just like Neil Armstrong. If the baby doesn't want to play hockey, maybe he'll want to be an astrophysicist."

I snorted a laugh. "That won't be happening if he inherits my math skills."

"How was Stephen at math?" Mom asked Judith.

"He was better at playing hockey, but he wasn't awful at math."

I managed to contain my laugh this time. Math wasn't Stephen's favorite subject either...not that it mattered when it came to Love Bug. Stephen could've been a mathematical genius, yet Love Bug wouldn't have appreciated those genes.

And I had no idea if Grayson excelled at math. It was one of those topics that never came up that night.

But heck, if I had known the condoms would fail us, I would've asked him all kinds of questions. Questions that Love Bug would probably want answers to when he got older.

"Look, sweetie, there's Daddy." Emma pointed at the

players on the TV screen. They were standing on the blue lines for the American and Canadian national anthems.

Kat, her toddler daughter, bounced up and down, her feet never leaving the floor, and cheered.

The shopping trip the evening before with my mom and Judith?

Don't worry, you didn't miss anything exciting.

Other than Judith adding more names to her list of potential options. Only none of them did anything for me.

She also bought Love Bug his first hockey skates. And a toy hockey stick.

And an entire collection of Rock jerseys and baby onesies and a stuffed bear sporting the team's jersey.

Nope, no pressure whatsoever for Love Bug to live up to the man whose genes he didn't share.

Logan was also on the ice for the national anthem.

My breath accelerated, and my body tingled. Neither, I suspected, had anything to do with the national anthem. My thoughts flicked to Sunday afternoon when Logan gave me the orgasm—an orgasm that put to shame the ones I'd experienced since the ball.

My purple vibrating buddy did a good job, but nothing like what Logan or Grayson could achieve.

Not even close.

Curiosity bubbled in my veins about something I had wondered ever since Logan told me about his divorce. "What's it like being married to an NHL player?" I asked Emma after the puck drop.

Before you get the wrong idea, I wasn't asking because I'd suddenly envisioned myself walking down the aisle with him.

Because I wasn't thinking about that.

At.

All.

But that didn't mean I wasn't curious about what Emma's life was like as the wife of an NHL player. And what Travis was like as a father and husband.

Logan blamed his dedication to hockey instead of his family for ultimately ending his marriage. But what about the other side of the fence?

What about those players who could balance both?

A smile curved onto her face. "Is there a particular reason you're asking?"

"Nope. Just curious."

"So, you're not interested in Logan that way?"

"He's just a friend." Who happened to be an incredible kisser.

"I can't speak for all NHL wives, but it's good. It definitely has its ups and downs, as you can imagine. Travis is away a lot during hockey season, and when he's not away, he's home late because of his games.

"It will be tougher once Kat is in school. Then she'll see him even less than she does now. She's used to talking to him on FaceTime when he's away, so hopefully, she'll adjust to it just fine. Plus, it's not all the time. Once the play-offs are over, he has lots of free time to spend with us. That makes up for him not being around as much during hockey season.

"The hardest part—as you can probably guess—is the possibility of your husband being traded to another team. It means uprooting your family. And in my case, if Travis is ever traded, I would have to figure out what to do with my store."

"Do you know what you would do?" I asked.

"I have a great manager who I trust to look after the shop while I'm away. I worked hard to make it the success that it is, so selling it if Travis is traded isn't high on my list of options."

The puck went sailing into the Oilers' net, and the three of us were on our feet, cheering. Except it took me a little longer to get to my feet than it did for Emma and Kat.

"It also helps having the support of the other players' wives and girlfriends," Emma said once we'd sat down again. Kat remained on the floor. "They understand what it's like being married to a player or dating one. We've become a family."

She smiled at me, her eyes sparkling with an emotion that went deeper than happiness and understanding and love. "So no, it's not easy being married to a hockey player. But I wouldn't trade being married to Travis for anything. It's worth the sacrifice."

A smile grew on my lips. "I'm glad that things are great with you two."

"Travis mentioned that Logan's divorced."

"That's right. Stacy, his ex-wife, is happily married and is expecting a baby with her husband later this year."

"You know his ex-wife?" Emma asked, helping Kat onto the cushion next to her. The little girl was clutching a bunny wearing a Rock T-shirt.

"Yes, she's the mother of one of my students."

"I didn't realize Logan's daughter is one of your students." Her eyebrows danced comically above her eyes. "This is getting more and more interesting. Do you see him often?"

"You mean as the father of one of my students?"

She threw me a *You-know-what-I-mean* look, and I laughed.

"He was volunteering when he could during the regular season." Which had only been two times. "As for what you're really asking, yes, I've been seeing him lately—but strictly as a friend. He's helping me out with the fundraiser. Remember?"

The fundraiser that Emma and I had been talking about before the game. She had even found a venue to hold the event and cater it.

"Well, you know what happened with the hockey player who helped me with my fundraiser." She wiggled her ring finger at me.

"Honestly, it's nothing like that," I told her. "He's just a supportive friend."

"Who took you to your ultrasound appointment *and* showed up at your gender reveal party."

"Travis and Wes showed up at that party, too," I said in Logan's defense.

"That's because they're married to Hannah and me. They didn't have a choice." She grinned, and I chuckled.

A memory of what Logan and I had done in the bathroom wiggled its way in. I tried pushing it away. The memory didn't budge.

It only became more insistent, reminding me of that mind-numbing orgasm—an orgasm that worked wonders at the time but had since left me, sadly, even hornier.

Last night, I might have even imagined it was his fingers getting me off.

And let me just tell you, my fingers were a poor substitute compared to his.

I could feel the temperature in my cheeks rise from thinking about it.

"Oh, wow, there's more to it than that, isn't there?" Emma grinned at me as if I'd turned into a giant sparkly diamond. "And don't try to deny it. I can see it in your eyes, and"—she shrugged—"you're blushing."

Dammit. No more thinking about Logan. No more...

"Okay, I like him as maybe more than a friend. But don't get any crazy ideas." The last part came out in a big rush. "Our situation is complicated."

"Daddy, Daddy!" The TV had flashed to the Rock's bench, and Kat had spotted her father next to Logan.

My traitorous body released a dreamy sigh. Logan might've been all sweaty from playing hard, but that didn't seem to bother my body. If anything, it made me hornier.

Emma snickered next to me. I didn't dare glance at her to check the reason behind it.

There was no point. Emma was aware of what I was going through.

"How did you survive being pregnant while Travis was on the road?" I asked.

"Oh, God, it was the worst. If he had been home, we could've fire-trucked every night. But I was pregnant during the regular season and had to endure his road trips, some of which were long. I pretty much jumped the poor man every time he came home from being away."

I laughed. "I can see how that would happen."

"I take it no one warned you before you became pregnant with your husband's little swimmers that, thanks to your hormones, your sex drive would go into overtime?"

I stretched my lips in what felt like an awkward grin. "No, that definitely wasn't in the fertility clinic's information pamphlet."

Emma giggled, seeming not to notice my sudden discomfort at the line of questioning. "Hannah complained about the same thing. But fortunately for her, she found a solution."

"What did she do?"

"She had a friends-with-benefits deal with a guy she was friends with."

"What happened to the guy?"

The corner of Emma's mouth twitched. "She married him."

Good thing I wasn't looking for a husband or a baby

daddy for Love Bug, because what happened between Hannah and Wes wouldn't happen to me.

There would be no wedding vows.

All I had to do was wait for Logan to return, and everything would be all right in the department of horny hormones.

For now, anyway.

27

KIERA

The day after the Rock played in Edmonton, I stood in the elevator of Logan's building, willing it to move faster. If I wasn't twenty-one weeks pregnant, I would have sprinted up the stairs to his condo.

Of course, if I hadn't been pregnant in the first place, I wouldn't have needed to see Logan, *stat*.

Each floor the elevator climbed, my palms grew clammier. Logan knew my reason for visiting him. We had agreed at the party to temporarily add "benefits" to our friendship.

But I had no clue what he was expecting.

This wasn't like a typical one-night stand. And it wasn't as if I could google instructions on the topic.

Yes, I did try doing that, which was how I knew about the lack of etiquette protocols for situations like this.

Online, anyway.

The elevator eventually opened after what my horny body deemed to be several lifetimes. I walked down the hallway, my fingers itching to start removing my clothes to save time.

Luckily, my brain still had some control over my body—by a sliver of a margin.

I knocked on his door. It swung open a moment later.

"Hi—" That was the only word Logan managed to say before my lips found his.

My hands shoved the hem of his T-shirt up his body. In the recesses of my mind, the etiquette police told me to at least say hi to him.

"God, I want you so badly," I murmured instead, barely pausing long enough to inhale air into my lungs.

Logan didn't argue or protest or say the same. He reversed, his mouth on mine. I could only assume we were headed for his bedroom. At least we were in agreement there.

He paused our kisses long enough to yank his T-shirt up over his head before his mouth was on mine again.

There was something familiar about his kiss—like I was coming home after being away for a long time.

I couldn't explain it.

And at this point, I didn't even want to try.

I had more important things to do.

Like getting Logan naked.

Logan bumped into the wall behind him.

I would've said oops, but I was a little preoccupied. My fingers were now on the button of his jeans. His were busy sliding the fabric of my maternity top over my belly. I helped him remove it and tossed it somewhere on the floor in his room.

His gaze dropped to my purple lace maternity bra that I'd bought yesterday, just for this occasion. I might be pregnant with a stranger's baby, but that didn't mean I couldn't feel sexy.

But not for Logan's benefit.

Completely for mine.

But the way he was looking at it, eyes dark, he definitely approved. "*Christ*, you're fucking gorgeous."

My breath caught at his words. His voice was rough like gravel, and something about it caused a fluttering in my chest like a thousand butterfly wings beating in harmony.

"So are you. I mean...not gorgeous...but hot." *Oh, God.* Now I sounded like a babbling fool.

Logan smiled indulgently and ran his thumb lightly over the lace, not touching my nipple but still managing to cause the bud to pebble.

He ran his thumb, again, across my now aching breast. The tip grazed my nipple, and my legs almost buckled under me.

As though sensing what I needed, Logan crouched, his hot, moist breath causing my breasts to beg for everything he was willing to give me—and more. They tingled with want, tingled with desperation.

Oh, God. Please.

Logan's face turned up to mine, and a smug smile met my gaze.

"I said that out loud, didn't I?" I asked.

He laughed. "No one ever accused me of not aiming to please." He sucked on my nipple, bra and all.

I released a whimper and knotted my fingers through the soft strands of his hair.

Logan continued to tease me, taking me to the edge, until I could barely stand upright any longer. While he did that, the other hand was busy pinching the otherwise neglected nipple. All I could do was groan.

And thank my lucky stars, solar system, and galaxy that at least for the next several months, Logan was mine.

Not mine in the sense that he was my boyfriend or husband.

He wasn't even a lover.

He was so much more—in a way, I couldn't even define. Not even to myself.

He straightened and guided me to his bed.

"By the way, congratulations on winning Tuesday's game," I said, palming the hard length in his jeans.

The hard length that I'd been fantasizing about since Sunday, when we'd agreed to be friends with added perks.

Was this the first time I'd congratulated him?

Nope. Not at all. I'd texted him as soon as the Rock won the game.

But hello? Thanks to the team winning the series, they had advanced to the next round, so he deserved all the congratulations he could get.

And I planned to congratulate him in a moment in a way that words alone couldn't convey.

"Thank you," he husked, his voice as strained as his cock was against his jeans.

Unable to wait any longer for the next part, I quickly removed my maternity pants and socks, leaving me in only my bra and matching panties.

Correction...leaving me in only my bra, panties, and a slip fashioned from awkwardness.

In college, when I'd had a thing for Logan, I'd imagined a few times what it would feel like to make love to him.

This was before I met Stephen, during those months of my secret Logan crush that even my close friends hadn't known about.

But never in any of those fantasies had I imagined myself standing in front of him while pregnant with another man's child.

All right—I'd never imagined myself pregnant with Logan's child, either.

Not that I was pregnant with his child, but you know what I mean.

I tilted my head to the side, trying to get a read on Logan. But it was hard to tell what he was thinking. The only light in his room came from the faint moonlight glowing through open slats of the blinds. Dark, blurry stripes slanted across my belly.

He stepped closer to me—until he was barely an arm's length away—and brushed his thumb across the swell of my belly. "You still want to do this?"

There was uncertainty in his tone, but I couldn't tell what it was directed at. Was he having second thoughts?

Some people think pregnancy is sexy, although I assume those people weren't pregnant when they said it. There was nothing sexy about needing to pee every five minutes or having swollen ankles.

Logan could be one of those who didn't believe pregnant women were sexy. I mean, sure he thought my bigger-than-normal boobs were great. But what man didn't appreciate big breasts?

I caught my lower lip between my teeth and nodded. Fear that he would change his mind cut through the air like a knife through a jelly donut. "Do you…?"

He chuckled and stripped his body free of his jeans, leaving him in nothing but his briefs, which were tented with his arousal. "What do you think?"

He closed the rest of the distance between us and trailed the pad of his thumb across my lip. "I want you more than you can possibly imagine, Kiera. But I want to make sure this is really what you want."

"It is." As far as I could tell, us having sex was the smart thing to do. It solved the issue of my horniness (when Logan was around). And we were friends who could be mature about the situation because we understood what the other person wanted when it came to a relationship.

This thing between us was temporary—while I was pregnant.

Once Love Bug was born, I would no longer be horny... and I wouldn't have time for a relationship. My son would be my number one priority.

"It really is what I want." Leaning in, I kissed him—proving with more than words what I needed, what I craved.

While our lips were still touching, our hands exploring, we stumbled to the bed and lay down. Somewhere between my declaration that this was what I wanted and the bed, my bra bailed on my body, assisted by Logan's skilled fingers.

His lips moved from my mouth to my jaw and neck, kissing and gently biting my flesh. He skimmed his fingertips along my ribs. I squirmed, my body now super ticklish. A soft laugh escaped me.

Logan chuckled. "I don't remember you being this ticklish."

I paused my squirming, momentarily confused by his comment. But then brushed it off. I must have misunderstood him. Maybe he was referring to when he'd seen Stephen and me together.

"Maybe it's a side effect of being pregnant," I said. "I've never been this ticklish until now."

"I'm not complaining." His mouth returned to mine, and he continued dragging his fingers over the curve of my hips.

A moment later, we were both free of our underwear and lying naked on the bed, limbs entwined. A foil wrapper sat on the bedside table.

The bundle of nerves between my legs pleaded for sweet relief. He didn't even have to touch them for the tinder to ignite. Just the taste of him, the feel of his naked skin beneath my fingertips, his smell was enough to create the spark.

My hands were no less idle than his. After they'd finished exploring his body, inventorying each valley and ridge of his muscles, they drifted south to the part of him that I'd been more curious about.

I wrapped my palm around his hard cock and grinned at the effect it had on him. His moan did more than just make me smile, though. The nerves cushioned between my legs grew more excited.

Luckily for them (and me), they didn't have to wait much longer for relief. Logan's fingers slipped between my sex. "God, you're so wet," he said.

I swallowed, willing my body not to explode just yet. Although I suspected once his fingers found my clit, I'd be done for.

I widened the space between my legs, giving him better access.

Turns out I was right when it came to how close to the edge I was hovering. One touch of my clit, and I went right over.

"*Oh, God,*" I cried out, my body floating skyward, stars sparkling in welcome.

It took several moments before I no longer felt like I'd been turned to Jell-O. I kissed Logan once more and returned to my fun of making him groan from my touch... to the point where he couldn't last any longer.

"I want inside you." He shifted me, my back to his chest. A moment later, the condom was rolled onto his length, and his fingers were working their magic on my clit, again.

They continued creating magic as he inched his way inside me.

"*Fuck,* Kiera," he groaned.

"*Yes, please,*" I replied on a moan, needing him more than I'd ever needed anything else.

He chuckled and plunged inside me until he was fully seated, hitting all the right places.

It would seem that I wasn't the only one balancing on the edge of the precipice. With only a few thrusts of his hips, we were both tumbling over the ledge.

I AM A FRAUD.

Those four words bobbed on the surface of my mind like a piece of chum before Jaws turned it into a midnight snack.

Logan was asleep next to me, exhausted from our three rounds of sex. The early shades of dawn painted faint shadows on his face.

You would have thought that I, too, would be sleeping. And under any other condition, I would have been.

But instead, all I could do was dwell on how it was time to contact Grayson.

No matter what the outcome, I couldn't drag my butt on this any longer.

This thought had briefly crossed my mind when Logan had tenderly swept his thumb over my baby bump. But the thought had been like wisps of white cloud, barely brushing my mind. I hadn't registered it until now.

It might not be possible for Grayson to physically be here for me since he lived in Chicago and I didn't, but I could live with that. And if he didn't want anything to do with his son, then fine. I could live with that, too.

I carefully wiggled out of Logan's bed and searched his room in the dim light for my clothes. It took me several minutes to locate everything and put them on.

Logan remained asleep the entire time.

I had fallen asleep for a short period after our third bout of sex but had woken up from a weird dream. I didn't remember most of it, but I did remember the part about Stephen in a halo and wings and playing a harp (Yeah, I don't know why he was playing the harp, either. In real life, he hadn't played any instruments).

Dream Stephen had told me I was ready to tell Grayson he was going to be a father.

Except, Stephen told me by song...like some sort of weird ode.

That was when I woke up.

The rest of the dream was fuzzy.

"Bye," I whispered to Logan. "I'll talk to you later."

The memory of the last time I sneaked out of a man's room after having sex tip-toed in. But unlike then, I would see Logan again soon. Although I had no idea if he would still want to be my friend once the truth came out about Love Bug's daddy.

I'd told him that his best friend was the baby's father. Hopefully, with time, he would forgive me for lying.

I slipped out of his apartment and clicked the door shut behind me. Silence greeted me, the day too early for anyone to be up.

I pressed the elevator down button and sent Ava and Chloe a group text while I waited.

> Me: I'm finally ready to contact Love Bug's real daddy.

28

LOGAN

I passed the puck to Eli, who shot it at the goal. Kai, our goalie, easily deflected it.

Normally, I'd be thrilled if that happened during a game (the goalie deflecting part). It meant the opposition was robbed of a goal.

But when you were practicing a specific setup with your teammate during the morning skate, the missed goal smarted.

We sprinted to the end of the line of players and performed the drill, again and again and again, until the coaches brought us in for feedback. Then we were on the ice again, practicing a new drill.

The best part about all of this?

It meant I had to shut out everything that wasn't hockey —including last night with Kiera.

But as soon as practice ended, my memories of last night power-skated back into my thoughts.

I'll admit I hadn't been too thrilled when I woke up in the morning to discover Kiera had snuck out during the night.

Like she had the night of the ball.

We hadn't set any ground rules for what we were doing, but I figured that she would leave in the morning given she was pregnant and needed her rest.

Perhaps that was something we needed to discuss.

Possibly that afternoon, since I was due to volunteer in her classroom shortly.

That was one advantage of winning our series when we did. It gave me a few extra days to help out. Fortunately, Joyce, the classroom volunteer coordinator, was happy to slip me into the schedule.

"I don't suppose your ex-wife has a woman friend I can borrow this summer for my cousin's wedding," Eli asked once we'd finished showering and were getting changed.

I laughed. "Borrow? We're talking about a person, not a car."

"All right, let me rephrase that. Someone who would be happy to go to a wedding as my fake girlfriend, so my mom and aunts don't try to play matchmaker."

"Would they really do that?"

"My mom and aunts are taking full credit for how my cousin met her husband-to-be. And since that match-making scheme worked, I'm now their next target."

"And you don't want that." I couldn't help the smirk on my face. I'd been lucky no one had ever tried setting me up with anyone. But it also helped that Stacy and I got married relatively young.

Had Mom been happy when Stacy and I divorced?

Not at all.

She had hoped for more grandchildren. But I didn't have to worry about her ganging up with my aunts to set me up with someone.

At least not yet.

"Look, I'll ask Stacy if she knows anyone who might be

willing to help you, but I can't promise anything. Don't you know anyone who you can convince to be your fake girlfriend?"

"Something tells me asking a one-night stand to help me out might not be a brilliant idea."

"Probably not. Don't you have any female friends you could ask?"

He shrugged. "Not really. I know females...but that's because I know their husbands or boyfriends. I wouldn't exactly call them friends."

Honestly, none of this surprised me. Unlike a lot of guys on the team, Eli was shyer when it came to women. Sure, he had no trouble finding women who wanted to hook up with him. But they weren't looking to be friends with him, nor were they looking for a relationship with him.

In a way, he reminded me of myself in college. If I had been more like some of the other guys in the room—or like Stephen—I would have told Kiera how I felt about her before she met my best friend.

As it was, it was a damn miracle I'd sat next to her in class one day and started talking to her. My shyness around women had kept me from striking up easy conversation with them.

The exception was Kiera.

Something about her had compelled me to sit next to her during our first week of classes and make a lame joke.

She'd actually laughed, and we'd talked while waiting for the professor to begin his lecture.

And from then on, I sat with her, and just like that, our friendship grew.

So I could totally see where Eli was coming from—but that didn't solve his dilemma.

"Is the wedding in San Francisco?"

"No, it's in a small town in Montana."

"So, you need a woman who can go with you to Montana for a day or two and pretend to be your girlfriend?"

"More like a week. There'll be several family get-togethers before the wedding."

I chuckled. "Well, good luck with that. I can ask around, but I can't make any promises. Maybe you could hire an actress to help you out."

"Do you know any actresses?" Hope bled into his tone like ink from a pen.

"Sorry, can't help you there either. Maybe you'll get lucky with the silent auction, and the highest bidder will be happy to spend the week with you in Montana." Naturally, I was joking.

He let out a This-is-useless huff. "I'm not that desperate." He might have said that, but the look in his eyes clearly stated the opposite.

I checked the time on my phone. *Shit.* I had to get going since I didn't want to be late. I yanked on my clothes.

"Logan," the assistant coach said from the locker room door. "Coach Fusco needs to talk to you."

I nodded that I'd be there in a second, while mentally cursing the delay.

But telling your head coach you had somewhere you needed to be that was more important than talking to him never went down well.

I practically sprinted to his office, praying whatever he wanted to talk to me about wouldn't take long. "You needed to see me?" I asked, entering through the open door.

He waved for me to sit.

Fuck. This wasn't going to be quick, was it?

I did as requested.

"How's your leg doing?" he asked.

"My leg?"

He leaned forward, folded arms on the desk. "The one you injured near the end of last season."

"It's fine. I spent the summer increasing my strength and flexibility so it doesn't happen again." I'd strained my left quadriceps muscle, but thanks to physical therapy and the work I'd done with the strength and conditioning coach, things were better.

"I'd like you to spend some extra time with Fredrick"—the Rock's conditioning coach—"to make sure the same thing doesn't happen during the playoffs. The team can't afford to lose you to an injury. And you might want to focus on your speedwork. That seems to be dropping slightly."

Have you ever felt like the forces of the universe were working against you? You had one simple goal, and the universe had other plans.

There was nothing wrong with my speed. And I was at no greater risk of being sidelined with an injury than any of my teammates.

See what I mean? The universe was screwing around with my plans of spending more time with my daughter.

It didn't want me to get to her school in time to volunteer.

"Okay," I said, hoping that was the end of it.

"I told him he can expect you after practice." He nodded, dismissing me. I unfolded from the chair, ready to leave.

"Before I forget." He picked up a manila folder from his desk. "You're doing that fundraiser for children's books, right?"

"That's right. I'm helping a friend who's organizing it."

"My wife's interested in donating artwork for it." He held the folder out to me. "It contains pictures of the sculptures she's donating."

I flipped it open. The top image revealed a young

woman made of bronze, wearing a long dress like a night-gown blowing in the wind. A wolf stood next to her—her own personal bodyguard.

"There are some hockey statues, too. Do you think your friend will be interested in them for the silent auction?" His expression softened, probably for the first time since I'd been traded to the team.

"I'm sure Kiera will love them. Did your wife make them?"

"That's right."

"They're really good." You didn't need to be an art critic to see that.

He dismissed me with a reminder to see Fredrick.

I texted Kiera to let her know I would be late, but I had no idea if she'd see it in enough time.

Fredrick was in the weight room when I entered, working with one of the younger guys, who had been side-lined until recently with a lower-body injury.

Hockey players were used to playing through injuries. We did our best to ignore the pain, often pushing our bodies past the limit. It was part of the game—the sacrifice we made to be the best.

Were our bodies vindictive assholes after we retired?

You'd better believe it.

But that didn't stop us from taking the abuse—for the love of the game.

"Hey, Fredrick. I'm supposed to see you about upping my conditioning."

"So I've heard." He looked me over, the overhead lighting gleaming off his bald brown head. The man easily towered the tallest of my teammates by a good two inches. We referred to him as the friendly giant for good reason. "You don't look like you're planning to do any plyometrics today."

"That's because I'm supposed to be volunteering in about twenty minutes in my daughter's classroom. Fusco just told me the part about upping my conditioning."

"Why don't you come and see me after practice tomorrow morning?" He lowered Brent Conway's leg. "But before I set it up, I need to know, are you experiencing any problems with your leg? Anything that you've neglected to mention to the trainers?"

"Nope. All is good. I haven't had any issues with either leg since the end of last season."

"That's what I thought. We're too late in the periodization cycle to really work on this without putting you at risk of injury. But I'll see what I can do."

THE RAIN THAT HAD BEGUN DURING PRACTICE WAS NOW coming down in diagonal sheets. The wind wasn't much better, imploring the trees to bow to the gale-force winds.

I raced to my car, hoping to avoid being soaked by the time I got to it. Wetter than I'd have liked to be, I climbed into my vehicle and drove to Livi's school. I left the arena fifteen minutes later than planned, and her school was on the other side of the city.

And because the galaxy was having fun toying with me, it made sure traffic wasn't cooperating. The rain could be partly blamed for that.

By the time I entered the classroom, I was forty minutes late. Even though the room was buzzing with activity that masked the sound of the door clicking shut behind me, Livi's gaze turned in my direction.

And for a second, disappointment stared back at me, poking me in the gut with a dull pencil.

Her expression then transformed into relief. Grinning, she waved at me.

But despite that, the disappointment jabbing at me didn't relent. I'd let her down enough times when she was younger because I'd put my career above her. Things were only slightly better now that I'd learned from my past, but even though I was living in the same city—which made things easier—I was still screwing up.

Sure, I was fucking things up less than before, but it was still tough balancing hockey and my daughter.

Thank Christ, once the season was over, I'd have the whole summer to dedicate to her.

Kiera was bent over a table, pointing to something in front of a student. The little girl grinned and nodded, and Kiera straightened. Her eyes found mine, and she smiled.

That smile, complete with my favorite dimples, had my heart skating around the classroom several times, breaking all NHL records.

My heart wasn't the only thing that reacted at the sight of her. My breath came in faster, and my gut felt the way it did during the puck drop at the commence of a game.

If we hadn't been in a classroom with kids, I'm sure my cock would have come to life, too. Fortunately, it chose to behave.

Fuck. She was even more beautiful compared to yesterday. Even though I doubt I was responsible for it—as much as I would've like to take credit—she glowed more than before.

I wanted to talk to her, but there was someone I needed to apologize to first.

Kiera seemed to recognize that. She smiled and nodded.

I walked to Livi's table and crouched next to her.

"Hi, Logan." Beaming, Tyler snatched up his book from the table. "Do I get to read to you first?"

"Of course." That was how it usually went when I volunteered. Tyler went first, and Livi was the last student to read to me. "Livi, I'm sorry I'm late."

"That's okay, Daddy. You're here now." She gave me a hug, which I returned, squeezing her a little tighter than I would've typically done.

"Let me talk to your teacher first, Tyler. Then we can go in the hallway to read."

I joined Kiera at the front of the class. What I really wanted was to kiss her, taste her. But now wasn't the right time for that—not when over two dozen pairs of eyes were watching us.

"I got your text," she said.

"Sorry I'm so late. The head coach needed to talk to me." My fingers itched to run my thumb across her lower lip. "But I have some good news to tell you after class."

"Mrs. A, the computer isn't working." The boy pointed to the one he was referring to.

Kiera flashed me an apologetic smile and went off to perform whatever computer-repairing magic she needed to do.

Leaving me to watch her sweet ass as she walked away.

29

KIERA

The final bell of the day rang.

"Don't forget you have a spelling test tomor-row," I reminded the class. The chatter and laughter and scraping of chairs drowned out my words.

The man who had turned my body into a horny mess the moment he'd entered the classroom earlier approached me, Livi by his side.

Livi's presence meant he and I couldn't kiss, which we probably shouldn't be doing to begin with, regardless if she was here or not. Logan was the father of one of my students.

A divorced father, but her father all the same.

"You said you have something to tell me?" I asked.

He wasn't the only one with something to say, but this was neither the time nor the place for the news about Love Bug's biological father.

"The wife of the Rock's head coach wants to donate some bronze statues she made to your silent auction." Logan handed me his phone. On the screen was a picture of a statue—a young woman next to a wolf. "The photos are all in my car. These are a few of them."

I flipped through the collection of images. "They're gorgeous. She's really donating them to the silent auction?"

"According to Coach Fusco, she is."

"Can you thank them for me?" I studied the statue of a little boy in skates and holding a hockey stick. He must have been about four years old.

I ran my finger over the image, imagining my son playing hockey one day. He might not have had Stephen's genes, but that didn't matter. Maybe just loving the sport would be enough.

Inwardly, I smiled at the picture now painted in my head.

"Have you called your sister yet?" Chloe asked, walking into my classroom. She stopped abruptly, her eyes on Logan, her mouth forming a silent, *Oops.*

"I'm calling her tonight." Right after I told my parents the truth. Brittany was friends with Grayson's grandmother and was my best way of tracking him down. I could ask Ava's husband for help, too, but at this point, I wasn't ready to do that.

"Let me know how it goes." She smiled reassuringly at me. At least one of us believed everything would be all right after I dropped my Jolly-Green-Giant-sized bombshell.

"Livi's hanging out with me tonight," Logan said after Chloe left the classroom, "and we're watching a movie. Do you want to join us?"

Livi flashed me a hopeful grin. "We're even having popcorn and hot chocolate with marshmallows."

"I'd love to, but I'm having dinner at my parents' tonight." Now that Stephen's parents had returned to North Carolina, I could breathe easier again when I visited my family. Between my all-over-the-place emotions and

Stephen's baby and toddler photos that Judith had insisted on showing me, I was surprised my tears hadn't flooded San Francisco.

"Rain check?"

I smiled at them both. "Sure, I'll take a rain check."

"How about Saturday? Livi and I are going to the beach to explore the tide pools and build a sandcastle."

The hopeful expressions were back on their faces, making it impossible for me to say no. "That sounds like fun. Count me in."

"Yay!" Livi bounced around on the spot.

Logan beamed at me, and my insides did a little bouncing of their own. "Are you heading to your car now?" he asked. "Or do you need to work a little longer?"

"I'm taking stuff with me to work on after dinner at my parents'."

I also needed to knit more mittens to send to my aunt. Once Love Bug was born, I wouldn't have much time to work on them.

"We'll walk you to your car."

"Daddy said you're having a boy," Livi said in the parking lot. "I'm hoping for a brother, too."

Logan affectionately stroked his daughter's hair. "But a sister will also be great."

She shrugged, not too convinced with her father's assessment. "Sure." She perked up. "What's his name going to be?"

"I don't know yet. I'm working through my options." None of which were on Judith's list.

"How about Tyler?" she asked.

"I like that name. I'll definitely add it to the list. But don't you want to save it in case you have a brother?"

"They can both be Tyler."

"True." Although it would get a little confusing every

time she mentioned the name, given that Tyler was also her best friend's name.

Once we reached my car, an awkwardness blanketed the air around Logan and me. If Livi hadn't been there, I was positive we would have kissed. I couldn't even kiss him on the cheek or hug him. That would've also been inappropriate.

Of course, the same could've been said even if she hadn't been with us.

"Have fun tonight watching the movie," I tell them.

"Bye, Mrs. A." Livi waved good-bye and tugged on her father's hand to get him moving.

It didn't work. He subtly rubbed my upper arm with his thumb, the closest he could get to being intimate with Livi there. "I guess I'll talk to you later."

I PARKED MY CAR IN FRONT OF MY PARENTS' HOUSE AND GAZED up at it. "You lied, and now you have to face the consequences," I reminded myself, my stomach churning at the thought.

It was like in the book Livi had been reading in March. *Max Thunder and the Ocean of Secrets*. Max had lied about what the Fates had told him, to protect those he loved.

The result?

As Livi had put it, the outcome was a huge disastrous mess.

Sound familiar?

While I wouldn't say my life had become a disastrous mess like Max's—no mythological creature would be stealing my best friends away because of a lie—the white lie I had blurted to my parents when I'd initially told them I was pregnant had morphed into a monster of its own.

A little monster.

Nothing too deadly, but still problematic all the same.

I wasn't ready yet to tell Judith and Joe and everyone else the truth until I'd spoken to Grayson first, but I did need to talk to my parents.

Did I think my parents were going to disown me?

Not at all.

They'd be disappointed that I lied—a disappointment that would hurt more than all the owies in the world combined.

And I didn't even want to dwell on what their opinion would be when it came to my one-night stand with a masked stranger—the reason I had blurted out the lie to begin with.

I inhaled a deep, fortifying breath and slowly released it. Then climbed out of the car.

Mom was busy weeding when I entered the yard through the side gate. Dad was sitting on a deck chair, reading a book.

Mom pushed herself to her feet and brushed her dirty hands against her green and brown tie-dyed skirt—not that you could see the dirt among the swirl of colors. "Hey, sweetheart."

I hugged her, even though it came at a cost.

She examined the brown smudge, now residing on my light-pink maternity top. "Oh, darn it. I'm sorry."

"It's okay, Mom." It was nothing compared to what I was about to share with them. "I have something I need to tell you and Dad."

There are two sentences that should probably be banned from the English language (or any language). The first one is when you tell your girlfriend or boyfriend, "We should talk."

That one rarely ends well.

The second one is when you're pregnant and announce to your parents you have something you need to tell them.

Mom's face paled, and she pressed her hand over her heart. "Is something wrong with the baby?"

"Oh, no. Nothing like that. But you might want to sit down."

She shared a glance with Dad, then did as I suggested.

Okay. Here goes.

"Stephen and I weren't seeing a fertility specialist before he died." The words rushed out so fast, if they'd been solid and with wheels, they would have won the Daytona 500.

Mom's eyebrows crinkled together, and her gaze dropped to my stomach. "So how did you freeze his sperm if you weren't seeing a specialist?"

"That's the thing. We didn't. We had just started trying to get pregnant, but then...well, you know what happened."

This time Mom's eyebrows shot up her forehead, giving her an owlish appearance. "Are you telling us that you got pregnant, thanks to a sperm donor? But why did you tell us that it was Stephen's baby?"

For a second, the idea of letting her believe that didn't sound half bad. Plenty of women chose to have a baby via IVF—like Hannah—because they were in the right place in their life for having a child, but they hadn't found a partner they wanted to settle down with.

My parents were liberals. They would have stood behind me if that had been my choice.

That story certainly was the more favorable option than the truth—that I'd had a one-night stand with a stranger.

But while it was one thing to blurt in a moment of panic that Stephen was Love Bug's father, it was another to tell them I was pregnant due to an anonymous sperm donor.

"Love Bug wasn't conceived via a sperm donor or in

vitro. There was definitely a man involved. It just wasn't Stephen."

Dad's expression?

Imagine for a second a father who'd forgotten his child was thirty years old, and in his eyes, she was still sporting pigtails and scraped knees.

Yep, that was the expression.

"What man?" His voice rolled in like thunder over the desert.

"Remember how I spent the weekend in Lake Tahoe with Brittany and her family just before Christmas?"

Mom and Dad nodded in unison.

"I went to the Jingle Balls ball with them. It was the charity event that raised money for testicular cancer awareness."

They nodded again, this time with the universal sign for "Go on."

"Well, I met a man that night." I pinched my lower lip between my teeth, hoping I wouldn't have to spell out the rest of what happened.

"Have you told him about the baby? What was his reaction?" Mom's questions tumbled out in a big rush, making it hard to tell where one ended and the other began.

I swallowed. "I haven't told him. Not yet, anyway."

"But you are going to tell him?" Dad asked.

"*Well*, I'm going to try to. All I know is that his name is Grayson, and he lives in Chicago."

Mom and Dad stared at me for a long moment as if I'd just told them that I was moving to Antarctica to live with a colony of penguins.

Although given I was about to tell a near stranger I was knocked up with his baby, the Antarctica option didn't sound so bad.

"Let me get this straight," Dad said, frowning. "You had sex with a man, and you had no idea who he was?"

Mom didn't say anything. She just slowly shook her head in a never-ending loop.

"And you let us believe that Stephen was the baby's father? You let Judith and Joe believe the baby is their grandson?"

With each word, my stomach felt as though someone were turning it into a piece of origami artwork.

A dove soiled with black ink.

I tried drawing air into my lungs—and failed. "I stupidly told you Stephen was the father because I knew you would be disappointed that I got pregnant from a one-night stand. And I didn't want my baby to suffer from that stigma. I hadn't counted on Mom talking to Judith. They were never supposed to find out I was pregnant. And when I saw how happy they were when they showed up, I didn't have it in me to break their hearts by telling them the truth.

"I can't take back what I did when it comes to the lie I let them believe, but I might be able to find the father. Brittany knows his grandmother. I was...I was wondering if you think it's a good idea. That I contact him."

I thought it was a good idea. Chloe and Ava definitely felt it was a good idea. I just wanted to know if my parents were also on board with my decision.

"He has the right to know," Dad grumbled. "And he also has the responsibility to support his child. The last I heard, it takes two to make a baby."

"Well, most of the time, it takes two," Mom said. "Assuming the baby wasn't created in a fertility clinic...like we thought our grandson had been."

I flinched. "I'm sorry I lied to you about who the father is. I...I just didn't want to disappoint you."

"Disappoint us?"

"Because I got pregnant from a one-night stand."

Their silence was hardly reassuring on that front.

I swallowed. "I made a mistake. And I promise I'll fix it."

That move to Antarctica? It was beginning to sound better and better.

Mom's eyes went round, and she began pacing. "*Oh, God. Oh, God. Oh, God.*"

"What?" I asked.

"Judith called me today." Mom stopped pacing long to give me the exciting news. "She and Joe sold their house. They're moving to San Francisco. To be closer to their grandson."

"No, no, no. They can't do that." Now Mom wasn't the only one who was pacing.

Except, we were walking at a ninety-degree angle to each other—participants in the Olympics' synchronized pacing event.

And our duet was expected to win a gold medal.

Mom stopped abruptly. "When are you going to tell them?"

I followed suit. "Soon. I just need time to figure out how best to do it. I don't want to hurt either Judith or Joe. But I will tell them. I promise. But I don't want you to say anything to her. This is my mess, and I need to be the one who cleans it up."

She studied me for a moment, then gave me a brief nod. "Okay, I trust you to do what's right for you and everyone else."

"But preferably before they actually move to San Francisco," Dad said. "They need to cancel their plans."

Mom took the seat next to him. "Judith is from the Bay Area. She's been wanting to move back here for a while. They finally decided to make the move now that Joe is retired. You said the baby's father lives in Chicago?"

I nodded. "That's right."

"Are you planning to move there if he decides to be part of his kid's life?"

"No, this is my home. And I have a job I love here." And friends whom I adored.

The idea of moving away left me feeling as though I'd been transformed into a giant snow cone.

On top of that, I didn't even know him all that well. He was just a stranger I'd had sex with. Great sex, mind you, but you couldn't base a long-term relationship on that.

A small, relieved smile spread on Mom's face at my answer. She didn't want to be separated from her grandson any more than Judith wanted to be separated from hers.

Only in Judith's case, there was no grandchild.

The sensation of a warm breeze filled me at Mom's reaction. While she wasn't thrilled with how her grandson had been conceived, she wasn't going to ignore him because Stephen wasn't his father.

***

THE NEXT MORNING, BRITTANY RETURNED MY CALL AS I walked through the school parking lot to the front entrance. After leaving my parents, I'd phoned her and told her I needed to talk to Grayson's grandmother.

Naturally, she had asked why, but I wasn't ready to tell her the truth. Not yet. The next person who needed to hear it was Grayson.

And he needed to hear it from me and not his grandmother.

"Did she give you Grayson's number?" were the first words out of my mouth when I answered the phone.

"And hi to you, too," she said on a laugh. "I take it pregnancy has tampered with your politeness gene. No, 'How's it going, Sis?' "

"Hi, Brittany, how's your day been?" There was no missing the mocking in my tone.

She snorted. "I'm good. But not as good as Lucinda Mathews is right now."

"What do you mean?"

"It would seem that she and her husband are at a spiritual nudist retreat in Argentina." Brittany laughed. "Who knew those two had it in them to do something like that? I know I wouldn't have the guts to do it."

That made two of us.

"When are they coming back?"

"Not for another month."

"A month!"

Curious glances turned in my direction. I flashed them an It's-all-right, nothing-to-see-here smile. "Is there any way I can contact her before then?" I asked, keeping my tone more neutral this time.

"I've left a message with her personal assistant, but that's all I can do until she returns. Unless it's an emergency, her assistant has been given strict orders not to contact her. And by emergency, we're talking the world is about to end, or Chris Hemsworth has been spotted at another nudist retreat. And if the latter is the case, please get her reservations ASAP at the retreat." Brittany chuckled. "I want to be like her when I'm her age."

Despite the panic spinning inside me like a dog chasing his tail, I couldn't help but laugh at her comment. "I'll be sure to tell your husband that."

"You do that." She laughed again. Her tone then changed to something a little more serious. "You're not going to give me a hint why you want to talk to Grayson?"

"Nope."

"But I'm your sister. The girl who changed your diapers when you were a baby."

"You changed my diaper *once*. You were three years old, and you put the diaper on my head." Or so went the family legend.

"But at least I figured it out before Emilia was born." Her daughter was probably thankful for that.

Not one to give up so easily, Brittany said, "I really am curious why you want to talk to Grayson. It can't be about your fundraiser because he lives in Chicago. And you left early from the..." Her words came to an abrupt standstill, and I could imagine her standing in her kitchen, eyes widening as she started slotting together pieces of the puzzle.

"Oh. You didn't leave early because being in Lake Tahoe was too much for you, did you?" Her voice was free of judgment. It held a wince from knowing how hard it had been for me to return to the area where Stephen had died.

In the seconds that my brain spun like a wheel stuck in the mud, rendering me speechless, Brittany found that final piece of the puzzle.

"You had s-e-x with Grayson?" she said in a hushed tone.

I burst out laughing and pulled open the door to the school. "You don't need to spell out the word. I can guarantee your daughter doesn't know what it means."

"I'll take that as a yes."

Crickets chirped merrily in the background.

"*Ohmygod!*" She pretty much shrieked at my nonanswer. I was certain cats in her neighborhood wailed in protest at the noise. "He's the father of your baby, not Stephen."

But it wasn't a shriek of dismay.

Not at all.

"Are you doing a happy dance?" It certainly sounded that way.

"I might be."

"Why?"

"Because I thought it was odd that you would decide to become pregnant with your husband's sperm when he was dead. Plus, you had only recently come off the pill before he died. You hadn't been trying long enough to worry about fertility clinics."

Busted.

"How do you know when I stopped using the pill?"

"I'm your sister. Of course, I know these things."

Did her comment come as a surprise?

Nope. Even when we were kids, it was scary how many times she knew my secrets without me saying anything.

I used to think she was a witch.

Or a fairy.

"You can't tell anyone," I was one step away from pleading my case.

"Do Mom and Dad know?"

"I told them last night."

"What about Stephen's parents? Mom told me how excited they've been ever since finding out you're pregnant with their grandchild—who isn't really their grandchild."

I quickly caught Brittany up on the conversation with Mom.

"Oh, crap," she said once I was finished.

"You've got that right....I have to go now, Brit. Class starts in a few minutes. Just promise me you won't say anything to Grayson's grandmother about why I want to talk to him. He needs to hear it from me and no one else."

"All right. Let me know if you need anything, sis. And let me know if Lucinda gets a hold of you once she returns to Lake Tahoe."

And if she didn't? Then I'd have to consider the option of having Ava's husband track Grayson down. But I didn't want to go that route yet.

We ended the call as the first bell rang. Several minutes later, the initial wave of kids strolled noisily into the classroom.

Livi approached my desk, holding a manila envelope. "Daddy asked me to give these to you."

"Thanks." I took them from her and pulled out the three tickets for that night's game. It was the Rock's first playoff game against the Vancouver Canucks. Chloe and her boyfriend, Landon, were joining me for it.

A scribbled note was stuck on the top ticket:

Hope to see you tonight after the game.

To the average person, the note looked innocuous. But to me, innuendo clung to each letter like whipped cream, and I smiled in anticipation.

My lady bits weren't quite so subtle.

I mentally cursed them for flashing the image of a hot and sweaty and equally satisfied Logan in my head.

30

KIERA

"This is our row." Landon strode down the row of plastic arena seats, an excited Chloe in tow. We found our chairs and sat, my best friend sandwiched between us.

When Logan said he could get us tickets for the game, I hadn't expected such great seats. We were only five rows from the ice, between the players' bench and one of the goals.

The teams were warming up on the ice. As luck would have it, the Rock players were skating at our end, so I could easily make out their faces.

Cue the sighing lady bits.

A group of kids who could have been in second and third grade flocked around the plexiglass, hoping their idols would notice them. Three of them held up poster boards, but I couldn't see what was written on them.

Logan skated past them and waved. That got the kids excited. They cheered, elevating their banners higher.

And those lady bits?

They swooned.

"Daddy!"

Logan waved at someone to my left, in the direction where the cheering had come from. Livi was skipping toward me, followed by Stacy and a good-looking man who I assumed was Livi's stepfather.

My gaze flicked briefly to the ice again. Logan was back to shooting pucks at the goal.

"Hi, Mrs. A." Livi didn't sound all that surprised to see me.

While the lack of surprise might've been true for Livi, the same couldn't be said for either Stacy or me if Stacy's expression was any indication.

"Hi, Kiera," Stacy said. "Wow. What a coincidence that we're sitting together? What are the odds of that happening?"

Her initial shock at seeing me had passed, and the friendly smile I was familiar with took its place. The three of them sat next to us.

Like me, Stacy was wearing a Rock jersey, but her baby bump was hidden under the fabric. My bump looked like I was either pregnant or had smuggled in a small bag of popcorn.

I smiled at her. "Probably not that much of a coincidence if Logan gave you your tickets."

Her eyes widened to the size of pucks. "Logan gave you tickets?"

"That's right. Livi gave them to me this morning."

The players skated off the ice. Logan waved at his daughter before his gaze landed on me. He smiled and disappeared onto the bench.

For some reason, I turned my head toward Stacy.

This time her emotion was clearly stamped on her face. She was jealous.

Oh, God. She might have been happily married to her

new husband, but something told me she hadn't stopped loving her old one.

Was she one of those women who ended a relationship and expected the guy she dumped to remain loyal to her? He wasn't allowed to date other women?

Not that Logan and I were dating.

We were having a fling.

Well, not even a fling.

A fling would imply the quickening of your pulse, clammy palms, electricity humming happily under the skin whenever you touched each other.

Don't get me wrong. That was exactly how it was for me—thanks to my out-of-control hormones.

But that wasn't how it was for Logan.

I was nothing more than the woman he was friends with, the woman he had sex with because he wasn't looking for a relationship but didn't want to become a monk.

Probably just as well.

There weren't too many monks in the NHL.

All right, there were no monks, but you get my point.

Stacy had no reason to be jealous of me.

Besides, I couldn't see our fun-between-the-sheets relationship going on for much longer. I was pregnant. At some point soon, I wouldn't be so desirable as a fuck buddy.

Some guys had a fetish for pregnant women. Logan wasn't one of those men.

The pregame ceremonies commenced, drawing my attention to the ice and the two people I came with.

Landon's hand was resting on Chloe's thigh, and part of me released an Oh-that's-so-sweet sigh. The other part ached, longing for that level of loving intimacy I had once shared with a man.

THE WORST PART ABOUT BEING PREGNANT?

I mean other than the swollen ankles, the insatiable sex drive—which was only an issue if you didn't have someone to help relieve it—and waddling around like a duck.

I was usually ready to crash by eight p.m.

The best thing about the playoffs?

The adrenaline rush that pretty much lasted the entire game. The only break I got from it was during the intermissions. And even then, I was too excited to be tired.

All right, I'll admit it. The second intermission interview on the Jumbotron with Logan might have helped me there, too. I'd sat there rapt with each word and watched those lucky beads of sweat kiss his cheeks, his jaw, his chest. (Yes, I know I couldn't see that part about his chest, but the fantasy was there all the same.)

But even though I was amped up on adrenaline, I was hoping the game wouldn't go into overtime—which looked to be the case as the final minutes of the third period ticked away.

And the teams were tied.

Even Livi looked like she wouldn't last much longer. She was fighting to keep her eyes open.

The announcer proclaimed the last minute of the game. We were all sitting on the edge of our seats, willing the puck to not fly into the goal.

Okay, maybe that wasn't what the Canuck fans were thinking. The players were battling around the Rock's goal. One well-aimed tip or shot and the game would be over. Vancouver would win the first game of the second series.

A Canuck player hit the puck, and it sailed toward the goal. It was as if the world stood still while we waited with bated breath.

One of the Rock defensemen—I couldn't tell who it was

from my angle—blocked the shot. Another Rock player intercepted the puck and sprinted down the ice.

He wasn't the only one. Logan and Eli were with him as the Canuck players chased after them. The player passed the puck to Logan.

Logan went to make the shot on goal, but at the last second, changed his intent and passed the puck to Eli. The Canuck goalie couldn't get into position fast enough, and the puck snuck in behind him.

Game over.

The fans leaped to their feet, cheering, whistling, applauding, high-fiving. Hugs were exchanged as if we had done all the work instead of the players.

"Are you sure you don't want us to wait with you?" Chloe asked a short time later, Landon's arm around her waist.

"I'll be fine. You guys go home."

They knew I was meeting up with Logan. They escorted me as far as they could go without needing security clearance. Chloe hugged me good-bye, and I joined the large group waiting for the players to leave the dressing room.

From what Logan had told me, they were family members, wives, girlfriends...and me.

The odd one out.

"What are you doing here?" Stacy asked, approaching me. Her tone was ripe with curiosity and something else I couldn't get a firm grasp on.

I hadn't noticed the trio when I'd arrived, but it made sense that they were here.

Livi was in her stepfather's arms, head resting on his shoulder. She peered at me through tired eyes and smiled. "Hi."

What's the best way to get out of an awkward situation when facing questions you'd rather not answer?

That's right—create a diversion.

Sounds simple, right?

Normally, it would have been.

Normally, I wouldn't have been ready to curl up in a corner and fall asleep. That energy high I'd experienced a short time ago?

It had long since left the building.

The only thing that came to mind was yelling out, "Look, the Easter Bunny." But considering Easter was two weeks ago, that probably wouldn't have worked.

Realizing I'd been silent a little too long, I blurted the truth—which I probably should have done to begin with. "Logan asked me to meet him here after the game."

Stacy opened her mouth, possibly to say something, but the loud cheers from the dressing room entrance prevented her from getting that far.

We all looked over to see what was going on and spotted members of the team strolling out, huge grins on their faces.

Like everyone else, we applauded. Livi covered her ears with her hands.

Logan exited the dressing room, his gaze scanning the crowd, his hair damp from the shower. My heart rate picked up at the sight of him, playing a fast tempo against my ribs.

And my palms? Definitely sweaty.

Damn. Why did the man have that effect on me?

He walked toward us, purposefully.

I expected him to go straight to his daughter and Stacy, soak in their adoration. Hug Livi.

But expectations don't always meet reality, and in this case, I wasn't complaining. His arms went around me, and his lips met mine in an all-consuming kiss.

Despite the loud noise echoing in the area, I got lost in the kiss...and didn't want to be found anytime soon.

I rested my hands on his chest. His heartbeat thumped steadily under my palms—which was more than I could say for me. My heart was still beating fast, but it had sped up the moment our lips touched.

Logan's hand drifted from my waist and gently caressed my baby bump. My heart took a moment to swoon. Love Bug didn't belong to him, but that didn't stop him from treating the baby as though the child were his own.

But I wasn't deluding myself. The action was nothing more than his caring nature because he thought Love Bug belonged to his best friend.

The exuberant chatting of people around us slowly brought me back to where we were standing. I was also vaguely aware of Livi asking why Mrs. A was kissing her daddy.

Oops.

Smiling softly, I pulled away. "Congratulations on the big win. You were incredible out there."

He returned my smile. "Thanks."

There wasn't a chance to say anything else after that. Livi flung her arms around her father's waist. "You were great, Daddy."

Logan bent down and hugged his daughter and gave her a big kiss on the cheek. She giggled.

Then yawned.

"Okay, sleepyhead," Stacy said. "Time to get you home to bed." She gave Logan a hug and a quick kiss on his cheek. "I'll see you soon," she told me with a small, uncertain smile.

I had no idea what to make of it.

Tony congratulated Logan on the win and scooped up

Livi. "Bye, Daddy." She waved to her father, and the trio walked away.

Logan threaded his fingers with mine. I could feel the adrenaline pour from him in waves. Unlike me, he was wired. If he had been three years old, he would've been bouncing off the walls.

The crowd didn't appear to be in too big a rush to leave, and the players milling around the area, absorbing the congratulations, looked ready to go out and celebrate.

Numerous people came over to reminisce about some of Logan's big moments. I had no idea who they were. Several players I recognized...like Eli Lawson.

He definitely looked ready to celebrate.

I'd met him at the Jingle Balls ball, but his face didn't hold a note of recollection at seeing me. That was hardly surprising. I'd been wearing a mask. He hadn't.

"We're heading to Rusty's," Eli said to Logan. "You're coming, right?"

Logan shook his head. "Not tonight. I've got to get Kiera home."

"Oh, you don't have to do that. Go out with your teammates. You deserve to go celebrate." I didn't drive here, but I could always catch a cab.

Eventually.

"I'll celebrate next time." He spoke it with such confidence, not doubting for a second they would win more games in the series.

I had to agree with him there.

"Are you sure?"

"Positive."

I wasn't sure if Eli noticed the gleam in his eyes, but I certainly didn't miss the innuendo it held. He wasn't interested in going out with them because he was looking forward to the promised sex that would happen once we got to his place.

The two players glanced between us, then shrugged.

"By the way, Eli," Logan said, "this is Kiera Ashdown. She's the one who's organizing the silent auction you're participating in."

Eli perked up at hearing that and flashed me a boyish grin. "I'm looking forward to it."

After I thanked him for helping out with the auction, he bailed to join the rest of the players who were going out to celebrate the win.

It took Logan and me several minutes after that to escape the building and the crowd. The cool April air was damp from the earlier rain. Large puddles dotted the ground and gleamed in the streetlights.

Logan held my overnight bag in one hand, the fingers of his other hand threaded with mine, as we wove between the puddles. "So, you enjoyed the game?"

"Very much. But I'm glad you didn't go into overtime."

He laughed. "That makes two of us."

It was after midnight by the time we arrived at his condo building. Once we were inside the elevator, he pulled me against him. I rested my head on his shoulder. It felt nice—and familiar.

Logan's typical post-game routine involved food, TV, then sex.

Sometimes he couldn't be bothered with the food, and we went straight to the sex.

This time he pulled me into the kitchen and removed several containers from the fridge. "You good with chicken stir-fry?"

"That sounds delicious."

And in no time, we were sitting on the couch, enjoying the food and watching TV.

It felt comfortable. Like we'd been doing this for years.

That nagging voice whispering in the recesses of my mind?

It nudged me to tell Logan the truth about Love Bug. And maybe it was right. Except now wasn't the time, not when I was tired and likely to say the wrong thing.

All right, I'll confess, I was a coward. But I had been lying to him for the past few weeks. This wasn't something to blurt after he won a game.

When was the right time to tell him?

Good question. But I bet if I googled it, even the Google gods wouldn't know the answer.

Tomorrow.

I'll tell him tomorrow.

Naturally, he'd have questions.

Questions I couldn't answer until I talked to Grayson.

And that would have to wait until after his grandmother's romp at the nudist retreat.

But at least I could tell him tomorrow, and the rest I would deal with once I spoke with Love Bug's father.

My vision blurred, and I had to fight to keep my eyes open. I set my empty plate on the coffee table and settled my head against Logan's shoulder.

Just for a second, I promised myself. *I'll close my eyes for only a second.*

I was vaguely aware of several characters talking on TV, but don't quiz me on what they were saying.

The shoulder I was resting on shifted, and the voices stopped talking. Silence wrapped around me like a fluffy blanket.

Or a cloud.

That was it. I was falling asleep on a cloud, sinking, sinking, sinking into dreamland.

The cloud shifted again. "Kiera?" Oh, the cloud also had a voice.

I didn't realize clouds could talk.

"Okay, let's get you into bed."

Since we were discussing things I didn't know, I also didn't know that clouds had deep, sexy voices.

Voices similar to Logan's.

No, not Logan's. There was something else familiar about it. Like I'd heard it before in a fairy tale.

Maybe he had been a prince.

Or a frog.

No, definitely not a frog.

Logan repeated something, and this time I managed to pry open my eyes. I blinked him into focus.

He was smiling at me with the kind of smile that made my insides feel like Jell-O.

Delicious.

Sweet.

Wobbly.

"C'mon, Sleeping Beauty. Time for bed." He helped me to my feet and led me into his room.

I sank onto the bed, barely fighting the urge to flop backward and fall asleep, and reached out to unbutton his jeans.

My hands felt like stone weights attached to the ends of my arms. When had they turned to stone?

Interesting.

Logan pulled away and walked to his closet. He returned a moment later with a T-shirt. "Here, you might want to wear this...or not."

My eyebrows tugged together in a frown. "You want to have sex with me while I'm wearing your T-shirt?"

He laughed my favorite sound. "As much as I want to have sex with you, Kiera, you're tired and pregnant and need sleep more than you need me inside you." He kissed my forehead, and my lady bits released a dreamy sigh.

Normally, I would have disagreed with him there. But he did have a point.

"A T-shirt," he said, scratching the back of his neck. "Definitely a T-shirt."

He helped me change into it, removing my clothes and my bra. The only thing of mine that remained on my body was my panties.

With his assistance, I climbed under the covers. He left the room for a minute before joining me, his chest a whisper of a touch against me. His arm went around my waist, keeping me close.

My last thought as I drifted asleep?

I was in heaven.

31

LOGAN

Kiera was asleep, curled up on her side when I awoke the next morning. It took a second for the previous evening to come into focus.

The last moment goal that saved the game from going into overtime.

Skipping on celebrating with the team so I could be with Kiera even though she was too tired to fuck.

Instead, I held her while she fell asleep, listening to her soft breathing. She hadn't even stirred when I caressed her bare stomach; she'd been that worn out.

It had taken me another hour to finally drift off, only to wake up with a morning wood that wasn't too interested in being dealt with in the shower. Not when I had Kiera's soft, warm body next to me.

The rhythm of her breathing shifted, and she muttered something I couldn't make out. She looked upset for a second, but then the frown faded, and her eyes slowly opened.

She blinked, her eyes still slightly dazed. "Hi. Have you

been awake long?" Her voice was husky with sleep, but it also held an edge of amused satisfaction.

"A few minutes." I reached for her, and she wiggled her way over to me.

As if sensing my predicament, she cupped her hand against my hard length. "You're not wearing underwear."

"So I've noticed."

A shy smile slipped onto her face, dimples and all, and I swear my cock hardened some more. "I take it someone was disappointed we didn't have sex last night," she said.

My mouth tugged into a one-sided grin. "Which someone are you talking about?"

"Maybe we need to do something about that."

"Maybe you're right." I slipped my fingers between her legs and stroked the seam of her sex, hidden under her panties. She opened her legs more, giving me further access.

"Oh, God," she moaned. "Is it possible to stockpile horniness overnight? Because if it is, I think I've accumulated enough to outdo ten teenage boys."

I laughed. "I'm not sure how to take that. But I would certainly be happy to release some of it...before it gets to a dangerous level."

"Like a pipe that's about to burst if not relieved of the built-up steam?"

"Exactly."

I slipped a finger under the lace of her panties. "*Christ*, you're wet." And hot. *Shit*. I wasn't sure how much longer I could last, and her state of arousal wasn't helping things either.

Kiera sat up, yanked my T-shirt off over her head, and shimmied out of her panties. She shifted to straddle my legs.

I pushed myself to sit and pulled her head down to

mine. "Fuck, I want you so badly," I husked in her ear. My fingers found her clit and circled it, making each turn tighter and tighter, the pressure increasing with each spiral.

Her panted breath brushed hot against my ear. "I want that, too, just as badly." A slight desperation clung to her words.

Yes, she was usually turned-on and hungry, but this was different.

"Are you okay?" I asked.

She looked slightly startled by my question. "Why wouldn't I be?"

I shrugged; it was just a feeling I had, but I couldn't explain it.

"I promise you I'm fine, Logan. But I won't be in a second if we don't do this soon. I'm dying here."

"Isn't that usually the guy's line because he wants to get laid?"

"Blue balls here, Logan. I'm definitely suffering from the female version." She circled her hips, grinding her sex against my fingers.

"No one could ever accuse me of letting a woman suffer from something like that." With a grin, I knotted my fingers in her hair and brought her head down to mine. I kissed her hard.

Or maybe she was the one who kissed me hard.

We both needed this, and we needed it now.

I swiftly rolled on a condom.

Kiera wrapped her hand around my rock-hard length and lowed herself, her wet heat swallowing me whole.

"Fuck," I growled out.

Kiera giggled. "Yep, that pretty much sums it up."

She circled her hips again, bringing us to the edge of insanity in record time.

With only a few upward jerks of my body, her inner muscles grasped me tight in a wave of euphoria.

"*Oh, God,*" she moaned, her forehead resting on my shoulder, our breaths coming in rapid and shallow.

The win last night?

That had been great. This was something else.

I kissed the side of her head.

Smiling, smug satisfaction on her face, she sat upright. My gaze caught sight of her growing belly, and a wave of guilt rushed through me.

Stephen's dead, I reminded myself. *You're not betraying him. She's pregnant with his baby, but she's his widow, not his wife.*

A murmur of a voice echoed in my head, pointing out that she wasn't my wife either. What she and I had was a friends-with-benefits arrangement.

For now.

But that would change once her baby was born. At some point, she would want to find someone who would be there for her and her son.

Someone who would be his stepfather.

The voice came in stronger when it spoke this time. *Why can't that be you?*

I shoved it away with a well-earned shoulder check.

It knew the answer to that. It was just being a dick.

"I'm going to have a shower..." I grinned down at her, ignoring the debate that had been battling in my head. "Unless you want to join me."

"We don't exactly have time. Don't you have a morning skate you have to leave for soon?"

⎯⎯⎯⎯⎯

KIERA WALKED INTO THE KITCHEN A SHORT TIME LATER TO the smell of brewing coffee and breakfast. Her blonde hair shone in the morning light, giving her an angelic appearance.

That was assuming, of course, that angels wore maternity jeans and long-sleeved T-shirts proclaiming, "Bump's First Hockey Season."

I waved my spatula at her top. "Nice T-shirt."

"Stephen's mother gave it to me." Kiera chewed on her lower lip for a second, uncertainty warring on her face. "She's assuming Love Bug will be a hockey player like Stephen."

"And you don't want that?"

"I don't want him to feel as though he has to live up to the footsteps of a man he's never met. Plus, if Stephen had been alive, he would've been there for his son, coaching him, encouraging him. I can cheer for Love Bug and be a supportive hockey parent. But beyond that, I have no idea what I'm doing. He doesn't have the hockey role model in his life that he would've had if Stephen was alive. Like Stephen had with his father."

The entire time she was talking, her gaze went everywhere but to me.

"You know, as long as I'm playing for the Rock and I'm still in San Francisco," I said, "I'd be happy to do my best to fill in for Stephen when it comes to being a hockey role model. I won't be able to do as good a job as he would've because I'm on the road a lot, but I can certainly help whenever possible."

Kiera smiled softly, the look of uncertainty not entirely erased. "That would be great, assuming Love Bug wants to play hockey. Thank you."

AFTER THE TEAM WAS FINISHED FOR THE MORNING, LIVI AND I picked Kiera up at her house. I had already stopped at the deli and loaded up on sandwiches and other supplies for our picnic.

"I don't know about you two, but I'm starving." I lowered the icebox onto the sand after scouting out a spot that wasn't too busy. It was also located near a stretch of sand ideal for castle building.

Livi waved her bucket and shovel in the air. "Me too!"

"How about we eat first, then create a sandcastle that will be the envy of all Disney princesses?"

Both agreed with that suggestion.

Kiera and I laid out the blanket. Livi went to search for shells near the water's edge. She returned a minute later to show us the one she'd found.

"That's really pretty," Kiera said, smiling at my daughter. "Do you collect shells?"

Livi rapidly nodded and plonked herself on the blanket.

I passed out the sandwiches, and we ate while Livi filled us in on her day so far. Kiera and I listened and laughed and asked lots of questions.

Curious glances steered in our direction, but I couldn't be sure if it was because the individuals recognized me or due to Livi's flamboyant storytelling. Her arms flailed about as she talked, and there was a fair amount of acting out what she was saying.

The salty breeze blew a strand of hair across Kiera's face, and my fingers itched to brush the strand aside. But that wasn't the thing you did when you were with your daughter's teacher.

Right, taking your daughter's teacher to the beach wasn't exactly on the list of normal parent-teacher activities either. However, this didn't count. Kiera and I had been friends long before Livi was born. So that negated all other rules on the matter.

Or so I kept telling myself.

A seagull strutted across the sand toward us, confidence making him cocky. He eyed the sandwich in Livi's hand and moved closer like a spy trying to act nonchalant.

A dog's bark from farther down the beach, heard over the faint crashing of waves, momentarily distracted Livi from the bird.

As if sensing this, the bird lunged for the sandwich and tugged it from her hand.

Livi shrieked in surprise.

The bird decided this would be a great time to make its getaway. It flew a couple of feet from us, dragging the sandwich with it.

Kiera burst out laughing and scrambled to her feet, as did Livi. They chased after the bird, reclaiming bits of the sandwich left behind.

And damned if something didn't stir deep inside me at seeing them like this.

After we finished eating our lunch, Kiera and I packed everything away, so the seagulls couldn't steal our food while we were distracted with the sandcastle.

Then the three of us commenced work on the castle. Hanging out with Kiera felt as natural as it had in college. We didn't talk much, our focus entirely on our project.

"It should be this big." Livi held her hand at chest height.

"How about we build it this high?" I demonstrated what I had in mind, which was knee height. At most. "Otherwise, we'll be here all week, and I'm not sure my head coach"— or GM—"would appreciate that."

Livi pondered that for a moment before agreeing to the compromise.

We'd been working for at least twenty minutes when I heard a man ask, "Aren't you Logan Mathews?"

I glanced toward the voice.

A man and his son stood to the side of our castle. I hadn't even noticed them until he'd spoken. Both were wearing Rock T-shirts. The boy couldn't have been much older than Livi.

"That was a nice play you made yesterday, late in the third." The man proceeded to recount it as if I hadn't been there.

But that wasn't all.

He told me what I'd done wrong and what I should do next time.

Yep, he was one of those fans.

The kind you could only roll your eyes at.

They had never stepped on the ice as an NHL player or coach or scout, but they seemed to think they could do a better job than anyone else.

His son nodded rapidly at everything his father said. However, I couldn't miss that his gaze kept shifting longingly to the ocean.

Livi stared at the man the way she looked at broccoli when Stacy cooked it for dinner.

Livi had never been a fan of broccoli.

"Daddy, help me make the moat." She passed Kiera and me our buckets.

"Oh, that's a great idea. We need a big moat to keep out the scary beasts." Kiera smiled sweetly at the man, and I inwardly chuckled. Even if her comment was lost on him, I knew exactly what she was referring to.

"One moat coming up," I said cheerfully. "Nice to meet you." I gave the man and his son a nod and walked off with Livi and Kiera to the water, even though we weren't ready yet to fill the moat.

"Is it often like that?" Kiera asked as we scooped up seawater. She and I were calf-deep in the ocean. Livi was closer to shore, playing leapfrog over small waves.

Kiera nodded in the direction the man and his son were walking. "Do strangers often come up to you to tell you how to play the game?"

"Most fans aren't like that, but yeah, there are a few who think they'd do a better job than the coaches of whatever team I'm playing for."

"I've had parents like that." She smiled sympathetically at me.

"Hey, Daddy." That was the only warning I got. Cold water hit me in the chest, catching me off guard.

Still holding her bucket, Livi giggled, the sound warming my heart.

Kiera burst out laughing as water streamed down my bare legs from my drenched shorts.

Not to be outdone, I scooped seawater into my bucket and tossed the contents at Livi.

Except, she darted out of the way at the last second. The water hit Kiera full-on, leaving her tank top clinging enticingly to her body.

She let out a shriek that was more laughter than anything, then filled her bucket and hurled its contents at me.

I lunged at Kiera. She tried to get away from me, but a rogue wave had different plans, almost knocking her off her feet.

I grabbed hold of her and pulled her to me.

My body instantly reacted, thrilled to have her in my arms again.

For a second, it was as though we were suspended in time. I peered into her beautiful blue eyes, filled with all kinds of emotions, some I didn't have a label for.

Without thinking things through, I cupped her face with my hand and brushed my thumb along her soft cheek. I didn't hear her gasp as much as felt the movement with my hand.

Kiss her, you idiot.

So I did.

I didn't care who saw me or if the kiss ended up on social media. The only thing I cared about was the feel of her lips against my mouth.

Mine.

The kiss lasted for a few seconds before the ocean pranked us, tossing another rogue wave at us.

Or maybe this was its way of telling us to get a room.

We pulled away from each other, the awareness of where we were standing coming back into focus.

Livi was working on the castle when Kiera and I joined her a moment later.

Had she witnessed me kissing her teacher?

I couldn't say. She beamed at us, then resumed constructing her tower.

Kiera kneeled beside her.

Mine.

I pushed that thought away.

"How about I take a photo of you two with the castle?" I removed my phone from my shorts pocket and instructed them where to sit, so I could fit the huge castle and the two of them in the frame. Luckily, my phone had been in my back pocket during the earlier water battle and had avoided getting wet.

"If you'd like, I could take a photo with all three of you in it," a soft female voice said behind me.

I turned to find an elderly couple watching us and smiling. I could tell they weren't hockey fans. Neither held a hint of recognition on their faces.

"You should be in the picture, too," she said.

"That would be great, thanks." I handed her the phone and kneeled between Kiera and Livi.

"Squeeze in together a little more." The elderly man made a gesture with his hands to indicate what he wanted us to do.

Livi and Kiera shuffled closer to me. He looked at the phone in his wife's hand and waved for them to move in closer still. It wasn't until Kiera was pressed against my side that we got the thumbs-up from him.

His wife lowered the phone. "Perfect."

I retrieved it from them and glanced at the screen, with the great photo of the three of us together still on it. The unexplainable sensation in my gut from earlier returned, but I couldn't put my finger on what caused it. "Thank you."

"It's such a lovely castle," the woman said. "You all did a great job."

The pair said good-bye to us and shuffled off down the beach, hand-in-hand. I could practically see the longing on Kiera's face as her gaze followed them for a moment. It wasn't hard to guess what she was thinking. That was supposed to have been her and Stephen—growing old together.

Tearing my gaze from Kiera, I sent Stacy the photo.

> Me: Impressed? Our daughter might have
> a future as a sandcastle architect.

> Stacy: You might be right. Looks great.
> This was followed by a heart emoji.

Livi, Kiera, and I spent a few more hours at the beach,

playing frisbee and exploring the nearby tidal pools. Then we went to Livi's favorite restaurant to eat burgers, fries, and ice cream.

By the time I drove Livi home, she was barely able to stay awake. I dropped her off at Stacy's before returning to my condo building.

The moment Kiera and I had left Stacy's house, excitement thrummed through my body, knowing that Kiera would be in my bed again that night.

That same excitement played through my veins as we stepped into the elevator.

So could you blame me that the first thing I did the moment the elevator doors closed was to kiss her like I had in the water?

I needed her like a plant needed sunlight and rain.

We were still kissing when the metal door slid open.

And we resumed making out once inside my condo... only this time it was accompanied with wandering hands and my lips tasting her salt-kissed skin.

All the way to my bedroom.

32

LOGAN

When I woke up the next morning, memories of the day before at the beach played in my head like overtime in the playoffs.

At least during the regular season, overtime was sudden death or five minutes of play, whichever came first.

If the latter happened, you were looking at a shootout.

During the playoffs?

That meant sudden death for as long as and for as many periods as it took.

So yeah, the memories of yesterday at the beach had just hit the fifth overtime period as Kiera slept next to me.

Mine. That was what the voice in my head had claimed.

But she wasn't mine.

And I had to stop pretending that she was.

She needed a man who would be there for her and her son.

What she needed was a man who didn't play in the NHL. A man who wasn't away most of the time.

Kiera's eyelids slowly fluttered open. She blinked and smiled sleepily at me. "Hi."

"Hey. Did you sleep well?"

"I did, thanks."

My morning wood was screaming for relief, preferably in the form of being buried deep inside Kiera.

My brain had other thoughts.

And unfortunately, my brain won the mental coin toss. "Have you thought about what you'll do once the baby is born? I mean...what you're going to do about dating. Stephen would want you to move on, for the sake of his baby. He would want you to find a good father for your son. I'm sure Stacy knows some great guys who—" *Who Stephen would approve of.*

"Don't even think of completing that sentence, Logan." Kiera began moving off the bed, her drowsy expression instantly vanished. "I'm not looking to be set up on a blind date or anything like that. For starters, no, just no. Plus, I'm pregnant. No man wants to date a woman who's pregnant with another man's child."

"There might be. You never know."

I couldn't think of any offhand, but there must've been some men who weren't fussy about something like that. Travis's friend, Wes, had dated Hannah when she was pregnant with another man's child, and now they were happily married.

Sure they were already friends before she became pregnant, but the idea was still the same.

Kiera hurriedly pulled on her panties and jeans. I climbed out of bed and grabbed my underwear.

"I've got a lot going on, and the last thing I need is to worry about finding the right father for my child." Her tone held a strange note to it, but I couldn't figure out what it meant.

"I didn't mean to upset you—"

"If you don't want to have sex anymore," she said,

pulling on her Rock jersey, without bothering to put on her bra first. "You just have to tell me. I know that..." Her gaze went everywhere but to me.

"You know what?"

Something about her expression made me think of a cornered small animal, vulnerability pouring off her in waves.

"It's nothing. But don't worry, I totally understand."

"Understand what?"

Why did I feel like I was missing a huge chunk of the conversation? Like when your friend talks on the phone, but you can't hear what the person on the other end is saying.

Kiera started walking to the door.

"Understand what?" I repeated, yanking on my briefs.

Still walking, she waved dismissively at me over her shoulder. "It's really nothing."

I quickly pulled on my jeans and raced after her. She was already opening the door to my condo.

"I was going to make us breakfast first," I said.

She grinned at me. "That's okay. One of my friends lives in the neighborhood. I texted her, and she's expecting me." Kiera kept on grinning, but it was as though the smile had been glued on. Even her dimples weren't interested in being on display.

"Give me a second, and I'll drive you."

She shook her head, the smile exactly as it was before, something still off about it. "It's not that far. And I could use the exercise. It's good for Love Bug."

"I'll walk you there."

"No, no. That's not necessary." For a heartbeat, she looked as though she was deliberating something. "Logan, there's something I need to tell you. I was going to tell you yesterday, but then—"

My phone rang from the kitchen table. "Give me a second. That's Stacy."

I hurried to the kitchen and grabbed my phone. "Hey, Stace. I'll be there in an hour."

"Can you pick up eggs on your way? And red pepper."

I laughed. "Is that the real reason you invited me for lunch, so I can pick up your groceries on the way over?" I vaguely heard the apartment door click shut.

As I strode to it, Stacy was listing several other items she needed from the store. I opened the door and raced down the hallway...in time to see the elevator shut.

"Logan, are you still there? Logan?" Stacy asked.

"Yes, I'm here." For a second, I thought of chasing after Kiera, but she would be gone by the time I made it to the main floor.

I returned to my condo. After Stacy repeated the grocery list so I could jot it down, I sent Kiera a text.

Me: Did you make it to your friend's okay?

"So, what's going on between you and Livi's teacher?" Stacy asked the moment I walked into the kitchen. Livi was sitting at the table, drawing a picture. Tony was busy chopping vegetables on the counter.

"Oh, boy," he muttered and flashed me a have-fun-with-that smile.

I set the grocery bags on the counter next to the sink. "Is there something specific you want to know?" I asked her.

"I'm just curious because you gave her and her friends tickets to Friday night's game, kissed her in front of your daughter after the game, and then she was with you and Livi at the beach yesterday."

"Was I not supposed to do any of those things?" Was there some rule I didn't know about?

"I just don't want you getting in over your head, Logan."

"What do you mean 'getting in over my head'? I'm a big boy, Stace. I think I know what I'm doing."

She flashed me a look I had no idea how to interpret.

The next one, though, I didn't need a translator to figure out.

She thought I was a clueless dumbass.

Why I was a clueless dumbass was beyond me—which was precisely why, in her opinion, I fell into that category.

"She's pregnant and single and no doubt looking for a father for her baby," Stacy said. "And I'm worried she might see you as the one to fit the shoes, especially since she's carrying your best friend's child. I mean, in her eyes, it's probably the perfect solution."

I inwardly cringed at how much her assessment of the situation mirrored what I had believed a short time ago, while Kiera was still in my bed. "She doesn't think that."

"How can you be so sure?"

Livi had stopped coloring and was watching us with rapt interest.

"Hey, baby girl, what are you drawing?" I walked to the table and peered over her shoulder.

Livi had drawn a picture of her holding two babies, one on each palm. Her arms were stretched to the side as if she were a balance scale.

One baby had on a light-blue outfit; the other was dressed in pale pink.

My gaze shot up to Stacy. "You're having twins?"

She laughed. "The last I heard, no."

"Why did you draw two babies?" I asked Livi, happy for the distraction from Stacy's interrogation.

"Mommy doesn't know if she's having a girl or a boy, so

I'm covering my bases and drawing both." She went back to coloring the picture.

"Okay, that makes sense." *I guess.*

I kissed the top of her head. She grinned briefly at me.

"Don't think you're getting out of the conversation that easily, young man," Stacy said, her hands fisted on her hips.

Tony burst out laughing.

"Did you really just 'young man' me?" The last person who did that was my eighty-two-year-old grandmother. "Are you going to send me to my room without any supper?"

That only made Tony laugh harder.

Livi peered at us, bemused.

"You don't have to worry that Kiera is expecting anything beyond friendship." As long as you didn't count the part where I was helping her with her pregnancy-enhanced sex drive.

And who knew how long that would last?

"How can you be so sure?" Stacy wore an expression I was only too familiar with. She wasn't dropping this until she was satisfied with the answer.

"Because she told me she's got a lot going on, and the last thing she needs to worry about is finding the right father for her son."

"When did she tell you this?"

"This morning in..." I pulled the brakes on my words. Livi didn't need to hear the next part.

Stacy folded her arms across her chest, waiting for me to continue.

"Hey, Livi," Tony said, resting the knife on the plastic cutting board. "Why don't we go in the backyard and check how the seeds are doing?"

"Okay." She pushed her chair away from the table, and

the two of them headed outside. Livi's merry chatter followed them out the kitchen door.

"Are you sleeping with Livi's teacher?" Stacy asked as soon as the door clicked shut. If her words could have crossed their arms in front of themselves and glared at me, they would have.

"I'm not sure how that's any of your business, Stace."

"She's our daughter's teacher."

"What difference does that make?"

"It just does. That's all."

"You forget Kiera was my friend long before she was Livi's teacher."

"So, you took that as an invitation to have sex with her?"

I snorted a laugh. "I think you're blowing things out of proportion. Yes, I'm having sex with her, but that has nothing to do with our daughter."

Although if it weren't for Kiera being Livi's teacher, Kiera and I wouldn't be having sex. Not unless I had decided to contact her now that I was living in San Francisco.

"So what else did she say after you two had sex this morning?"

"I didn't say we had sex this morning."

Stacy's mouth curled to one side. "You didn't need to. It's practically written on your face with colored markers. So what else did she tell you that makes you so sure she's not interested in you taking over the role of being her baby's daddy?"

"She told me if I didn't want to have sex anymore, I just have to tell her."

Stacy pondered this for a moment and grimaced. "She told you this after you had sex this morning?"

"We didn't have sex this morning."

"Okay, so you had it last night. Don't even try to deny it,

Logan. So do you no longer want to have sex with her?" She removed the carton of eggs from the bag on the counter.

Was this a trick question?

Answer it wrong, and purgatory would start to sound like a day at the spa?

"Do you really want to discuss my sex life?" Because hell if I wanted to hear about her sex life with Tony.

"Well, not in any particular detail. Thank you. But we're friends, and this is the kind of thing friends talk about."

I grabbed the two Spanish onions from the other bag and started juggling them. "Are we painting each other's toenails, too?"

The smirk was back on her face. "If you would like to. I'm sure I can find you something pretty that will go with your hockey gear. So, do you still want to have sex with her?"

"Yes, as long as she's still interested."

"She didn't say anything else? Possibly give you some reason why she believed you're no longer interested in having sex with her?"

"Nope. Nothing. She just acted a little strange when she brought it up."

"Were you two naked?"

"Seriously, Stacy?" I groaned, close to dropping the onions. "Most ex-wives don't want to talk about these things with their ex-husbands."

"Right, but we're not your typical exes. We're still close friends. So spill it. I want to understand better what went down this morning."

"Yes, we were naked when the conversation started. She was getting changed when she told me to let her know if I didn't want to have sex with her anymore."

"And did you tell her you're still interested?"

"Stace—"

"Just stick with the facts." From her tone, I almost expected her to slam a gavel on the kitchen counter. I barely held back from sliding the carton of eggs away from her just in case.

"I didn't have a chance. She started saying something else but changed her mind. I pushed to find out what she was going to say—"

"Which was what?"

"I have no idea. She told me it was nothing, not to worry, and that she totally understood."

"And then what happened?"

I put the onions on the counter. "You want to remind me why you never went to law school?"

Stacy chuckled. "I know. I totally missed my calling. So what happened next?"

"She wouldn't answer my questions, and when I went to drive her home, she told me one of her friends lives in the neighborhood, and she was going to visit her."

Stacy dropped her face in her hands. "Logan, Logan, Logan." She shook her head, face still covered, as she repeated my name. "Why do men have to be such idiots?"

"And yet you still marry us," I said dryly.

She removed her hands from her face. "I guess that makes me an idiot, too....Kiera's pregnant and probably a little insecure about her body because she has no husband telling her how sexy she looks."

I started to argue that she was wrong, but Stacy cut me off. "Maybe Kiera is telling herself that she'd rather not go through the pain of losing someone else she loves, and that it's easier being a single parent than risking her heart again. But her hormones are all over the place, and she may feel differently once the baby is born. But you won't. You're not interested in settling down with another woman until you've retired from hockey."

I grunted. "What are you saying? Just spit it out."

"You'll end up hurting her, Logan. You two want different things—even if Kiera doesn't realize it yet. And in the end, she'll be the one who gets hurt."

"So, what am I supposed to do?"

"You need to end whatever is going on between you two before it's too late. I care about you, Logan. You know I do. But I don't want to see Kiera get hurt either. She has more at stake in this than you do."

Have you ever been hit in the gut by a speeding truck?

I haven't either, but Stacy's words were that vehicle, their impact felt clear to my bones.

"Are you saying she and I can't be friends anymore?"

"If you can be strictly friends with no mixed signals, sure, why not? But I've seen how you look at her."

"I look at her like she's my friend."

I didn't think I'd ever seen Stacy as smug as she was at that moment. "Hate to burst your bubble, but I've never seen you look at any of your teammates that way. Are you certain you don't want something more with her than just sex or friendship?"

"Positive."

"Then it's time you end the friendship before it's too late."

That speeding truck?

It just got upgraded to a speeding train—even if she was right.

33

KIERA

I spread out the assortment of stationery on the coffee table, and dropped onto the couch, doing my best not to dwell on the conversation I'd had with Logan that morning.

The conversation where I'd almost told him that Stephen wasn't Love Bug's father.

But then Stacy had called, and I'd had second thoughts. I'd been hurt by what he had said and couldn't bring myself to tell him the truth.

After much deliberation about that and everything else, I'd come to the conclusion that while it was preferable to tell Judith and Joe about Love Bug's father to their faces, I couldn't wait that long.

But how did you tell someone on the other side of the country that they weren't really your baby's biological grandparents?

Phoning them didn't seem right.

Texting was definitely out.

So was sending them an email.

Messenger pigeon was always a possibility.

Except I didn't know any.

No, it was better that I wrote them a letter.

Yes, you heard me correctly.

Wrote.

Not typed.

Hence the stationery paper I'd bought earlier.

But I'd purchased the collection of paper from a store near where I worked, and their selection was impressive, which made deciding what to buy next-to-impossible.

So I bought way more paper than I could possibly need in a lifetime.

There was the plain linen design that was elegant and simple.

There was the light-blue paper with a baby theme.

Hmm. In retrospect, that probably wasn't the best choice for my news.

There was some pretty pink floral paper.

And there was one with a comical cartoon kitten on the bottom.

It was adorable, and I couldn't resist it when I saw it. But again, probably not the best choice. Or maybe it was the perfect choice. The cute kitten might soften the news.

I had also purchased a few other options, just in case.

I removed a sheet of linen paper from the pile and picked up my pen.

Then stared at the blank page.

Which pretty much summed up my thoughts on what to write.

As I continued staring at the paper, the sound of a clucking chicken played in my head.

It was the sound Stephen used to teasingly make whenever he attempted to convince me to try something new.

My gaze shifted to the ceiling. "Hey, you're not helping me here. I know I'm being a chicken by not calling your parents. But I think I'll do a much better job telling them in a letter. I mean, look what happened the first time I tried to tell my parents about my baby.

"Knowing my luck, if I try telling your parents on the phone or in person, I'll probably just blurt something idiotic...like I'm having twins."

I could almost imagine Stephen in heaven, laughing his head off at that.

"I don't suppose you could help me out here. At least give me a hint on how to start this."

I sighed when the request was met by silence.

"That's what I thought."

With another sigh, I began writing.

Dear Judith and Joe,
It is with great regret

Not exactly the best way to start. Too formal, and it sounded like I was about to tell them their application to be grandparents had been denied.

I scrunched up the page, tossed it onto the coffee table, and picked up another piece of paper.

Dear Judith and Joe,
It pains me to tell you that you aren't
going to be grandparents.

I cringed at how bad that sounded.

Which was no better than how the next letter started:

While it is true that Stephen and I had

been trying to get pregnant, we'd never actually visited a fertility clinic.

And while "I hope you are doing well" sounded like a great way to start my next sorrowful attempt at writing the letter, it seemed too upbeat for what I was about to tell them.

That piece of paper joined the rest of the crumpled pages that were forming quite the impressive pile on the coffee table.

Maybe I would do a better job telling them the news via a poem.

Or a sonnet.

Or an ode.

Or possibly even a riddle.

Except, Shakespeare made writing sonnets sound a lot easier than was the case in reality.

And I wasn't very good at solving riddles, never mind writing them.

An hour and a half later, the only thing I'd accomplished was creating the Great Wall of China from the pile of scrunched up rubbish on the table, depleting my supply of stationery paper, and the lack of a letter to send Judith and Joe.

Well, that was it. I just had to buy more paper.

34

KIERA

May

The timer on the microwave dinged. I pulled on the oven mitts and removed the mozzarella sticks from the oven, the cheese oozing from cracks in the golden crust.

In the background, a hockey commentator was discussing what the Rock needed to do to win the series.

If San Francisco won the game, they would win the Campbell Bowl and progress to the Stanley Cup finals.

If they lost? It meant the end of the series and the end of hockey season for the team.

Cassie toddled over to me, a blue and yellow daisy painted on her cheeks. Like Ava, Chloe, and me, she was wearing a Rock jersey.

Liam and Landon were away on a mission, so it was just the four of us watching the game.

The game wasn't even in San Francisco. The Calgary

Flames were hosting it. All the girlfriends and wives and family members were there, ready to (hopefully) celebrate the conference win with the team.

And since I fell into none of those categories, I got to watch Logan in action from the comforts of Ava's couch.

Which—when you considered the past month—pretty much summed up how often I'd seen him. If the Rock game was on TV, I got to see Logan.

And nothing beyond that.

Don't get me wrong. He had checked in from time to time to see how I was doing.

Well, more like inquired on how the final plans for the fundraiser were going. Giving him the opening to end our fuck-buddy arrangement had definitely been the smart thing to do.

I should have been relieved. I'd been getting too comfortable with him—letting my guard down when I'd known that what he and I had was nothing more than a fleeting moment.

A way to deal with my horny hormones.

That wasn't to say I didn't miss him.

It felt like a woodpecker had pecked a crater-sized hole in my heart because of how much I missed Logan.

Which meant we were doing the right thing, keeping our distance. In time, the pain and loneliness would fade away.

Or maybe I was just using it as an excuse to delay telling him the truth about Love Bug's parentage.

I needed to tell him soon.

Preferably before Love Bug was born.

He had the right to know.

"You look adorable," I told Cassie. "I think the rest of us should have painted pretty flowers on our cheeks, too.

What do you think?" The toddler grinned at me, giggled, and returned to the living room.

I placed the hot cheese sticks on a plate and carried it to the coffee table, where we already had an impressive array of food spread over the wooden surface.

"So I've got some big news," Ava said. She'd been beaming ever since Chloe and I arrived.

I ventured a hopeful guess. "You're pregnant?"

Still beaming, she nodded. "I'm eight weeks. So we're not telling everyone quite yet. But I've been dying to tell you two."

As I hugged her, my phone rang from the end table by the couch. I checked the screen.

The number wasn't familiar.

"Hello?" I said, answering the call.

"Hello, this is Lucinda Mathews. May I speak to Kiera, please?"

Shock passed through me, an electrical current kick-starting my heart. I had been counting down the days until Grayson's grandmother called me, but when they passed without a word from her, I had given up hope of finding him that way.

"Hi, Lucinda. This is Kiera. Thank you so much for getting back to me. I hope you had a nice trip."

"I did, thank you. There's nothing more exhilarating than staying at a nudist retreat for a month."

I'd have to take her word for that.

"Your sister said you would like my grandson's phone number because you need to talk to him. Can I ask why you need to contact him?"

I could have told her the truth about the baby. I could have told her I wanted him to know that he was going to be a father. I could have even just told her I wanted to see how he was doing...but none of those words are what flew from my mouth.

"Grayson gushed about a squid recipe he had made." *Seriously? Squid? I didn't even like squid.* "I tried googling it but couldn't find anything that came remotely close to what he'd described. So, I was hoping he could tell me where to find it."

Shaking my head, I covered my face with my hand, as if that would magically snatch back the words.

"That wasn't quite what I was expecting," she said with a laugh. "I'll let him know that you called, asking for the recipe."

"Okay. Thank you."

"You're welcome, dear. Now, you'll have to excuse me. I have an appointment with my masseuse." She ended the call.

I looked up to find Chloe and Ava gawking at me.

"You seriously didn't just tell her you need to talk to him because of a squid recipe, did you?" Chloe asked, clearly not sure if she should laugh or groan.

I cringed and nodded. "I hadn't planned to say that. But my mind went blank, and the recipe excuse kind of came out."

"What did she say?" Ava asked, appearing a little more sympathetic about my screw up.

"That she would tell him I called, asking about the recipe, and he would return my call."

"You guys didn't talk about a squid recipe or any recipe that night, did you?"

I figured my expression said it all. "What do I do now? He's going to think I'm crazy. And he definitely won't call me after his grandmother tells him why I want to talk to him. I can't believe I lied to his *grandmother!*"

Ava handed Cassie her bunny from the couch. "You

never know. He might call you. He might be curious why you wanted to talk to him but felt you had to lie to his grandmother about the reason."

"Do you think he'll be able to tell I'm pregnant because I lied?"

The corners of Chloe's mouth twitched. "Because you lied about squid? I don't think you have to worry about that. It just sounded like you were interested in him and wanted to talk to him again."

Ava nodded in agreement. "But maybe you should have told her the truth. If he only thinks you're interested in talking to him because you can't stop thinking about him, he might not return the call. It's been five months since the ball. That's a really long time for you to suddenly get the urge to contact him."

I slouched back on the couch. "Well, in my defense, I did attempt to contact him a month ago. I can't help that his grandmother was hanging out at a nudist retreat for the past month." Surely, I got credit for that time.

Right, that still left me four months before I contacted him.

Although, if you think about it, I was almost three months pregnant by the time I learned I was knocked up. So if you did the math, it was really only one month before I contacted Grayson.

And one month was a lot better than five.

"What will you do if he doesn't call you back?" Ava asked.

"What can I do? If he doesn't return the call, it means he's not interested in talking to me. For all we know, he has a serious girlfriend now. He might not want to mess that up by talking to the woman he"—I glanced at Cassie, who was attempting to climb onto the couch with her bunny—"firetrucked the night of the ball. He might have even forgotten all about it." Who knew how many women he'd had sex with since that night.

"But what if he doesn't return your call? Have you changed your mind about telling him about the baby?"

I picked up my orange juice from the coffee table. "What if he's got a girlfriend now? Maybe he proposed to her on Valentine's Day, and the news that he's going to be a daddy will destroy them?"

Momentarily at a loss for words, Chloe and Ava simply stared at me. "Wow, you really do have all your bases covered when it comes to excuses," Ava said, the first to recover from my romance-filled logic.

"I've had time to think."

"You mean you've had a month to chicken out when it comes to telling him the truth."

Yeah, that, too.

"Oh, look, the game's started." I nodded at the TV.

Chloe and Ava weren't so easily distracted. They continued to regard me with worried expressions.

"Look, there's nothing we can do about it for now. I just have to wait to see if Grayson contacts me to find out the real reason I called him."

"And if he doesn't?" Ava asked.

"I'll cross that bridge when I come to it."

"Have you told Stephen's parents yet?"

"I'm working on it." I grabbed a cheese stick from the plate and bit into it, preventing further discussion.

The truth? I was no closer to telling his parents about Love Bug's father than I had been a month ago.

But I did have some new pretty paper that I hoped would soften the blow.

Right. Nothing was going to soften the blow.

No matter what I did or say, I would end up hurting them.

At that thought, I crammed another cheese stick in my mouth.

The five Rock players quickly gained control of the puck, and within the first minute, Logan scored.

The four of us jumped to our feet and cheered, although I had a feeling Cassie wasn't sure what she was cheering about.

An odd sensation fluttered low in my belly. I'd felt it before, but it was stronger now. My heart thudded in reply.

Grinning, I pressed my hand on the spot where I'd felt the sensation. "I think Love Bug just kicked me. Looks like I might be having a hockey fan after all."

While the players on the ice celebrated their first goal, Chloe, Ava, and I celebrated something even more monumental.

But as the game resumed, a heaviness settled in my chest because Love Bug's father wasn't here to appreciate the moment.

Logan stepped onto the ice, and the heaviness expanded. Even he wasn't here to share it with me—and wouldn't have been even if the team hadn't been on a road trip.

The days of us spending time together were long over.

35

LOGAN

The team's plane landed at the San Francisco airport, and I turned on my phone the moment we were allowed to do so. A bunch of texts popped up on the screen, but instead of reading them, I re-read the ones that shouldn't have meant anything to me but still did.

Because as much as Stacy had been right about putting distance between Kiera and me, I still missed being her friend.

> Kiera: I felt Love Bug kick! He was so
> excited when you scored the first goal.
>
> Kiera: BTW, congratulations on the big
> win!!!!

She had sent them after yesterday's game, but that didn't stop me from checking them again.

The news that she'd felt the baby kick, once more caused a bucket load of emotions to twist inside me: happiness for her, regret and relief I hadn't been there with her when it happened, sadness that Stephen wouldn't get to experience the moment either.

My fingers paused over the keypad as I tried to think of the best way to respond to her texts. I hadn't been able to come up with the right thing to say last night either.

Next to me, Eli was talking on the phone to someone. I heard the word "wedding," but didn't hear anything beyond that. My phone rang.

Temporarily giving up on replying to Kiera's text, I answered the phone. "Hi, Grandma. Let me guess, you were brushing up on your ESP while at the resort, and that's how you knew I just landed?" No way in hell I was saying out loud that she'd been at a nudist retreat.

I was still having nightmares thinking about it.

That wasn't to say I subscribed to the belief that elderly people weren't allowed to go to nudist resorts or beaches. But this was my grandmother we were talking about. That was an image I didn't want in my head.

Ever.

She laughed. "I'm your grandmother. I know everything."

I really hoped that wasn't true.

"So, you know my team won yesterday?"

"Of course. Did you think Edward and I and all our party guests wouldn't be watching the game? Congratulations on winning the Campbell Bowl."

"Thank you. But that's not why you're calling, is it?" I knew my grandmother better than that. There was something in her voice that had nothing to do with the Rock making it to the Stanley Cup finals.

"Do you remember that pretty girl from the Jingle Balls ball you spent most of the evening with? The one you were talking to about the squid recipe you liked?"

Huh? I don't remember talking about recipes with any woman, period. Not at the ball, not anywhere.

"You mean Kiera Ashdown? The sister of the woman you're friends with? Brittany?" I couldn't remember Brittany's last name.

"That's the one."

"What about her?"

The plane pulled up to the airport terminal. We would be disembarking at any moment.

"Her sister called while I was away. Kiera is excited to try out that recipe herself, but she couldn't find it online." Undeniable laughter sat squarely in my grandmother's tone. I wasn't sure why she was so amused, other than she had seen right through Kiera's farce of a lie. "She asked if you could call her so she could get it from you. She made it sound so good, I wouldn't mind trying it out myself."

"Kiera wants me to call her?"

Why the hell would she want Grayson to call her?

The last she'd heard, he was living in Chicago. I knew she wasn't interested in some fictitious recipe she was claiming I'd told her about.

"Did you tell her I now live in San Francisco?"

"No, that's not my place to tell her. That's up to you. Do you want me to text you the number?"

"Sure," I told her even though I already had it.

Fuck. What was I supposed to do? Kiera hadn't figured out I was Grayson when she and I first bumped into each other at Livi's school.

My secret had been safe.

When things first progressed in the direction of us having sex together after I was traded to the Rock, I had thought there was a slim chance she might recognize I was Grayson.

But that hadn't been the case.

I'd even been close to telling her about that night several times. But either something prevented me from saying anything (like Livi vomiting on my shoes), or the timing wasn't right, or the words failed me because I didn't want to risk our friendship.

Except in the end, I'd walked away from our friendship anyway...all because I was worried she wanted more from our relationship than I could give.

As far as I could tell, there was no reason for her to suddenly want to talk to Grayson. She'd never mentioned him to me. She hadn't even mentioned attending the ball.

The only possible reason for wanting to contact him was because she'd discovered the hotel had erroneously sent her pendant to him, and she wanted it back.

Everyone in the plane stood, the signal we were ready to exit the aircraft. "I have to go, Grandma. Thanks for letting me know she called."

"You're welcome. I'm looking forward to trying out that recipe." The laughter had returned to her tone.

I ended the call, silently cursing Kiera because now I had to find a squid recipe to send to my grandmother.

"Mom, I swear you'll like my girlfriend," Eli said next to me, earning a double take from me. Seeing my expression, he shrugged. "Yes, she's looking forward to the wedding and meeting you. I've gotta go now. We're getting off the plane. Yes, I love you, too." He ended the call and groaned.

"So when do we get to meet your mysterious girlfriend?" Travis asked. "And why is this the first time I've heard about her?"

Good question. The last I'd heard, he was looking for a fake date for his cousin's wedding.

"I don't have one." Eli shoved his phone into his trouser pocket. "And I'm running out of time to find one for my cousin's wedding."

Travis laughed. "So what, you're claiming you have a girlfriend because you need a date for your cousin's wedding?"

"Yep. That about sums it up. If I want to avoid my matchmaking mom and aunts from making my life miserable, I need a fake girlfriend for the wedding. Maybe I'll have to contact a call service and hire someone."

"Yes, but if that gets out, it could cause you all kinds of nightmares," I pointed out. This was the kind of thing that the media and social media would've loved to get their hands on.

"I guess my only solution is to take whoever wins the date with me to the wedding."

Travis and I exchanged glances, then burst out laughing.

"You're not seriously thinking of doing that?" The corners of my mouth twitched in unsuppressed laughter.

"What can I say? At this point, I'm desperate."

"You must be. It's not like you're guaranteed that a hot woman your age will win the date. You could end up on a date with someone your grandmother's age."

Eli laughed, looking none too worried at that possibility. "Then I'd say I would be the talk of the wedding."

"I bet the bride and the groom wouldn't be too thrilled with that," Travis said.

"I thought finding a fake girlfriend would be easy. But so far, the women I've talked to haven't been interested in being my fake girlfriend. They've only wanted to date me for real."

"So date them for real," I suggested. "I'm assuming you're not allergic to dating since you're giving away a date with you in the auction."

"Not allergic, but also not interested in dating. Hence my need for a fake girlfriend."

"Well, you might change your mind when you see who wins the date with you."

Eli lifted his shoulder. "Hopefully not, because I've run out of options."

"Here's a piece of advice from someone who's been there." Travis smacked him on the arm. "Sometimes, those fake girlfriends can turn into something real." With a smug look, he walked toward the exit.

"That's not going to happen," Eli called after him. Travis just laughed.

I checked my phone and typed a quick text to Kiera.

Me: That's great about Love Bug. Clearly, you've got yourself a future hockey fan.

As for Grayson—as far as Kiera was concerned, he was just a masked stranger she'd met at the ball.

Someone from her past.

Someone who had moved on.

36

KIERA

June

The first day that went by without me hearing from Grayson?

I brushed it off that he was busy with work.

Same with the days two, three, four, and five.

By day six, I was convinced that Grayson was on vacation.

With his hot girlfriend.

A girlfriend who wasn't pregnant with the product of a one-night stand.

By day twelve, I came to a firm conclusion: Grayson wasn't going to contact me.

He would never know he was going to be a father—unless Ava's husband was able to track him down.

Which leapfrogged me back to my original dilemma: did I want to do that, or was it better to let people believe Love Bug was the result of Stephen's Popsicle sperm?

Pros:

1. My son would have two loving sets of grandparents.

2. My son would grow up believing he was the product of love. Both Stephen and I had wanted to have a baby.

3. My son would never know he was the result of my dirty little secret. (By dirty, I meant a naughty roll between the sheets, complete with masquerade masks.)

Cons:

1. My son's existence was based on a lie. And what would happen if one day he discovered I'd been lying to him all this time?

What were the negatives of telling people the truth about Love Bug's father?

I didn't even want to contemplate them. There was no point.

My decision had been made.

For the sake of my child.

The only exception was, I still needed to tell Judith and Joe the truth.

They had the right to know.

I just had to figure out the best way to do that because the letter I had been working on just wasn't happening.

Too bad there wasn't a Dummies guide for such an occasion.

I stepped out of the elevator and walked to Logan's apartment.

Sorry to disappoint. I was here on official business. Fundraising business.

I knocked on the door. A moment later, it opened, revealing Livi and two younger girls: five-year-old Everly (Hannah and Wes's daughter) and two-year-old Kat.

All three were beaming at me. All three were dressed as princesses, complete with tiaras and fancy gowns.

"Hi, Mrs. A," Livi opened the door wider.

"Thank you, your royal highnesses." I curtsied. But it was hard to look graceful curtsying when you were five months pregnant. They giggled and ran off to tell the adults I had arrived.

"You look amazing," Emma said a moment later, hugging me. Hannah did the same, with equal exuberance. The three of us had become good friends in the past two months.

I removed my shoes, and we walked to the living room.

Hannah and Wes's two-year-old son, Cameron, was on the floor, building a rickety tower with large blocks.

Travis was also here, talking to Logan. Both men looked a little worn around the edges. Not too surprising, considering they had already played four games of the final series of the playoffs. San Francisco and Tampa were tied at two games each.

"Hey, you made it," Travis said. He gave me a quick hug. In the short time I'd known both Emma and her husband, I had fallen in love with them and their fairy-tale story of how they ended up together.

Unlike Cinderella (and those two), there was no fairy-tale ending for me.

Of course, Cinderella also hadn't managed to get knocked up by Prince Charming.

So, there was always that.

"Sorry, I'm late." My gaze drifted to Logan, and my heart squeed a little. I hadn't seen him in person in over a month but my heart hadn't forgotten how it felt about him.

I really wished it would.

My lady bits weren't much better. They longed to savor the feel of his fingers against them, to feel him buried inside me.

It had been a long time since we'd been together that

way. Now, I just had my memories and my friendly purple dildo to help me out.

My breath released as if I'd sprung a slow leak. In the past month, I had lost the man who I'd thought was becoming my close friend, and I had lost hope that somewhere in Chicago was a man who'd be happy to discover he would soon have a son.

Okay, I'll admit it. I'd foolishly been fantasizing that not only would Grayson be thrilled to hear he was going to be a father, he would be eager for us to become a family.

True, I hadn't known him very well—all right, not well at all—but the Grayson I'd met that night had been a nice guy. Friendly. Funny. Sweet.

Pretty much like Stephen.

And Logan.

He'd seemed like the kind of man I wanted as the father of my child.

"You're just in time." Logan gave me a simple nod from behind the three girls.

My squee-ing heart?

It sagged in my chest. I had no idea what I'd done wrong, but it felt like he was moving on from our friendship and had forgotten to send me the memo.

Oh, well. We just had to survive the fundraiser together, after which he would be free of me.

Tomorrow was the last day of school. Livi would no longer be one of my students, and Logan would never have to see me again.

And *splat.* My heart was now a sorrowful mess on Logan's hardwood floor.

Oops.

"The pizza arrived a few minutes ago," Hannah said. "We're giving the kids theirs, then we can get to work."

A short time later, the kids had finished eating their

dinner and were watching the live-action *Cinderella* on TV in the living room. We were discussing the final details for the fundraiser, making sure nothing was missed. Even Wes had been recruited by Hannah to help us out.

"The stage will be set up for the MC to present the different prizes up for auction," he reminded us. "The Rock players and the local celebrities participating in the auction will go on stage one at a time. Because let's face it, they're the reason the tickets sold out."

He was right about that. Excitement toward the event was far greater than I had initially anticipated—all thanks to everyone in the room and the individuals who had generously donated the prizes.

"Mrs. A, can you put this on me, please?" Livi held out her hand.

I carefully picked up the gold chain and gasped as it untangled, revealing the scripted letters that spelled "Believe."

It looked exactly like the one Logan had given me many years ago. The one I'd lost the night I was with Grayson.

Did Stacy have one, too? Or had he only given them to Livi and me?

"This is beautiful, Livi. I used to have one like it. A friend of mine who I cared a lot about gave it to me as a graduation gift." I fought against the urge to look in Logan's direction, to see if he remembered what I was talking about. "Unfortunately, the clasp came undone one night while I was wearing it, and I lost the pendant." I smiled at her and flipped it over.

My gaze dropped to the "B," to a groove in the gold.

The air in my lungs froze, and my eyes went wide.

It can't be...

My pendant had the exact same marking—a marking that hadn't been there when Logan gave it to me.

It had happened a few years ago, completely by accident.

What were the chances that two identical pendants had the same groove that wasn't part of the original design?

"When did you get this?" I asked Livi, doing my best to keep the panic from my voice. My pulse thumped in my ears, *It's not what you think, it's not what you think, it's not what you think…*

"It's Daddy's," Livi said proudly.

The entire table was quiet, watching us. All the adults appeared curious at my question.

All the adults except for Logan.

A flock of emotions flickered on his face, the most prominent one being *Fuck*.

There was only one way he could have ended up with this.

Oh, God. How could I have been such an idiot? Yes, Grayson's hair had been shorter than Logan's, but the style was similar. The waves were similar.

And they both had light-blue eyes. I just hadn't been able to tell they were the same eyes because his mask had affected my perception of them.

As for the bruises that were standard issue when it came to being a hockey player? It had been too dark in the cabin for me to have properly registered them. In the flicker of firelight, they were easily brushed off as shadows.

It also explained why my body had reacted the same way to both men when they touched me.

When they kissed me.

When they fucked me.

My body recognized what my brain had failed to acknowledge.

But if I hadn't realized Grayson Mathews was actually

Logan Mathews, did that mean he hadn't known it was me that night either?

"No," would have been the easy answer, but I suspected it wasn't as simple as that.

For starters, his voice had been different that night...like he had been altering it slightly so that I didn't recognize it.

All this time, he had to have known, but he never said anything.

His expression confirmed I was right. He *had* figured it out that night.

"Did you know?" My voice splintered into a thousand pieces. "The night of the ball, did you know it was me?"

I could feel everyone's rapt eyes watching me, but my gaze was locked on Logan, the blood rapidly draining from my face.

Love Bug picked that moment to poke an arm or a foot into my side, reminding me that my pendant's loss wasn't the only consequence of that night.

I lightly pressed my palm against the spot, letting him know that everything would be all right. He and I would be all right.

Logan and me? Not so much.

Logan's lack of a reply was hardly comforting.

You wanted Love Bug's father to know that the two of you are having a baby, a voice in my head reminded me. *Now's your chance to tell him.*

Right. But that was when I believed the man had been a stranger, someone I could tell the news to over the phone, and then move on with my life—regardless of whether he wanted to be part of Love Bug's life.

That was prior to finding out that Logan had lied to me.

And you didn't lie to him? You didn't tell him you were pregnant with your dead husband's sperm?

"That night...when did you figure out it was me?" The

words felt like they were being pushed past a block of gritty sandpaper. "Was it before or after we...?" I let the rest of the sentence hang, knowing full well that the other adults in the room could easily fill in the blanks.

It was Livi who I wanted to remain oblivious to the truth.

Uncertainty blanketed the air, suffocating me.

Logan had made it clear he didn't want to be in another relationship until he retired from hockey. He wasn't interested in having any more kids until then, either. His hockey career and his daughter were his first priorities.

The best thing about being pregnant?

That's right, the predictability of my unpredictable hormones. One minute I could be horny, the next a crying mess.

Any other time, I could have walked out of that condo, keeping my emotions in check until I was safe from prying eyes.

Unfortunately, pregnancy obliterated that option.

My gaze blurred as hot tears pushed their way to freedom. I sniffed and shoved away from the table. "I'm sorry... I...just remembered I need to be somewhere else."

Like on another planet.

Jupiter looked like a nice place to inhabit—once you got past the part where it was composed of gas and was super cold.

Livi watched me with wide eyes.

Even Max in *Max Thunder and the Ocean of Secrets* had it easier than this. He just had to deal with a pissed-off kraken.

Easy-peasy.

Logan stood up from his chair. "Look, Kiera, I'm sorry I didn't tell you then that it was me. I didn't know how you would feel if you found out."

This just kept getting better and better.

Math had never been my best subject, but even I knew that the compounding of lies was never a good thing.

It just made for one big explosion.

Useful for when tackling the kraken.

Not so helpful here.

Everyone else shifted in their seats, clearly uncomfortable at the turn of events. They weren't the only ones. I was beginning to have a new respect for how zoo animals felt with people staring at them, waiting to be thrilled with some daring stunt.

"We should leave you guys to talk," Emma said.

"No, that's okay," I rushed to say. It wasn't like Logan and I could talk anyway, not in front of Livi. I brushed my hand against my cheek, smearing the mess of tears, and sat. "We need to finish finalizing everything." Preferably before I had another hormonal meltdown.

Emma and Hannah shared a glance. I could tell they had a billion and one questions. Questions I didn't want to face.

Cradling my belly, I resumed our previous discussion, doing my best to pretend the last five minutes hadn't happened.

Doing my best to pretend the father of my child wasn't sitting at the table.

What I needed was to conference with my two besties.

What I needed was to pee. *You're a genius*, I thought, sending the mental message to Love Bug, hoping he could read minds while he was in my belly.

I stood up. "Excuse me for a moment. My son's been busy kicking my bladder."

I grabbed my phone and bailed.

Once inside the safety of the bathroom, I pulled my panties down and sat on the toilet.

I didn't have much time until everyone would start to wonder what happened to me, so I needed to multitask while peeing.

I called Ava first. "I'm going to do a conference call with you and Chloe," I told her as soon as she answered. My voice was low so no one outside the bathroom could hear me. "Hold on a second."

Thirty seconds later, I had them both on the line. "Logan is Grayson," I whispered, my gaze taking in the gray color scheme of the room—the wooden rack holding small jars of shaving supplies, combs, cotton swabs.

"Why are you whispering?" Ava asked.

"Because I'm in his bathroom, and Emma and Travis Hamilton and Hannah and Wes Chiasson, and Livi and a bunch little kids are in his living room. I discovered that Logan is the man I had sex with in Lake Tahoe. He's Love Bug's father. What do I do?" The words came out in one hot, sticky mess. I'd be surprised if Ava and Chloe understood anything I said.

"How do you know he's Grayson?"

"I lost my 'Believe' pendant when Logan and I were... you know..."

"Fornicating?" Chloe asked.

Despite everything, I laughed. "Yes. That. Anyway, his daughter has the pendant. She said it was her father's. I recognized it because it's damaged in exactly the same spot as mine. And when I asked him if he knew it was me the night of the masquerade ball, he didn't deny it."

If I wasn't sitting on the toilet, I'd be pacing in the small bathroom as I spoke. Maybe then I'd had a better chance of piecing everything together.

"Did you tell him he's Love Bug's father?"

"No."

"What did you tell him?" Ava asked.

"That I had to go to the bathroom. I don't know what to tell him. What do I tell him?"

My breath was coming in fast and shallow. I really needed to pace. That would help me think things through.

"Breathe, Kiera. It will be all right."

"No, it won't!" My whisper came out louder than planned. I closed my eyes and fought to regain control of my emotions. "It was okay when I thought my baby's father lived in Chicago, and I had no idea if he would want to be part of Love Bug's life. But I know Logan, and I know he doesn't have room in his life for our baby. And he's made it perfectly clear he's not looking for a girlfriend."

Which would be fine if my body didn't respond every time he was near me and if my heart wasn't falling for him.

I did have to admit, though, if you examined way, way, *way* deep inside me, a tiny part of me—that had come to grips with Logan's betrayal—was happy he was my baby's father.

Because despite my recent discovery, there was no one else I'd rather be the father of my child, other than Stephen.

He was certainly more preferable to some stranger who lived over two thousand miles away.

"You need to tell him, Kiera," Ava said. "If he's still going to be part of your life, you need to tell him the truth."

"But that's the thing, I don't know if he'll be part of my life. Things were great between us, and then suddenly, he pulled away. The only reason I'm even here is because of the fundraiser. Once that's over, there won't be any more reasons for us to be together."

"Hello, I think you have a good reason growing in the stomach."

A light rap on the door intruded on the conversation. "Kiera, are you okay in there?" Logan asked.

"I'm fine," I squeaked. "I'm almost finished. I drank more water before coming here than I realized."

"Are you talking to someone on the phone?" His voice sounded bemused.

"Yes, it's Chloe. She's having, um...boyfriend issues."

"Hey, I'm not having boyfriend issues," an undignified voice in my ear grumbled.

"I know that," I whispered, "but he doesn't."

"Right."

Logan's footfalls moved away from the bathroom door.

"Kiera," Ava said. "You have to tell him the truth. He has the right to know he's going to be a father."

"At least he lives in the same city as you and Love Bug," Chloe pointed out. "He can be part of his son's life. More so than Grayson from Chicago could've been."

"Right." That was more for my benefit than anyone else's, but she did have a point. Except... "I will tell him. But I can't tell him yet."

"Why not today? The sooner you tell him, the better. As it is, he thinks his best friend is really the father of his son."

Yes, that did make things slightly trickier.

Okay, a steamy-pile-of-manure trickier.

"I don't know when I'll be able to tell him. His daughter's here, so even after everyone else leaves, I still can't say anything. She needs to hear from her father—not from me—that she's going to have a half brother. And I can't tell him for at least the week. Not with his team in the finals. He doesn't need that kind of distraction."

"The longer you wait to tell him, the harder it will be for everyone concerned," Ava pointed out. "Now that you know the truth, you can't keep pretending Stephen is your baby's father."

"Sure I can. I've been doing a great job." Other than my sister figuring out the truth before anyone else did. "I should probably get back to the meeting." I promised them that I'd call them later and ended the call.

After finishing up in the bathroom, I walked to the now empty living room. "What happened to everyone?"

Did aliens abduct them while I was peeing?

"They took the kids to the playground," a deep voice that caused my heart to catapult into my throat said.

37

LOGAN

You've heard the phrase "a deer caught in the headlights."

At the sound of my voice, Kiera spun around and forget that deer. She resembled a herd of deer caught on the train track with the express hurtling toward them.

She made a move to the apartment door.

I gently grabbed her arm, not wanting to freak her out any more than she already was. "You and I need to talk."

She grimaced. "That's probably not a good idea."

I released her arm. "Look, I'm sorry about letting you believe I was someone else. I should have been honest with you."

"You think? What I don't get is why your grandmother kept calling you Grayson." Her brow wrinkled adorably, although I suspected that wasn't the look she was aiming for. "Do you have a relative called Grayson that she keeps confusing you for?"

I chuckled. "More like she was never a fan of the name Logan. She doesn't think it sounds as dignified as Grayson, which is my middle name."

"So, she only calls you Grayson?"

"That's right."

"And your voice? Why didn't I recognize it at the ball?"

"I altered it slightly. Not a lot—I'm not an actor—but enough that you didn't recognize me." Clearly, I'd been a better actor than I realized.

"But why not tell me the truth as soon as you figured out that Kiera was me? And when exactly did you figure out the Kiera at the ball was the same one who had been married to your best friend?"

"I saw you checking into the hotel with your brother-in-law."

"And you were never going to tell me you were Grayson, the man I had sex with?" Her voice cut like a kiddy knife aimed at my nuts. Ready to maim if my answer pissed her off.

"I didn't think I would see you again, and you seemed happier not knowing anything about me. In case you've forgotten, it was your idea that we keep the masks on during sex."

"Yes, but that's because I thought you were a stranger."

"If you had known it was me, would you still have wanted to have sex with me?"

She slipped her lower lip between her teeth, her tale-tale sign that she was contemplating the question.

The clock on the mantel ticked away the seconds, and yet she remained silent.

I guess I had my answer right there.

"So I was only good enough to have sex with once you were pregnant? Is that what you're telling me?"

She grimaced again and tugged at the fabric of her maternity top. "No, that's not what I'm saying. I've already told you, Logan, that I liked you when we were in college, even before I met Stephen. Honestly? I have no idea what I would have thought if you had been honest with me.

"My goal that night was to kiss a stranger under the mistletoe. It was my first step in moving on with my life after losing Stephen. I hadn't planned to have sex. Things just progressed that way." Her gaze dropped to her belly.

That was what had me confused. She said that night the kiss was her first step in moving on, and yet that contradicted her decision to keep his memory alive by getting pregnant with his sperm.

Did anyone else think that hardly sounded like moving on?

"And now that you know it was me, you regret it?" Christ, I should have tossed that damn pendant instead of hiding it in my drawer.

Though to be honest, the last thing I had expected was for Livi to go searching in the drawer and ask Kiera for help putting the pendant on.

But none of that changed anything. She was still pregnant with Stephen's baby, and Stacy was right. I needed to remove myself from Kiera's life before things became more complicated.

Kiera's gaze flashed to mine. She let out a slow breath, her hand caressing her belly. "There are a lot of things I could regret about that night. Having sex with you wasn't one of them."

"That's good to hear. I'd hate for you to regret that. I certainly don't."

She grimaced once more, and something about her reaction gave me pause.

"Am I missing something?" I asked.

She glanced away, but not fast enough to keep me from catching her expression. A sensation in my gut, like a fish flopping around the bottom of a boat, warned me whatever she wasn't telling me was huge.

Blue-whale huge.

"Kiera, whatever it is, you can tell me."

"I'm pregnant."

I laughed because that was the last thing I had expected her to say. "Yes, I think we've already established that. You're having Stephen's baby, thanks to his frozen sperm."

She didn't say anything. She just kept staring at me as though she was waiting for me to slot in the final piece of the puzzle.

The clock continued to tick in the background, mocking me for not getting why she was stating the obvious.

And then it hit me like a transport truck falling off the Golden Gate Bridge and landing on an unfortunate rowboat.

Except it was my stomach falling off the bridge.

I frowned. "You're telling me you're not carrying Stephen's baby? It's my baby? How do you even know it's mine?"

Kiera's face paled, much like it did when she first realized I was Grayson. "Because I haven't been with anyone else since Stephen died."

"I believed you were pregnant with his Popsicle baby. Now you're saying it's mine?" *Shit.* I really needed to sit for this conversation; it was making me feel dizzy.

But despite thinking that, I remained standing.

"I hadn't meant to tell people that Stephen was the father. I panicked when I told my parents I was pregnant and kind of told them that I'd gotten pregnant with Stephen's frozen sperm. And then I only told people that Stephen was the father because it was less awkward that way," Kiera said. "Or at least I thought it would be less awkward. Turned out I was wrong."

I snorted a laugh. She got that right. Her mother-in-law threw a gender reveal party, thinking the baby was her grandchild. "Let me get this straight. I'm the father of the baby, and you weren't going to tell me?"

How did I feel about the news I was going to have a son?

Let's circle back to that after I've recovered from the shock.

"In case you've forgotten, you didn't exactly give me your phone number that night. I asked your grandmother for it so I could tell you about the baby. She said she would give you my number. I can't help that you didn't return my call."

"You told my grandmother that you wanted some fictitious squid recipe. Not exactly a reason for me to return the call."

Her eyes narrowed. "And why didn't you call me once you'd heard I was trying to contact Grayson, the man I'd slept with that night? You knew I wasn't looking for a recipe." She folded her arms, wearing a smug, don't-call-me-the-kettle expression. "Was it because you didn't want me to find out the truth about that night? You knew if you called me, your dirty secret would be exposed."

Her smug expression upgraded to a "So take that."

Okay, she had me there. Although if I had known she was pregnant with my child, I would've been honest from the start. I would have admitted that I was Grayson.

I wouldn't have let her go through this alone for as long as she had.

"I thought you would be angry with me if you found out I had kept the truth from you," I said. "I came close to telling you a few times once I was traded to the Rock, but then figured you'd hate me, and I didn't want that either."

"There's a word for that, Logan. It's called a lie. Omission of the truth is still a lie."

"Says the woman who's been telling everyone that my baby genetically belongs to her dead husband. If you had told me the truth when I found out you were pregnant, I would've told you then that I was the father."

She grunted. "I only told you that because I wanted people to think he was the result of the love that Stephen and I shared, and not the product of a one-night stand with a masked stranger. Can you blame me for that?"

I shrugged even though I could see her point. It would've been better for the child if he believed his father had wanted him, even though Stephen was dead, than to believe his father was a stranger who breezed in and out of Kiera's life.

She released a defeated breath. "I never meant to lie to anyone. I did it to protect my baby. I never expected everything to become such a big sticky disaster."

"Me—"

The apartment door opened before I could finish that sentence, and a tornado of little kids came rushing in, giggling.

None were aware of the storm-cloud of tension in the room.

"I should go now." Kiera walked to the closed door, where the other four adults were standing. Emma and Hannah exchanged a silent message with her as she slipped on her shoes, asking if everything was okay.

I couldn't hear what Kiera said to them, but from their reactions, I didn't think she'd just announced I was Love Bug's father.

"Wait, Kiera," I called out, but it was too late. She had already shut the apartment door behind her.

I sprinted down the hallway, yanked the door open, and

raced to the elevator—in time to catch a final glimpse of Kiera as the metal door sealed shut.

Fuck.

I ran back to my condo, shoved my feet into my runners, and hastily tied the laces.

"Is everything all right?" Travis asked.

"No, I royally fucked up everything. And now I have to race the elevator to the ground floor. Can you stay with Livi till I return?"

I didn't wait for a reply. I bolted to the nearest exit and practically hurled myself down the steps.

When I first moved into the condo, I was thrilled I lived on the twentieth floor. The view was spectacular, and I appreciated the stairs for the extra training they afforded me.

Now?

I was mentally cursing in several different languages—thanks to the teammates I'd played with over the years—the number of floors.

By the time I made it to the ground floor, it was a damn miracle I'd arrived in one piece. Which was a good thing. Coach Fusco (not to mention the team's general manager) would've skinned me alive with a hockey stick if I had injured myself.

Breathing hard, I pulled open the door and rushed to where the elevators were located. The door for the one Kiera had been on was closing. I was too late. She was gone.

I turned around the main lobby, but there was no sign of her.

Dammit.

I raced out the front entrance to the visitor parking lot.

Taking a chance that she had parked in her usual stall, I kept running.

At the end of the row, a familiar red car was reversing from the spot.

I wasn't too late.

It was as if the clouds had separated, allowing beams of heavenly light to reach the earth, accompanied by the strains of a harp.

All right, none of that happened, but it might as well have. The universe had granted me a second chance, and fuck if I would screw it up this time.

Kiera finished pulling out of her spot and drove toward me.

At first, I wasn't sure if she saw me or had no intention of stopping.

I was fairly confident, though, that she wouldn't try to run me over.

She was upset that I had lied to her, but murder wasn't her thing.

Or at least it wasn't her thing when she was five months pregnant. Hiding my body would be a little tricky when she had my son in her belly.

But after he was born? That might've been another matter.

That gave me four months to prove to her that it might not be a bad idea to keep me around and spare my life.

Panting hard, I banged on the driver-side window and indicated for her to climb out of the vehicle.

With what I guessed was a huffed sigh, she turned off the engine and opened the door.

I still have no idea how I felt about her being pregnant with my baby. In another lifetime, I would've been thrilled.

But in this lifetime? It made things more complicated.

Way more complicated.

You would think that while I was racing down the stairs, I could've spent the time figuring out what to say to her. But even if I had come up with something, it would have vanished due to the lack of oxygen plaguing my brain.

I bent over, palms on knees, and fought to regain my breath. I felt like I'd just played back-to-back shifts, and the coach still wanted me on the ice.

"Did you just run down the stairs?" Kiera asked.

"Yes," I panted. "Wanted...to talk...to you."

I also wanted to kiss her, but I needed to wait a second before that became feasible.

Kiera didn't say anything. She stood there, patiently waiting for me to catch my breath. "You're really having my baby?" I finally asked once I had enough oxygen going to my brain. This time my voice wasn't heavy with shock; awe filled it.

She nodded, uncertainty creasing her forehead.

I wanted to erase it, but I didn't know how. Her news had knocked me on my ass, and I was still coming to terms with the fact that I was going to be a father again.

Livi wasn't about to have one half sibling. She was going to have two.

The thought of that made me laugh.

Kiera's frown deepened. "And you find this funny because...?"

"Livi's thrilled to be having a little brother or sister. Now she'll have a brother for sure. Maybe two brothers, depending on what Stacy's having."

The frown faded, and a smile twitched at the corners of her mouth. "People might think she has twin siblings because they'll be the same age."

And then, because I couldn't wait any longer...I kissed Kiera.

It began as a tender kiss but quickly morphed into something more heated. The slide of my tongue against hers, hers returning the gesture.

I wrapped my arms around her waist, pulling her to me. Christ, how had I survived this long without her—without kissing her, without holding her?

A horn blasted, yanking us from the moment. I looked over at the annoying vehicle and realized the problem. Kiera's car was blocking it.

I held my hand out to Kiera. "Give me your keys, and I'll park your car. We need to talk. Not to mention, tell Livi the news."

"I can park my own car." She waved apologetically at the driver and climbed into her vehicle. A minute later, she and I were returning to my condo.

"Is everything all right?" Hannah asked Kiera once we stepped inside. Her worried glance darted between us.

Was everything all right?

I had no idea.

I'd fucked things up when it came to Stacy and Livi, and I was positive I would fuck things up, once again, when it came to Kiera and our baby.

That was just a given.

38

KIERA

After I let Hannah and Emma know that everything was hunky-dory, they filed out of the condo, with husbands and kiddies in tow.

Did I tell them that Logan was Love Bug's father?

No, I was still trying to wrap my brain around that myself.

It would take several days for the news to fully sink in.

I just couldn't believe I hadn't pieced things together sooner. To start with, both men had been living in Chicago at the time of the Jingle Balls ball.

Yes, I understood that Chicago's population was well over two million. The odds that the two men had been the same person were only slightly greater than the odds of Grayson being related to Winnie-the-Pooh.

But I had skipped over so many similarities between the men. Similarities that would've had me questioning things sooner.

Sure, in retrospect, it was easy to say I should have known Logan was Grayson, but that would've been a lie. There had been no reason to believe that Grayson had moved to San Francisco. There had been no reason for me to wonder if every tall, dark-haired, athletic man I came across could be him.

There had been no reason for me to add one plus one and come up with Logan as the answer.

But where did that leave us?

He was finally becoming the father he wanted to be for Livi. Hockey and his daughter were his top priorities. Love Bug and I were a complication he hadn't counted on.

And even if he did manage to balance his two kids, where did that leave me?

The same place as Stacy—one day married to a man who wasn't Love Bug's father?

That was if I ever fell in love again.

I was lucky that I'd fallen in love twice already.

What were the odds of me falling in love a third time?

That's right. I was in love with Logan—had been ever since the day at the beach with him and Livi, only I hadn't realized it until now.

But I didn't tell him that. It was the last thing he'd want to hear.

Like I said, I was a complication that he didn't need, a complication my heart hadn't counted on.

"Livi," Logan said, "Kiera and I have something we need to tell you."

He smiled at her, but that didn't stop the sinking sensation in my stomach that rivaled the Titanic. What if she was upset with the news I was pregnant with her half brother? Until just a day ago, I had been her teacher. She wouldn't be my student next year, but she would still be at the same school. Would that be awkward for her?

"What, Daddy?" She gazed expectantly at us, curiosity curling her mouth up at both ends.

"How about we sit down?" He pointed to the gray armchair.

She sat. I stood where I was, unsure if it would be better if I left so he could break the news to her in private.

Before I could say anything, he pulled me to the matching couch and gestured for me to sit. He sat next to me, hand resting protectively on my upper back.

If Livi thought this was odd, her expression didn't show it. She just looked at us in turn, smiling eagerly. Like she was expecting her father to tell her he was buying her a dog...or a pony.

Logan cleared his throat. "Livi, as you know, Kiera is pregnant, like your mom."

"They're both going to have babies," she proudly announced.

"That's right. Well, they aren't the only ones who are going to have babies. Your stepfather and I are also going to have babies."

Livi's expression twisted to one of confusion, and I had to choke down a laugh.

"You and Tony have babies in your tummies, too?" She leaned to the side to get a better look at Logan's stomach, hidden behind me.

"No, no. That's not what I meant. How much has your Mommy told you about how babies are made?"

She shrugged.

"Well, making babies is a lot like cooking. If the mommy and daddy add the right ingredients together at the right time, it makes a baby."

She pondered this for a second. "You mean like making chocolate chip cookies. I love helping Mommy make cookies."

"Yes, exactly like making chocolate chip cookies." He cast me an amused glance. "I love making cookies, too."

I chuckled.

I knew firsthand how much he loved the action of making cookies. It was the rest of it I wasn't optimistic about.

"Okay, so we've established how babies are made," Logan said. "Well, Kiera and I were playing around with cookie dough a few months ago, and that's why she's having a baby."

A pleased smile slipped onto his face, and he released a hard breath.

While he might've been happy to get that out, Livi didn't share the sentiment. Her face twisted into a deeper shade of confusion.

"What your father means," I said, attempting to rescue the situation, "is the baby in my belly"—I rubbed said belly—"is your brother."

Some more pondering from Livi. "What about the baby in Mommy's tummy?"

"That will be your brother or sister, too," Logan explained. "Your mommy and Tony also love making cookies."

"Does that mean if I make cookies with you or Tony, I'll have a baby in my tummy, too?"

The blood in Logan's face drained.

Yeah, maybe he shouldn't have gone with the cookie-making analogy.

"No, only adults can make babies," I told her, even though that wasn't entirely true.

I mentally apologized to her future teacher who would be covering sex ed. Hopefully, Logan hadn't just made her life a whole lot more challenging.

"So I'm going to have two baby brothers...or a baby brother and a baby sister." Her face brightened. "I'm going to have twins! Katie has twin sisters."

"They would only be twins if they're born at the same time and have the same Mommy and Daddy," I said.

Disappointment scrunched on her small face. "Oh."

"But you'll still be a great big sister," I told her.

She nodded, then grabbed Logan's hand and tugged him off the couch.

"Where are we going?" He asked as she pulled him down the hallway.

"To pack your stuff."

"Pack my stuff? I'm not going anywhere."

"You and Mrs. A are moving in with me and Mommy and Tony. We need to pack your stuff."

Logan stopped walked.

Livi yanked on his hand, trying to get the laws of motion to work in her favor. But her father's larger mass compared to hers prevented that from happening. "C'mon, Daddy."

"We're not moving in with you, your mommy, and Tony."

She pouted. "But how will I see my baby brother every day if you and Mrs. A don't move in with us?"

Logan snickered. "I'm sure your mom and stepfather would have something to say if the three of us moved in with you."

Livi released Logan's hand. "At least I'll see the baby when I live with you." She glanced between the bedroom doors. "Which is the baby's room? Is he sharing mine?"

"The baby will be living with me," I said.

Logan whirled to me. "What do you mean the baby will be living with you?"

"Just that. He'll need his mother, especially since I'll be nursing him. You might have donated to the cookie dough, but there are some things you won't be able to do." I wanted to wait as long as I could before introducing Love Bug to the bottle.

I had assumed that if Grayson had ever returned my call, he would've visited and FaceTimed us like Logan did with Livi when he was away. I hadn't planned on our son living with him.

Just because Grayson turned out to be Logan and he lived in the same city, it didn't mean my original plans had changed.

The apartment door opened and Stacy entered.

"Mommy!" Livi ran to her and threw her arms around her mom's waist.

"We'll be circling back to the part about where the baby will be living in a moment," Logan said to me.

Stacy's gaze landed on me and her eyebrows raised. "I didn't realize you two were still seeing each other." There was no malice in her tone, but there was something in it that made me squirm. Why? I had no clue.

"Daddy and Mrs. A were baking chocolate cookies together."

Stacy smiled at her daughter. "That's nice, sweetie. I hope you didn't eat too many. You don't want to ruin your appetite before dinner."

Livi released an exaggerated huff. "Not *those* kinds of cookies. They made the baby kind of cookies."

"You mean they made small cookies?"

Livi rapidly shook her head. "No, *baby* cookies. You know, when the mommy and daddy add their ingredients at the right time and make a baby." She glanced over her shoulder at Logan. "Isn't that right, Daddy?"

He groaned, the sound so low that only I could've possibly heard him.

Stacy wasn't looking at her ex-husband. Her gaze was zoomed in on me. "You're pregnant?"

I blinked, digesting her shock. What did she think the baby bump was? Me devouring a small basketball in a single bite?

"I mean, I know you're pregnant," she spluttered and gestured at my belly. "But I wasn't aware that you and Logan had..." She glanced at Livi and back at me. "Had been baking cookies together."

All this talk about cookies was making me crave a plate of ginger snaps. The kind Mom baked.

To-do list item #1 once I left here? Text Mom for the recipe so I could make them once I got home.

Something warned me I would need them after this conversation—and it had nothing to do with my craving.

Stacy swiveled to Logan. "How could you have been baking cookies together? Until you were traded in February, you were living in Chicago. And she's definitely further along than three months."

"I'm twenty-seven weeks tomorrow," I helpfully pointed out.

"Don't you remember? Chicago played the Rock in San Francisco in December?" he told her. "Kiera and I could've baked cookies then."

"Could have?" Stacy said. "But that's not when the cooking lessons happened, is it?"

I pressed my fist against my mouth, curtailing the laugh that was pushing its way to the surface at the ridiculousness of the conversation.

"Can Daddy and Mrs. A move in with us so I can see my baby brother all the time?" Livi earnestly asked her.

"You don't have to call me Mrs. A when we aren't in school," I told her. "You can call me Kiera."

I was the mother of her half brother. It didn't feel right for her to keep calling me Mrs. A. At least for now. At least until I returned to teaching after my maternity leave.

"Kiera and I won't be moving in with you guys." Logan's gaze flicked from Livi to me. "But *you* will be moving in with me."

He made it sound like I didn't have a choice.

I had news for him.

Stacy burst out laughing. I'd been so busy silently telling him with my eyes I had no intention of moving in with him, her laugh startled me.

"Well, you two have fun figuring that one out. Livi and I are going home now." She grinned at us, her gaze moving to each of us in turn. "And congratulations on the new addition."

If I'd thought her laugh had surprised me, that was nothing compared to her comment. She genuinely did look happy for us.

She hadn't even questioned why I'd claimed Stephen was Love Bug's father, and now Logan and I were admitting that *Logan* was the father. She'd just accepted it.

Which meant she couldn't have been jealous the other day like I'd initially believed. She wouldn't have suddenly done a one-eighty after learning Logan was going to be a father again.

Livi hugged Logan good-bye before she and Stacy left.

No sooner had the door clicked shut, Logan folded his arms across his chest. "Like I said, you're moving in with me."

"Sorry to disappoint, but no, I'm not. I like my home." It had memories in it that I wasn't ready to let go of yet. Plus, it had a backyard. Not a huge one, but it was more than Logan could claim. He just had a balcony twenty stories up.

"I like my home, too."

"Problem solved. You stay in your condo, and I'll stay in my house."

"How is that solving the problem? I can't see my son whenever I want if you two aren't living with me."

"I'm not looking to be your roomie, Logan. And we want different things in life right now." I wanted to make a loving home for my son, and one day find someone who would love us both. Someone who would make us his priority.

And by love, I meant it went both ways. I was in love with Logan, but he wasn't in love with me.

"I don't know about that," he said. "I'm positive we want the same thing."

I shook my head. "Sorry, not happening. We're friends who have sex. That's not the same thing as being in a committed relationship. I want what I had with Stephen. What Stacy has with Tony. That's not what you want."

"Says who?"

I laughed. "You. Remember? You made it clear that Livi and hockey are your top priorities. You aren't looking to settle down until after you retire from the NHL." Which could still be many years away.

"We'll play strip poker. The loser moves into the winner's home."

"Didn't you hear a single word I just said?"

He smiled the cocky grin that always had an annoying effect on my body. Things hadn't changed in that respect since college.

"I did, which is exactly why we're playing strip poker."

"And if I say no?"

"You don't have a choice." He cradled his palm against my belly. "Love Bug votes that we give this a chance."

Easy for Logan to say. His heart wasn't vested in this relationship like mine was.

"All right. We'll do a trial run and see how things go."

If Love Bug's father had actually been a stranger instead of someone who I'd known for years, I would've insisted we got to know each better before making such a giant leap of living together.

But this was Logan.

Plus, I knew that even though he hadn't planned on being a father again quite so soon, he didn't want to miss a single minute with his son if he could avoid it.

Us living together definitely helped in that department.

"Is that your way of saying yes, you'll move in with me?" he asked.

"No, it's my way of saying, 'Where do you keep your cards?' "

YOU KNOW HOW KENNY ROGERS USED TO SING ABOUT HOW you've got to know when to hold your hand in cards, know when to fold, know when to walk away and when to run?

Great advice—if you knew how to play poker.

It had been a while since I'd played it in college, and even back then, I hadn't been very good at it.

"Okay, what do you have?" Logan asked. He still had all his clothes on, sans a pair of socks.

I, on the other hand, was down to my underwear and maternity top. Not that I had begun with much on. He'd removed his socks to make things even. I'd already lost my shorts.

I laid out my cards. "Two pairs."

He set his cards on the kitchen table. Two aces.

Oh, right. Did I mention Logan hadn't been any better at poker than me?

He yanked his T-shirt over his head, exposing his muscled abs and chest.

Not to mention several bruises from his last game.

I'd seen his body plenty of times, but I still hadn't gotten used to seeing the game's physical aspect laid out on his body like an atlas.

Stephen had frequently been bruised from playing in the competitive league, but nothing like this.

Typically, I would've kissed them as if that would make them better. But not this time.

This time, there was more at stake than making his owies feel better.

He shuffled the cards and dealt out our new hand. I made my bet, doing my best to adopt something of a poker face.

He hummed...and raised me.

I bit my lower lip. Then caught myself and released it.

We went back and forth until I was positive I was going to win this hand. I had a good feeling about it.

"You might as well start removing your jeans." With a smug grin, I lowered my cards onto the table. "Straight flush."

"Sorry, sweetheart. Not going to happen." He lowered his three Fours onto the table, followed by two Queens. "I'll take your top now."

I rolled my eyes and shimmied the striped fabric over my head. I folded it and placed it on the kitchen table, on top of my folded shorts.

I glanced at Logan to find him staring at my stomach. It wasn't like this was the first time he had seen it, but it was the first time in over a month. A lot had changed. Love Bug was rapidly growing.

But the expression in his eyes wasn't of someone who was seeing a woman's pregnant belly for the first time. This was something else, something that melted my heart further for this man.

He kneeled in front of me and caressed the baby bump with his thumb, sending a shiver through me. "I can't believe this is my son." His voice came out as a reverent whisper, and he leaned down and kissed my stomach.

I swept my fingers through his hair, loving the soft feel of it on my skin. There was nothing about this man I didn't love.

And while he might've been scared that he wouldn't be enough for his son, that he would fail him in the way he believed he had failed Livi, he had nothing to worry about.

I'd seen how much he loved his daughter. He would do anything for her, and it would be the same for our son. No matter what, they would always be a priority for him.

I smiled at Logan as he sang "Twinkle, Twinkle Little Star" to my belly. His deep voice was a warm brush against my skin. This wasn't the first time I'd heard him sing, but it was the first time he'd sung to Love Bug.

"Did you used to sing to Livi when Stacy was pregnant with her?" I asked once he was finished serenading his son.

He nodded. "I still sing to her whenever she's sick. I used to do that when she was little."

"That's so sweet." I could easily imagine Logan doing the same for Love Bug. "We should probably get back to our game. There are high stakes in jeopardy."

He shook his head. "I have something better in mind. And once the playoffs are over, I'm moving into your house. Assuming you still want me there."

"I do."

He pulled me to my feet. "We've got a lot to discuss once the playoffs are over."

I nodded because he was right. We did have a lot we needed to figure out, but now wasn't the time to do that. Not when his energy needed to be on the remaining games of the final series.

He kissed me. I'd missed his kisses. They left me feeling like every part of me was lit up from the inside, all the way to my soul. I was surprised he didn't need sunglasses to look at me.

His kisses slowed enough for him to peer at me, a question in his eyes. I nodded my reply, and he led me to his bedroom.

He guided me to the bed, and then his mouth was on mine again. The kisses were sweet and hungry, passionate, and intense. They left me naked and vulnerable. They built me up, made me stronger.

No matter what happened between Logan and me, he had given me that. He had given me the strength to go on with my life, even though Stephen was no longer physically part of it.

While we kissed, my adventurous fingers undid his jeans button and slid the zipper down. They brushed his hard length, and Logan sucked in a soft breath.

I grinned at him. His kisses weren't the only thing I missed. My purple dildo just hadn't been the same as the real thing.

We quickly removed what remained of our clothes, and Logan reversed onto his bed. With his pillows propping him up, I straddled his hips.

And then we were kissing again as his fingers teased the sensitive nerves between my legs.

It wasn't long before the condom was on, and I was sinking onto his length, hugging the part of him that I'd wondered if I would ever experience again.

"I missed you," I murmured against his lips. I hadn't understood just how much I'd missed him until now.

I rocked along his length; he moved his hips, thrusting into me, taking me higher and higher, until I could practically reach the stars.

And just as I thought I couldn't go much higher, my orgasm rocketed through me and proved how wrong I was.

Logan came moments after me, uniting us in a way that hadn't happened the night of the Jingle Balls ball. Taking us to a whole new level.

As I floated back to Earth, all I could do was pray that it would be enough to show him that even though we hadn't planned for things to go this way, Stephen would have approved.

Logan had been his number one choice for me to move on with.

He'd believed in Logan, even though I suspected he had known Logan's marriage was failing.

He had known Logan was the right man for me.

But even though I told myself this, a small part of me was still annoyed that Logan had lied to me the night of the ball.

He had known the entire time who I was and had kept it a secret.

A secret that had resulted in such a knotted mess, I didn't know how to start untangling it.

39

KIERA

Were competitive sports my thing?

When it came to playing them, not at all. When I first learned that Logan was actually Love Bug's father, I'd hoped that Love Bug would be lucky enough to inherit his father's genes.

But as the Lightning player smashed into the plexiglass, with Logan sandwiched between them, I changed my mind. Maybe it wouldn't be so bad if Love Bug inherited my lack of hockey prowess.

I guess Stephen's mom had been right all along about Love Bug possibly one day playing the sport at an elite level, like Stephen and Logan.

Had I broken the news yet to Judith that Love Bug wasn't her biological grandson?

Was the moon made from strawberry cream cheese?

I know, I know, the longer I waited to tell her, the worse the heartbreak would be. I needed to yank off the Band-Aid, and do it soon.

Very soon.

They were moving to San Francisco in a few weeks.

Except, I had no idea how one went about breaking someone's heart without actually breaking their heart. Hence why I hadn't gotten far with my letter-writing campaign.

Once again, I mentally cursed Logan for the predicament he'd put me in when he kept his true identity a secret at the ball—and continued keeping it a secret after moving to San Francisco.

Yeah, I know, it wasn't totally his fault. I was the dummy who told everyone Stephen was Love Bug's father. I'd panicked and hadn't thought of the consequences until it was too late.

As it was, only a few people were aware that Logan was Love Bug's father—and my parents weren't part of that privileged group.

I planned to tell them after the playoffs were over.

Yep, I was a pregnant chicken.

I was positive they'd be thrilled that the father was someone I'd known for ten years. We weren't two strangers having a baby together.

My parents were only starting to come to terms with my reasons for lying about Stephen being Love Bug's father. This news would help things along.

"Yay, Daddy!" Livi bounced in her seat as Logan battled for the puck near the Lightning's goal.

The final game of the playoffs was halfway through the third period, the score tied.

And my heart had been sitting in my throat, beating faster than hummingbird wings, since before puck drop at the beginning of the game.

Even Love Bug couldn't miss that something big was happening in his daddy's life.

Logan flicked the puck to Eli, who nailed it at the goal.

The darn Tampa goalie blocked the shot with his stick,

sending the puck toward his teammate. The forward gained control of it and sped down the ice.

Logan and Eli chased after him.

"If you lean any farther forward, Kiera," Stacy said, grinning at me, "your center of gravity will cause you to fall off your seat."

I grinned back. "I can't help it. I'm nervous for them."

Whoever won this game won the Stanley Cup. It was the moment Logan had worked hard for all these years.

It was also the turning point in our relationship. No matter how the game went, he was moving into my house tomorrow.

"You're lucky your baby isn't due during hockey season," Stacy said. "Logan will be around for it."

"Wasn't he there when Livi was born?" I asked, even though I knew the answer.

On the ice, tempers got heated, and a penalty was called on the Rock for tripping.

Eli was sent to the sin bin.

Or as Livi liked to call it, the time-out box.

"Livi came two weeks earlier than expected. Logan was away on a road trip." Sadness crossed Stacy's face like a cloud pushed by a strong breeze. "I hope you're ready for being the girlfriend of an NHL player. I didn't know what I was getting into when I married him. Turns out, it was something I wasn't prepared for."

Was I ready? I had no idea.

If Stephen had been recruited into the NHL, I probably wouldn't have been ready for it either. It had been tough enough when he played collegiate hockey. But I would've liked to think I'd grown up since then. I'd spent the last seventeen months alone, the last six months pregnant.

I was a strong and independent woman.

Hear me roar!

Of course, it was easy to think that. As my granny used to say, "The proof is in the pudding."

Although now that I thought about it, she meant that in the more literal sense.

As in, she put rum in the pudding...

"I guess we'll find out soon enough. But I'm not sure that I'm technically his girlfriend. I'm the mother of his baby, and he's moving in with me"—*and we have sex*—"but he hasn't actually said anything about me being his girlfriend. For all I know, he's the father of my baby and my roommate."

She laughed as Logan stepped on the ice for his shift. "I've known Logan for over eight years. He definitely thinks of you as his girlfriend. Can I tell you something, just between us?"

I nodded.

The puck flew toward the Lightning goal.

"He's always been in love with you, Kiera. I don't think that's ever changed, even when he and I were married."

I opened my mouth to protest.

"It's true," she said, preventing me from denying it. "He and I might not have realized it at the time, but in retrospect, his feelings for you were always there. He just respected Stephen, you, and me too much to risk admitting the truth to himself and everyone else. You need to—"

Logan tipped the puck into the goal.

Whatever Stacy had planned to tell me was lost to the noise of the entire arena jumping to their feet, cheering the goal.

The energy had been high before, but that was nothing compared to now.

"And the winner of the Stanley Cup..." the NHL commissioner announced, "the San Francisco Rock."

Weightlessness filled me over what the team had accomplished. They had done it. All the sacrifices the team had made—that Logan had made—had been worth it.

The fans screamed and cheered their appreciation. Tears were running down Stacy's and my smiling faces. Livi covered her ears with her hands and bounced on the spot like a hyped-up kangaroo.

The team captain skated to the table, which held the large trophy. The commissioner handed the coveted prize to him, and the captain hoisted it above his head. He skated a short distance before handing it off to the next player.

I caressed my side where Love Bug had last kicked me. "What do you think of that?" I said to my belly. "And your daddy scored the winning goal."

That resulted in more tears. I was so happy for him, for his team.

Stacy, Livi, and I had vacated our seats while waiting for the Cup to be carried onto the ice. Now, we were with the rest of the players' families—including Logan's parents— waiting to join the players on the ice.

Logan's parents had flown in for the game, and Logan had put them up in a hotel. They had no idea that I was pregnant with their future grandchild. They also had no idea he was moving in with me soon.

If they wondered why I was with Livi and Stacy, they never said anything.

The players each took their turn skating around the ice while holding the cup for all to see. Livi continued to keep her ears covered until it was her father's turn to hold the Cup. Then she was as loud as everyone else.

Once they finished the skate and the team photo, we were allowed to join the players. Stacy and I cautiously walked along the ice to where Logan was standing with a sports reporter, doing our best not to slip. We kept our distance while the pair talked.

Logan looked too excited to pay attention to her questions. His energy level rivaled Livi's from a moment ago. Apparently, the hyped-up kangaroo thing was an inherited trait.

Logan spotted us and said something to the woman, then skated toward us.

*Play it cool. Play it cool. Play it...*I told myself as he approached us.

All I wanted was to fling my arms around him, kiss him, and let him know how proud I was of him. But I couldn't exactly do that in front of his parents...in front of anyone.

No one was aware of his pending double fatherhood status.

Not yet, anyway.

I might have been thinking that, but Logan had a different plan in mind.

Without even acknowledging his family first, his mouth was on mine, almost startling my feet out from under me. His sweaty arms engulfed me as much as they could, given my swollen belly.

Any other time, I would have been severely grossed out by his dripping body pressed against me. But this was Stanley Cup sweat, so it was totally worth it.

Our kiss was brief but intense, the result of his adrenaline high. We hadn't seen each other for the past four days, and we had lost time to make up for. But that would have to wait since his parents were in town.

His parents.

Oops. I guess the secret was out of the lockbox.

I beamed at him. "Congratulations. Love Bug and I are so proud of you."

His grin widened, and he spread his hand on my belly.

Behind us, I heard Livi declare, "That's my baby brother."

"It is?" That sounded like Logan's mother. "You must be excited."

I turned to see Livi nodding enthusiastically.

Logan's mother peered at me with more curiosity than before. "I take it congratulations are in order, you two. And when were you planning to tell me the big news?" She closed the distance between her and Logan and hugged him.

Whereas Logan and his father were tall, his mother was petite. Her size difference almost caused him to topple over.

Laughing, he returned her hug. "Mom, Dad, this is Kiera, my girlfriend."

I exchanged a glance with Stacy, who wore an I-told-you-so smug smile.

"Well, I've got a billion questions to ask you two," Logan's mother said, "but they'll have to wait until tomorrow. You've got a Stanley Cup win to celebrate."

40

LOGAN

Three days after the Rock won the playoffs and I moved in with Kiera, I was standing in Stacy's kitchen. She handed me two glasses from the cabinet to set on the tray next to me on the counter. Outside the kitchen window, Livi and Tony were searching for the soccer ball. The three of us would be playing a game once they'd finally located it.

"Don't say anything to Livi," Stacy said, "but Tony and I have decided to get a puppy."

"A puppy? Won't you have your hands full with the baby?"

"Absolutely. But we're not getting it quite yet. We're checking out breeders first."

"Is this your way of making sure Livi will want to spend more time with you and Tony than with me?" I grinned at her so that she knew I was kidding.

She returned the grin. "No one is saying you can't get a puppy. Oops. I forgot. You're living with Kiera now. She can say no to a puppy."

That might've been true, but Kiera had always wanted a

dog. Her mother was the one who hadn't been interested in getting one when Kiera was growing up.

But that was all I knew. We hadn't discussed the possibility of us getting a dog at some point.

We hadn't discussed a lot of things since discovering I was the father of her baby.

"How are things now that the two of you are living together?" Stacy asked.

"You mean since we've become roommates?" At her confused expression, I clarified. "Kiera decided that I would be living in her guest room."

Stacy's eyes and mouth went comically wide. If it weren't for the embarrassment hanging out in my gut, I would have laughed at her expression. "You're not sharing the same bed?"

Good, I wasn't the only one surprised at that.

That's right. When I won the poker game that had me moving in with Kiera, I thought I'd at least get to share her bed with her.

Nope.

Not at all.

Don't get me wrong, we were still having sex. Kiera's horny hormones had practically demanded that.

But I was expected to do the walk of shame every night back to the guest room.

All right, it wasn't precisely the walk of shame, but the sentiment was the same.

"Why do you think we didn't work out?" I blurted, not really interested in continuing the bed-sharing conversation. Based on Stacy's shocked expression, that clearly wasn't what she'd expected me to say. That made two of us. "We were in love when we got married. What changed?"

She appeared to consider my question for a moment, then removed the pitcher of strawberry lemonade from the fridge. She placed it on the tray with the glasses. "You're right, we were in love when we got married. But it takes a lot more than being in love to make it work."

"I guess my hockey career didn't help much since I was never around."

She shook her head. "It's true that your career didn't exactly help things, but that meant we needed to try harder to make sure we didn't drift apart. Neither of us did that. I was busy putting Livi first. And then later, I was so intent on starting my own business because I felt like I was nothing more than a hockey wife and a mother. I had no identity beyond that."

Her answer startled me. "I didn't realize you'd felt that way."

"That's because I didn't tell you. I thought I needed to be the perfect mother and perfect NHL wife, and that was all that mattered. And at first, that was true. But then, as we began drifting apart, and I realized I wanted more in life. I wanted an identity that was all mine. And that only caused us to drift even further apart.

"Only neither of us clued into that at the time. We were so focused on our own needs, we forgot about our marriage." She gave me a sad smile. "I know you think you were the one at fault for our failed marriage, but that's not true, Logan. A marriage is about two people who feel complete together. Two people who are confident in who they are and can both contribute to a healthy, loving marriage.

"I learned that lesson the hard way. And because of that, I won't make the same mistakes with Tony that you and I made. Now it's your turn to do the same...with Kiera. Don't repeat the mistakes you and I made.

"You're a good man, Logan. You deserve the best. But if

you screw it up this time, I will hunt you down and kick you in the ass." She slugged me in the arm. Hard.

Then she kissed me on the cheek, and I chuckled.

She nodded at the kitchen window. Outside, Livi was waving the missing soccer ball at me. "I think they're ready to whoop your ass."

THE BEST THING ABOUT THE ROMANTIC COMEDIES THAT GIRLS drag their boyfriends to see?

All right, there's nothing great about them...other than the fact that they're educational.

Yep, you heard me correctly.

For example, they teach men how to get the big moment right when they're declaring their undying love to the woman they're dating. Girls lap that stuff up.

Don't believe me?

Then why are they so popular?

Good. You see my point.

So this was why—the day after hanging out with Livi, Stacy, and Tony—I was using my limited knowledge of romantic comedies to plan the proposal that would (metaphorically) knock Kiera off her feet.

No, you don't need to get your hearing checked. You heard me correctly that time, too.

Kiera was the mother of my unborn child, and us getting married was the right thing to do.

But because we had done things backward (and inside out), I needed to pull out all the cannons and go huge.

Just like they do in romantic comedies.

Have you ever watched the movie *Enchanted*?

Okay, I'll admit I hadn't paid a lot of attention to it when

I watched it with Livi a few years ago. I did remember there were a lot of singing and dancing numbers.

And that kickass fight with the dragon at the climax.

And "true love's kiss" after the redheaded heroine ate the poisoned apple.

But since Kiera and I had already kissed more than once, I figured "love's first kiss" no longer applied to our situation—especially since Kiera hadn't eaten any poisoned apples.

So my conclusion from what I remembered of the movie?

That I needed to go big with the proposal.

Yes, I realized Robert didn't actually propose to Giselle, but since fire-breathing dragons weren't (fortunately) part of our agenda either, I figured that was okay.

Would a musical number factor into the proposal?

Hey, let's not get too crazy.

There wasn't enough time to pull that together. But if there had been, then yes, I would have also included a big musical number.

Had Kiera and I talked about getting married? Not in so many words.

But it was the right thing to do for our son.

And I knew she would agree with me.

Stephen would have done the same if our places were reversed.

How did I propose to Stacy? Nothing like what I'd planned for Kiera.

We'd been talking about marriage and our plans for the future and how our friends were all getting married. I figured the timing was perfect and got down on one knee to propose.

Maybe that was part of the reason our marriage hadn't worked out in the end. The proposal had been lackluster.

That wasn't to say our marriage had been that way, too, but I figured it certainly contributed to the problem.

A foreboding, so to speak.

There hadn't even been an engagement ring at the time.

And so that was why I was standing outside of Tiffany's, preparing to buy the perfect ring.

When I'd bought Kiera the "Believe" necklace, it was because I had cared a lot for her in college. I still cared a lot for her, only things were more complicated now.

My feelings were more complicated.

Of course, if I'd been honest with her from the start, things would never have gotten to this point, with us discovering I was the father of her son.

Our son.

And yes, if I could do the night of the ball over again, I would. Only this time, I'd tell her the truth. I would give her the choice of deciding if she wanted to have sex with me, knowing full well who I was.

But it was too late for that.

As for the billion-dollar question: how was I planning to balance two kids with different mothers while playing hockey? It had been difficult enough as it was balancing Livi and my career. Now I had to balance two kids in two separate homes, a girlfriend, and my career.

The universe's take on this?

It was having a great laugh at my expense.

Couldn't say I blamed it.

But that was why I was here.

Looking at engagement rings.

Proposing was the right thing to do.

A way to tell the universe it was mistaken.

And with my plans to go big with the proposal, all the universe could do was pat me on the shoulder and give me its blessing.

It was romantic—and I had those dumb chick flicks to thank for that.

41

LOGAN

"And the next item up for auction is a date with San Francisco Rock forward, Elias Lawson," I announced into the microphone to the sold-out audience in the hotel conference room.

Bright stage lights shone down on Eli and me as he strutted across the stage like it was a catwalk, and he was a Calvin Klein model in a suit. Cheers and hoots followed his every move, and I explained what the date would entail.

The women began entering bids on the app that Wes Chiasson had designed for the event. The man was a programming genius.

Eli walked to where I was standing and flashed the audience what Kiera had described as his smoldering look.

I had no idea what that meant.

"The date will include a delightful dinner at Bonterra Ristorante for two," I said. Nowhere on the card did it mention the part about attending a wedding with him.

As desperate as he was to find someone to fill the role of fake girlfriend, he'd finally conceded I was right about waiting to ask the winner if she'd do it. There was no point in asking someone to do it if he couldn't stand being in the same room with them for more than five minutes.

That would be one helluva disastrous wedding date.

We gave everyone a chance to bid on the prize, and I moved on to the next item.

Once I'd finished introducing the items in the auction, we waited while Wes determined the winners. Waiters handed out the desserts in the meantime.

Kiera was talking to an older woman when I approached.

"Logan, this is Kristina Lugwig," Kiera said. "She works with family services and will be helping to distribute the box sets."

The woman shook my hand. "I can't even begin to tell you how much I appreciate the work you and Kiera have done on this. It will make a big difference for many of the kids when it comes to literacy."

I wrapped my arm around Kiera's waist. "This project was all Kiera's idea. I was just her helper."

Beaming at my girlfriend, I kissed her temple. She really was something. The work she had done to make the event a success was tremendous. And it wasn't just tonight's event.

She'd been working hard, figuring out how to help increase the reading skills of the kids who might otherwise lack the necessary resources.

The woman was relentless when it came to something she was passionate about. But that came as no surprise. She'd been that way in college, too.

We chatted with Kristina for several more minutes. The entire time, the box with the engagement ring weighed heavily in my pocket.

The grand gesture?

Don't worry, it was coming shortly.

Not much longer and I'd be able to breathe again.

I kissed Kiera, doing my best to keep things PG-rated. "You did it. From what I can tell, you exceeded your expectations."

She smiled sweetly at me, her excitement vibrating off her in waves. "It might not be the same as winning the Stanley Cup, but I'm thrilled with the outcome."

"I think this is bigger than winning the Cup." Although I was confident my teammates and the coaching staff would've disagreed with me. "What you've accomplished will make a huge difference in the lives of a lot of kids."

"Thank you." She returned my kiss.

"Kiera, Logan?" Hannah said behind me. "Wes is ready with the winners' names."

She handed me the list of the items and the winning bids.

Out of curiosity, I flipped to the page where the date with Eli was listed. "Holy shit."

"What?" Kiera asked, looking over my shoulder.

I showed her the winning bid, and she whistled. "That's a lot of money." She scanned the room. "I wonder who the lucky woman is."

"Nala? Isn't that Simba's girlfriend in the Lion King?"

She snorted a laugh. "Yes, but I somehow don't think a lion bid in the silent auction."

"I guess we'll find out who she is soon enough." I walked onstage to the mic. "Before I announce the auction winners, I'd first like to ask the event organizer to join me." I held my hand out to Kiera, and her cheeks reddened.

She looked goddamn adorable, but now wasn't the time to tell her that.

At the thought of what I was about to do soon, my palms grew clammy. I slipped my hand into my pocket to make sure the ring box was still there.

During the playoffs, each game I'd played had been more important than the last, yet somehow the momentary case of nerves I'd felt then was nothing compared to now.

Applause filled the room as Kiera walked to me, and she gave a shy wave.

I handed her the mic. Her responding grin was wobbly.

"Thank you, everyone," she said, "for coming out and supporting the fundraiser. The money will ensure that foster kids of lower-income families have access to the series of books that are so gripping, kids can't help but want to read them. And as you know, the love of reading is key to learning and having opportunities that might not otherwise be possible. Thanks to your generosity, we've raised thirty thousand dollars, which will go to the Reading for Tomorrow Literacy Program." Kiera had recently decided that if the auction were a success, she would extend the program to all families who otherwise couldn't afford kids' books. It looked as though that would be the case now.

The crowded room broke out in cheers, and she practically thrust the mic at me as if it had turned to lava.

"Don't go anywhere," I told her.

Confusion flickered on her face, but she did as I asked.

Like with her joining me onstage, this, too, hadn't been part of her plan.

I started announcing the auction winners.

"And the winner of the date with Elias Lawson," I said as I reached the end of the list. I gave a dramatic pause. "With the winning bid of one thousand and twenty-nine dollars...Nala Johnson from table nineteen."

Applause rose throughout the room, but it was the cheers from one table that outshone everyone else.

All the women at the table were high-fiving and laughing.

All the women except for one.

The pretty Black woman with shoulder-length, curly hair looked stunned.

Not the *Wow-I-really-won?* kind of stunned. This was more of a *Hell-what-just-happened?* stunned.

Her three friends—in their late twenties to early thirties—nudged her forward. She looked at them and vehemently shook her head. They began quietly arguing among themselves.

Eli sat at a table near the front of the stage with our teammates who contributed to the auction. A mix of emotions—relief, curiosity, nervousness—flickered on his face, noticed only by me because I was looking in his direction.

The redhead at Nala's table stood up. "She's coming." Grabbing hold of Nala's wrist, she dragged her reluctant friend to her feet and tugged her to where the winners were supposed to pay for their prizes.

I exchanged glances with Kiera. She just shrugged. "I should probably make sure she really does want the date in case we have to award it to the next highest bid."

She turned to leave the stage.

I wrapped my fingers around her wrist. "Don't go anywhere yet." I lifted the microphone to my mouth and looked out at the audience. "Not only—" I started to say, the words sounding like they'd just marched through the Sierra Desert. I cleared my throat. "Not only is this beautiful woman the organizer of today's fundraiser, she's the mother-to-be of my son." I pulled the ring box out of my pocket and dropped to one knee.

It was time the world found out I was going to be a father again. And I wanted to make sure Kiera knew how much I loved my son even though he hadn't been planned.

She already questioned our relationship due to my stupid lie the night he was conceived, so I wanted to make sure she knew how excited I was that he would be part of our future.

Kiera's eyes widened, and she paled.

"She's not carrying *your* son," a woman yelled out. "That's *my* grandson she's carrying."

All eyes turned to the woman.

Judith. Stephen's mother.

Who—if her expression was any indication—hadn't heard the news yet about who was the true father of Kiera's baby.

Fuck.

42

———————

KIERA

Why is it every time you want to disappear into a hole, there's never one handy?

It doesn't matter how much you will for it to happen; the universe just laughs at you.

Only in this case, I wasn't sure what exactly it was laughing at: the part where I kept putting off telling Stephen's parents the truth, or the part where Logan had been about to propose to me.

I assumed that was what the ring box was for, and why he'd gotten down on one knee.

In front of everyone.

There was also a chance I was wrong. We hadn't even discussed getting married. He'd only recently discovered I was pregnant with his child—that the baby was his, not Stephen's. He was still dealing with that shock.

We both were.

And while I might've been in love with him, he had never given any indication he felt the same way about me.

Okay, I know what you're going to say. And you're right. I hadn't said it to him either. But I had an excuse. I was still

struggling with how he'd withheld the truth about his identity at the ball.

I watched in horror as my mother-in-law made her way
from where she'd been sitting with Mom, past the jungle of
tables, toward the stage. My mind was working a mile a
minute to come up with an explanation for why I'd lied
to her.

*Try telling her the truth. Like you should have done to begin
with.*

It was time I pulled up the big girl maternity panties.
My parents had eventually understood why I had lied to
them about Stephen being Love Bug's father. They eventually forgave me for being less than honest.

Hannah and Emma had been the opposite. Both
women had understood right from the start, more than
anyone, why I had lied. Both were also thrilled that Logan
was Love Bug's biological father.

But I had a feeling it wasn't going to be the same for
Judith.

It suddenly dawned on me that the universe hadn't
been laughing at me after all.

It had been throwing me a bone.

I'd never believed that being proposed to in public was
romantic. Having strangers stare at you, waiting for your
reply, felt intrusive. And what if you weren't in the same
place in the relationship as the individual proposing? What
if you didn't love them the way they loved you?

Look at those men who propose on Jumbotrons while
at a sports game, and their girlfriends said no. The video
goes viral, and everyone who sees you on the street knows
of your humiliation.

Proposals in front of a bunch of strangers were best
reserved for movies.

So yes, Judith might've been distraught—but she'd just saved me from saying "no" to Logan in front of everyone.

I could have hugged her for her brilliant timing.

Although something told me that hugs were now off the table.

"Why are you lying about who's really the father of Kiera's baby?" Her voice was soft, her glare sharp like a knife dipped in lime juice.

Ouch.

Several people at a nearby table watched us, their interest no doubt piqued because of Logan's celebrity status.

Oh, who was I kidding? The entire freaking room was watching us, stunned into silence. Peering at us like we were an accident on the highway you couldn't look away from.

I didn't know what to say.

And that's what you get for lying to her.

Judith glanced around us, seeing all the curious faces staring at us.

She removed a piece of paper out of her purse and handed it to me. "This is our new address. Come over after you're finished here."

My mouth didn't even have time to flop open before she marched away, heading for the exit.

And leaving me to face the man who was about to propose to me.

It was too bad *What to Expect When You're Expecting* didn't cover situations like this.

At least I assumed it didn't. I hadn't exactly read the book from cover to cover yet.

I looked briefly at the piece of paper and sighed that sound you made when you had just dodged a bullet, but plenty of others were headed your way.

"I should go see what's going on with Eli's reluctant winner," I told Logan. Nala was standing with her friend next to Wes, looking all shades of uncomfortable. Her redheaded friend appeared to be paying for the date while chatting amicably with Wes. "I have a feeling he's going to have a hard time convincing her to be his fake girlfriend for his cousin's wedding. He might have an easier time convincing her friend."

"You might be right about that," Logan said, chuckling. He turned to me. "About what happened on the stage—"

I was kind of hoping he had forgotten about that.

"You mean that part where you held out a ring box and got down on one knee? How about we pretend that didn't happen?"

Sounded like a plan to me.

That expression on his face?

I would have felt better if it looked like I had just kicked his puppy (if he had one). Instead, it was free of emotion.

"Are you saying you don't want to marry me?" he asked, tone even and unreadable.

I nodded thoughtfully. "Yep, that sounds exactly like what I'm saying."

"But we're having a baby together, Kiera. Don't you want us to be a family? A family living in the same house?"

And that was when I got it—what was really the problem.

If it wasn't for Love Bug, Logan and I wouldn't be together. He wasn't looking for a serious girlfriend until he'd finished playing in the NHL. He didn't live with Livi full time, and I knew how hard that was for him.

I smiled with what I hoped was a reassuring grin. "We'll still be a family, and you're welcome to live with us for as long as you want, so you can spend as much time with your son as possible. I would never deny you that."

He frowned. "You mean like a roommate?"

No, like a boyfriend, the man I love. "Yes, like a roommate. With benefits." I danced my eyebrows.

He still looked confused, so I spelled it out for him. "When I marry again—*if* I marry again—it won't be because someone got me pregnant. I'm not interested in getting married because the condom failed. That's no way to begin a marriage. If I marry again, it will be because I love him and he loves me. It will be with someone who is not only there for my son, he's there for me."

I wouldn't be a distant third place like I would be with Logan. I wouldn't come *way* down the line after hockey, Livi, and Love Bug.

I smiled at him, assured that I had addressed his fears, and walked away.

43

LOGAN

"*When I marry again—if I marry again—it won't be because someone got me pregnant. It will be because I love him and he loves me. It will be with someone who is not only there for my son, he's there for me.*"

Kiera's words replayed in my head as we drove to Judith and Joe's new home.

You're probably screaming at me to just tell her that I love her.

But telling her that after everything that had happened tonight would have sounded like an afterthought, a moment of panic.

And that was the last thing I wanted Kiera to think.

I had a better strategy in mind.

One I hoped to hell would work better than how I'd fucked things up with the proposal. Maybe things would have gone better if I'd arranged that musical number. And perhaps relying on my memory of the romantic comedies I'd seen a while ago hadn't been a bright idea, either.

What did I need to do?

Spend the next few months with her re-getting to know me, becoming her close friend again, being her lover, doing all the little things to show her that I loved her, to show her we were perfect together.

And I needed to have her fall in love with me.

Because in case you were too distracted by Lawson wiggling his ass onstage, Kiera still hadn't said anything about being in love with me. I did realize, though, that I hadn't said those words either.

Don't worry, I planned to eventually tell her I loved her. But first, I needed to regain her trust. I had fucked up badly the night of the ball.

I wasn't making that mistake again.

Especially since Stacy had made it clear that my ass was on the line if I hurt Kiera one more time.

And I took my ex-wife's threats very seriously.

The last thing I needed was to end up with chocolate pudding loaded with hot sauce.

Yep, that did happen once during our marriage.

"You don't need to come in with me," Kiera said after I'd parked on the street in front of Judith and Joe's Victorian-style house.

"I'm not letting you face them on your own. This is very much my fault."

She flashed me a You-have-a-point-there smirk.

"I swear that's the last time I lie." Of course, anyone could make empty promises, which was why I would be spending the next several months proving that I deserved more than a second chance with Kiera.

But ultimately, the decision was all hers.

Unfortunately, history was a pain in the ass when it came to my life. I'd screwed up in so many ways, and Kiera knew it.

Stacy hadn't enjoyed being the wife of an NHL hockey

player. There was a good chance Kiera would feel the same way and not want our relationship to go beyond our current roommate status. She might not want to risk being with a man who could be traded at any moment.

And if that were true, I had no idea what I would do.

If I wanted to keep her, my only option would be giving up the career I loved.

The only career that I knew.

We walked up the porch steps to the front door. Kiera rubbed her palms against the cotton fabric of her floral dress. I slipped my fingers between hers, letting her know she didn't have to go this alone. I would do anything to protect her.

Kiera didn't say anything or look at me, but her shoulders relaxed slightly at my touch.

I took that as a positive sign.

I rang the doorbell. A moment later, the door swung opened, revealing Judith, her tear-stained face pale.

Her gaze dropped to our joined hands.

Kiera pulled hers away from mine, and I suddenly felt naked, uncertain.

And for the hundredth time since discovering her baby was mine and not Stephen's, I mentally cursed myself for not telling her the truth the night we hooked up.

Judith gestured for us to enter.

Joe stepped into the foyer, looking fifty years older. Unlike his wife, he managed a hesitant smile. "Thank you for coming. Judith explained what happened at the auction." The smile widened. "Congratulations on it being such a success." And then the smile faltered. "Stephen would have been so proud of what you accomplished, Kiera."

Judith snorted but didn't say anything.

"Why don't we go into the living room, and you can

explain what's going on." Joe pointed to the rear of the house. We followed Judith and took a seat on the couch. They were clearly in the middle of unpacking. Moving boxes were stacked all over the room.

Judith sank onto one armchair. Joe sat on the other one.

She glared at me, and I inwardly shuddered. I had faced some of the fiercest hockey players in the NHL, and none of them had intimated me like Stephen's mother did at this particular moment.

I suddenly understood why Kiera had been so reluctant to tell them the truth once she found out I was Love Bug's father. But despite that and her anger at how I had kept the truth from her about being Grayson, she couldn't be pissed at me for what happened. When it came down to it, *she* was the one who'd told everyone Stephen was the father of her unborn child.

Silence surrounded us like the eye of a hurricane as Kiera and I waited for Joe or Judith to speak. Or maybe they were waiting for us to begin.

But what could I say that didn't involve throwing Kiera under the school bus?

It wasn't my idea that she lied to everyone.

I was only responsible for accidentally knocking her up.

After an uncomfortable minute that seemed to stretch an eternity, Joe spoke. "Am I to take it that you and Stephen never went to a fertility clinic? Or do his sperm still reside in a freezer somewhere?" He squirmed in his chair and scratched the back of his neck.

"No, there are no frozen sperm and never was." Kiera's voice was as small as a field mouse. And just as squeaky. She coughed. "I'm sorry I let you believe that. Stephen and I had started to try for a baby before he died. There were no fertility clinics involved. I said that it was his sperm because I didn't know who the real father was."

Judith scowled. Kiera stiffened.

This was exactly what she had feared when she found out she was pregnant.

It was why she had lied about who the father was.

And now I understood why.

"That was my fault," I said. "We both attended a masquerade ball in December. I saw Kiera without her mask on but didn't let on I was the man she was talking to. My grandmother was also there, but she only uses my middle name, Grayson. So when Kiera discovered she was pregnant, she had no way of contacting the baby's father. Our baby."

I skipped on how she'd later contacted my grandmother to tell Grayson she was pregnant with his baby. I had further screwed things up by not confessing even then that I was him.

"I never meant for you to find out that I was pregnant," Kiera said. "I told my parents..." She swallowed hard. "I told my parents that I used Stephen's frozen sperm. It sounded a lot better than admitting I got pregnant from a one-night stand, especially when I had no idea how the man would react to finding out about the baby. I wasn't aware until you showed up to throw the gender-reveal party that you and my mother were still in contact."

"So why didn't you tell us the truth then?" Judith asked, finally finding her voice. It cut like a hockey puck to the face. "Why keep lying?"

Kiera's fingers fidgeted with the fabric of her dress. "Because you were so happy to have a grandchild, a part of Stephen in your life again. I couldn't tell you and hurt you more than you already were from losing him. I couldn't break your heart again." Her voice cracked.

A small understanding smile curved at the corners of

Joe's mouth. The same smile wasn't duplicated on Judith's face.

Not even close.

If I didn't know better, I would've sworn the woman had turned into an ice statue.

Her expression had the warmth of one.

Knowing how much this was costing Kiera, I settled my hand on hers, attempting to calm her fidgeting. As much as Judith and Joe were upset with the turn of events, my first priority was protecting Kiera and our baby.

"I take full responsibility for what happened," I told them, meaning it. "I don't expect you to forgive either of us, but I hope in time you understand why Kiera lied to you about whose sperm was responsible for creating her baby. Neither of us meant for anyone to get hurt."

I looked at Kiera with a message in my eyes that I hoped she understood: *I never meant for you to get hurt either.*

That was the last thing I ever wanted to happen.

I stood up, pulling Kiera with me. "We should go now."

Joe walked us to the front door. Judith stayed where she was.

"Thank you for coming over," he said, voice low. "And congratulations on your son." He shook my hand. "I'm positive Stephen is smiling from heaven, happy the truth finally came out."

I was positive about that, too.

Of course, if Stephen wanted to throw pointers my way on showing Kiera how much I loved her, I'd be more than grateful.

44

KIERA

August

Tuesday morning, my doorbell rang, and I waddled to the front door.

I opened it to find Stacy standing there, yoga mat in hand.

That's right. For the past two months, Logan's ex-wife and I had been bonding over our biweekly prenatal yoga sessions.

It gave Logan extra time with his daughter when she came over with her mother.

But instead of doing their own thing together, they usually joined us, in my backyard, practicing our poses. Travis had been the one to convince Logan to give it a try. It had become part of his daily routine after Emma had taken yoga when she was pregnant.

Which was why Emma was also here—as our pseudo

yoga instructor—along with Ava and her five-month-old baby bump, and Chloe.

Now that it was the end of August, Livi was in school, and I had officially commenced my maternity leave. Where was Logan now?

Training. Hockey preseason was rapidly approaching.

And with it came the realization. As great as these past few months had been, the real test when it came to our relationship was about to begin.

So how had things gone ever since he tried to propose to me at the silent auction?

If you're asking if he had told me he loved me, that would be a big no.

Nor had I told him that I loved him.

But I had been close to blurting it several times.

As for the past three months? They had been incredible.

We had spent a lot of time together. Sometimes it was just the two of us. And other times, Livi was with us.

We'd gone to the beach, had picnics, explored San Francisco together. He had found places I hadn't even known existed even though I had lived here longer than him.

We also cuddled together a lot. In bed. On the couch.

And the kissing and sex got better and better—even when I looked like a beached whale. I still had the rule about him sleeping in the guest room, although there were a couple of nights where the rule had been forgotten when I fell asleep in his arms.

He was everything I had imagined he would be when we first became friends. He was sweet and attentive and funny.

He worked hard at making me feel like I was his

number one priority—along with Livi, which was only to be expected.

But despite that, the nagging feeling that it was only temporary still lingered. It had been easy during the off-season, but would he slide back to old habits once hockey was back in full force?

Would Love Bug and I only get to appreciate him being in our lives during those few precious off-season months each year, or would things be different than they were for Stacy?

"How are you doing?" she asked, entering my house.

"Other than feeling like a walrus, not bad." My due date wasn't for another ten days.

But who was counting?

"And how are things between you and Logan?" Her voice held a bright and cheery smile to it.

"They're good. He's getting excited for hockey season to start." He was like a little kid on Christmas morning. I was positive if an advent calendar for hockey season existed, he'd be all over it.

She tilted her head to the side, giving me an appraising look. "Are you ready for that?"

I lifted my shoulders. "As ready as I'll ever be."

She nodded. "Logan told me you've been making friends with the hockey wives and girlfriends."

"That's right. They're nice and super supportive." Emma had introduced me to members of the group two months ago. Not all of them had been in town at that point. But now that the season was gearing up again, I'd had a chance to meet them all.

"When I was married to him," Stacy said, "I never bothered getting to know the wives and girlfriends. Yes, I participated in the obligatory activities that went with being the wife of a hockey player, mostly the charity events, but I never made an effort to get to know the women." She made a wry face and shrugged. "Instead, I spent my time with friends who didn't get what it was like to have your husband away so much, for him not to have weekends off from his job. They didn't understand the late nights, the loneliness. That played a role in ending our marriage.

"I'm glad to see you're not making the same mistake I did. Loving a hockey player—or any professional athlete— is never easy, but loving Logan definitely is."

She was right. It was easy to love him.

AS WE USUALLY DID WHEN WE PRACTICED YOGA TOGETHER (unless it was raining), Stacy and I rolled out our mats in the backyard. Emma, Ava, and Chloe had already staked claim to their area of the grass. Cassie and Kat were busy giggling and playing with their toys on the nearby blanket. The sky was blue, but the air was cool.

Not that I noticed it with the way Love Bug had caused my body temperature to skyrocket.

"Looks like Emma lost on the baby pool." Chloe grinned. From the way she said it, I almost expected her to rub her hands in glee.

"Baby pool?" This was the first I'd heard of one.

"That's right. We took bets on when Love Bug would be born. Emma predicted yesterday."

Emma snapped her fingers. "Well, there goes my career as a fortune-teller to the stars. What can I say? I'm better at predicting what will sell well in Aphrodite than I am at predicting due dates."

"What about you three?" I asked Ava, Chloe, and Stacy. "When did you predict Love Bug is going to make his grand entrance?" I rubbed my lower back, which was already begging me to lie down.

"Oh, we can't tell you," Ava said. "Not until you've passed the predicted date."

I laughed. "Why not? Do you think I'm going to pick favorites and make sure Love Bug is born that day?"

Because the last I heard, the popular wives' tales for inducing labor didn't exactly have much scientific merit.

I eyed them each in turn...until they finally gave in and told me.

"How do I get in on the bet?" I asked. "And how much is it?"

"When do you think it will be?" Chloe asked. "And the bet is fifty dollars."

Damn, those girls didn't play around.

I didn't need to ponder the answer. "I've always been a punctual person. So I'm going with my due date."

This was one bet I was confident I was going to win.

"Mornin', ladies," Logan said, walking into the yard. His hair was damp, but since his T-shirt wasn't, I figured he must've already had his shower after his run.

"Hi," I brightly responded.

The five of us were still on our yoga mats, but we had just finished our final resting pose. I struggled to get to my feet, which always took several extra steps when you had a baby who was getting close to pushing their way to freedom.

Logan helped me up. Before I could say anything, I was in his arms, his lips on mine.

It was a sweet kiss, but that didn't mean my heart rate didn't soar.

He gently cupped my watermelon-sized belly and lovingly stroked it with his thumb.

"Aaand, that's our cue to leave." Stacy laughed.

The four women collected their mats and supplies.

"We'll see you Friday, Kiera. Have fun, you two." Chloe waved and headed for the side gate, followed by the rest of our posse and the two little girls.

"How was yoga?" Logan's thumb continued stroking my belly.

Love Bug gave him an answering kick, and Logan grinned. Feeling his son move never grew old for him. For either of us.

"I missed you this morning," I murmured, gazing into his beautiful blue eyes.

"I missed you, too." He brushed his lips against mine again.

He understood exactly what I was talking about. It wasn't that I missed seeing him when he got up to train with Travis and the guys. It was the waking up alone because we slept in separate rooms.

And I was done doing that—at least while he was at home. I would just have to get used to it once he was on the road.

I inhaled a slow breath, trying to calm my revved up heart rate. "I was thinking that maybe if you want, we could get rid of the rule where you sleep in the guest room. You can sleep with me."

The smile on his face? It was brighter and more beautiful than a hundred sunrises. My heart rate tripped over itself.

"I get to move into your bedroom?"

I nodded. "If you would like to."

He didn't answer with words. He didn't need to. His kiss said it all.

Unlike the other ones, this kiss wasn't sweet. It was deep, possessive, body-tingling divine.

For several minutes, we stood in the backyard kissing, and then we weren't in the backyard...but we were definitely still kissing.

Logan sat on my bed—I meant our bed—a few minutes later, naked, when I stepped from the master bathroom. Only I wasn't naked.

I was wearing the black lace negligee I'd bought at the sex party earlier this year. Had I worn it for Logan yet?

Not at all.

Somehow it hadn't felt right until now.

I couldn't explain it, and since the man I wanted to make love to was waiting for me, I wasn't interested in wasting time analyzing it either.

Fortunately, the top had a slit down the front that allowed the lace to flow open on either side of my belly, so I didn't feel like a whale shoved into a sardine can.

If the expression on Logan's face was any indication, he approved of the negligee.

Very much so.

I climbed onto the bed and straddled his hips.

He swallowed, the bob of his Adam's apple slowly ascending and descending. "Christ, you're like an early Christmas present."

My lady bits tingled at the rough rumble of his voice.

I smiled. "Well, your gift *will* be revealed in ten days, give or take a day or two."

The answering grin warmed me from the inside out. I was certain even Love Bug was fanning himself due to my temperature skyrocketing at Logan's words.

"I can't wait." He threaded his fingers in my hair and brought my head down to his.

The kissing that ensued was gentle and heated and

sublime. Every inch of me buzzed at how much I loved this man.

His talented fingers that scored game-winning goals sought out another prize. They moved between my legs and found the eager throb that had been building toward the crescendo ever since Logan kissed me in the backyard.

"Oh God," I moaned. "I want you so badly." I meant it in so many ways, but for now, I left him believing there was only one way I wanted him.

Preferably with him inside me.

I quickly removed my panties (looking no more graceful than I had crawling across the bed) while he rolled on the protection. Then I positioned myself on the tip of his hard length and slowly lowered myself until I was fully seated. We both groaned at the feel of my soft heat hugging his hard length.

Logan settled his hands on my hips and rocked me back and forth, taking things slowly. Savoring each deliberate stroke.

Our eyes remained locked the entire time, and the love in his was unmistakable.

The pressure between my legs grew steadily to the point of no return. My inner muscles tightened around him, and a white light filled every part of me, turning me inside out. I cried out my release, along with his name.

This was accompanied by his own grunted release, so desperate, so needy, so satisfied.

I'd had plenty of orgasms in the past, so I was more than familiar with the sensations rocking through my body. But this time it felt different, and the overwhelming desire to reveal how I felt about him pushed the words to my lips.

"I love you," I whispered.

"I love you, too." He rested his forehead against mine. "So very much."

My heart practically swooned in my chest at those words. Words I had longed to hear but had believed would never happen. "You do?"

"I've been in love with you since the first time I sat next to you in our geology class, Kiera. I was just too much of an idiot at the time to realize it. And the same deal when you came back into my life again the night of the Jingle Balls ball. I was still denying my feelings for you when I was traded to the Rock. But I can't do that anymore. I love you, Kiera. And I hope you'll give me a chance to prove that I can be the man you need and the father our son deserves."

He tenderly kissed me.

I smiled softly, still a little dazed at his words. Stacy had been right after all. "Okay, I'll give you a chance."

Since the real test was yet to come.

And I hoped with everything inside me that neither of us would fail it.

Because when it came down to it, Stacy was right about that, too. The success of what Logan and I had didn't fall on his shoulders alone.

It took two to make a relationship work.

But it only took one to damage it.

45

LOGAN

"I heard you have a sparkling kitchen," Travis said the next morning as we ran along the hilly path in what felt like the middle of nowhere. Tall trees bordered either side of us, the sweet scent of decay and the coming fall lingering in the air.

The indication that hockey season was almost upon us.

"Kiera went crazy cleaning the other day when I was out with Livi," I told him.

"Emma did the same thing right before Kat was born. I think she called it nesting. Isn't Kiera due any day now?"

"Next Friday."

"Didn't your ex-wife go through the same thing with your daughter?"

"I have no idea. If she did, I was away on a road trip when it happened. Just like I was away when Livi was born."

Livi had come slightly earlier than expected. But even then, I hadn't even requested family leave for around her due date, to ensure I wasn't on the road when Stacy went into labor.

This time?

You'd better believe I would do everything in my power to be there for the birth of my son and to be there for Kiera.

"How are things going with Kiera?" Travis asked.

He didn't have to say it, but I knew what he was thinking. He was referring to my failed attempt at proposing to her during the silent auction.

"Things are definitely better between us."

"So, she knows that you love her?"

"Yep. I told her yesterday."

My plan to begin from scratch and not just assume we should be together for our baby's sake had paid off. I had shown her over the past three months that she meant more to me than that. We had dated like a typical couple would have. Sure, we'd had sex probably more often than a typical couple when they started out, but I had also respected Kiera's boundaries.

And during that time, I'd fallen even deeper in love with her. I'd thought I loved her the day I proposed. I'd been wrong, and Kiera had known that.

What I felt for her now was nothing compared to what I had shared with Stacy. The love I felt for Kiera went deep to the core. It was like having your soul taken apart and then put together in the best possible way.

I couldn't imagine not being with her.

When Stacy and I were married, I didn't feel like I'd left a part of me behind every time I went away on a road trip. If I didn't talk to her for a day or two, it hadn't been the end of the world.

Something told me it wouldn't be the same with Kiera.

I would miss her down to the marrow of my soul every time we were apart.

Travis and I ran for another mile before I finally asked what had been lurking at the back of my mind. "How do you do it? You and Emma have been together for a few years, and you have a daughter. I've seen a lot of players fuck up their relationships because of the sport. Whereas players like you have no problems balancing everything. How do you do it?"

"Nothing worthwhile is easy. Love isn't easy. It's complicated and messy—as you know. You just need to keep doing those things that are special between you and Kiera, and those things that are special between the two of you and your son. Don't lose sight of them.

"Hockey is our job. A job we're lucky that we feel passionate about. The secret is to remember that it's just a part of you. It's not everything that you are. It won't be there for you when the days are tough. It won't be there for you on the good days. Your family—Kiera, your son, and your daughter—are the ones who will be standing behind you, supporting you."

I smirked at him. "Wow, that's really poetic."

He grinned at me. "See? There's more to me than just a hockey player and artist."

An artist who recently painted a colorful mural on my son's bedroom wall. A colorful mural that resembled the coral reef in *Finding Nemo*.

"Either way, thanks for the advice."

We completed our run and stretched out our muscles.

After we were finished, we returned to Travis's car. He was checking his phone as mine rang.

Without looking at the screen, I accepted the call as Travis said rather breathlessly, "Kiera's in labor."

46

KIERA

For the record, labor hurts.

Whoo whoo.

Hee hee.

"Did he answer this time?" I asked Judith after the latest contraction subsided. I resumed bouncing softly on the exercise ball I was sitting on in my living room. The ball I'd bought to use during labor.

Except when I got it, I hadn't imagined things would progress so quickly.

When I'd had the twinges of discomfort this morning, I assumed it was Love Bug growing bored of his position and squirming to get comfortable again.

Logan had been home at that point. He'd made me breakfast, given me a foot and ankle massage, and kissed me.

And because that man gave great massages, I groaned, "God, I love you." It felt amazing to be able to say it.

And that had led to us making love again.

Because we could.

Did I keep expecting him to realize he wasn't cut out for

long-term relationships, and once Love Bug was born, he would break up with me?

Yes, I'll admit it, the nagging doubt was still there. It was probably the hormones talking, but they were kind of tough to ignore.

"He's on his way." Judith placed my phone on the coffee table. "Are you sure you don't want me to drive you to the hospital?"

"No, I'm good. I still have plenty of time."

Logan and Travis had left for a run over two hours ago. An hour later, the twinges had upgraded to contractions.

"I can't believe I'll be a grandmother soon."

Yes, about that. After I came clean the day of the auction about everything that had happened, Judith eventually forgave me for lying about Stephen being Love Bug's father. She understood why I had initially lied.

I'd even told her about Stephen's and my conversation regarding who he wanted me to move on with if he should die before me. The conversation I still hadn't shared with Logan.

After she forgave Logan and me, she asked if it would be okay if she and Joe could still be Love Bug's grandparents.

So that was how Logan's and my son ended up with three sets of grandparents.

And I couldn't imagine it any other way.

I smiled at Judith. "You're going to be an amazing grandmother."

Oh, I forgot to mention, she was also an amazing party planner. She truly outdid herself when it came to the baby shower.

"I should probably call your mom and give her an update."

"Good id—" The word was cut short with a long groan.

And a gush of fluid coating the ball.

Whoo whoo.

Hee hee.

"Change of plans," Judith said. "Looks like I'm driving you to the hospital."

I nodded through the pain, mentally telling her, *Great idea.*

She helped me to my feet. Liquid trickled down my legs.

"I'll just change first into something not so wet. Can you tell Logan we're going to the hospital?"

"Will do. I'll call your mom, too."

I hurried off to change. Well, hurried as much as one could go when carrying a watermelon-sized baby in your belly while said belly wanted to squeeze it out.

By the time I was finished, Judith was standing by the door, her outstretched hand holding my phone. "Logan wants to talk to you. I'll drive. You talk."

Her other hand held her own phone. "We're leaving now, Beth. We'll see you soon."

Ahh, my mom.

"I need my suitcase." I accepted my phone from her.

"It's in my car. Now, let's get you to the hospital before I wind up delivering your son in my vehicle."

That got me moving.

Correction—that got me waddling in the direction of the front door.

"Hi," I said into my phone as another contraction hit, and my hi turned into a prolonged groan. Not the sexy groan Logan was used to when I came. This was more of an *I'm-going-to-kill-whoever-screwed-up-making-that-condom* sound.

I stopped moving and doubled over, clutching the corner of the hallway wall.

Whoo whoo.

Hee hee.

"Just breathe through the contraction," Logan instructed me. "You can do it, babe. I'm staying on the line the entire way to the hospital."

"Logan?"

Whoo whoo.

Hee hee.

"Yes?"

"Shut up for a moment."

Whoo whoo.

Hee hee.

The contraction eased, and I let out a cleansing breath. "Okay. I'm good now." That was more for Judith as I resumed my waddle to the door. "And sorry about being a... for being rude." That was for Logan's benefit.

Judith helped me into the passenger seat, and I buckled myself in.

"How was the run?" I asked Logan just so I'd have something to focus on other than the part where I was in labor.

And so I could hear his voice.

"It was good. There weren't many people out there. The scenery was great. And now I'm sweating all over Travis's car seat."

I laughed because Emma had insisted they cover the seats in plastic whenever Travis and Logan drove to Muir Woods for their run. "I'm sure the hospital staff will be especially excited to see you sweating all over the—"

I had to pause for a moment as a new contraction swept through my belly.

Whoo whoo.

Hee hee.

God, I really wanted Logan with me. "I miss you," I

whispered even though I'd only seen him less than three hours ago.

"I miss you too, Kiera." The smile in his voice made me smile.

"Will you sing to the baby and me?"

And he did exactly that, with me holding the phone so even Judith could hear him.

"That was so sweet," she said once he was finished. "No wonder Stephen listed you as his number one replacement."

Oh, shit.

Judith seemed to realize at the same time as me that she had said too much. She winced.

I put the phone to my ear before she could accidentally say anything else.

"What's she talking about?" Logan asked, sounding both amused and bemused.

"Nothing…I'll explain later."

"Not much longer, Kiera. You're doing great."

Easy for the OB to say. She wasn't the one attempting to squeeze a watermelon through a hole the size of a lemon.

She had the easy job.

I groaned out my misery, mentally cursing the makers of the brand of condoms Logan had used.

He leaned over and kissed me on the forehead.

"Eww, you're all sweaty," I said with a slight sigh, my contractions giving me a momentary reprieve.

Although if there were a contest as to which of us was sweatier, I had a feeling I'd be the clear winner.

I had to admit, though, that Logan was far from fresh smelling, thanks to his run. But if given a choice between him leaving to have a shower and him being here and smelling slightly stinky, I'd opt for the stinky, thanks.

Another wave of contractions bulldozed through me before Logan could respond.

And then the doctor said the most magical words that ever existed: "And here's the head."

All right, not quite as magical as I would've liked, but it was close enough.

I closed my eyes with the next contraction and pushed with all my might.

I could vaguely hear the cheering and chanting from the doctor and the nurse and Logan, encouraging me to keep going.

For a second, they flashed in my mind as three individuals wearing cheerleading uniforms and waving pom-poms.

Give me a push.

Give me a baby.

Give me a "You did it!"

"Just one more push, Kiera."

Collecting everything inside me—the love I felt for my baby and the love I felt for Logan—I pushed with all my might.

I was positive even Logan's grandmother in Lake Tahoe heard my battle cry from the effort.

"And here he is..."

Smiling and weary, I opened my eyes and peered up at Logan.

Even though he looked a little green (which wasn't too surprising given what he'd just witnessed), he was grinning at his son. His eyes shone with so much pride that *my* eyes teared up.

There was no doubt in my mind about how much he loved his son.

That same pride and love in his gaze were then directed at me.

But this wasn't the first time I'd seen it. I'd witnessed it daily for the past three months.

I'd just chosen to ignore it until yesterday.

"I love you." My voice came out raspy, thanks to the flood of emotions.

His smile widened, stealing my breath. He brushed a kiss against my lips. "I love you, too."

"Would you like to hold your son now?" the nurse said.

As if she even had to ask.

She set him prone on my chest. Logan crouched beside the bed and studied the little boy he'd helped create.

He lightly stroked the dusting of dark hair on his son's head. "Hi, Daniel Stephen Mathews."

We'd already had a discussion about Daniel's last name. It didn't feel right to give him my married name when he was biologically Logan's and not Stephen's.

The little boy smiled at hearing his daddy's voice.

I know what you're thinking. Daniel wasn't really smiling. It was gas. And maybe if he had been any other baby, that might've been true.

But you're wrong.

He was definitely smiling at his father....But how could he not?

"I should probably go share the news with everyone and phone my parents," Logan said.

"Don't forget to text Travis so that he can tell Emma." She would update everyone else—including Chloe and Ava —with our news.

A SHORT TIME LATER, DANIEL AND I WERE SETTLED IN OUR hospital room when the door opened, and two sets of grandparents entered. Logan was by the window, his son in his arms, singing to him.

"And a quack, quack here, and a quack, quack there."

I giggled because it was the funniest sight to behold.

"Let me see my grandson." Mom rushed over to us, Judith right behind her.

Dad and Joe followed, knowing they wouldn't get to see Daniel for a while longer. The two grandmothers had called dibs on him first.

Logan's parents had already booked their flight for the following week. However, from what Logan had laughingly told me, his mother had pressured his father into moving their flight up several days.

His grandmother and stepgrandfather would be driving in from Lake Tahoe on the weekend to visit. Logan had finally admitted to her that I hadn't contacted her because of a squid recipe Grayson had told me about.

Even though she had figured that out for herself, she certainly hadn't expected to learn I was pregnant with her great-grandchild.

She had called me right after that to tell me how happy she was about the news.

I could tell Logan wasn't in a big rush to relinquish his son anytime soon. But despite that, he carefully handed Daniel to my mother. And for the next ten minutes, the two women gushed over the sleeping baby while their husbands grinned knowingly.

Logan sat next to me on the narrow bed, his arm around my shoulders, and gently kissed me. "How are you doing?"

"Tired, a little sore." I gave him a quick peck on the lips. "Happy."

Mom and Judith peered at us in the same way I'd seen them do more and more during the past few weeks. They always did it when they thought I wouldn't notice.

Both had witnessed the proposal that had fortunately been interrupted. They also knew not to bring it up. But even though they tried to act like they weren't feverishly hoping Logan would propose to me again soon, there was no denying that was what they wanted.

Me?

I was happy the way things were.

We still had to see what would happen once hockey season officially began.

He had learned how to balance his hockey career and Livi, but balancing the three of us with his career would be a whole new challenge.

And I wasn't sure if it was a challenge he was up for.

A small knock came from the door. Even before Logan opened it, I knew who it was.

Livi strode into the room without even saying hi to her father. She marched over to her new brother, now in Judith's arms. Stacy hugged Logan and congratulated him. Then waddled to my bed to give me a big hug.

"She couldn't wait any longer to see him," she said, smiling at her daughter.

Judith was sitting in the armchair and happily showed off Daniel to his big sister. Livi proceeded to excitedly tell him all the things they would do together once he was a little older.

And for now, everything seemed great as I tried not to dwell on the rapidly approaching hockey season.

47

LOGAN

October

"How's my little boy doing?" I said to my phone screen. Daniel was in Kiera's arms, peering wide-eyed at me. His fluff of dark hair stuck up in all directions.

I had no clue if my six-week-old son could focus on me yet, but he smiled as though he knew my voice belonged to his daddy.

"He's doing great," Kiera said. "He misses you. We both do."

I'd been away for the past four days on a road trip.

And as promised, I'd called Kiera every day.

I had also called Livi and her baby sister, Hailey.

"I miss you, too," I told Kiera and Daniel. "I can't wait to return home to see you both." Only one more day; then the team was flying to San Francisco for several home games.

I couldn't make love to Kiera yet, but that didn't stop me from making out with her and cuddling with her once Daniel was asleep.

Daniel started rooting around for dinner. Kiera put him on her breast, and we continued our conversation while he contentedly had his meal.

"Remember, those are on loan," I told him, and Kiera laughed. That wasn't the first time I had pointed that out. I was eagerly waiting for them to be mine again.

<hr>

November

THE IMAGE OF MY TWO-MONTH-OLD SON CAME INTO VIEW ON my phone. He was snoozing peacefully in his crib, looking adorable in his Rock team onesie and navy sweat pants.

I wanted to say something to him just to see him smile at me. But I restrained myself because waking him from his nap would be cruel to both him and Kiera.

Kiera let me stare at my son for a few minutes, then quietly tiptoed to our bedroom.

"I saw my physician today." She smiled my favorite grin.

"And?"

"And...I can finally have sex with you once you get home."

My mouth twitched to one side. "We don't even have to wait that long."

This was met by her shy smile. "What do you have in mind?"

So I told her exactly what I had in mind, explaining where and how I wanted her to touch herself as she told me the same.

And in no time, we were two writhing bodies on beds in

two separate countries, each appreciating the sounds of the other person as we brought ourselves to euphoria.

———

December

"Look, Daniel, there's Daddy," Kiera said. The two of them were on their stomachs on the living room floor, doing tummy time. Kiera was holding the iPad in front of them.

I was also on my stomach on the hotel bed.

Daniel grinned like he always did when he and I did tummy time together. He also loved to watch when Kiera and I played tummy-time hockey.

What was tummy-time hockey?

It was a game I'd invented where Kiera and I passed a small ball to each other with novelty hockey sticks.

While we were on our stomachs.

Like our typical daily conversations while I was on the road, I told them about my day, and Kiera told me about hers and Daniel's. And then we planned our next family outing for when I was home.

And later, once Daniel was asleep, Kiera would text me to let me know so that we could have phone sex.

"I love you," I told Kiera.

"I love you, too."

I ended the call.

For the past three months, Kiera and I had been doing everything in our power to make our relationship work, to make our little family work.

It hadn't been easy. But nothing worthwhile ever was.

Even though I'd messed things up with Stacy and Livi

when Stacy and I were married, things were different when it came to Kiera, Daniel, and me.

Did I believe that if we got married, we could make our marriage work despite my hockey career?

Absolutely.

There wasn't a single cell in my body that believed otherwise.

Now, I just hoped Kiera felt the same way.

48

KIERA

"What do you think of the Christmas tree?" I asked Daniel. He was in my arms, waiting for his daddy to come home. "Look at this decoration. Do you think Daddy will love it?"

The decoration in question?

It was a hockey goal with a cute bunny goaltender guarding it.

Daniel giggled and waved his hands at the decoration, eager to grab it from me.

"You don't want to put this in your mouth." Which was exactly where it would end up. Daniel was at the age where he loved to put everything in his mouth.

The doorbell rang.

"You're not expecting anyone, are you?" I asked him with a big smile.

He rewarded me with one of his.

I opened the door to find Mom on the porch. Before I registered what was happening, she had Daniel out of my arms and was gushing over him. "How's my big grandson today?"

"Mom, don't get me wrong, because I'm always happy to see you, but what are you doing here?"

She stopped fussing over him long enough to do a quick perusal of my clothes. "Oh, heavens, that outfit won't do."

I glanced down at my black yoga pants and long-sleeved nursing top. My hair was pulled back in a sloppy bun, and I barely had any makeup on.

I might have been a million miles from glamorous, but Daniel and Logan didn't care. I didn't have spit-up on me, so that was always a bonus.

Before I could respond, Judith entered the foyer, a dress bag on one arm and a small suitcase in her other hand. She, too, looked me over. "Oh, that outfit definitely won't do. Okay, upstairs with you. Have a shower, and I'll meet you in your bedroom."

I glanced between the two women. "Will someone tell me what's going on?"

"You'll find out soon enough." Judith tried to nudge me forward.

"Do you have any idea what's going on?" I asked Daniel. He giggled and waved his arms at me.

With a little more prompting on her part, Judith ushered me upstairs.

Once I'd finished my shower, Judith had me sit on a chair in my bedroom and began applying my makeup. All I had on was my underwear and bathrobe.

"I know how to do my own makeup," I said as she rummaged through her supplies.

She just grinned at me. Did that make me slightly nervous?

You'd better believe it. What the heck were she and my mother up to?

I kept expecting to hear Logan walk into the house, but

that never happened. If he had texted to tell me he was delayed, I wouldn't know because my phone was downstairs on the coffee table.

Thirty minutes later, my hair was styled, and makeup was applied. Judith slid the zipper down on the garment bag, revealing a blush-pink gown with gold sequins sewed on the bodice and the skirt's gauze overlay.

I sucked in a ghost of a breath and stared wide-eyed at the delicate dress. A thousand thoughts and emotions spun inside me, creating a fragile web.

I reached a shaky hand toward the bodice and traced a finger along the lacy design. "Really, Judith—what's going on?"

"You'll see. We have to hurry. The car will be here soon to pick you up."

"Pick me up for what?"

The grin returned to her face. "I'm your fairy godmother, and I've been sworn to secrecy."

Realizing there was no point trying to get an answer from her, I let her help me into the gown. It fit perfectly.

She opened my closet door, revealing the full-length mirror.

"You look gorgeous." Tears thickened her voice the way they had the day I married her son.

I had to admit she was right. The V-neckline plunged to below my breasts, two thin straps holding it up. The sequins in the floor-length dress formed patterns in the skirt like raindrops trickling down a window.

I had thought the gown I'd worn the night of the Jingle Balls ball was beautiful. That had been nothing compared to this.

Mom walked into the room, carrying Daniel. "You do look gorgeous, sweetheart." Her voice was as choked up as Judith's.

I laughed under my breath. "You mean compared to my usual jeans and nursing tops?"

Fortunately, I'd nursed Daniel a short time ago. I had a feeling breastfeeding him while I was in the gown wasn't on their agenda.

"I'm going to make a wild prediction here. Is Logan meeting me somewhere? And you two are looking after our son while we're gone?"

Both women nodded enthusiastically, smiles wider than before.

I gave them instructions about Daniel's routine even though they already had it memorized.

The limo pulled up to the front of the house, ready to whisk me to wherever Logan was waiting for me.

I kissed Daniel on the cheek. "Make sure your grandmothers keep out of trouble, okay?"

He gurgled in reply and smiled his toothless grin.

The driver helped me into the vehicle, and we drove to a small restaurant that Logan and I had been to several times since we'd begun dating.

It was one of our favorite places to eat.

Logan wasn't waiting for me outside when we arrived. I entered the building. The man waiting at the host booth smiled at me. "Kiera Ashdown, I assume?"

"That's right."

"Let me show you to your table." I followed him through the restaurant. I couldn't see Logan anywhere. Maybe he wasn't here yet.

Instead of taking me to a table, the host led me to a door and gestured for me to enter a private dining room.

I stepped inside the spacious room and was greeted by a sight I hadn't expected. Tall, leafless trees covered in fairy lights formed a pathway to the dance floor and the single table in the center of the room. It was like stepping into a magical wonderland.

But as beautiful as it all was, that wasn't what had me gasping.

Logan was standing next to the table, wearing a tuxedo and a mask, like the one he had on the night of the Jingle Balls ball.

The door clicked shut behind me, and I walked to Logan. He bowed, and I smiled, every part of me feeling warm, tingly, and dazed.

"Happy anniversary," he said, holding out his hand to me.

The ball had taken place a year ago. I'd known that, but I hadn't realized Logan had paid attention to the date.

The only difference was, last year he and I had both been masked. This time it was only Logan who was wearing one.

"Happy anniversary to you, too."

He lifted my hand to his lips like he had that night. Despite everything that had happened since the first time he'd kissed the back of my hand, I couldn't help but blush.

Which made him chuckle. "A year ago, I was given a second chance to be with you. Before you met Stephen, I'd planned to tell you numerous times how I felt about you. But each time I tried, I chickened out. A year ago, I saw you at the ball, but I didn't dare tell you it was me. I made love to you that night, but I screwed up by keeping my identity a secret.

"When I first saw you in Livi's classroom, I figured it was too late to tell you the truth. I couldn't turn back the calendar. And then when you told me you were pregnant with Stephen's baby, I figured there was no point in telling you the truth.

"But I was wrong. I should never have kept my identity

a secret. So I'd like to have a redo of that night." He removed his mask. "Hi, my name is Logan Grayson Mathews. And I'm in love with you, Kiera."

I glanced around the room. The only similarity to the ballroom that night was the Christmas tree, and both had been decorated differently.

Everything was different.

And I wasn't just referring to the decorations and my dress.

I couldn't believe he had done this. For me.

I turned back to him. "Hi, I'm Kiera Claire Ashdown. And I'm in love with you, Logan."

His arms went around me, and he pulled me in for a kiss.

DINNER WAS INCREDIBLE. WE TALKED, WE LAUGHED, AND WE reminisced.

A song we had danced to at the ball started to play from the speakers in the ceiling. Logan stood up and offered me his hand. "Would you like to dance?"

Smiling, I accepted it. "I would."

He led me to the dance floor. I wrapped my arms around his neck. His went around my waist, and we swayed to the music.

"The day Daniel came into the world," Logan said, "Judith mentioned that Stephen listed me as his number one replacement. You said you would tell me what she meant later. Are you ready to tell me now?"

I couldn't believe he'd remembered that. I had forgotten about that conversation.

I felt the heat in my cheeks raise once more. "It's kind of silly."

"Will you tell me anyway?"

I smiled and nodded. "Stephen once told me that if he died before me, he wanted me to eventually fall in love again. He listed the options for men he felt would be great husband material—should they also be available at the time. You were his number one choice."

"When was this?"

I told Logan when Stephen had jokingly told me his list of potential candidates.

"So, after Stacy and I were divorced."

I could tell what he was thinking. "He never mentioned you were divorced, but he knew you had been a better husband than you'd given yourself credit for."

Stacy and I had talked a lot about our former marriages after we'd become close friends. She loved Logan, but only as a friend. She had also admitted their failed marriage was as much her fault as it had been his.

For the past three months, Logan had proved just how different our relationship was in comparison to what his marriage had been like. He had proved he could balance what he and I had between us with his hockey. He had proved he could balance our family and his career.

Now, I just needed for him to see that.

Yes, it wasn't easy making sure nothing was remiss. But we were aware of what we needed to do to succeed when it came to our family and our love. And I knew, with every ounce of my soul, we would triumph.

As long as we continued to make each other a priority, I had no doubt our love would remain strong till our dying days.

"Do you believe that?" he asked, referring to what I'd told him about Stephen.

I nodded. "I do."

I had witnessed firsthand how much Logan had grown

since he'd first become a husband and a father. I'd seen how hard he'd worked at being a great father to both Livi and Daniel.

And I'd seen how much he'd made me a priority, even when he was on the road.

Logan smiled, and as usual, when he looked at me that way, my heart galloped in my chest, destination unknown. "I originally said I wasn't interested in settling down again until after my hockey career is over, but I was wrong. Ever since you stepped back into my life and ever since Daniel was born, I realized how wrong I'd been in thinking that I could wait. I don't want to wait."

Logan stepped away from me, slipped his hand into his trouser pocket, and removed it, fisted. "I want to wake up to find my *wife,* the woman I love, next to me. I want to come home from road trips to be with my wife. I want to grow old with my wife now and not starting in four or five or six years.

"I know you believed that I only wanted to marry you because we were having a baby together. But the truth is, even if Daniel had been Stephen's, I would still want to marry you. I love you." He opened up his hand, revealing a simple gold ring with a breathtaking diamond. "Kiera, will you marry me?"

The love and honesty on his face stalled the air in my lungs, and my heart stopped beating.

It took two to make a relationship work. I understood his career and the demands it placed on him. It was something that Stacy said she hadn't been prepared for, and that was what had ultimately caused their marriage to be like a seesaw, never finding a balance between everything.

It wouldn't always be easy. But neither would be not being his wife.

Because there was nothing I wanted more than that.

My mouth widened into a big grin, and tears blurred my vision. "Logan, I would love to be your wife."

Logan had barely gotten the ring on my finger before we were kissing.

It was a simple kiss—a kiss to seal our love—but it also melted me down to my soul and beyond. It left me feeling complete in a whole new way.

I rested my head on his shoulder, and we swayed to the music.

"Did my Mom and Judith know you were going to propose tonight?"

I felt Logan's chuckle more than I heard it. "No one knew. Tonight was about us and no one else. Just like it was a year ago. Just you and me."

Just us.

EPILOGUE
LOGAN

Six Months Later

When Stacy and I had gotten married, it was a lavish affair. Kiera and Stephen's wedding had also been big.

"You ready?" Travis asked as we took our places next to the pine-bough and white-tulle archway. Over two dozen guests sat chatting on white chairs arranged in rows on the hotel patio.

My grandmother had suggested that Kiera and I hold our intimate wedding at her house, but both of us had agreed this was the perfect place for it.

The hotel was where our second chance for a new start had begun, where our son was conceived.

The son currently content in my mother's arms.

Dad sat on one side of her, making goofy faces at his grandson. My nine-month-old son giggled at him.

Stephen's mother was sitting on the other side, laughing at something Mom had just told her.

"Definitely ready," I told Travis, my best man.

The two of us, along with Eli, my groomsman, wore light-sage-green suits and ties for the low-key event. Ideal for the daytime wedding. They also perfectly complemented the mountains and pine trees overlooking us.

"It's not too late to change your mind," Eli said on a chuckle.

I threw him a look that said that wasn't going to happen. It might have taken Kiera and me quite the journey to get to this moment, starting from the first time I sat next to her in our geology class, but there was no other place I would rather be than here. Now.

We'd done a lot of talking since we'd gotten engaged about everything when it came to making sure our marriage worked. And this included details of what would happen if I were traded to another team.

I had no doubts whatsoever our marriage would last and be a happy one.

Eli laughed again. "Yeah, I didn't think that was the case."

Stacy stepped onto the patio, her baby daughter in her arms. She walked down the aisle to where we were standing with Tony, Kiera's and my officiant for the ceremony.

If someone had told me two years ago I would one day be marrying the woman whose wedding I'd been the best man for, and my ex-wife's husband would be the one marrying us, I would've wondered what drugs they'd inhaled.

But now, I couldn't imagine it any other way.

"They're ready," Stacy said, smiling at Tony and me. She gave me a quick hug while keeping her drooling daughter away from my suit. "I'd say good luck, but you really don't need it. You've totally got this."

She wasn't talking about the wedding. That was the easy part.

She was talking about what came after that.

After the honeymoon.

But she was right. I did have this. It wouldn't be easy. But the best things in life never were.

Easy was boring.

Hard—that was what made things worthwhile. It didn't matter if it was the Stanley Cup or falling in love. The harder the work to achieve them, the greater the prize.

And for me, Kiera was definitely the best prize of them all.

Stacy gave Tony a brief kiss, nodded at the cellist, and sat in the front row with my parents, Stephen's parents, and my son.

The classical music began to play, and a moment later, Livi walked down the aisle, toward me. Her white dress was simple with a dusty-rose sash.

Did I really know the difference between dusty-rose from regular rose?

Nope. Livi had excitedly shown me her dress (because that wasn't bad luck) and explained the color's name.

Grinning broadly, she continued to the end of the aisle and flashed me a comical thumbs-up with the hand not holding a small bouquet of flowers.

I returned the gesture, which resulted in chuckles from those who noticed.

She sat next to Stacy.

Ava was the next to walk down the aisle and take her place at the altar. Her two-year-old daughter called out, "Hi, Mommy," and waved at her. Ava waved back to her daughter and baby son, who was asleep in his father's arms.

Chloe, Kiera's maid of honor, came after her.

And then the moment I'd been waiting for...

The music changed, and the guests stood.

My heart slammed against my ribs to the slow rhythm of the song as Kiera stepped onto the patio, her father at her side.

She'd been beautiful the day of her first wedding, in her long white gown. This time she was beyond breathtaking.

Our first weddings had been what some would call fairy-tale events—this time we'd chosen to keep things simpler, more casual.

Her effect on me? It was anything but that.

Her off-white, lacy dress brushed just above her knees and dipped low enough to reveal my favorite cleavage. The short, barely-there sleeves were pure lace. Her hair hung loosely around her shoulders and blew slightly around her face in the warm June breeze.

The sun shone down on her, turning her blonde hair into a halo as she approached me. Everything about her resembled an angel.

A fucking gorgeous angel.

A chorus of sniffling came from our mothers' direction, but I was too busy staring at the woman who was soon to be my wife to check which of the trio was crying.

I had a feeling, though, it was all three of them—including Judith.

Kiera had shared with me a few months ago the love note Stephen had given her. In it, he'd told her that he wanted to be the star in the sky that granted all her wishes.

So it was only fitting that the brightest star in the sky—the sun—was shining down on us.

Granting Kiera's and my greatest wish.

Kiera stopped in front of me and beamed at me, her dimples on full display.

Tony nodded for everyone to take their seats, and the music faded away.

"Who's giving away the bride?" he asked.

"Her mother and I are," her father replied.

More sniffling from the three smiling mothers.

Her father left to join them and their husbands.

It turned out that Tony wasn't just a great husband and stepfather—he was also one helluva wedding officiant.

Things went smoothly, and then we got to our vows.

"Kiera and Logan have written their own vows." He nodded for me to go first.

Travis passed me Kiera's wedding band, and I took her hand in mine. "Kiera, from the first time I saw you in our geology class, I knew I wanted to be your friend. But you gave me so much more than just friendship. You gave me the stars and the moon, not to mention our beautiful son." I indicated with a nod at Daniel, who was contently watching us as if he knew this was a big moment in all of our lives. "And now I want to be your everything. To grow old with you. To be your today and your tomorrow. To be your forever. Do you, Kiera Claire Ashdown, take me to be your husband?"

She smiled at me, and my heart couldn't help but soar. "I do."

I slipped the ring onto her finger.

Chloe handed her the other wedding band. "Logan, from the first moment you sat next to me in class, I have cherished our friendship. Our path to ending up together wasn't typical, but I wouldn't change it in any way. You are my best friend, my love, my world. You are my sun on good days and the bad. I want to grow old with you, for us to build sandcastles together, and for me to always be there for you, loving you, worshiping you. Logan Grayson Mathews, would you do me the honor of being my husband?"

I grinned at her. "You better believe I do."

How I kept from sweeping her into my arms and kissing her was beyond me. But I'd be patient...for now.

But as soon as we could sneak away and be on our own for a short time, I'd kiss her the way I wanted to and make love to her.

Guaranteed.

Kiera slipped the ring onto my finger.

I didn't wait for Tony to announce, "By the power vested in me..." My lips were already on hers.

I did, though, manage to keep the kiss PG-rated for the benefit of the guests and young kids.

When it came to my restraint in the kissing department, I deserved a trophy worthy of a Stanley Cup.

The guests laughed as Tony said the line of the ceremony I had ignored in my need to kiss my beautiful wife.

But the best part of that?

It meant I got to kiss her again.

This time the guests cheered our union.

I rested my forehead against Kiera's. "Are you ready to begin the rest of our life together?"

That beautiful smile of hers? It became that much brighter.

READ ON FOR AN EXCERPT FROM
DECIDEDLY WITH WISHES

NALA

A man with dark-blond hair and wearing a smoky-gray suit stepped onto the stage. He was the same blond man I had literally bumped into at the children's hospital last month.

The bright stage lights glinted off highlights in his hair, and my body tingled at the memory of his hand on my arm. Only this time, my heart decided to get in on the act and it sped up.

"And the next item up for auction is a date with San Francisco Rock forward, Elias Lawson," Logan announced into the microphone.

Elias strutted across the stage like it was a catwalk, and damn, he was swoony in that suit. Whoever his tailor was had done a great job with the fit. I didn't know much about men's suits, but I did understand that much from working with Robert and working with the male models on Ayanna fashion shoots.

I wasn't the only one who felt that way about Elias's swooniness. Cheers and hoots and lovesick sighs followed his every move.

"The date will include a delightful dinner at Bonterra Ristorante for two," Logan explained.

I scanned the other tables. Some women were practically drooling on their phones in their haste to bid on him via the phone app. Others were staring openmouthed at him, too stunned to bid.

Could you blame them?

Elias walked to where Logan was standing and flashed the audience a look that turned all knees wobbly. God, if he played hockey as well as he smoldered, it was no wonder the Rock won the Stanley Cup this year.

"Aren't you bidding on him?" Rachel asked me.

"Even if I did bid on him, I doubt I'll win. Besides, my bucket list only says the hockey player has to be hot. It doesn't say anything about him being on an NHL team." Thank the good Lord for that. "I'm sure I can find someone who plays recreationally and who won't cost me over a thousand dollars."

Because based on the eager expressions on some women's faces, I wouldn't be surprised if their bids were that high.

The auction continued. Eventually, Logan ran out of items, and the waitstaff served dessert while the auction organizers determined the winning bids.

"*God*, this tastes amazing," I moaned, trying to ignore the temptation to lick the chocolate sauce and whipped cream that clung to my plate. Around us, excited chatter and laughter filled the air like the noise from a troop of monkeys hanging out in the rainforest trees after spotting a banana on the ground.

"I was never a fan of chocolate cake until this moment," Amelia said, creating the same moaning sound I'd just made.

"If I end up in heaven"—Dani waved her dessert fork at us—"this will be dessert for every meal."

"Forget dessert. This *will* be my meal."

My friends couldn't argue with me there.

After the plates had been cleared from the table, Logan Mathews strutted onstage.

"Before I announce the auction winners, I'd first like to ask the event organizer to join me." He held his hand out to the pregnant woman at the side of the stage, who promptly blushed.

Applause filled the room as she walked to him and waved shyly at us.

Logan handed her the mic. She smiled at him and turned to the audience. "Thank you, everyone, for coming out and supporting the fundraiser. The money will ensure that foster kids of lower-income families have access to series of books that are so gripping, kids can't help but want to read them. And as you know, the love of reading is key to learning and having opportunities that might not otherwise be possible. Thanks to your generosity, we've raised thirty thousand dollars, which will go to the Reading for Tomorrow Literacy Program."

The crowded room broke out in cheers.

She passed the mic back to Logan.

"Don't go anywhere," he told her and began announcing the auction winners.

Dani and Rachel each won an item they'd bid on.

Did I win the French cooking lessons?

Unfortunately not. I missed it by a few dollars.

"And the winner of the date with Elias Lawson," Logan said with a dramatic pause. My friends' faces lit up with anticipation, their bodies leaning forward as they hung on to his every word.

Did a laugh escape me at their expressions?

Maybe.

They weren't the only ones acting the same way. Several hopeful women near our table shared identical reactions, some of whom were practically falling off their seats under the weight of the suspense.

"With the winning bid of one thousand and twenty-nine dollars...Nala Johnson from table nineteen."

Huh?

Applause rose throughout the room as I scanned the crowd, searching for another Nala Johnson. That had to be the only explanation for why he'd said my name.

I had to admit, though, the part about her being at our table was slightly perplexing. He must've gotten the numbers mixed up.

And I might have continued believing that if not for the cheers from my table. My other hint? Amelia, Dani, and Rachel were high-fiving and laughing.

When they realized I wasn't moving, Amelia and Dani attempted to nudge me out of my chair.

I vehemently shook my head. "I didn't bid on him. There's obviously something wrong with the app."

"We know you didn't bid on him," Amelia said, looking pretty proud of herself. "We did. He's perfect. And now you'll be able to cross an item off your list."

"Yes, but that's just one item. You're forgetting I still need to ride a horse, kiss someone in front of the Eiffel Tower, learn to make a breathtaking cake—"

She raised a perfectly arched eyebrow. "You only said it had to be beautiful, like a wedding cake."

I ignored her. "Go on a hayride. And the biggie, find a husband. Plus, I can't justify that kind of expense for a single date." Even if it was for a great cause.

Amelia stood up. "She's coming," she called out and grabbed my wrist. "Don't worry about the amount," she said to me. "This is our treat. We chipped in to win you the date."

If I'd thought I was stunned before, that was nothing compared to now. Which was why she succeeded in dragging me to my feet and tugging me toward where the winners paid for their prizes.

"I can't accept the prize," I told her. I wanted to stop moving, but I also didn't want to make a scene. "You and Sarina need the money more than I need to go on a date with Elias. It's not even a real date."

"It counts when it comes to your grandmother's deal. Your list only said a date with a hot hockey player. It didn't say you have to kiss him. And we screenshot the page from the website that listed the winner would win a date with him. What more does your grandmother need?"

She had a point there.

"Also, I met him when he volunteered with Sarina's wheelchair hockey team. He's a really nice guy. So you can't do much better than him. *And* it's for a great cause. So everyone wins in the end."

"But it's over a thousand dollars."

"Yes, and you've sewn Sarina lots of beautiful dresses over the years, so this is the least I can do. You'll have a fun night out with a nice guy—God knows when the last time you went out with a guy was —and the charity benefits. What more could you ask for?"

We approached the table tucked away in the corner of the room where you paid for the prizes.

"Hi," Amelia said. "I've come to pay for the date with Eli Lawson."

"God, that sounds so bad," I mumbled under my breath. Behind us, from the loudspeakers, Logan was mentioning something about a baby.

"Is everything all right?" A deep man's voice rumbled in my ear.

My skin tingled, and my heart rate picked up its pace again. I didn't have to turn around to see who the voice belonged to. My body's reaction said it all.

I also didn't have to turn around to know that his eyes were the deep blue of the sky just after sunrise. His smell—all man and the crisp scent of a pine forest at dawn—brought forth a clear memory of those eyes.

"Everything's great," Amelia said as I finally swiveled around to face him. "Nala can't wait to go out with you. Isn't that right?" The question was directed at me.

ACKNOWLEDGMENTS

First, I want to thank everyone who has fallen in love with the By the Bay series and asked me to write more stories for it. I was lucky to meet a group of amazing romantic comedy authors at a romance author conference (Romance Author Mastermind) in November 2019. Christina Hovland and Dylann Crush were looking for rom-com authors to participate in a charity anthology that would raise awareness and money for the Testicular Cancer Awareness Foundation. It was a no-brainer about joining them.

When I polled the members of my Facebook group (Stina's Sweethearts) as to where I should go next with the By the Bay series, the majority asked for more hockey romances. All right, the majority also asked for books for Drew and Holly's two brothers (all from *Decidedly with Baby*). When it came to baby names for Hannah and Wes's newest addition in *Decidedly with Luck*, I asked my Facebook group for suggestions. That's how Hannah and Wes's son Riley came to be. So thank you to everyone in Stina's Sweethearts for always being eager to help me out when I'm looking for a name or ideas for pets to include in my books.

I want to thank my content editor Bev, as well as Hope and Jessica for their copyediting and proofreading wizardry. All three individuals helped make this book sparkle. Naturally, I can't forget rom-com author Brenda St

John Brown, who always shares her brilliant wisdom when it comes to my romances. She's the best.

Finally, I would like to thank my husband, our two young adult sons, and our teenage daughter, for their love and support. And I can't forget our cat, Callie, who loves to jump on my desk in the morning (thereby blocking the computer screen) to absorb all the attention she can get. The words "I'm busy right now" mean nothing to her.

ABOUT THE AUTHOR

Born in Brighton England, Stina Lindenblatt has lived in a number of countries, including England, the U.S., Finland, and Canada. This would explain her mixed up accent. She has a kinesiology degree and a MSc in sports biological sciences.

In addition to writing fiction, she loves photography, and currently lives in Calgary, Canada, with her husband and three kids.

For news about her books and to sign up for her newsletter, check out her website at stinalindenblattauthor.com.